The Crescents

Joseph R. Lallo

ISBN-13: 978-0999708132

Table of Contents

ACKNOWLEDGMENTS

I would like to acknowledge, as always, Nick Deligaris for his work on the cover, and Tammy Salyer for her excellent work in editing the story.

Prologue

The sun had only just risen. It had yet to chase the cold of night away. That was for the best. This close to the desert, it didn't take long for the heat of day to become punishing. Best to get to the shore quickly and start fishing. Dillydallying only meant traveling under the baking sun before finally reaching the relief of the cool breeze of the North Crescent Sea. And so he hopped onto his horse and set off toward the pier, where his fishing boat and the rest of his crew would be waiting.

Blindol squinted at the sky, eying a cloud creeping toward the sun. He tried to will it there, to reduce the glare upon the white sand that made up the path. Sometimes he questioned why he'd moved away from the forest. The desert—even the very fringe of one—was no place for an elf. Indeed, neither was the sea—though of the two he preferred the waves. But then, that was the point, wasn't it? So few of his countrymen had ventured beyond the isthmus and braved the wilds of North Crescent; every day of work here was worth a dozen back home. Fewer boats vying for fish, fewer suppliers for local markets. It was trouble, to be sure, but it was worth it.

A long, dark form swept along the ground. He grinned; finally, a cloud was braving the sun. But no… When he looked to the sky, there was no counterpart anywhere near the sun. Moreover, the shadow moved too quickly to be a cloud. He tugged the reins of his horse and watched the mote of darkness flitting over the dunes of the desert that opened up like a sandy sea to the north. He shielded his eyes. A shifting, dancing distortion hung in the air above the dunes. It blurred and curled the view of anything near the surface of the sand. He couldn't be sure, but there seemed to be little puffs of sand bursting into the air and wafting away in the wind.

"You're seeing things," he muttered to himself.

The shadow slid along until it was gone from view, but he couldn't bring himself to resume his journey. Instead, he remained atop his horse and strained his vision. Scattered puffs of sand continued to erupt in the distance. They traced a path… the same path the shadow had followed.

"Childish superstition," he chided, shaking his head at the notion. "But it will bother me all day if I don't see for myself."

The answer was a simple one. It was a herd or pack of some kind. The desert was home to any number of little scampering creatures. They were the same color as the sand, easy to miss at this distance. Those little puffs of sand were kicked up by desert hares, or perhaps those odd little foxes he'd seen about. All he had to do to set his mind at ease was find the tracks they'd left behind. After all, rare was the morning he didn't spot trails crisscrossing the road to the pier. This was simply the first time he'd seen the creatures *making* one.

He waited until he saw one of the puffs beside an isolated bit of scraggly desert grass. With it as a landmark, he could be sure he'd found the right spot. His horse snuffed irritably when he guided it from the packed path to the uneven sands, but it was only a short detour. In minutes he reached the grass and hopped down to investigate.

"That's… curious…"

He knelt and scrutinized the ground. There were no tracks. If anything, there was the *opposite* of tracks. The sand was unnaturally smooth. The little dips and furrows dug by the breeze had yet to disturb the surface, though each gust shifted things a bit more naturally. If he'd been a minute or two later, the wind would have wiped away any semblance of the bizarre patch of sand, but for the moment it stretched forward like a neat little ribbon rolled across the desert. It traced a perfectly straight line, the same path the shadow had traced. And now that he stood upon that very path, he saw that it led *directly* to his own village in the distance.

Whether it was childish or not, he didn't think twice about what to do next. He climbed upon his horse and spurred it back toward his home. It was better to feel foolish and be certain of it than to feel wise and fear that he wasn't.

He kept his eyes on the village, barely visible through the rising heat. It wasn't that he didn't know the way. He could find his way to the pier and back with his eyes shut. But something deep in his soul demanded he not look away. He fixed his eyes upon the watchtower. It was right at the edge of the village, a short distance away. Each day one of the townspeople would climb the tower and watch for danger. Just yesterday *he* had been the one in the tower.

"It's Logali on lookout today," he said, snapping the reins to quicken the horse. "He's a good man. I'll have a word with him, see what he saw, and then be on my way."

Those words were still on his lips when he saw darkness descend upon the tower. At this distance, he could just barely see Logali lean out over the railing to check the sky. Then, in place of the unnatural darkness… searing flame.

A brilliant tongue of fire enveloped the tower, consuming it from roof to foundation in a single monstrous column of churning red. It appeared in the blink of an eye coalescing from the air itself. By the time he'd spurred his horse to a gallop, the wooden tower was blackening. He was near enough to hear the sound when it finally splintered and collapsed. Next, he heard the screams. The town was in the grip of a full panic. Horses, mad with fear and lacking riders, scattered into the desert to escape the madness. Men and women rushed to the streets. A chain formed from the well he and the others had dug the previous year when they'd founded the town. Buckets traveled along the line, dousing the burning tower and the nearest buildings lest they join the blaze.

"What happened?" Blindol shouted when he was within earshot.

"It was no one! There was no one!" replied a woman, his neighbor.

"It was the Aluall!" replied a younger man.

"Never mind who it was. They've gone now. Help us put out the flames!" urged an older man.

Blindol leaped from the back of his horse and joined the line, passing buckets and extinguishing the remnants of the watchtower. If he'd not seen it burst to flame before his own eyes, he would have sworn the tower had been burning for hours. It was nothing but a pile of cinders now, reduced to char and ash. There was no sign of the lookout.

The fire may have done its work quickly, but it was still slow to die away. He and the others worked for more than an hour before the smoke stopped rising and they were free to investigate what had happened. Soon subtler happenings revealed themselves. Market shelves were empty. Pantries were stripped bare. It was as though a horde of locusts had descended upon the town and devoured every scrap of food and scooped up anything of value. Blindol made his way to his own home, where his wife was looking in dismay at the shambles it had become.

"How did this happen?" Blindol said, lifting the lid of a crate once filled with bolts of fine fabric his wife had woven. "Who did this?"

"There was no one! Not a soul!" she said. "I helped tend to the fire, and when I came back, *this…*"

"Have you been through every room?" he asked.

"No. No, I've just come through the door," she said.

He looked to the door to the pantry. "Stay where you are."

Blindol pulled a short, sturdy knife from his belt and stalked into the pantry. Like every other room with so much as a scrap of food, it had been stripped utterly bare. He found a lantern and lit it, then held it to the floor. It was clean. Even his own footprints from when he'd fetched the ingredients for breakfast had been wiped away.

"How… how could this happen without anyone seeing?" he said, marching out to his wife again.

She stood silently, one hand over her mouth as she pointed at the door. She'd shut it behind Blindol when he'd arrived. Doing so had revealed something they'd not noticed before. It was a message carved into the wood. Though the language was his own, it was poorly rendered. The looping and intricate glyphs of the elven writing were coarse and angular, but not so badly mangled that he couldn't read what it said. He gritted his teeth and threw the door open. Others, having returned to investigate their own homes, were gathering in the street again, voices harsh and frenzied.

"Friends!" Blindol called. "I've found a message."

"On your door?" called the nearest man in response. "So have we."

"All of you?"

"There is one on every door in the village."

"There!" called another villager. "Even on the city gate!"

They turned to the southern side of the town, where the gates stood. As small and new as the village was, they'd yet to build a wall. They scarcely saw the need. But it was a tradition in the elven villages of South Crescent, when first breaking ground, to erect a village gate to signal to travelers their entry into elven lands. They'd seen no reason not to continue the tradition in this tiny step into North Crescent. And so a great arch straddled the road leading back to their homeland, and the same crude carvings marred it with the same ominous message.

The Crescents
Leave this place. This is only the beginning.

Chapter 1

Six weeks later…

Five Point Hall was a magnificent structure by any measure. Its foundation straddled the precise point where the two kingdoms, which now collectively bore the name the Northern Alliance, met the two kingdoms that had long ago joined to form Tressor. The landscape around it was vibrant and green yet free of the overbearing heat Tressor frequently suffered. Its stone had been hauled from the far corners of the continent. Artisans and architects from both the Northern Alliance and Tressor had collaborated on its design. Hundreds of workers representing nearly every major city and village of both nations had gathered to build it, constructing the marvel in mere months. Everything about the building was an attempt to embody the very concept of unity, and it succeeded brilliantly. It stood with the elegance and grace of a cathedral, built with the sturdiness of northern buildings and the artfulness of Tresson ones. Great carved columns held its vaulted roof, and its massive polished wooden doors shone in the morning sun. On any other day, Five Point Hall would be the most remarkable thing for miles around. Today, that honor belonged to its visitors.

The duke and duchess of New Kenvard, Myranda and Deacon, were dressed in ceremonial garb. Acting as they were as ambassadors from their land, they had to look their best. Myranda's long red hair was gathered with a dark blue ribbon. She wore a silver circlet on her brow and topped her elegant gown with an azure fur-lined cloak. Deacon was similarly dressed, though the simple crown atop his head wreathed a somewhat less orderly mane of brown hair. Majestic though they were, the eyes of the assembled crowd of servants, soldiers, and dignitaries rested with a mixture of curiosity and concern on the other two guests.

The first was Myn, a full-grown dragon. She too was "dressed" in her ambassadorial finest. In her case this meant thin silver rings around each of her horns. A sash the size of a military banner hung about her neck, blue with silver thread. In addition, she wore a small and rather simple amulet reminiscent of her own head rendered in brass and amber. It hung from a darkened metal chain, and beneath it a small, shiny stone with gold marbling dangled in a mesh pouch. The dragon had trained her gorgeous gold eyes on the southern sky. Every few moments, she shuffled her feet in place, churning up the earth beneath her and nearly dislodging the final member of their party, who was still perched on Myn's back.

"*Easy*, Myn," chided Ivy from her perch between the dragon's wings. "He'll get here when he gets here. Look at this nice new building. They built it this big for *you*, you know."

Ivy was dressed a bit more simply than Myranda and Deacon but still looked every bit the part of an ambassador. She wore a fine dress of elegant blue but lacked any crown or other sign of nobility. Her outfit was, of course, not the reason curious onlookers gawked when they thought she wasn't looking. Ivy was a malthrope, a vanishingly rare sight these days. If not for her role in the end of the war and the ongoing defense of both the Northern Alliance *and* Tressor, a creature of her kind would scarcely have been tolerated in civilized society. They were, it was believed, monstrous killers and thieves by their very nature. Ivy was waging a one-person war against such notions and had achieved a limited but measurable degree of success. Indeed, she'd not had to dodge a thrown stone in months.

Myranda removed her heavy cloak and folded it over one arm. Though necessary when soaring through the sky on Myn's back as they ventured from their home in Kenvard, here at the border the cloak was a bit heavy for the pleasantly warm day.

"It really is a remarkable hall," Deacon said, shedding his cloak as well. "It still smells of green wood and fresh paint. These days it seems everything smells of such things."

"I wouldn't have it any other way. For a city, that is the scent of healing and growth," Myranda said.

Ivy wrinkled her sensitive nose. "I could do with a little less of the paint, myself. It's a beautiful color, but blue paint smells *awful*."

"Duke Deacon, Duchess Myranda. Guardians Ivy and Myn," remarked a voice from within the hall. "So fine to see you again."

An ornately armored man with the perpetually youthful face of an elf marched from within the hall and descended the stairs. He was flanked by servants, who eagerly took the guests' cloaks.

"Captain Lumineblade," Deacon said with a courtly bow. "Always a pleasure."

"Yes. It is a rare treat to see you in formal attire without the continued peace of our land hinging upon the outcome of the gathering, Croyden," Myranda said. "Is the queen waiting inside?"

"No. Only some of the lesser dignitaries are present. You are the first of the guests of honor to arrive. I believe Queen Caya has grown weary of being upstaged by your arrival and has chosen to make a grand entrance of her own once the stir surrounding you has run its course."

"Caya wears the title of 'Queen' like it was tailor-made to suit her," Myranda said. "You'd think she was born on the throne."

"I believe it is specifically the adoring crowd to which she's become most accustomed," Croyden said.

"It's nice to be adored," Ivy said, hopping down from Myn's back. "Good to see you, Captain." She turned to Myn and bopped up and down. "Practice on him, Myn!"

Croyden took a step back and eyed the dragon uncertainly. "What precisely are we practicing?"

"You'll see," Ivy said brightly. "She's been practicing for *weeks*. It's *adorable*. Come on, Myn."

The dragon turned reluctantly from the sky and looked first to Ivy, then to Croyden. At her gaze, he took another cautious step back. Becoming accustomed to locking eyes with a predator several times one's own size required more experience than Croyden had. She sidled into position before him, shut her eyes, and angled her head and body in a respectful bow.

"Come on…" Ivy prompted.

Myn rumbled a bit in irritation, then took a slow breath. "*HELLO*," she said. Her voice was deep and resonant, and her pronunciation somewhat breathy, but the word was clear and distinct. Croyden raised an eyebrow and took a step back.

"She speaks?" he said.

"Just a few words," Myranda said, vigorously scratching the brow on Myn's lowered head. "But she's learning so quickly. My heart practically *sang* when she first spoke. I was sick with the thought that somehow in raising her myself I might have robbed her of her voice."

"Now me!" Ivy said, trotting over to look Myn in the eye.

Myn looked at her and, with visible concentration and difficulty, intoned, "*IVY*."

Ivy squealed and threw her arms around the dragon's neck. "I'm so proud! She can say my name, and she can say Myranda's name. Not Deacon, though."

"If I recall her disposition toward you correctly, this doesn't come as a surprise," Croyden said. "Would you care to wait inside?"

"If it isn't too much of a breach of protocol," Myranda hedged, "I'd like a moment to stretch my legs. I'm sure Myn would prefer to wait outside until our friends from Tressor arrive."

"They're here!" Ivy said, pointing to the southern horizon.

Myn's head snapped toward the sky, her eyes lighting up. She practically danced in place when she spotted the small speck approaching just beneath the clouds. Her wings spread and tensed, but she looked longingly at Myranda.

"Go, Myn," Myranda said.

The dragon launched herself skyward with a single bound, causing a bit of a stir in the crowd.

"Admittedly, I've not yet fully learned the nuances of diplomatic occasions such as this, but is it typical for Dragon Riders to attend summits such as this one?" Deacon asked.

"It is not typical for Dragon Riders to attend *anything*," Croyden said. "But the attendance of Grustim and Garr was specifically requested by King Mellawin."

"Why?" Myranda said.

"If my time with Queen Caya has taught me anything, it is that no sane man attempts to plumb the depths of the whims of royalty." He took a cleansing breath. "How, may I ask, are things in New Kenvard?"

"The reconstruction is coming along nicely. It is beginning to feel like a city again. Though…"

"Has something not gone well?"

"Turiel's attack has not been without consequences," Deacon explained.

"How so?" Croyden asked.

"She churned up the spirits of a very dark time," Myranda said. "Some of them have been reluctant to return to their rest. I suspect, when the time comes to rebuild the palace, its halls may never feel quite empty."

"I personally consider it an asset," Deacon said brightly. "One of the things that made Entwell such a potent mystic environment has been the spiritual presence there. In communing with them, we can learn much, and if we can calm their torment, New Kenvard could become a beacon of mystic learning and focus."

Croyden looked at Deacon. He masked his incredulity well, but not quite well enough.

"Have I said something unusual?" Deacon asked.

"I suspect I would be hard-pressed to find another person in all of the Northern Alliance who would consider the literal spirits of a catastrophe haunting the halls of their future home a positive development," Croyden said.

"I see… Every day it becomes more apparent to me just how fundamentally my upbringing has shifted my point of view in different ways from those raised outside Entwell."

Myranda held his hand and gave him a kiss on the cheek. "It helps to have an outsider's eye sometimes. It lets you see the things we've become blind to."

The small crowd of servants and onlookers murmured, then hurriedly parted as not one but two dragons descended from the sky. The first was Myn, landing somewhat heavily. The second was Garr, an armored dragon of green and yellow who landed with a lightness and grace that belied both his massive size and his raw strength. Unlike Myn, Garr had no semblance of formal attire. He wore the same battle-scarred steel helmet with ancient green enamel, a match for the distinctive armor worn by his Dragon Rider. He paced toward the hall with dignity and discipline. Myn lacked the same decorum, prancing around him like an excited puppy reunited with a playmate.

Croyden watched the dragons approach and sighed lightly. "If this kingdom becomes any more absurd, I suspect sanity will become a liability for me."

When the dragons reached the entrance to the hall, the armored Dragon Rider, who had been practically invisible in his place atop the dragon, hopped to the ground and offered a reverential bow.

"Duke, Duchess. It is a privilege and honor to be called upon once again to serve my nation by your side," said Grustim.

He lacked the diplomatic experience of some of the other attendees, and thus was not quite as skilled at hiding the underlying tone of voice that suggested the privilege and honor were tempered somewhat by inconvenience.

Myranda stepped forward and held out her right hand. He mirrored the motion, and each placed their hand on the shoulder of the other, a traditional Tresson greeting. Grustim greeted the others in the same way, then exchanged handshakes and bows as protocol required.

"Always fine to stand beside you, Dragon Rider Grustim. And for once without battle looming over our heads," Myranda said with a respectful nod.

Grustim removed his helmet to reveal his dark-skinned face and sweat-soaked hair. "It is rare for a Dragon Rider to stand beside *anyone* outside of combat. We are soldiers, and we were never meant to be more."

"It is the duty of any good soldier to rise to the challenges of their service. I certainly never imagined I would be hosting such *diverse* functions with any regularity." Croyden gazed down the road that curved to the north. "At least the relevant parties are reasonably punctual."

Myranda and Deacon turned to see the royal procession approaching. Queen Caya had curious tendencies for a royal, and nowhere did they show more clearly than when she traveled. Many nobles would assemble a veritable caravan. While she still sent Croyden ahead with anything deemed indispensable by ceremony or tradition, Caya had swiftly reduced her personal entourage to what others might consider an impossibly austere minimum. She kept her honor guard, of course. While impeccably equipped, they still had the bearing and demeanor of the rogue band of misfits they'd been when known as the Undermine. The only other addition was a small wagon stocked with certain supplies she made certain she was never without. Most prominent among these supplies were barrels of strong drink to share with any and all who were fortunate enough to have an audience with her. This, perhaps more than any other quirk, had made her frequent tours of the kingdom *very* popular with the people. Thus, while they were not officially a part of her procession, a short train of curious or thirsty locals followed like dolphins playing in a great ship's wake.

"Trumpeters! Fanfare!" Croyden ordered the waiting attendants.

Myranda, Deacon, Ivy, Grustim, Garr, and Croyden arranged themselves and stood at attention. The trumpeters lifted their instruments to their lips. As the queen's carriage neared, a hulking man with a worrisome ax rode ahead on a formidable steed and encouraged the locals to keep their distance. He was named Tus, and his reputation alone was more than enough to give any would-be troublemakers second thoughts.

The carriage stopped in front of the receiving line. The queen's driver hopped down from his seat and opened her door. The trumpets blared.

"Yes, yes, enough of that," Caya said, waving her hand and holding the other to her head.

The trumpets abruptly silenced.

"Your Majesty," Myranda said with a curtsy and a grin. "Feeling under the weather?"

"I may have overimbibed," she muttered. "It wasn't a problem until those blasted trumpets. Fanfare is delightful for the ego but murder when fighting the drink. Nonetheless, delightful to see you all. If you'll give me a moment…"

She paused to gather herself, and any irritability or discomfort slid from her expression. She stepped from behind the carriage and turned to the crowd. "Hello, my people!" she crowed.

They raised their voices in response, their adulation washing over her. Caya stepped forward to address some of the nearest people directly, much to the chagrin of her guard.

"It is nothing short of miraculous how she holds a crowd in her hand," Deacon said.

"I can't think of a more important thing for a queen to be than beloved by her people," Myranda said.

"I respectfully submit." Croyden growled, "that a queen should also be wise enough to be of sound mind and body when meeting with the monarch of a foreign power for the first time in recent history."

Myranda nodded. "As much as I've seen her enjoy her wine, I don't know that I've ever seen her feel its effects before."

"There are matters weighing upon her mind, though she has not seen fit to share them with me." Croyden raised his voice. "Your Majesty! If you would come inside, there are matters to attend to."

"Yes, Captain, of course," she called over her shoulder. "Duty calls, my good people. Your queen must serve her subjects."

She pivoted and stepped lightly toward the steps to the hall. When her face was out of the crowd's view, the benevolent and enthusiastic expression she had affected faded somewhat, but it was clear she was still riding high on the love of her people.

"Anyone who says there is no cure for a hangover should try being adored by the masses for a while. It really perks a person up nicely," she said. "Onward! Let's see this new hall of ours."

"There is a proper ceremony and order to—" Croyden began.

"I know that, Croyden, there is *always* a proper ceremony for this and an order for that. We're nobles. It seems all that really means is that every waking moment is codified by some almighty book of protocol written gods know when by gods know who, just to make things difficult. But I've come a long way, my head is throbbing, and I mean to get out of the sun. We'll do the official ceremony when King Mellawin arrives. So says the queen."

"Yes, Your Majesty…" Croyden rumbled with what little patience he had left.

#

The inside of the hall was as magnificent as the exterior. Most of it was a single massive room with vaulted ceilings. Tall windows facing east and west filled the room with sunlight. Chandeliers and sconces bearing white candles chased away the shadows in those places the windows couldn't illuminate. Most impressive, though, were the murals. There were three. To the left of the massive entryway was a grim and foreboding illustration of the Battle of Five Point, the skirmish most considered the first true battle of the Perpetual War. A brighter and more triumphant painting on the opposite side of the door immortalized the Battle of Verril. On the far side of the room, a symbolic representation of the reunion of the North and South filled an entire wall with images of the greatest sights of both the Northern Alliance and Tressor.

"There! There I am!" Ivy said, eagerly pointing at a streak of blue and white rushing among the streets of the Battle of Verril painting. "I sketched this myself, you know. They did a *wonderful* job. And look. There's Deacon above the bell tower. And Caya right there with him. And Myranda, you're on Myn's back! Oh, I wish they'd let me paint it myself…"

Floorboards creaked as Myn padded lightly through the massive doors, curling her neck to investigate the painting.

"Not bad, eh?" Caya said, nudging Croyden. "I become queen, and scarcely a year later we're finishing halls large enough to host *dragons*."

"Indeed," Croyden said. "If you will all follow me, ours is the table at the far end. The platforms on either side are for the dragons. Our thanks to Dragon Rider Grustim for, after a fashion, sharing with us the proper means to seat a dragon."

"My superiors are not in the habit of discussing our methods of care and treatment for our dragons. It was difficult to convince them to part with even so simple a piece of information," Grustim said. "I assume Garr is to be seated to the right, beside me?"

"Indeed."

Grustim turned to his mount and gestured with his head. The green dragon strode inside the building. His posture suggested he was more accustomed to navigating smaller, more cramped spaces when indoors. The platform waiting for him was built from thick timbers and bore a trough filled with cool water and a platter awaiting his meal. He plopped down on his haunches and respectfully awaited further orders.

Myn, on the other hand, was less inclined to wait for instructions. She plodded over to Garr's platform—maneuvering with a grace and speed that suggested she was far more comfortable in human-built surroundings, and wedged herself onto the same platform. It groaned under the additional weight but held firm.

"Guardian Myn," Croyden said. "If you would, the platform on the opposite side is for you."

Myn looked evenly at Croyden, then settled down to get more comfortable. Garr shuffled aside slightly, but between the two of them, there wasn't a spare inch of platform.

Croyden looked nonplussed. "The Tresson representatives are on the right, the Northern Alliance on the left, and the South Crescent here along the front. It has all been laid out to assure each representative is given their proper place and treated as indicated by protocol."

Myn huffed a breath, blinked once, then deliberately swished her tail aside to curl it around Garr's.

"Croyden," Queen Caya said. "For now, I think 'let the dragon sit where she wants' is a worthwhile amendment to protocol. And good advice in general. Garr and Grustim are the only two Tresson representatives anyway. Putting another dragon on their side will even things out."

Myn huffed again, this time with an air of self-satisfaction, then leaned against Garr contentedly.

Garr, trained from birth and every bit as military as his Dragon Rider, was subtle in returning her affection. A trained eye, though, would note the way his muscles eased and his claws flexed, proving he was every bit as pleased to share her company as she was to share his.

"Grustim, my boy," Caya said. "I must say I was a bit surprised to learn the king of Tressor would *not* be attending or sending any other representatives. This is, after all, the first anniversary of peace between our lands. One would imagine he would be as eager to celebrate as I."

"I am not certain anyone is as eager to celebrate as you, Caya," Myranda said.

Caya threw her head back in a laugh. "You might be right at that, but the question remains."

Grustim crossed his arms wearily. "The ambassadors sent their regards and their explanations. I am certain they are better suited than I to answer."

"Bah. They wove some superficially true tale about prior engagements and the like. That's the purpose of ambassadors. You can give it to me straight. Does the man not enjoy my company?"

"It isn't my place to say, or to speculate," he said.

She shrugged. "I'd expected as much. Word has it the king isn't much for traveling. Though a single year isn't much time to shrug off the weight of a century and a half of war, I choose to believe it's more to do with a bad back than lingering bad blood between us. Tell me, have you met with King Mellawin before?"

"Few have."

"So I'd gathered. Myranda, Deacon, I don't suppose you spied our wayward representative from across the sea while you were flitting in on Myn, did you?"

"There was a sizable procession approaching from the east. I would be very surprised if it wasn't the king. I suppose we can expect his arrival in two hours or so," Myranda said.

"Fine, fine. Time enough to do a bit of brushing up on any quirks we are likely to face from the king. I'd very much like to make a good first impression."

Caya and the others made their way to the first available seats. As if by magic, the moment they were seated, servants arrived with bottles of wine and pitchers of ale. Captain Lumineblade gave her a pointed glance.

"Out with it, Croyden," Caya said, filling a tumbler with ale.

"Perhaps Her Majesty would prefer a glass of water, suffering as she is from the effects of whatever drink she imbibed in to excess last night."

"The ale around here is near enough to water for me," she muttered beneath her breath.

"Begging your pardon, Your Majesty?"

"I said Her Majesty will do as suits Her Majesty. And for your own sake, would you stop referring to me by the honorifics? Honestly. You are making me feel as though I am a crown drifting about without a head beneath it."

Croyden fetched a passel of pages from a satchel on his belt. "I would have liked to discuss matters with Tresson dignitaries, if they'd seen fit to attend. The information we have of South Crescent is spotty, and all comes from well before the start of the Perpetual War. I've gathered a bit more from the Tressons in preparation for this occasion, but it is still quite limited. They keep to themselves."

"Anything new since last we discussed them?"

"Not much."

Caya sipped her ale. "Best to share it all anyway. If we are going to acquit ourselves well in this venture, we'd do well to ensure we are all working from the same information."

"This will be fascinating," Deacon said. "I've known my share of South Crescent elves, but most left for Tressor hundreds of years ago."

"We will begin there, I suppose. South Crescent is home, primarily, to elves. A handful of human traders have set foot there, and there may be some dwarfs about, but all would be considered foreigners. We can expect a delegation entirely composed of full-blooded elves from some of the oldest and most storied clans in history."

"Quite an asset to have our own Northern Alliance elf to help get relations off on the right foot."

"No. They will not see things that way. As far as they are concerned, South Crescent elves are the *only* elves. An elf native to the Northern Alliance, like myself, is merely a long-lost offshoot of some South Crescent family who has yet to visit his or her homeland. They will consider me one of them, not one of you."

"Ah. Even so, I trust having you among us will reflect well upon us."

"As much as anything *could*. If what I've been told is accurate, they have something of an obsession with their own superiority as well."

"Not so different from the local variety of elves then." The queen shook her head. "As well as half of the nobles I've known. What do we know about the king himself?"

"He has been in power since shortly before the start of the war. All we really know is that he brokered a deal after hostilities had been running high between Tressor and the Northern Alliance for a few years." Croyden lowered his voice. "Our friends to the south were understandably vague regarding the *nature* of that deal, but it is reasonable to assume that South Crescent provided considerable support to the Tresson army in the form of weapons and supplies over the entirety of the conflict."

"Yes…" Caya said, eyes narrow and face stern. "It will be interesting to see how they regard the people they have effectively been helping to kill for a few generations."

"We have worked hard to heal our relationship with Tressor. I see no reason why we cannot foster a relationship with South Crescent," Myranda said.

"Indeed," Caya said. "I truly hope we can. The last time their monarch ventured across the sea, Kenvard, Ulvard, and Vulcrest were separate. I can't imagine he would make the journey unless he felt he had something to offer and something to gain. And now that the war isn't sapping every last bit of our resources, I wouldn't mind a bit more trade. Do we know what they have to offer?"

"The Tressons have not been forthcoming about it, but we know the elves cultivate a variety of plants unavailable in any reasonable quantity on our continent." Croyden referred to his notes briefly. "They are also skilled craftsmen and probably produced some specialty weapons."

"We can make our own weapons, and so long as I do my job, we won't have much need for any more of them. But if they have something that can grow a bit farther from the front—"

"Border," Myranda corrected.

"… Right. Best to avoid a slip like that in front of the ambassadors…" Caya said. "But the point is, much as it's lovely to have Tressor able to sell us food, and to repay them with minerals and lumber, it would be ideal if we could bolster ourselves with a few new crops. It seems we can't get *anything* to grow in farms that were bountiful when I was a little girl."

"We can only hope such things will be on offer. And that we will be able to meet their price," Croyden said.

"And what might that price be?" Caya asked.

"There is no indication that they need *anything* from us. Again, the Tressons have not been straightforward about the terms of their own trade, but it was clear that negotiations were difficult. South Crescent cuts a hard bargain."

Caya rubbed her hands together. "So do I, Croyden. So do I."

#

Caya sat impatiently as the official greeting ceremony rolled into its second hour. Despite her best efforts, she'd had very little success in convincing those in the loftiest positions of her kingdom that diplomacy could be greatly improved through the removal of some of the surrounding tradition. Naturally, it was only right to treat visiting nobles with respect, but mandating where they sat and who entered first, and reading out an exhausting list of titles and accomplishments for each, turned even a brief discussion into a night-long ordeal. King Mellawin certainly hadn't made it any easier. The man had a *massive* entourage. For the last half hour they'd been introducing and seating an interminable sequence of advisers.

"And now entering, Personal Poet to the King," Croyden announced to the assembly, "Lualil Cossoran."

"A personal poet. Of course. What trade negotiation or memorial anniversary would be complete without a personal poet?" Caya said, delivering the line with an impressive degree of mock sincerity.

Myranda, seated beside the queen, gave her a gentle look of rebuke. "I am quite certain it is a long and beloved tradition of the South Crescent people."

She turned to the elven woman seated across from her. The woman had been introduced as Silla Lorekeeper, though it hadn't been made clear how much of that was her name and how much was her title. She had long features, an inscrutable and stony expression, and a gown and headdress as ornate and frail as a spider web.

"Is that so?" Myranda asked.

"As it happens, no." Silla spoke with the careful, deliberate diction of a non-native speaker who refused to flavor her speech with an accent. "King Mellawin, some seventy years ago, made some additions to his entourage. Personal poets, tasters, and artists are among them."

18

"Personal poet*s*? He has more than one?" Caya said, her expression dropping a bit.

"Owing to the *length* of this journey, he saw fit to include only one of each."

"Ah. Good. I do admire a monarch with the capacity to endure personal hardship for the sake of his duties." She leaned aside to Myranda and whispered, "Wonderful. He's *eccentric*. That bodes well."

The introductions continued for several minutes more. Finally, all in attendance stood as the six trumpeters of the elven king's personal procession raised their silver horns to their lips. The fanfare they played was a softer, more complex one compared to Queen Caya's. The king himself appeared in the doorway unaccompanied, and from the first glimpse, the courtly nobility was astonishingly apparent. His robes had been spun of gold-colored silk. They billowed and flowed as he moved. He wore a silver-gray wooden crown, grown rather than carved. It lacked the symmetry of something crafted by hand, curling left then right with individual pointed branches. Tiny jewel-like leaves dangled from threads affixed to the tip of each branch of the crown. He gripped a short scepter of the same wood in his right hand, a lump of naturally smooth amber cradled in the forked branches at its end. The color of the gem was milky-gold, and a large occlusion marred its heart, vaguely visible when illuminated from behind.

Elves tended toward long, slender features, but King Mellawin was an extreme example even among his own people. He was a head and shoulders taller than Queen Caya, taller even than her hulking bodyguard Tus. His cheeks were slightly sunken, his black hair threaded with a scattering of gray. The robes hid his physique, but his fingers were long and quite slender, hinting at the gauntness of his frame.

As he moved with an otherworldly grace, almost seeming to float down the hall's floor, he raised his left hand, palm facing Queen Caya and fingers slightly curled. She responded in kind.

"Blessed greetings to you on this auspicious occasion of our first meeting," Caya said in a practiced tone.

"And continued blessings to us all on the promise of meetings to come," he replied in a voice oozing with refinement.

Unlike his representatives' voices, his was flavored with the faintest hint of an accent. Caya didn't have the proper ear to place the accent precisely. The only word that seemed a proper description was "regal."

Queen Caya and King Mellawin took a seat, followed by the rest in the assembly hall.

"I am sure everyone in attendance is relieved to know there are no speeches planned for today," Caya said, eying the servers as they set out the first of the banquet's many courses.

"Yes. These events can become so tiresome, don't you agree?" he said.

"Thoroughly. But then, as I am *frequently* reminded, tradition is tradition. And that alone is reason enough to cling to it, evidently," Caya said, bolstered by what seemed to be a common belief.

"If you think *your* people cling to tradition, I formally invite you to visit my own court. A terrible curse of the long-lived, Queen Caya, is the stunning inability to see the value of change."

"I suppose knowing you may not live to see the end of change that comes slowly *does* motivate one to seek it aggressively."

"Quite." He gazed about. "This is truly a remarkable hall. Cut stone. Your people do have an affinity for cut stone. Stacking it into whatever shapes you require."

"Do you not build of stone?"

"We prefer to coax nature into obliging us, rather than inflicting our will upon it with hammer and chisel, but seeing artful edifices such as these might just change my mind on the subject. It is a union of sculpture—which we most certainly *do* embrace—and accommodation. Delightful." He glanced about, fixing his eyes briefly on the pair of dragons, who still shared the same platform. "Oh! By the heart of the trees, I've become so numbed by the drudgery of office I'd nearly forgotten the thrill that has sustained me through the entirety of my sea voyage and my trip through the fair land of Tressor. The Chosen!"

"Yes, of course, you were not present for the introductions, allow me to—"

He raised a hand. "No, please. I am keen to guess. Now let me see. Most of what I know is second- and thirdhand. There *is* a sea separating us, after all. But there was a dragon. *Presumably* one of the pair you've seated at the table. Might I guess… the green one is Myn?"

"I am afraid not," Caya said. "Guardian Myn is the red-and-gold creature cuddled up with him. And presently intimidating the server unfortunate enough to be carrying the boiled potatoes, I see. Croyden, please instruct the servers to see to the dragons first. Best not to have hungry beasts worrying our guests."

"Ah, blast it. It was the armor, you know. I'd imagined a warrior would be dressed for battle. Nonetheless, it is so charmingly absurd to see such beasts seated at the table. You are to be commended for the level of training you have achieved. But back to the game, eh? I find myself at the disadvantage. There is a wizard, and now a duchess, by the name of Myranda. And that must be this exquisite crimson-haired beauty."

"A pleasure to meet you, Your Majesty," Myranda said with a nod.

"Ah!" the king said with a delighted clap. "And so I have balanced the scales. The pleasure, Duchess, is entirely mine. This young and studious gentleman by your side is Deacon, correct? Not one of the Chosen, as I recall, but still nearly so in his significance to the fulfillment of the prophecy."

"That is I, Your Majesty," Deacon said.

"You present yourself with considerable pride and confidence in spite of being overshadowed by so many members of the fairer sex."

"... Thank you," Deacon said, somewhat bemused by the statement.

Mellawin handed his wine aside to be tasted by a man to his left. "Now, now, now. I already know that *two* of the Chosen were malthropes, and that the male lamentably lost his life, so that leaves us with this ivory-furred creature here." He touched his fingers to his head. "Oh, the name escapes me."

"I'm Ivy," she replied. "You sure do know a lot about us."

"Oh, yes. We have listened with interest to every scrap of information our Tresson friends could share. For months I have been positively replete with anticipation of the opportunity to meet you. As you might surmise, I've never met a malthrope before, so you can imagine my amazement at learning not one but *two* of the beasts had been tamed and made to serve so noble a cause."

Ivy's expression sharpened. "*Tamed?*"

"Yes, yes." Mellawin sipped from the glass of wine, which his taster had deemed safe to drink. "Oh, this wine is quite good. But as I was saying, it has been ages since the claim could credibly be made that a malthrope had been seen on our shores. Of course, the stories persist. And they do *not* paint a picture of a warrior who would fight in service of its world. No, not at all. Indeed. Malthrope. Do you know that it is one of very few words that is common to nearly *all* languages? Such was their monstrous nature that the word passed unchanged from one culture to another, again and again. But here we have a dragon and a malthrope put to work. A sign that no matter their dire instincts or simple intellect, any being can be made useful if guided by the right hands.”

“Yeah. Even a closed-minded lout can be king,” Ivy muttered, thankfully beneath her breath.

Mellawin continued. “And that leaves the most troublesome one. Ether, the shapeshifter. It could be anyone, I suppose…” He pointed to Grustim. “It must be you. You are entirely unremarkable otherwise.”

“No,” Grustim said flatly. “I am Grustim, Dragon Rider.”

“Oh, *oh*! Yes, I know the name. A rare Tresson addition to the quests of legend to defeat the otherworldly foe. Of course. I should have supposed as such. Your gear matches that of the dragon, which I now realize must be Garr. I give up, then. Which of you is the shapeshifter?”

“Ether, unfortunately, was unable—or rather, unwilling—to attend,” Caya said, pouring a fresh drink. “A shame; you share her capacity to alienate others with extreme efficiency.”

Rather than displaying shame or irritation at the assessment, King Mellawin grinned. “I take it that I have not made the best of impressions. Please accept my apology. Several of the members of my court were insistent about accompanying me in an advisory role to, in effect, speak for me. I refused. I wanted my contact with the locals to be unfiltered.”

“You brought a poet and an artist and a taster, but you left your cultural advisers behind?” Deacon said.

“Indeed. Who better than the king to decide how the king should behave? But now I see the folly in that thinking, as I’m left to fumble my way through these first steps. I am lamentably inexpert in my direct dealings with lesser races.”

“As a first step toward greater expertise, may I recommend you forgo referring to us to our faces as ‘lesser races,’” Caya said.

“There, you see? I am learning already!” Mellawin said, raising his glass. “Though I am utterly comprehensive in my knowledge of my own lands, I make no claim of anything more than ignorance of this lovely and mysterious continent of yours. Thus far, my dealings with your people have been nonexistent, and my dealings with those of Tressor have been entirely in the realm of business. I have far leveler heads than mine to deal with such matters, and so I have left it to them.”

"Am I to take it, then, that this meeting shall *not* be to discuss business?" Caya said.

"Not in the traditional sense, no. The nature of the currency involved is far more exotic. You see, what you have to offer is the *Chosen*."

"You will have to clarify what I hope is a misguided metaphor."

"Naturally." He turned to his people. "Mingle among the others. This is matter between myself, the queen, and the instruments of fate."

Without a word of question or a moment of delay, Mellawin's people stood and left the table. After a pointed glance and a conspicuous silence, Croyden left as well, along with any other members of the Northern Alliance procession. All that remained were the king, the queen, the Chosen, Deacon, Grustim, and Garr.

"I shall be frank, Queen Caya… May I be informal and call you all by name rather than linking them with titles? It makes for cumbersome conversation."

"You'll afford us the same courtesy?"

"For the duration of this private chat, certainly."

"Then I'll agree to those terms, Mellawin."

"Much obliged. As I said, I shall be frank. I have among my court any number of truly skilled diviners and seers. And few aspects of our world are more visible to such mystics as the framework of the prophecy. Different minds interpret in different words, but the broad strokes are the same here as they are at home. A great war, a threat to the world, divinely anointed warriors, and eventually salvation. I became king some number of years prior to the war that, in short order, clearly represented the one that had been foretold. That much we had anticipated. There is no questioning Tressor was the largest of the world's nations. Anyone who would challenge them and last any amount of time would surely do so *only* if empowered through some unexplained means. We thus did what we believed to be necessary in rendering aid to the side we believed to be the most virtuous… for a modest compensation, of course."

"Of course," Caya said.

"Now, it is only natural for us to assume most, if not *all*, the Chosen would come from among my people."

"Oh? And why would that be?"

"Any number of reasons. Elves have a natural mystic affinity greater than any other race, to name but one."

"I would counter that fairies have a greater mystic affinity, and a strong argument can be made that mermaids do as well," Deacon interjected. "And furthermore, I have found that with sufficient training and discipline, nearly any race can rise to a similar—"

"I am sorry, Deacon, but as you are at best tangentially connected to the individuals in whom I am currently interested, I would prefer you did not interrupt or contradict me." He said sharply.

Deacon blinked, slightly taken aback. "Of course. My apologies."

"As I was saying, ours were at the very least a *likely* people to provide divine warriors, if not the *exclusive* race likely to provide them. Imagine our concern when it slowly became evident that the Chosen *had* arisen, the prophecy *had* been fulfilled, and my people and land played no role. Many among my subjects believe this can only be a sign that we have fallen out of favor with our gods. And as my family holds the throne by divine right, there have been murmurings that some deed of my own is to blame for fate turning its back on us. This is, of course, laughable. Nonetheless, I would not be serving my people to the fullest of my duty if I did not investigate. So to begin, I have questions that *may* be of a sensitive nature regarding the finer points of the fulfillment of the prophecy."

"So long as it won't endanger our people, I naturally defer to the Chosen to decide whether they wish to answer," Caya said.

"I will be as forthcoming as I am able, as will the others, I'm sure," Myranda said.

"First, the most blunt of questions. Are we *certain* that residents, past or present, of my beloved South Crescent have played no role in the fulfillment of the prophecy?"

"I don't know that any fought among us…" Myranda said, her eyes drifting as she thought back.

"There are some…" Deacon paused. "In my education I was taught by some elves who journeyed from your lands. And I lent a hand in both training Myranda and in defeating—"

"I am not interested in something a half-dozen links removed on the chain of glory, Deacon," Mellawin cut in. "Were there, at least, any elves in a role of any importance? I speak of hands on weapons, feet on battlefields, drawing blood and shaping history."

"Croyden's mother and my godmother, Trigorah, might satisfy your requirement, though perhaps not in a way you would prefer," Myranda said.

"Trigorah. Interesting. A strong name, and one with some history among my people. From what family did Trigorah hail?"

"Teloran."

"Teloran! I have no fewer than three Telorans in my personal guard! This is delightful news. What role did she play?"

"She was to be a Chosen; she bore the mark."

Mellawin slapped the table. "There! You see! Already my journey has borne fruit. But that you speak of her in the past tense, and that she does not have a seat at this table, suggests perhaps an unenviable fate?"

"She was rendered impure, unworthy, due to service to the D'Karon."

"… She was a traitor to our world?"

"Through no fault of her own, and she eventually turned her back on them. It was that act that claimed her life."

Mellawin considered this. "The principle contribution of our land to the fulfillment of the prophecy is a treacherous failure. We shall not speak of her again, if you don't mind."

"Forgive me if I am overstepping my bounds, Mellawin, but surely information such as this could have been provided via dispatch or surrogates," Deacon said. "And frankly, if I'd known it would be the subject at hand, I could have much more thoroughly prepared."

"I do believe we were to be discussing business, not history," Caya added.

"Quite so, quite so. A show of what I have to offer is called for." Mellawin turned and gestured vaguely at one of his attendants lingering nearby. "Fetch the satchel."

The attended hurried from the hall.

"One topic that has been discussed at length in the months since the remaining Chosen and the intrepid young Grustim defeated the misguided follower of the D'Karon… this… *Turiel* was her name. I always forget it. At any rate, the subject has been the expansion of the Southern Wastes. I understand Deacon and Myranda have investigated the topic as well."

"Yes. Turiel's attempt to open the—" Deacon began.

"Yes, yes. We know the tale. The important point is that significant damage has been done to the vitality of the land. Its strength has been sapped, and its ability to support life is terribly diminished."

"Very much so," Deacon said.

"What determination have you made about how to *reverse* this effect?"

"The land *will* heal itself, if nothing else," Deacon said. "It took over a hundred years to do the damage, and it will likely take over a hundred years to heal from it."

"Hmm, yes. But as Tressor is primarily peopled with *humans*, and as I understand it, the race has a distinct lack of patience for anything that takes more than one of their lifetimes to complete, there has been some interest in speeding the recovery, and no simple answer has been forthcoming."

"None that is within our… power…"

Deacon trailed off and turned toward the doorway with interest. A moment later Myranda matched his gaze. The attendant entered holding a satchel not much larger than a coin purse. Both wizards watched it intently as the attendant delivered it to the table. Mellawin grinned at their reaction.

"My people had informed me you were both wizards of the highest renown. I suppose I would have been disappointed if you'd not felt the power of this before I showed it to you," Mellawin said.

He tugged a plate from the place setting beside him and unfastened the thread cinching the satchel shut. The contents were anything but impressive. From the look of the stuff, Mellawin had reverently revealed a bit of dried tobacco. Deacon was visibly enthralled by the substance.

"Is that… dried moon herb?"

"Moon herb. I suppose that is one name for it. My people call it 'nara leaf.'"

"I'm quite familiar with this. The tea of these leaves is profoundly restorative to one's spirit. The plant is also the source of moon nectar," Deacon said.

"Indeed. Again, if what I have been told is accurate, the city of Verril owes its freedom and safety at least in part to the less-than-judicious application of moon nectar."

"I consumed a rather inadvisable dosage of it in defense of the city, yes," Deacon said.

"Setting aside for a moment the question of where you acquired any quantity of the stuff, I am pleased to inform you that nara leaf is a small but well-cultivated part of the royal gardens. Some quality of the plant, not yet fully understood despite our great efforts, motivates benevolent spirits to gather themselves about this herb. We value it above almost any other product of the land. Every drop of nectar, every leaf, every stem, every pinch of soil is carefully collected and processed. It is my understanding that these D'Karon, or their agents at any rate, drank the land dry and left it a wasteland in this plane and the plane of spirits. This has caused the spread of the Southern Wastes of Tressor, and I must assume a similar blight has befallen much of the Northern Alliance. My court mystics believe, and I have every confidence in their assessment, that if this quantity of the leaves could be spread across an area the size of a small farm, within a year or two the blighted nature of the land would begin to recede. That, I suspect, is enough to satisfy even the most *impatient* and *short-lived* of races. It certainly beats the century or more you are currently anticipating."

"How much of that substance do you have?" Myranda asked.

"Not enough to solve your problem overnight, or even over the course of the next few years. But more than enough to markedly improve the land both north and south of the border."

"And how much will it cost us?" Caya asked warily.

"Pleasant to see there is at least one business-minded individual at the table."

"The way I figure it, if you've been selling supplies to the Tressons for a century and a half, I've got to believe the income from the war effort has become a comfortable and reliable way to keep the coffers full. Now that peace has robbed you of that, you'll either be searching for the best way to replace it, or the best way to start the war back up."

"You injure me with the insinuation that I would seek to resume the horrific bloodshed that, indeed, had served as a valuable but distasteful part of our trade. My people are implicitly peaceful. That, as a matter of fact, is one large piece of the initial price I had in mind."

"You want troops?"

"In a way. A very small number of troops, and very specific ones. I request that the Northern Alliance loan to me the Chosen, and Tressor loan Grustim and Garr."

"Why?"

"There *is* a military aspect to the visit, but such details can be discussed later. There is no doubt a sumptuous feast awaiting us, and I have already prattled on far too long. Suffice it to say, it will be a rather small matter, well within your ample skills. The *primary* reason I request the aid of the warriors of myth and legend is one of popularity."

"Popularity," Caya said flatly.

"Yes. As I have said, my people are quite peaceful, so there is no war to unite us. And the trade with Tressor has kept us quite comfortably wealthy with very little effort. Through all of that time, I have been the king. I have had the most peaceful and uneventful rule of any monarch in the history of South Crescent. There are those who question precisely what role a king *has* in times of such peace and bounty. Pile upon this the matter of the prophecy passing us over, and my popularity is wavering markedly. If I were to return with the fabled Chosen aboard my ship, on the other hand…"

"It seems a rather frivolous reason to summon individuals with a great deal of work to do in their own lands."

"I am a king. It is my prerogative to be frivolous. And remember that in exchange you will be given the right to purchase the antidote to the plague of your land."

"We do not even know that this treatment will work."

"I have in my possession two more such satchels. Consider the three of them a gift. You are capable of traveling quite swiftly, as both the Tresson and Alliance representatives have dragons to ride. I will be making a direct visit to the king of Tressor before returning to my ship. More than enough time for you to test the veracity of my claims. The effects of the treatment while subtle, begin at the very moment of application. If you find them to be worthwhile, I shall at this moment commit to the whole of the first year of treatments to be delivered immediately in exchange for a brief visit by these remarkable individuals and the timely completion of the tasks to be discussed later."

Caya turned to the others, rubbing her hands together. "What do you say?"

"I do as I am ordered. If my superiors deem it a worthy assignment, I shall go," Grustim said simply.

"I've always wondered what things were like in South Crescent. And I've never been on a long sea voyage before!" Ivy trilled.

"If we determine it will help both the North and South to recover from the D'Karon damage, I don't think we have any choice but to oblige," Myranda said. "Though I would prefer to know a bit more about these 'tasks to be discussed later.'"

"Nothing that you haven't done before. Some investigation, and if that investigation turns up something troubling, whatever steps are necessary to deal with the situation."

"Will there be battle?"

"I certainly hope so!" Mellawin said brightly. "We don't anticipate it, but to have the Chosen do battle on our soil? My people would be delighted! It would be a divine acknowledgment."

Myranda looked at the queen, who offered a subtle but certain expression of encouragement.

"Again, if what you offer *can* ease the burden of our people, I don't think I can refuse."

"Splendid. Then we are in agreement! And to think that my advisers warned me humans were unreasonable and shortsighted."

"And mine warned me that elves were self-satisfied and blunt."

"Not all of us." He laughed. "Just the best of us. Enough! Commence with the food and drink. I want to see what revelry the Northern Alliance has to offer."

Caya raised a glass. "I'll drink to that."

#

Hours later as the ceremony was nearing completion, Deacon excused himself from the banquet and managed to encourage Myranda to join him. Much to the staff's confusion, the duke and duchess of Kenvard discreetly asked to be shown outside through the servants' entrance.

"Deacon, I appreciate that you are eager to test the capabilities of the nara leaf, but it may not be entirely appropriate to do so *during* the negotiations to acquire it," she said.

They stepped lightly through the courtyard between the rear of the hall and its stables, which made for something of an obstacle course to avoid ruining some very stately shoes. Deacon was notably less careful in this regard, guided entirely by his curiosity and enthusiasm.

"I've never worked with these leaves in their dried state. It wasn't my area of focus while in Entwell. Even if it was, the plant is so difficult to grow, knowing that it could be of aid in our current situation would have done us little good." He spotted a patch of withered earth a short distance past the stables. "There. I can feel the damage done in this place quite clearly. We need to test."

He held out his hand, and his gem obediently leaped into the air beneath it. A simple, weak spell wove into the left half of the barren patch of earth. Blades of grass reluctantly sprouted, struggling to flourish despite his mystic influence. When he was satisfied, he encouraged Myranda to hold out the bag of nara leaf and sprinkled the tiniest pinch of it onto the other half of the soil. A few rough rakes with his fingers mixed it in, and he resumed his spell.

The difference was pronounced and immediate. Grass rose in lush, thick tufts. A flower, its seed long dormant in the soil, extended from the ground and bloomed. Even a few fragments of dried leaf were enough for the magic to be restored, and thus for the life-giving nature to surge back.

"Look at it…" Myranda said.

"Like fertilizer, but for the *soul* of the land," Deacon said. "I don't believe it has enhanced the soil beyond what it would have been if not tainted in the first place, but it certainly wiped away the influence of the D'Karon… I wonder… The purpose of this proposed mission is to see if the D'Karon have had some sort of influence on North Crescent. If they *have* made a place for themselves there, that would mean that South Crescent and Entwell are the only places entirely untouched by them. And they are also the only places I know of with nara leaf. Do you suppose the leaf is somehow abhorrent to the D'Karon?"

"A question worth considering, but for another time. Even if there is nothing to be found, if lending our aid to Mellawin's people can forge a relationship between the Northern Alliance and South Crescent, *and* will afford us access to these leaves to undo the damage to our land, there is no doubt in my mind what needs to be done."

"Indeed. We should discuss terms immediately," Deacon said. "The sooner we can shake hands on this agreement the sooner both North and South will recover."

She glanced at his hands, now filthy from his experiment. "It might be wise, before shaking hands, to wash them. Mellawin may not find your enthusiasm quite as endearing as I do."

Chapter 2

Myranda took a deep breath of the cool air rushing by. Myn seldom had cause to fly near the sea. It was a rare treat for her. Where land met sea, where desert met plains, where mountains met forest, these were the places the young dragon most loved to soar.

"There, I see the port," Myranda called.

The dragon angled her head down and scanned the coast. An amber ribbon of beach turned steadily more gray and rocky as it wove northward. In the distance, the most southerly edge of the Eastern Mountains was just visible. The forbidding slopes and cliffs of those mountains left the people of the Northern Alliance without a single decent harbor in the Crescent Sea. That, among other things, was to blame for their utter isolation for the duration of the war.

Thread-thin roads traced their way toward a mottled patch of coast. It was too far below for the individual buildings or streets to be visible, but there was no doubt that the city below was Port Mataam. Ships drifted lazily on the churning waves, some throwing nets to haul in fish, others heading north or south with bounty from other coastal cities.

Myn spiraled closer. A trio of ships in the harbor stood out as utterly foreign in their design. The Tresson ships were artful, almost sculptural. These visiting ships looked as though they'd barely been touched by the hand of a carpenter. Their forms were smooth and organic, woven of thin branches, bound with vines. The masts were twisted, forked branches. Sails strung between them had the faded green color of leaves at the beginning of fall. One could almost imagine such things grew along the shores of South Crescent and simply drifted across the sea sometimes.

"It looks as though word of our arrival has not been adequately spread," Deacon said, gazing down.

The dragon watched the people below as they raised their heads. Myn had flown over dozens of cities. As different as the people throughout the continent were, they all seemed to react in the same handful of ways upon seeing a dragon flying over their homes for the first time. Most ran for shelter and encouraged others to do the same. The rest stood in awe at the majesty and size of the beast casting its shadow across the land. There were perhaps only two cities on the entire continent that didn't bat an eye at the comings and goings of dragons, and thanks to Myn, New Kenvard was one of them.

Myranda indicated a wide-open section of pier where a small assemblage of elves was loading things onto the deck of the largest of the three elven ships. As she was carrying Ivy, Deacon, and Myranda, along with some basic supplies, Myn's landing was a bit heavier than it might have been. This didn't bother Myn at all, but the shaking pier nearly pitched a pair of crew members into the water.

"My apologies!" Myranda called, hopping down from Myn's back. "Is everyone all right?"

The elven crew surveyed them silently, then continued loading.

"Ah! You have arrived! And not a moment too soon," called the king from the deck. "Come aboard, come aboard!"

"Look at the ship!" Ivy called, leaping from Myn's back after enduring the landing with her eyes shut tight. "I've never seen anything like it! And look at all of *those* ships! And the sun on the water! The sea this far south is so *different*. I miss the twinkle of the ice, but the warmth and all of the *birds*—I've got to get a look from down on the beach. I'll be right back!" She dashed off without waiting for an answer or permission.

"Not *perfectly* obedient yet, I take it?" the king called. "Still, that you've had any level of success in her training at all is quite impressive. But quickly, give the servants your things and come aboard. If you require, I shall have someone fetch the beast. My people will show you to your quarters for the journey. Oh, and do not trouble yourself asking them any questions. The majority of the crew has been instructed not to speak to you."

"Why not?"

"Because you are nobility of the highest order! Only personal representatives of the king and his court are permitted the honor of informal discourse."

"But what if we have questions or require guidance?" Deacon asked.

"Ah, yes… Stay where you are for a moment. Someone with the proper status will be along shortly. When your things are stowed, my people will show you to our communal meeting chamber. There is much to discuss."

Like Ivy, the king didn't see the need to linger long enough for a reply. Turning to Deacon as he slipped from Myn's back, Myranda said, "It seems King Mellawin has a rather firm view of hierarchy."

"In both political and natural order," Deacon said. "I fear if he does not adopt a more balanced attitude toward Myn and Ivy, this will be a very awkward journey."

"To say the very least."

A well-dressed and rather frazzled representative of the crown, who evidently had not anticipated the sudden need to meet with foreign dignitaries, rushed from the ship. It was Silla Lorekeeper. Her previously detached and disinterested attitude made the expression of borderline panic almost jarring in comparison.

"Guardians of the Realm and Chosen. I apologize wholeheartedly for any confusion or delay," she said hastily, fixing her hair. "I was not made aware of the king's instruction of the crew to avoid dealing with you directly and thus was not prepared to act in the capacity of a ship's guide."

"That is quite all right," Myranda said. "It seems the king, if you will excuse the observation, isn't well-versed in the finer details of such matters."

"King Mellawin has traditionally employed a sizable and well-trained staff to carry out his orders. Having him present to direct them personally has been… disruptive. This way, please."

She turned and paced back up the gangplank with as much grace and dignity as she could salvage. Myranda and Deacon followed, but as the gangplank was sized for humans and not dragons, Myn hesitated.

"Excuse me," Myranda said. "I beg your pardon. A few questions?"

Silla turned, now once again wearing the weary expression that was so natural a fit for her features. "Yes, Duchess?"

"How shall I refer to you?"

"Silla or lore keeper, as you prefer."

"Silla, what arrangements have been made for Myn during this journey?"

"There are cages for both Myn and the Dragon Rider's mount, if and when it arrives."

"Cages?" Myranda said, eyes narrowed.

"Indeed. Surely you do not intend that they be permitted to roam free. The crew is already quite understandably uneasy about a fire-breathing creature riding aboard a ship. Fire is a considerable concern for them."

"Myn can be trusted to behave herself so long as she isn't kept from me or Deacon. In our experience, she tends to act up when confined."

"I… see…"

"Perhaps if you could take us to this cage, we could determine how to make it more acceptable."

"It is on the main deck. This way," she said.

Myranda turned to Myn. "We'll call you up once we're there. Stay here and don't cause any trouble."

Myn gave Myranda a mildly reproachful look. She plopped down on her haunches, shaking the pier again and this time succeeding in spilling one of the workers into the water below.

"Myn!" Myranda snapped. "Now go get him."

The dragon slumped somewhat, a flicker of shame subtly crossing her expression before she thumped over to the edge of the pier. After a hesitant look at the water, she cautiously looped her tail around the floundering worker. She hoisted him up, set him down, and watched with satisfaction as he backed cautiously away from her. A few vigorous flicks shook away the unwanted seawater from her tail.

"That's better. Now behave yourself, please," Myranda said.

Silla continued along the gangplank. The wizards followed a few steps behind.

"I apologize again," Myranda said. "She's still a bit of a child."

"So it would seem," Silla said. "Not to worry. I am certain the king will overlook this minor act of assault against one of his people."

Myranda glanced to Deacon. A change of subject seemed in order.

"Tell me, Silla. What sort of quarters do you have for us? I can only imagine the sort of luxury a ship as grand as this one has in store."

"Naturally, when we arrive in our home kingdom of Sonril, we shall provide you with more appropriate hospitality. While aboard, your lodging will be quite simple by our standards, I am afraid. I have only traveled via our own ships in the past, but I am assured our people's interpretation of minimum acceptable accommodation is *vastly* in excess of the requirements of other races. My own room is not so different from the quarters I was given at the Tresson palace during our visit. Your rooms will be of a greater quality than mine."

"And what of Ivy?" Deacon asked.

"The malthrope, I understand, is treated as an equal member of your force. Thus, her room is a match for yours."

"And if we had not made her status among us clear?"

"Beasts are normally kept in the cargo hold. Were there room, that is where the dragons would have been stowed."

Myranda took a steady breath. "I hope you will see, as our own people have slowly come to realize, that Ivy and her kind are no mere beasts."

"No doubt under your expert guidance we shall learn much. Though the lesson, lamentably, is likely to be short-lived."

"Why?"

"Because Ivy and her people are short-lived, and unless I have misunderstood their plight, she is among the last. This way to the deck."

Myranda gave Deacon another look. There was a time when Deacon might have reached out with his mind to discuss his feelings silently. Now it was hardly necessary. She could read his mind from the look on his face, and he could do the same with her. These elves elevated superiority and dismissal to an art form, and it grated on Myranda's nerves terribly. Never before had she encountered someone who so expertly delivered peerless hospitality while looking resolutely down their nose at their visitors. The elves were so assured of the wisdom of their worldview that every interaction with another race had the distinct tone of humoring a child.

She tried to push the irritation from her mind and instead admired the unique surroundings. Just as was the case for the outside of the ship, the interior looked as though a massive, curling tree had simply chosen to grow into the shape the elves had requested. Here and there, doorways formed from arched branches. Each was a slightly different shape. Most had bark-like doors that had been fit precisely into the openings. The floor was a nearly flat mat, woven from thinner branches or vines. Light came from candles held in the forks of silver-leafed branches emerging from the walls. They burned with a curious, perfectly white flame. Myranda held out her hand as they walked past. The flames were almost free of heat, and each had a small but quite skillful enchantment upon it.

"Impressive," Myranda said. "I learned a fair bit of fire magic during my education, but I've never seen it put to such common and utilitarian use."

"Having not had to devote the talents and lives of our best spell casters to military conquest or defense, we have been free to weave the touch of magic far more deeply into the fabric of our society. I would share the details of the spells with you, of course, but they are—"

Deacon happily spoke up. "Oh, it is quite clear what's been done. The flame has simply been coaxed to feed upon the mana intrinsic to the ship rather than consuming the wood itself. I imagine some basic earth magic has been employed to guide and speed the growth of the trees into the form desired, and such an act would produce a plant with a very strong affinity to magic. The entirety of the ship acts as a weak mystic focus in much the same way a wizard's staff might, even in the absence of a focusing crystal. It is a rather brilliant application of magic, as it means the whole of the ship can be lit safely with self-sustaining mystic flame."

Myranda smirked at him.

"Oh! But I've interrupted you. Please continue."

She spoke with the slow deliberate tone of one hoping to make her irritation. "I was going to suggest that such matters were secrets of the Sonril sages. Perhaps not as carefully protected as they *might* be… Here, the main deck is just this way."

They ascended a set of stairs that was as wavy and irregular as everything else on the ship. It was a bit unnerving to move about on something so large and yet so free of the straight lines and regular curves Myranda normally associated with craftsmanship. If there was one place that had at least a semblance of a normal design, at least by Kenvardian standards, it was the main deck. The deck boards were broad and flat, quite possibly the only traditionally milled lumber so far, but even here the uniqueness of their workmanship showed through, as it was all assembled without a single nail. Instead, the boards, planks, and assorted mechanisms of the ship were connected with complicated joinery that spoke of absurd precision and patience.

"There, the cages," Silla said, gesturing to the far end of the deck. "As you can see, they should be more than adequate."

Myranda and Deacon surveyed the cell that Myn was expected to inhabit during the journey. It looked out of place surrounded by such elegant and natural beauty. Stout iron bars traced out a boxy chamber quite large enough to comfortably accommodate Myn. The roof was thatched to spare the interior the full brunt of the sun, and wooden troughs for both food and water were bolted to the floor near hatches that would permit them to be refilled without braving the interior. In truth it was probably larger than the converted stable that Myn slept in back in New Kenvard, but what it gained in size it lacked in hospitality. One would be hard-pressed to argue this was anything but a prison.

Deacon looked doubtfully at Myranda, then glanced back at the cell. There was a second identical one beside it awaiting Garr. He stepped up to it and inspected a heavy lock set into the open door. "I am not entirely certain this will be well received."

"We took great pains to have it made for just this purpose," Silla said. "This much hammered metal was difficult to come by in Sonril. As you may have observed, we believe metal has its place, and that place is *not* among the nobility."

"Is there something inherently ignoble about metal?" Myranda said.

"Gold, silver, the *noble* metals are of course well and good in polite society. But iron? It is the stuff of weaponry, armor, and tools. These are things best left to lower hands. To secure these cages, we had to contract the Workslag Clan, a rare dwarfish family worthy of collaboration."

"Interesting. I suppose those elves with whom I was educated were too far removed from their origins to maintain the same fascinating beliefs," Deacon said. "Or perhaps they occupied a lower caste. I wonder if—"

Deacon's musings were cut short by a brief, confused outburst from the pier, followed by Myn's form vaulting up to the edge of the ship. She touched down heavily on the thick branch that formed the railing, rocking the ship ever so slightly. The crew on deck scattered and shouted what Myranda suspected were the most elegant and musical profanities she'd ever heard. Myn looked uncertainly behind her at the water, as if fearful it was trying to sneak up on her. Satisfied it wasn't plotting something, she scanned the deck, spotted Myranda and Deacon, and hopped over to them. The flurry of motion and the unannounced arrival of the dragon once again caused a crack in Silla's dour demeanor. She leaped backward, one hand clutching her chest.

"Control your beast!" she blurted.

The dragon glared at her, unimpressed by the demand.

"Myn, I'm sure our hosts would appreciate it if you would wait until called," Myranda said. "But now that you are here, what do you think of your home aboard the ship?"

Myn turned to the cage and padded up to it. Her movements were cautious and measured, as though she expected the cage to contain some manner of trickery. She sniffed at the troughs, craned her neck up to inspect the thatched roof, and finally discovered the lock in the door. Her gaze slowly and savagely shifted to Silla.

"Naturally, the door would only be *locked* after Myn had retired for the evening," Silla said defensively.

The assurance must not have been sufficient for Myn, as she took this opportunity to put her burgeoning language skills to use.

"*No,*" she rumbled.

"It is a simple and reasonable precaution, and one that is *quite* nonnegotiable. We *must* take the safety of the crew into consideration."

Myn leaned down and came face-to-face with Silla. The lore keeper took a single step back, but tried to remain firm.

"*No,*" Myn repeated with force.

"I-it is simply *n-not* negotiable," Silla stated.

Myn released a slow, hissing breath, then turned to the cage. She stood just outside its open doorway, planted her feet, and curled her head aside. Her horns hooked through the bars, and she flexed her neck.

"What is she doing?" Silla asked.

"I suspect she is proposing a compromise," Myranda said. Normally, she would more vigorously chastise Myn for what she was doing, but the attitude prevalent among her hosts had already begun to wear on her. At the moment, a bit of disobedience felt called for.

The metal of the hinges creaked and groaned. Muscles visibly flexed and strained in Myn's shoulders and neck. The metal popped, tore, and finally gave way. Myn's head whipped aside, and the door hurled from her horns, spinning through the air until it disappeared over the starboard side of the ship to splash down into the water.

The job done, she stepped into the cage, turned to Silla, and plopped down.

"This is… how can… this is *utterly* unacceptable," Silla said. "The lock on the cage was a perfectly reasonable precaution."

"Perhaps so," Deacon said. "But in light of this demonstration, it would appear to have been an *insufficient* precaution as well."

"The king will *not* be pleased with this," Silla said.

As if beckoned by the mention, the king's voice boomed from a nearby doorway. "What is this commotion?"

"The representatives from the Northern Alliance *refuse* to control their beast. It has assaulted one member of our crew already, knocking him into the water, and now it has sabotaged our security precautions against it."

Mellawin surveyed the circumstances of the deck. "Has anyone been hurt?" he asked.

"Not for lack of *trying*," Silla said.

"I imagine the dragon tore the door from the cage?"

"With *ease*."

"Then I suspect if no one was hurt, it *was* for lack of trying, as she certainly wouldn't have had to try very *hard*. At any rate, she seems to be behaving herself now. Come, I grow weary of waiting. There are matters to discuss. We shall show you to your rooms after."

"As you wish," Myranda said. She turned to Myn. "We will return shortly. Do *not* cause any more trouble."

Myn tipped her head up and gave a short huff, then plopped down again.

#

Myranda, Deacon, and Silla disappeared below deck, leaving Myn alone with the crew. To the dragon, this was already beginning to feel unpleasantly like one of the many trips they'd had to make to the south recently. As nice as the flights were, seldom did she get to spend more time with Myranda and the others than when they were traveling. Once they arrived, there was little for her to do but laze about and await her return. Deacon, Ivy, and even Ether were sliding with varying degrees of success into their roles as ambassadors and role models for their people. Myn was as often as not left out in the cold. It had taken her some time to truly understand why it was necessary, but no amount of understanding would make her *like* it.

She shut her eyes and tried to doze. It *had* been a very long trip, and she was rather exhausted, but something seemed wrong. Now that she didn't have something to distract her, she became aware of the motions of the deck beneath her. It was pitching first one way, then the other. The bobbing and swaying was subtle, but she was utterly unaccustomed to the ground moving beneath her feet at all. She stood and plodded over to the edge of the deck. This was the side of the ship away from the pier, and thus the only things waiting below her were gentle blue waves lapping at the hull of the ship. She raised her head and looked out to the sea. The mere sight of so much water caused her heart to flutter with anxiety.

Myn did *not* have a good history with water. Though she had fond memories of a place called Entwell, both reaching it and escaping it had involved copious amounts of violent, rushing water. And then there had been an encounter with a frozen lake, one that had in a very real sense ended her life. Until now she'd been too preoccupied with these pointy-eared creatures who were telling her where to go and what to do to consider just what lay ahead. As the pieces came together, she didn't like the picture that formed.

Two waves slapped together and sent a spritz of water high enough to sprinkle her face. She stumbled back as if struck, then bounded to the other side of the ship. There she found a pier, but just more of the same water beneath it and around it. Crew members dove to avoid her as she dashed to the rear of the boat, then rushed to the front. Water all around. They were *floating* on the water… And the journey had just begun. Myn peered at the land to the west and realized it soon would be left behind. Her heart went from fluttering to hammering. The desire to be with Myranda and make her proud was floundering in the torrent of fear at just what that would require. She wasn't frightened of creatures she had to battle. No matter how large, they could always be beaten. But the water, the sea… once she was in its icy clutches, there was nothing she could do to overcome it. It could not be beaten.

"Myn! There you are," called a voice. "Did you see who threw that big metal thing into the ocean?"

She snapped her head toward the source. It was Ivy, and the young malthrope instantly saw in the dragon's eyes that she was troubled.

"Is something wrong?" she said.

Myn glanced to the water anxiously, then back to Ivy.

"Oh... *Oh*... Myranda was worried about this. Silly me, forgot all about how the water scares you. Well you don't have to worry about it. We're all here with you."

Ivy hopped to Myn's back and gave her neck a reassuring hug. "If I can get used to flying, you can get used to sailing. And look! You'll have more friends to keep you company."

Myn twisted her head and saw that Ivy was indicating the sky. That could only mean one thing. She darted her eyes about until she found the familiar shape in the sky.

"*Whoa*," Ivy giggled as Myn took a few steps along the deck, spread her wings, and launched skyward. She held on tightly, eyes shut, as the dragon made the impromptu trip upward and the ground dropped away beneath them. "Y-you've got to warn me before you do that, Myn," she said shakily. "I'm not *that* used to flying."

Myn caught a rising warm current and circled, climbing ever upward, until she was high enough to tuck her wings and glide toward a green dragon and its rider.

Garr offered little more than a glance in her direction, but that was enough. Garr was like her, but he'd seen more, done more. Like Myranda and Ivy, and even Deacon, being with him made her feel as if she belonged, but with Garr, there was something more. Something strong and familiar. Something she couldn't quite explain, but that she knew she needed.

Ivy briefly released Myn's neck with one hand to venture a wave to Grustim. Like the dragon, he offered only a glance. Myn felt a twinge of resentment when she thought of how closely they worked, how inseparable the two were, but it passed. Myn had her family, Garr had his. She wouldn't dream of giving up Myranda, so she would have to tolerate Grustim.

The pair of dragons and their riders wheeled downward again. The vast blue expanse of the sea sprawled out before Myn, cutting at her. She focused on the warm pressure of her rider, the confident grace of Garr, and the wisdom and friendship of those waiting below. It would not be easy. In truth, it would be beyond trying. But if they could do it, she could do it.

Garr landed on the pier. Myn landed directly on the deck of the ship, then leaned on the railing to see what was keeping him. The elves were exchanging words harshly with Grustim, then pointing in Myn's direction. Garr turned in her direction and unfurled his wings.

Ivy hopped from Myn's back and stomped over to the sturdy metal cells. Her eyes narrowed. "Why are there cages here?"

Myn replied with a glance at the nearest elf and a huff of irritation.

"Is this where they're having you stay?" The air around Ivy flickered with the faintest of red auras. "A cage? They're putting you in a *cage*?"

Garr touched lightly down onto the deck of the ship and allowed Grustim to dismount.

"They're having the dragons sleep in *cages*!" Ivy said, charging up to the Dragon Rider. "Can you believe that?"

"It is not ideal, but we must endure it for the sake of the mission. Few understand how to properly deal with dragons."

"You treat them like *people*, Grustim. It isn't hard."

"Not so. Dragons demand a great deal more respect than people. In a way, the cage acknowledges their power."

The Dragon Rider directed his mount to enter the still-intact cage. Garr obliged, then turned and sat within, coolly observing his surroundings and awaiting a fresh order. Several of the crew leaped at the chance to have at least *one* of the dragons properly locked away. They heaved the heavy cage door shut and latched it.

Being treated as a prisoner did not appear to bother Garr at all. Myn felt differently about the situation. She stalked forward, ignoring the objections of the crew, and once again locked her horns between the bars. The latched door didn't afford nearly as much leverage as the open one, but she was nothing if not persistent. A few seconds of creaking and groaning tore the door free. Myn let it drop to the deck, its twisted, bent bars causing it to wobble and rattle. She slipped through the empty doorway and coiled herself into what free space remained until she was squeezed pleasantly beside Garr, her head resting contentedly on his neck.

Ivy crossed her arms and looked to the dismayed crew. "There. Maybe next time treat *all* of your guests like guests and this won't happen."

"It was my understanding that you were an ambassador," Grustim said. "This does not appear to be diplomatic behavior."

"Part of being a diplomat is about making sure people don't mistreat your friends. Lucky for me, most of my friends can take care of themselves. Oh! Speaking of diplomacy, we'd better find Myranda and Deacon. They're probably waiting for us."

#

King Mellawin sat at the head of a large table, which, like the rest of the ship, looked as nearly as nature intended as the function would allow. It and the chairs surrounding still smelled of sap and lush growth. Deacon sat to his right side with Myranda beside him. Silla and a handful of other subordinates filled seats to his left, and servants stood at the corners of the room. The room itself, though nothing compared to a dining hall of a palace, was still a great deal larger than anything Myranda imagined she would have found on a ship. Servants set the table with hot tea and assorted fruits, breads, and cheeses from across the sea as King Mellawin grew visibly impatient.

"Shall we wait for your malthrope friend? She does not seem to be the sort to deal with the more complex, intellectual matters I hope to discuss with you today," he asked.

"If the task ahead of us concerns her, I certainly feel she should be present," Myranda said. "She is every bit as intelligent and capable as we. To be perfectly honest, I would have preferred it if there were some way Myn could be included as well."

"Lamentably impossible. Though my crew was handpicked for this trip, the matters to be discussed are not for their ears, and I simply cannot foresee anything good coming from attempting to find someplace private that is still accessible to that magnificent beast of yours." He tipped his head, brushing some of his long hair behind his ear. "Ah, but I do believe I hear the malthrope coming now."

"If you would, Mellawin. Her name is Ivy. I do wish you would refrain from referring to her by her species, even when she isn't present. I can't imagine you would be fond of the idea of Deacon and myself referring to you as 'the elves' behind your backs, nor do I imagine you would refer to us as 'the humans' either."

"Yes, yes. Of course," the king said. "A thousand and one pardons. It may be our most glaring fault that the people of my race are *quite* slow to change, but it is a failing I am keen to correct."

Ivy stepped through the door, accompanied by members of the crew. Her eyes were wide with wonder as she gazed at the veritable work of art the ship was.

"Myranda, Deacon! Isn't this place *gorgeous*? How do you think they got the branches to curve so perfectly to form all this? Was it magic? And—" Her expression hardened as though her mind had just caught up with her and reasserted her earlier indignation. "Did you see they wanted Myn and Garr to be in *cages*?"

"Yes, a misstep, to be sure," Mellawin said. "This journey is nothing if not educational regarding the many ways in which your people differ from our own."

Ivy's expression softened a bit. "Myn ripped off both doors, though, and now she's napping with Garr. Those two are so *cute* together."

She plopped down in the seat beside Myranda. One of the servants stepped up to fill her teacup and artfully assemble some refreshments on her dish.

"Oh, *thank* you," Ivy said. She wrapped her hands around the delicate cup and raised it to her sensitive nose to breathe in the aroma. "A hot drink will be lovely. Flying can really put a chill through you."

"I can only imagine. And I only ever *intend* to imagine, as I certainly do not intend to try it," Mellawin said. "Now that we are all present, shall we begin?"

"Grustim is getting changed out of his armor. It will take him some time to get here," Ivy said.

"Grustim and Garr were invited for completion's sake, as they were involved in the most recent acts of the Chosen. I didn't see much value in including him initially, but my advisers insist that leaving Tressor entirely out of this enterprise would have been inadvisable. One must maintain relationships with one's longtime allies, and so the Dragon Rider comes along. But we needn't delay on his behalf. He is a soldier, his training is to follow orders, not to understand their origins. You all, on the other hand, have precisely the expertise to help intelligently devise an appropriate stratagem. So let us begin. First, my lore keeper will explain the historical underpinnings of this dilemma."

Silla nodded. She dismissed the servants and what must have been the lowest-ranking pair of subordinates with a gesture, then fetched a small folio of pages from a satchel beside her chair.

"To understand the issue at hand, you must first understand the nature of the Crescents. Though they are a match in size, the North and South Crescents could not be more different from one another. South Crescent is nothing short of a paradise. It is almost entirely forested. It is chiefly populated by elves, and the only nation of any note is, of course, Sonril with Mellawin as its king. For our purposes, 'South

Crescent' and 'Sonril' may as well be spoken interchangeably. In addition to the elves, fairies are present in abundance, and a small community of dwarfs dwells within the foothills at the eastern shore. All exist in service to, in partnership with, or in isolation from our people. It is a peaceful and uncomplicated arrangement and has served us all well for generations.

"The North Crescent is another matter entirely. It is a land of extremes, in all ways a dark mirror of our own land. Where we have foothills, they have forbidding mountains. A great desert begins just north of the isthmus that connects the two continents. Beyond that desert, if our records are correct, lay harsh forests and then a biting, frigid tundra."

"If your records are correct? You do not know for certain?" Deacon said.

"All we have ever needed can be found within our own lands. We have seen little value in venturing far enough to the north to see for ourselves. Even if the land *were* inviting, its inhabitants would be reason enough to stay away."

"Who lives there?" Myranda asked.

"This, at least, we can speak of with a greater level of authority. We've had minor encounters with each as their mindless wandering has brought them near enough to our lands to be a threat. The place is besieged with chaotic, uncivilized races of all sorts. Its mountains are home to dozens of warring dwarf clans. The forests and deserts are overrun with fairies even less civilized than those in the southern forests. And the north belongs to the dragons. Our history is littered with skirmishes against each of those wretched collections of barbaric tribes, but after being turned away by our warriors and wizards for so long, they finally learned to keep to their own borders. We've had no more than passing sightings of the odd swarm of fairies or dwarfish mining parties near our borders for well over two centuries, and none has challenged us beyond some simple blustery posturing. There is one exception, though until recently it was dubious at best. The Aluall."

"What is the Aluall?" Myranda asked.

"If I recall correctly, in ancient Elven that can be roughly said to mean 'Those things of flesh that cannot be witnessed by eye or ear' or, more tersely, 'the Undetectable,'" Deacon said.

"I would have translated it as 'the Unseen,' but I must congratulate you on your knowledge of our language," Silla said. "For hundreds of years, the Aluall have been a superstition. They are said to lurk throughout North Crescent and punish those foolish enough to venture too far into that forsaken land. It was all rather childish, we believed. Nothing more than weak minds trying to explain away this or that minor misfortune. If a thing of value was misplaced, it was the work of the Aluall. If livestock vanished or ripe crops were stolen from the fields, they were taken by the Aluall. None had ever seen so much as a shadow lurking in the places where the Aluall had struck. There were no footprints. Hounds found no scent. They simply could not exist. That changed some weeks ago. Two small villages of our people, recently established a bit farther into North Crescent than any of our people made their homes before, were struck by creatures as undetectable as the Aluall are believed to be. And for once, even if their existence remains questionable, their actions are undeniable."

"What happened?" Myranda asked.

"In the first attack, a life was taken. It was a town called Treadforge. Witnesses say that the air itself turned to flame and consumed a watchtower, killing the elf within. At the same time, every storehouse, every cupboard, every scrap of food vanished, as did the goods in the markets and anything else of value. The attackers also left behind a message, a warning that other attacks would follow and a demand that the people leave the village."

The king crossed his arms. "It is not in the Sonril spirit to back down in the face of a threat, but what can we do against an enemy that we cannot see?"

Silla continued. "The people of Treadforge abandoned their homes and made their way to the second village north of the isthmus, Dusand. The following night, that village was also attacked in precisely the same way. No one was killed—this time the flames consumed only the gate, but once more the food and goods were taken. Many of the people nearly perished for lack of food or water as they retreated to the safety of our borders."

"Since then, there have been no further attacks of that scale, but the Aluall have remained bold. Soldiers patrolling the abandoned cities have been robbed, as have scholars hoping to learn what mystic works may have been utilized by the Aluall. Finally, we were forced to abandon the cities entirely and fortify the nearest towns, Rendif to the east and Twilus to the west. The Aluall have yet to come that far, but it may only be a matter of time."

"Forgive me if I presume," Myranda said. "But it sounds as though your only evidence that these Aluall are to blame is the lack of any *other* evidence. I've learned all too well that every legend sprouts from a kernel of truth, but surely you must have found *something* solid for you to believe you needed aid from the Chosen."

"Quite so, Myranda. Quite so," Mellawin said. "Our scholars may be pestered and burgled, but one cannot steal *insight* from a wise man with a good eye. One of our mystics noted there was *some* semblance of evidence. It was in the form of… of… Silla, please explain."

"We determined, though to a profoundly lesser degree, that there seemed to be a withering, weakening of the soil around the attacked cities that was quite similar to the afflicted soil from Tressor."

"I see…" Myranda said gravely. "And as the D'Karon were to blame in Tressor, and in the Northern Alliance, you believe they might also be to blame for these attacks."

The king nodded. "It stands to reason. Our land is every bit as remarkable and valuable as Tressor or the Northern Alliance. I dare say in *most* ways it is a good deal more so. It strains credulity to suggest that the vicious, otherworldly interlopers would invest centuries of their time and effort attempting to pillage and topple your own lands but leave ours wholly untouched. However! If they were to have lain dormant in North Crescent, nestled in a place so chaotic and wild that no civilized or virtuous people would ever tread there, then they just may have escaped notice. And now, with their defeat elsewhere, surely they have targeted our noble people as a final, desperate bid to defeat the forces of good in our world."

"I follow the logic," Deacon said. "Some of your conclusions require a bit of a leap, but I understand why you felt we could be of aid. If there exists the whisper of a D'Karon threat, it must be treated with all seriousness."

"I only hope our own investigation determines that threat, whatever it is, is *not* of D'Karon origin," Myranda added.

"Perish the thought, Myranda. Perish the thought that this crime is the work of any but our mutual foes. It is infinitely preferable to me that we discover Sonril and its people have finally come to blows with the enemies presaged by our scholars in the great prophecy. That, at least, would mean that my people have a place in history."

Myranda looked the king in the eye. "I understand your desire to have your land 'elevated' by its inclusion in this terrible conflict, but the D'Karon are not to be wished upon your worst enemy, let alone your own people. They are a heartless, savage, soulless blight upon the land. They bring nothing but misery and suffering in their wake."

He waved a hand dismissively. "Not since before my time have our soldiers been called upon to sharpen blades and draw bows for a meaningful clash. It is long past time we had a nice black-and-white conflict to prove our valor. Bring forth the evil, the morally corrupt, the malicious and vile. We shall face them unafraid. I have not called upon you to advise in that regard. What I ask is quite simple. Go forth into North Crescent. As none of our people have much knowledge of North Crescent beyond the most southerly reaches of its desert, there would be no sense in providing you with a guide. The attacks were clearly targeted at pushing us back, so I suspect sending along even *one* of my own people could easily trigger a fresh assault, but you are plainly *not* of Southern Crescent, so at the very least you shall cause some confusion. You shall unlock the secrets of the Aluall, and when you have done so, you shall instruct our troops and we shall fight beside you to vanquish these foes once and for all. Thus, our land will have played host to at least a postscript of the battles foretold in prophecy, and we can rest assured that the gods have not forgotten us."

"And if the D'Karon aren't to blame? If there is some other explanation?" Myranda asked.

"A pity, then, but so long as the attacks cease and my people know that the Chosen came to our aid, I shall be satisfied and your people shall have the treatment for your ailing land."

"Will we get to see much of your kingdom?" Ivy asked. "If your ships are any indication, your cities must be *gorgeous*."

"For the sake of expediency, we shall make port at Twilus, a city far from the capital and thus hardly among the grandest places within our borders. But rest assured, when you've completed your task, you shall be given a hero's welcome and a tour of every magnificent sight Sonril has to behold," Mellawin said.

"Great!" Ivy trilled.

"How long will the voyage last?" Myranda asked.

"I don't trouble myself with such details. Silla?" Mellawin said.

"If winds are favorable and weather is good, the trip will take three weeks," the lore keeper replied. "In that time, we hope to educate you as fully as we can regarding what little we know about North Crescent and its people."

"Splendid," Deacon said, reaching into his satchel beside him and withdrawing a book. "I relish the opportunity."

The ship rolled gently to one side. It creaked and groaned, not with the rigid feel of a human ship, but with the same natural tone of a large tree shrugging off a stiff breeze. Mellawin picked up his glass, lest it spill, and the others followed suit.

"Ah. And so we are on our way. If I recall correctly, on occasions such as this it is traditional among many human cultures to toast, yes?" He raised his glass. "To our voyage! May it be the final step in bringing our beloved world fully into the light of a glorious new day!"

Each raised their glass in turn, then drank. Ivy, notably, drained her glass entirely, then gathered a few handfuls of the assorted foods on the table and stuffed them into her pockets.

"You don't need me for anything else, do you? I want to see what it looks like to pull away from the shore!" she said.

Silla said, with a hint of exasperation, "Perhaps I was not clear, but it is our intention to educate you all, to the best of our ability, on the nature of North Crescent."

King Mellawin repeated the dismissive motion. The bulk of his royal duties seemed to center on applying the gesture when confronted with information that didn't please him. "Bah. What we know of that wretched place can be learned in an afternoon, and we both know our malthrope friend shan't get much good out of it. Let the beast run along and gawk at the view. Steadier minds shall deal with the fine details."

Ivy shot a brief glare of irritation at the king for his indelicate phasing, but as he was granting her exactly the permission she was seeking, she let it go without comment. She rushed out into the hall before the drudgery of diplomacy could deprive her of another moment of the glorious view. When her scampering footsteps vanished down the hallway, the king smiled.

"All of the enthusiasm of a child, and all of the manners as well," he said. "A bit more training may be in order for that one."

Myranda shut her eyes and stifled a tremor of anger. "Please, King Mellawin, I must again stress that Ivy has not been trained and is not a beast. If you expect our aid, I expect respect for *each* of our party."

"Of course, of course," King Mellawin said, little indication in his tone that he'd actually heard her words. "Silla, do begin."

The lore keeper fetched a very ragged book bound in thick, leathery paper. She set it out on the table beside a smaller, newer book with fresh notes taken in it.

"I had some prepared speeches regarding the broader points, but I'd written them with the expectation of addressing *all* of the Chosen. You will forgive me if I reference Ether."

"It is not a problem," Myranda said. "I am sure Ether would be pleased to know she was included."

"It worries me that she believed there was something so pressing that she could not join us."

Myranda smiled. "It is a family matter. Please, proceed."

Silla cleared her throat. "What we know of the North Crescent comes mostly from the records of the Workslag Clan, who migrated south more than four hundred years ago…"

#

On a side street in a bustling town deep in the Northern Alliance, an elderly woman pushed her way gratefully through the door of her modest home. It was little more than a single room over a bakery, but it was more than enough for her. The fires burning below took the edge from the cold even while she was away. Thus, the only thing she had to do to really make it livable was to stoke the small iron stove set against the stone wall. She tugged the door open with a poker and tossed in a small bundle of wood, then stirred the smoldering remains of the previous night's fire beneath it until it took to flame. It had been a long day of doing laundry at the nearby inn, and all she really wanted was to sleep, but today was a special one. She'd promised she would treat herself to one or two of her few remaining luxuries.

She nudged the stout wooden window open and brushed some fresh clean snow into a kettle, then secured the drafty shutter and placed the kettle on the stove. While the snow melted—there were few things that tasted as fresh and clean to her as pristine snow—she rummaged through the cupboard and found a clay jar sealed with wax. A quick slice with a dull knife carved away the wax, and she lifted the lid to breathe the delightful aromatic scent of well-aged tea.

For a few tantalizing minutes, she sat and enjoyed the scent while she let the warmth ease into her old bones and tried not to doze off. She'd very nearly failed at that last part when a knock at the door startled her to full wakefulness again.

"Coming, coming!" she called, her heart fluttering a bit at the unexpected sound.

She set down the tea leaves and, with some difficulty, hauled herself from the chair. Out of habit she took a stout copper soup ladle in hand when she answered the door. At her age, she didn't get many visitors, so she wasn't inclined to assume the person at the door had her best interests in mind. She gripped the handle tightly, planted a still-soggy boot on the floor as a doorstop, and opened the door a sliver. A single glimpse of who awaited her was enough for her to throw the door wide and wrap her arms around her visitor.

"It is so wonderful to see you again, Em—I'm sorry. Guardian Ether," the old woman proclaimed. "Come in, come in. Let me clear you someplace to sit…"

Her visitor stepped inside. She was a younger woman, her features elegant and beautiful, though her expression was cold and stern. She was a bit underdressed for the frigid northern weather, wearing little more than a light cloak over an exquisite tunic and leggings. Nevertheless, she didn't seem chilled in the slightest. She set down the small bag she'd been carrying and pulled back her hood. A trained eye would detect a family resemblance between the two, though the truth was more complex. The visitor *appeared* to be a soldier of the Alliance Army called Emilia. In fact, she was a creature of divine origin, a shapeshifter who had merely taken the form of the fallen Emilia. That Ether's travels had brought her and this woman together was perhaps evidence that the gods had a sense of humor, or at least a sense of pathos.

Ether gave the woman a measuring look as she moved folded linens from the only other place to sit in the whole of her home, the edge of the bed. "Are you well, Celia?" she asked. "You seem uneasy."

"It was the knock at the door. That sort of thing still startles me. You'll remember, until you introduced me to your dear friend Myranda, I'd not heard a thing for *years*. When one grows accustomed to the idea of never hearing anything for the rest of her days, it can take some time to get used to those everyday noises again."

"I apologize. When Myranda restored your hearing, it was intended to be a gift to show my gratitude for your insight. I did not intend for it to cause you distress."

"Oh, no. Heavens no. A little start here or there is nothing in light of hearing the crunch of snow beneath my boots. The crackle of fire. The murmur of half-heard conversations. You have no idea how *lonely* the world can be when you can't hear."

"Indeed I do not. Loneliness is something I had not considered until very recently…"

"Well, you needn't worry about that anymore. My door is always open for you. Sit, sit. Do you drink tea?"

"I do not drink at all," Ether explained.

"You really should try some. I know I've got another cup around here somewhere," Celia said.

"That will not be necessary."

"Oh hush. It's wonderfully soothing. I am a host and you are my guest. I can't have you sit there and watch *me* drinking tea. There is such a thing as hospitality. There, what did I say? A second cup. I knew I'd find it."

She wiped it clean and set it on a small table between the bed and the chair, then eased herself down.

"Just a bit more for the tea to boil, and then we can brew up a nice cup for each of us. Until then, tell me, what has been filling your days?"

"I have been ruminating on my purpose in this world."

"Ah. Still haven't worked that out, have you? I hear there have been all sorts of wonderful talks going on down south. There have certainly been plenty of traders heading north *and* south, passing through the inn and plying their trade." She leaned forward a bit. "After all these years of fighting them, I'm not so sure I trust the Tressons enough to not keep an eye on them when they pass through. But the ones I've met seem nice enough, and they've got some lovely blankets and such to sell."

Ether nodded, looking a bit more as though she were enduring the conversation than actually listening. Celia continued regardless. She'd met Ether often enough to know that such was simply her way. The shapeshifter wasn't much for social graces. Feigning interest or engaging in small talk was far beyond her expertise. That didn't stop the older woman. That her guest wasn't terribly interested didn't change the fact that she still *had* a guest, and thus a rare opportunity to chat.

"Come to think of it, the queen passed through here on her way south. Doesn't that normally mean *you'd* be headed south as well? Seems she doesn't meet with the Tressons without the Guardians of the Realm by her side."

"It was not a matter worthy of my attention. And one I suspect they would prefer I not discuss."

"Of course, of course. The affairs of the throne aren't for an old biddy's ears."

"Indeed."

"What brings you here, then? Not that I'm not happy to have you."

Ether straightened her posture, a flutter of uncertainty in her expression. "When you attended the reception at Five Point, in the course of conversation you indicated that this was the day of your birth. It is my understanding mortals celebrate the day of their creation."

"It *is* my birthday. So nice of you to remember! Not to sound rude, but it doesn't strike me as the sort of detail that would matter to you."

"It doesn't matter to me in the slightest," Ether said simply. "But I have observed that it is *also* a mortal tendency to celebrate matters that are of importance to others as a sign of respect. Such was the indication of Ivy when I spoke to her."

"Ivy. She's the malthrope." Celia shook her head. "These are interesting times, Ether. Interesting times. Such a time to be alive."

"Ivy also suggested it would be wise to present you with gifts. If they do not suit you, please inform me. I bring them based solely upon her recommendation, but I hesitate to trust her judgment completely."

Ether handed the cloth sack to Celia. The elderly woman carefully unwrapped it. Inside was a small wooden presentation box that held a soft, finely woven scarf. Beside it was a smaller sack filled with sweet buns.

"Oh…" Celia cooed, unfurling the scarf. "It's almost too fine to wear. And these. They smell wonderful. You'll have one with your tea, of course."

"I neither eat nor drink," Ether said, her perpetual tone of irritation just a bit sharper.

"I certainly won't eat them all myself." Celia wrapped her scarf about her neck, then transferred the hot water from kettle to pot and dispensed some leaves to steep. "There. Won't be a minute more. Plenty of time for you to tell me why you've *really* come here."

"I have said, I come celebrating your birthday."

"That would be a fine reason for anyone *else* to visit, but you? How do I put it? Bah. Heaven knows you are direct enough, Ether. No sense tiptoeing around it. You aren't the sentimental type. And though they may not be yours from birth, you still have my child's eyes, and I know a troubled look in them when I see it. I've had a long day, Ether. My bed is calling. Much as I love a visit, if you beat around the bush for too long, I am liable to doze off before you get what you came for."

Ether simmered with irritation for a moment. "I am uncertain."

"You don't know what you came here for?" Celia poured out two cups of tea. "That's just youth. I wouldn't worry about it."

"Youth?" Ether scoffed, taking the tea. "My years are uncountable. I walked this world when it was new."

"Then you really don't have an excuse," Celia said with a smirk.

Ether scowled. "I seem to recall you being much more deferential to my status in our prior encounters."

"You come to me with the problems and words of a child. You leave me with nothing to offer but the wisdom of a mother. Forgive an old woman at the end of a long day, but I know no other way to respond." She took a luxuriant whiff of the tea. "Drink, before it gets cold."

Ether, now weary of explaining the nature of her being, put the cup to her lips and sipped at the warm contents. She paused.

"Lovely, isn't it?"

"I had not anticipated the complexity of the flavor."

"I imagine there is a lot about the world you had not anticipated." Celia handed Ether one of the buns. The shapeshifter took it but did not partake. "But let us see now. You do not know what to make of your place in the world. I am afraid I cannot be of much help to you. My place was always clear, and it filled my life from one end to the other."

"Has your life fulfilled you?"

"Very much so."

"And what has been most fulfilling?"

"Family."

Ether looked aside in irritation. "So I have been told. That this yawning emptiness within me is the place where family is to reside. And so I have been told that those closest to you, those most important to you, take the place of family when you have no family of your own."

"Wise words."

"Wise for mortals, perhaps, but useless for me. Even those creatures with whom I have the most in common test the very limits of my patience. I was not created to cope with the petty details of a mortal life."

"Perhaps not, Ether, but if you think there is something special in being driven to wits end by your family, you understand even less about mortals than you realize."

"What are you implying?"

"Loving someone and liking them are very different things. You'll never hear a bigger row than a large family at a holiday meal."

"That is absurd. What good is a family if their mere presence infuriates you?"

"Sometimes your family will be there when you don't want them. But they will always be there when you need them. They're something solid and real in a world were very little can be relied upon."

Ether narrowed her eyes and sipped the tea. "Then clearly family is not what is missing. I *have* as near to a family as I will ever have, and still I feel empty and adrift."

"There *are* those we seek to—"

The shapeshifter raised a hand. "Do not. You will speak to me of finding a mate, of having a child. I have attempted to acquire a mate for just such a purpose. None have been receptive."

"You may not be going about it in the proper way."

"I have attempted it in the most direct and intelligent a manner. Is this yet another aspect of this ridiculous society that resolves into a pathetic dance and game, always playing at meaning without stating it?"

"Indeed it is, as all the best things in life are."

"I refuse to lower myself to such a level."

"That is your choice."

Celia munched on her own bun for a few moments. Ether became visibly impatient.

"Have we reached the end of your insight?" Ether asked.

"Have some of your bun, Guardian Ether."

Ether glared at Celia for a moment but grudgingly took a bite.

"Well?" Celia asked.

"It too has an unexpectedly pleasant flavor. Have I engaged in enough pointless rituals to receive your advice, or has this all been for nothing?"

"You want me to solve your problems for you, but I say you haven't *got* a problem."

"I have *told* you my troubles. You now say they don't exist?"

"Guardian Ether, your years are 'uncountable,' yet you've only today had your first sip of tea and your first sweet bun. You have your strength, and you have peerless powers, and you have the whole world to experience. That isn't a problem, that is a gift. A mortal would give anything to be where you are today. If you want to know where you belong, what you should be doing, I say stop thinking about it and start looking for it. You and the other Chosen have saved this world. Now would be a fine time to see what sort of a place it is you've saved. And who knows? Maybe in sampling the virtues of the land and its people, you'll find a role you'll be happy to fill."

"And if I don't?"

"Then you can at least come and tell me what you've seen. I haven't got many years left, and I haven't seen *half* of what I would like to. To hear it from you might be nice."

"You believe that somehow aimlessly wandering the land and passively absorbing what I find will somehow make me whole again?"

"Heavens no. I believe purposefully exploring and actively participating in what you find will make you whole for the first time. Ask questions, try foods, listen to music, look at the landscape. Live, Guardian Ether. You've earned it." She finished her bun, then held out the sack. "Another?"

"No."

"More for me." She finished her tea and yawned. "I do hope I've been a help, and I look forward to the tales and mementos of your travels, but my pillow has waited long enough. If I don't close my eyes for a bit, I'll be of no use to anyone tomorrow."

"Where do you recommend I *begin* this pointless journey?"

"Someplace far away. Someplace people around here would never dream they'd see."

"The others are at this moment traveling to Sonril."

"To where now?"

"An elven kingdom on South Crescent."

"Heaven's, Ether. What are you standing around here for? Go join them!"

"As you wish." Ether stood. "Rest well, Celia. I do not have high hopes for your advice, but as all other tasks at hand are equally pointless, I shall heed your words."

"Good, Guardian. Enjoy. And don't forget to come and tell me what you've seen and done."

Ether gave a stiff nod and took her leave. When Celia shut the door behind her, she shook her head.

"All the worst parts of a child and all the worst parts of an elder. I hope she can find the missing pieces. Really, something of a trick for a hero to have so little to redeem her." She stroked the scarf she'd been given. "But there's hope for her yet…"

Chapter 3

Time passed slowly as the ship made its way west. The elves had not been exaggerating when they'd indicated their knowledge of North Crescent was limited. The broad strokes of their information filled barely the first day. Another day or two of gathered hearsay and speculation brought Myranda and Deacon to the same level of knowledge as their hosts.

Myranda stood at the railing of the main deck and gazed over a sea that seemed to spread endlessly in all directions. She'd carefully braided her hair and tucked it into her hood, lest the wind play havoc with it. Deacon emerged from a nearby doorway and stood beside her.

"Ah, Myranda. There you are," he said. "Silla was curious where you'd gone. It seems our hosts expected us to stay in our rooms for the bulk of the trip. That is evidently *their* plan. I get the distinct impression they aren't terribly fond of the open sea."

"I can't say I'm overly fond of it either," Myranda said, clutching her stomach lightly. "The tossing sea has turned my stomach terribly. Particularly in the mornings."

"Seasick?" he said.

"I suppose."

He shuffled through his satchel. "I am certain I can find a spell of some sort to give you some relief…"

"No, no. The fresh air helps." She glanced about, ensuring there were no members of the crew near enough to overhear. "Tell me, does it strike you as strange that in all of this time it was not until very recently that the people of Sonril decided to break ground on villages in North Crescent."

"It *is* rather odd. But certainly Silla would have shared the reasoning if it was relevant."

"I'm not certain of that at all. Perhaps their behavior has soured my opinion of them, but I get the distinct feeling the elves only trust us with the information *they* believe we need. I can understand being ignorant of the continent to the north. After all, we in the Northern Alliance have barely given either of the Crescents a second thought since before the war began. But *we* are separated by a *sea*. They've merely been toeing a figurative line in the sand for all of these years. And some of the gaps in their knowledge seem a bit too convenient to be mere disinterest."

"You think they are hiding something."

"'Hiding' may be too strong a word. But I do think they know more than they let on. For a kingdom with countless residents who remember a time before the war, I can't imagine *none* of them has ventured into the heart of their sister continent unless they had a very good reason to avoid it."

"If such a reason exists, they must be very confident it won't be found, as they are sending us unsupervised."

"True. Perhaps I am overthinking things. This is a rare introduction that *hasn't* begun with strife and tension. I shouldn't be seeking to create it.... But I'm not pleased with the king's attitude toward the D'Karon either. The man seems to relish the idea of a clash with them as some means of soothing the bruised ego of his people for being left out of the Perpetual War."

"I've known a few elves. As they grow older, they *do* have the tendency to view the world and its people as some sort of ongoing game with a distant goal. Mortals tend to neglect the long-term consequences of their actions. Immortals neglect the short-term consequences. A bit of bloodshed now is a tragedy, but the glory and honor it brings will live on in song and story for ages."

"I thought I was through with people seeking glory through war..." She clenched her fist. "It is honestly as though the world doesn't know how to do anything else but squabble and kill."

"Myranda, if I may say, since this trip began you have been rather more out of sorts than I've seen you in ages." He placed his hand on her shoulder. "Is there something else that's bothering you?"

She took a breath and took his hand in hers. "I'm just feeling restless... Heavens, how long has it been since I've had nothing but time and no tasks to fill it? From my years wandering, looking for a place to say, then the discovery of the sword and my time on the run, then to Entwell, then in search of the Chosen... all of the battles, all of the trials. And when peace came, still more needed to be done. New Kenvard is a hive of activity, each day a new problem to solve. And yet here I am, at sea in a ship finer than most homes, pampered and spoiled as the guests of another kingdom. It feels so *unnatural* to have a chance to rest. I feel like I am neglecting my people back home."

"There is a great task ahead, Myranda, and many great tasks completed. A few moments to pause and reflect are the least fate could offer you from time to time."

"I suppose." She turned her gaze from the horizon to the air beside the ship and smiled.

Garr was airborne over the water, facing the rear of the ship. His wings caught the same breeze that filled the sails. A well-placed flap here or there allowed him to hang beside the boat as if he were dangling from a string. Grustim stood on his back, one hand holding his pike and the other holding a coiled rope affixed to its end. Myn watched the pair as they held their place beside the ship, though she'd yet to work up the courage to venture over to the edge. She sat resolutely in the very center of the deck, much to the chagrin of the crew that needed to work around her. Though she craned her neck and struggled to get a better view of what her fellow dragon was doing, she held her position as though it was the only safe place in the whole of the ship.

Grustim hefted the pike, then thrust it toward the water. The rope drew taut and the Dragon Rider dropped down to grip Garr's neck tightly. Garr flapped his wings and rose into the air. The pike emerged from the water, dragging with it a flailing fish speared by its tip. The fish was massive, nearly the size of a bull calf. Grustim secured the rope around Garr's neck to keep from losing his grip, and the pair swept over the deck to deliver their catch. The stricken fish thrashed for a moment, but Garr thumped down and finished it with a deft snap of his jaws. Grustim climbed down and drew a knife, slicing a goodly portion for himself. What remained was easily enough to feed the rest of the crew for a day or two, but Garr had other plans for it. He collected the fish in his jaws, took a few purposeful steps toward Myn, and set the kill before her. She sniffed curiously at the potential meal. Garr sat and patiently waited to see if the offering would be accepted.

The Dragon Rider paced over, his share in hand, and addressed Myranda.

"May I have a word with you, Duchess?" he asked.

"We have fought beside one another, Grustim. I believe we can dispense with the formalities."

"There are matters regarding Myn. The first, her fear of the water…"

"Yes. I'd hoped by this point in the voyage it would have begun to diminish. She's braved the water before."

"Rare is a beast who would take it upon herself to set aside what she perceives to be valid caution. The fear is genuine, there can be no doubt of that. On those times she ignored the fear, did she have good reason?"

"Once, at least, was to rescue me."

"Yes. That would be sufficient, but it would not begin to cure the fear."

"Why not?"

He beckoned her. "Come inside."

She and Deacon followed as he stepped into the shelter of one of the ship's corridors. When he spoke again, it was softly.

"In the generations that the Dragon Riders have worked with these noble beasts, we have learned much. It is not our custom to share what we have learned. But as you care for this beast, I am prepared to share some of our wisdom, on the condition that you do not share it with anyone else."

"Of course."

He lowered his voice further. "A dragon is a powerful beast. It knows this implicitly, from the moment it is born. There are few forces in nature that can truly be a threat to a dragon, beyond other dragons. They understand battle, and thus they understand that death can come by the claws or blades of a dedicated foe, but only at great cost. I… forgive me if I do not make myself clear. This is not something I've had to put to words before… Anything that might soundly defeat a dragon should have to work hard, should have to give it all, and furthermore should need more than a bit of luck. When something lays a dragon low without effort, this is devastating to the beast."

"A dragon does not understand what it is to be powerless," Myranda said.

"Yes! Yes. That is precisely the case. If ever a dragon is made to feel powerless, helpless in the face of something, it will shake the beast to its very soul. And if the creature cannot find its way through the fear, it can end poorly."

"How so?"

"For some, it will simply linger as a weakness. If the source of the fear is rare, this may be of little consequence, but among the Dragon Riders, we would never allow it to stand. It would be a liability in battle. Some fears, fears more constant in the beast's mind, they can fester. They turn to dark things or simply dominate the beast's life. Best to work through them before that can happen."

"Absolutely. I understand."

"It isn't enough that Myn would brave the water to rescue you. That your life was in danger only strengthens the threat water poses in her mind. This journey, to utterly surround her in water and show her she can survive unscathed, is a fine start. But she must be made to face her fear. It may seem unkind. It may hurt you to see her frightened. But she has a long life ahead of her. A bit of fear now is nothing to what the rest of her days will hold if you do not rid her of this."

"I'll do what I can. While we are on the subject of Myn's well-being, I wonder if you could help me with something?"

"If it is within my power and rights, I will do all that I can."

"We do our best to keep Myn busy, and to keep her company. But ever since she met Garr, she's… how do I say this…?" Myranda shrugged. "No sense being delicate about it. She's smitten with Garr. We've known that since shortly after they met. But…"

Grustim shut his eyes and lowered his head with a slow shake.

"I take it this isn't the first you've considered the issue," Myranda said with a grin.

"It is an unfortunate complication. One that has no real solution."

Grustim nudged open the door to the deck to offer a glimpse of the dragons. Myn was messily devouring the meal provided for her. Garr was patiently observing.

"The stone about Myn's neck. I imagine you fashioned the pouch for it because she carried it wherever she went?"

"Ivy fashioned it, actually," Myranda said.

"Regardless. A gift from Garr. There will be others. He presented it, pursuing her as a mate. She accepted. Until one rejects the other, there is no one else for either of them." He turned to Myranda. "We keep the males and females separate. We breed our dragons. Garr's mate was selected for him before he was hatched. The line has been cultivated for many thousands of years, as far back as our history goes. Three generations of dragons. Countless generations of Dragon Riders."

"I am terribly sorry if this has spoiled an ancient tradition."

Grustim shook his head. "Garr has clutch-mates. The line will continue. If I'd imagined this might occur, I would have taken steps to prevent it. But I have never seen a couple pair themselves so quickly. Myn is a remarkable creature. I only hope I live to see their offspring."

"You believe it will go that far?"

"I don't imagine we will be able to prevent it. When they both decide the time has come, I pity anyone who would try to come between them. At that point, they shall make their own decision, regardless of what we feel is right. Dragons, even properly trained, can be quite willful when it suits them."

"Perhaps if Queen Caya and I have a word with your superiors, we may be able to work out permission for them to visit one another," Myranda said.

"There would be no precedent for that."

"Very little in my life has precedent these days."

"Since our first encounter, I can say the same."

"Whatever it takes, we shall find a solution. Family is too important to let something like this stand in the way."

#

King Mellawin reclined in a chair of mystically woven wood and sipped at a chalice of fine wine. Set before him on the table he'd shared with the Chosen during their briefings was the rough map of the Northern Crescent that would serve as the guide for their investigation. A knock at the door stirred him from some self-satisfied thoughts of what praise he would earn upon his triumphant return.

"Yes?"

"It is I, Your Majesty. Silla."

"Enter," he said.

His subordinate opened the door and slipped inside. Since their arrival in Tressor, she'd been uneasy, but it was doubly evident since they'd begun their return voyage.

"Does something trouble you, Silla?"

"My liege, though the thought would never occur to me to doubt your judgment, I wonder if it might be wise to adjust your expectations regarding the capacity of our guests to perform their intended tasks."

"Have they done something to illustrate themselves as something less than their exploits would claim?"

"The duke and duchess show at least the veneer of civility and dignity, but the others… they are beasts. The lot of them. That the people of Tressor and the Northern Alliance would entrust their safety to such creatures is perhaps understandable in light of their lack of options, but we of Sonril should know better."

"Silla, please. Their behavior may be less than what we have come to expect, but their divinity cannot be questioned. It is evident to even the weakest of mystics and seers."

"I do not argue that they are products of the gods." She clutched her hands together and briefly bowed her head in reverence. "And I would no sooner question the will of the gods than slit my own throat. But… *dragons*? Two of them? And a malthrope? What next? Fairies? Dwarfs?"

Mellawin stood. "Silla, as elves it is our burden to perpetually associate ourselves with less dignified races. By virtue of our lofty place in the world, to reach beyond our borders at all is to find inferiority. But these warriors have proved themselves on the field of battle. War is a coarse enterprise that is served well by coarse creatures. And I have seen *much* to admire. Strength, loyalty. Even *artistry*. And, if nothing else, they bring the experience necessary to definitively determine the nature of the threat as D'Karon."

"And if it is not D'Karon?"

"Then it will be a simple, crude task as ably achieved by them as any. Blood will be kept from our hands, and the novelty of their presence shall suitably distract and entertain the people. I do not think even *you* can dispute their capacity for distraction."

"I only hope that distraction does not escalate to chaos."

"I entrust the task of avoiding such things to you, until such time as they are well within North Crescent. Once there, I could not care less if chaos descends. It would scarcely be noticed in that savage land."

"Perhaps if a small force of our people could accompany them…"

"Silla, on that there can be no debate. The Chosen and their Tresson associate shall *not* be accompanied or guided. You are the lore keeper, and thus your knowledge of our history and ways is second only to my own. But it *is* second to my own. Elements that shall not and must not be divulged have weighed upon my final decision. And that decision *is* final."

"Understood, Your Majesty."

"Good. Now go. Our guests are curious to a fault, I have noticed. I believe it would be wise to remain on hand to indulge their questions rather than to permit their minds to wander."

"Yes, Your Majesty. Of course you are correct. I shall do so immediately."

Silla hurried from room, leaving the king to enjoy his wine once more.

#

"Come on, Myn. It's fine," Ivy said, perched atop the dragon's neck. "We've been at sea for *days* and nothing's gone wrong. Just go near the edge."

"No," Myn rumbled.

"Seems like ever since you learned that word, it's the only one you'll use." She hopped down and trotted to the edge of the deck. "You can *fly*, Myn. Compared to that, swimming is easy. You could even take a dip and you'll be fine."

"No."

"But the sea is so nice and *calm*…. Except for back there…"

Ivy peered into the distance to the northwest of the ship. While she'd been impressed by the beauty of the sea when they'd first set sail, she'd quickly become disappointed by how little it changed as they traveled. During long trips overland, be they by foot or by wing, the scenery that greeted you at sunrise would be entirely different by sunset. Conversely, the sea was the sea. Perhaps a deeper green here, or a lighter blue there, but the change was terribly gradual. The only distinctive features were the odd glimpse of a distant shore or an island when the air was at its clearest… but right now the sea itself seemed to have something new to offer.

She glanced aside. Deacon had taken a seat in the shade of one of the sails. He was, as always, writing his thoughts and observations. The stylus in his hand was joined by a pair of others moving of their own accord.

"Deacon?" she said. "What is that?"

The books snapped shut, the styli stowed themselves, and he stood to address her "What have you found?" he asked.

She took him by the hand and led him to the port side of the ship. "There. In the distance there. The sea is so churned up."

It was truly uncanny. While the surrounding expanse of water twinkled and churned with the gentle waves, just at the edge of vision was a stretch of water that rippled violently. It looked like the result of a storm but was impossibly localized.

"Look at it," she said. "So much wind, but just in that one spot."

"Curious," Deacon said. He held out a hand, and one of the books flipped open and revealed a small but carefully rendered map. A point of light marked their present location. "I am not as skilled as I might be at judging such things, but it would appear that calm patch is quite near the center of the Crescent Sea." He summoned his stylus and marked the position.

"What matters trouble you?" called Silla, appearing from below decks.

"I do not find it troubling," Deacon said, "but I *do* find it fascinating. Do you know what that rough bit of sea is? Is it a permanent fixture of the sea at that point, or some other phenomena?"

Silla gazed into the distance. "It is certainly not a permanent fixture of the sea. If I am correct, at this stage in our journey the only feature of the sea we are likely to see is Deep Swell, and only if our navigator has strayed too far north."

"Deep Swell?" Deacon said, flipping to a fresh page and jotting down the name.

"The capital of the mer kingdom," Silla said. The statement seemed to put a bad taste in her mouth.

"That's where the mermaids live?" Ivy squealed. "Can we visit? Myranda and Deacon told me about their mermaid friend, Calypso. She seemed *so* nice. And she sounds *beautiful*. I'd love to meet some."

"We cannot, for a great many reasons, pay a visit to that place," Silla said. "And before you probe deeper, please be aware that it is not a matter relevant to your current visit, and thus not one I am at liberty to discuss."

Ivy leaned aside to Deacon and whispered, "Sounds like the elves and mermaids don't get along. Seems like *no* one gets along with the elves."

Deacon nodded and gazed at the choppy bit of sea. He finally decided to shut his eyes and put his mind to work. The answer immediately became clear. "It is Ether."

"Oh…" Ivy said, crossing her arms. "I thought it was something *interesting*…"

"Ivy, that isn't a very nice thing to say. I am pleased she's decided to join us," Deacon said.

She grinned. "It *will* be nice to see how 'diplomatic' she can be."

He raised his crystal, which pulsed lightly in what served as a mystical wave hello. It did the job, prompting the churning point in the distance to shift toward them. The sea beneath it calmed slightly as it approached, and when it was a short distance from the ship, an airy form became visible above it. Ether's tightly coiled wind fluttered the sails a bit as she drifted over the deck, then set down. She assumed her human form and gazed evenly about as the deckhands reacted, quite understandably, with more than a bit of confusion and dismay over her sudden arrival. Two of them drew weapons. Ether seemed unimpressed.

Silla hastily stepped forward. "You will lower your weapons. This is Guardian Ether. She is a guest of the throne." She fixed her hair, which had been stirred up by Ether's arrival, and offered a bow. "Welcome, Guardian Ether. We were concerned you would not be able to attend. I wish you would have announced your arrival so that we could properly receive you. You'll understand if we are unprepared for an honored guest to arrive while we are at sea."

"It is just as well. I have no interest in such things," Ether said.

"But you *must* receive the proper greetings!"

Silla turned and, in hushed, desperate tones, delivered some instructions to a nearby subordinate, who rushed below decks.

"Welcome aboard, Ether," Ivy said. "How was your visit to your mother? Did she like her gifts?"

"Yes. Both the scarf and the buns were well received."

"Those buns are *so good*," she purred, looking to Silla. "We had them at the feast, remember?"

"I wasn't entirely certain you would join us on this journey at all," Deacon said. "What inspired the change of heart?"

"And why did you meet us in the middle of the sea?" Ivy added.

"Celia suggested there was value in experiencing the world and, furthermore, suggested I do so in the farthest-flung places I could find. The Crescents seemed appropriate. That you all would be there as well was reason enough to be present, as you frequently require my aid."

The subordinate returned to the door, breathless, and signaled Silla.

"Ah, yes. If you will follow my associate, Guardian Ether, I am certain King Mellawin will want to meet you personally. The others have been formally introduced and have been educated on the task at hand. Surely you will want the same information."

Ether turned to Deacon. "Is this entirely necessary?"

He nodded. "I think it would be best to oblige our hosts and share their findings."

The shapeshifter's expression hardened somewhat. "Very well…"

She followed the underling below decks. When she was gone, Ivy gave Deacon a nudge.

"She wants to see the world. She's existed in the world since the dawn of time, but one little visit with Celia and she *finally* decides it's worth being a part of it."

"It is quite encouraging," he said.

"Funny. It turns out all it took to set her on the right path finally was a mother."

"Forgive the observation," Silla interjected, "but the reputation that has reached us regarding Guardian Ether's disposition suggests she can be difficult. We were unconcerned prior to meeting the rest of you, but now I wonder if perhaps I *should* be concerned."

"She'll behave herself," Ivy said. "Put probably there will be some hurt feelings and bruised egos. You'll never find anyone more full of herself than Ether."

"I was more concerned about the potential for physical violence. I will remind you of the altercations between your dragons and…"

She trailed off as her eyes came to rest on a rather sizable stain on the deck. It was scattered with bits of fish and more than a splash of blood, the messy remains of the fresh-caught meal the dragons had enjoyed. She recoiled in disgust. "What have you done to the deck?"

"My apologies. Garr, Grustim's mount, had a taste for fresh meat."

"Is that how things are done? The base desires of unthinking beasts are humored, leaving the horrid offal of the butchery staining the deck of the royal flagship?"

Her voice as almost shaking, as though if not for profound self-restraint she would be screaming. Her eyes danced between Myn, who remained an obstruction in the middle of the deck, and Garr, who was lazing in the shade of his cage, licking the last of his meal from his chops. Grustim, who had been silently watching the exchange between Silla and the others, stepped forward.

"Silla Lorekeeper, my kingdom has decreed that I must serve you for this mission. I am bound by honor and duty to do so. But I am similarly bound to care for my mount. I will not ask him to subsist on the food you have provided. And nor would I expect Myn to do so."

"I see. Perhaps you could see to it that they do not create such a mess."

"You sought the aid of dragons. If the steepest price you must pay is a smear of blood, consider yourself lucky it isn't yours."

Silla's expression hardened. "That sounded disturbingly like a threat, Dragon Rider Grustim."

He extended a finger toward Myn, who had finally stirred in order to plod toward Garr and slip into the cage beside him. The seas were rolling the ship a bit, but her movements were slow and graceful, absorbing the motion effortlessly, her claws clutching the gnarled wood of the deck.

"Every inch of those beasts is a threat, lore keeper. Do not forget that."

Grustim stalked over to the dragon cage and leaned against it. He carved off slivers of his share of the fish and popped it, raw, into his mouth.

"And thus the wisdom of my concerns of violence is illustrated. I get the distinct impression Dragon Rider Grustim has great hostility for me."

Deacon flipped through one of his books. "I am not entirely certain Grustim cares for anyone without fiery breath or a scaly hide. I suppose the state of mind necessary to thrive among dragons is different from that best suited to thriving among humans and elves. Tell me, this Deep Swell, have you—"

Silla turned away. "It is not a matter for discussion, and I must see to Guardian Ether's meeting with the king now."

She paced off into the ship. Ivy stepped up beside Deacon and crossed her arms.

"It seems like there's an *awful* lot that they don't want to talk about," she said.

"All kingdoms have secrets," Deacon said.

"I know. And it seems like the more secrets they have, the more trouble *we* have when we try to help." She glanced about. "Do you think *all* of the elves from South Crescent act like this? Because if they do, I'm not sure I want to help them. I'm used to people treating *me* like I'm something they'd scrape from their shoe. People have been taught to think of malthropes that way. But these elves treat *everyone* like that. They feel like the sort of people who deserve what they get."

"Now, Ivy, that is no way to think. If we all withhold our kindness and aid until others have shown us kindness and given us aid, then it will never begin."

"Sure, but what if we're nice and we lend a hand to people, and they continue to treat us awful and ignore us when we need help?"

"That is the risk we take, but we must never assume the worst of others. We live our lives assuming the best of our fellow creatures and doing all we can to help them, and we trust they shall do the same for us."

Ivy and Deacon looked to the door to the lower decks, where Silla was berating one of her subordinates and directing him to clean the mess the dragons had left behind.

"But when they show you their true colors, do not ignore it," he amended.

Chapter 4

Myranda and the others stood on the main deck beside the king and his entourage. They all watched as the ship eased its way to shore. Everyone was eager for their first taste of land in too long, but none more so than Myn. She'd gone so far as to climb atop her cage to gain a better view of the shore, and from her tensed muscles and partially unfurled wings, it was taking considerable restraint for her to keep from abandoning the ship to seek refuge on solid land.

The ship had been within sight of land for some time, but it was not until they were just a few minutes from port that the city became apparent. At first glance, Twilus seemed to be little more than a particularly grand stand of trees. Myranda wasn't familiar with the specific type of tree, but they grew tall and stout, with silvery bark and a complex forking structure. Their branches spread out as much as they reached up, most interweaving with the branches of nearby trees such that it was difficult to determine where one tree ended and another began. The size was deceiving as well. Without a point of comparison they didn't seem much larger than what Myranda had found in the oldest sections of Ravenwood, but as they drew nearer and the workings of the elves became apparent, she realized even the smallest of them was twice the size of all but the largest trees she'd ever seen in the Northern Alliance. Tucked among the glade were pathways and bridges strung between the trees. The delicate catwalks were formed of mossy ropes and stout vines. Here and there a door set into the base of a tree or a gate beneath a natural arch of branches marked a home or shop. The only overtly manufactured part of the entire port town was the row of piers stretching out into the water.

Dockworkers and a small receiving party marched to the longest and widest of the piers. Elven men and women dressed in finely woven, brightly colored garb welcomed the flagship of the fleet with music played on string and horn. Silla had carefully explained the precise order that all would disembark. First would be the king and his escorts, then Myranda and Deacon, followed by Ether, Ivy, then Grustim and the dragons. Perhaps not surprisingly, Myn's desire to be off the sea and away from the boat superseded the elven protocol. She flapped her wings while atop her perch, causing a wave of panic and yelling. When she could wait no longer, she bounded from deck to shore in one ponderous swoop. Myn's entire act of abandoning the ship was so smooth and so swift that by the time the line of archers had organized themselves enough to take aim, she was already solidly ashore and settled down to wait for the others.

Soldiers, archers, and dignitaries shouted orders in the oddly musical clamor of their nuanced language. It took a shouted command from the king himself to bring the crowd to order. A few more moments and Myn might have felt the bite of some very skillfully made arrows. Her relief at finally being off the horrid waves was such that she barely seemed to notice the threat the soldiers presented.

Once the stir settled, protocol fell back into place and the nobles and guests left the ship to be greeted by the elders of the town. A short ceremony conducted entirely in Elven welcomed them to Sonril. Deacon took it upon himself to translate for the others, and each stepped forward to accept a woven wreath of silver leaves. It was all very cultured. It did, however, lack the ring of sincerity. As reverent and respectful as their words and actions were, their eyes told a different story. All within view—and that included a few surreptitious onlookers hiding behind curtains and shutters as the Chosen toured the town—viewed the visitors with the combined wonder and revulsion of those seeing their first circus.

Officially, each of the visiting nobles was given an armed escort, but in light of Myn's breach of protocol and the comparative threat she presented, most of them had gathered around Myn and Garr. This left Myranda, Deacon, Ether, and Ivy more or less isolated in the center of the procession.

"I'd expected a visit from their king to divide their attention a bit more," Myranda said, "but we seem to have the dedicated interest of the townspeople."

Deacon nodded. "Indeed. It is a bit like when we visit Tressor, in a way."

"It is and it isn't. In Tressor, at least in the beginning, I could *feel* the distrust. There is a healthy dose of that here, but more so, I can feel the curiosity, disbelief, and even a dash of disgust. It is a unique experience, being judged by an entire town simultaneously."

"Not for me it isn't." Ivy stepped up between them. "This is how it always is for me. On good days, people are curious. On bad days, they're angry. Sometimes they're afraid, like they are when Myn shows up, but never so afraid that they run and hide like they do sometimes for her. At least the people here seem like they've got better manners than some of the towns in the Northern Alliance."

"How so?" Deacon asked.

"They aren't throwing things."

Myranda shook her head. "We've got a long way to go, Ivy…"

"It's fine. I'm the only malthrope most people have ever seen, or will ever see. People are supposed to stare." She threw her arms over their shoulders. "It's kind of nice to not be the *only* one getting looks like that. It's different, isn't it? You can see it in their eyes. They're not wondering if they should *trust* that person. They're wondering if you are even a person at all. But we'll win them over. Just follow my lead. I'm used to this."

Myranda smiled. "You've grown so much since we first met you."

"I had to. We all had to, right? No one *else* was going to do what we could." Her eyes brightened, and she sniffed the air. "Oh! I think they've got a feast prepared for us!" She clapped. "This is one of my favorite parts of big formal things like this!"

#

The great hall of Twilus, like so much else in the elven city, was at once familiar and foreign. All had gathered into a space beneath six of the largest trees in the town. Their branches had meshed into a dense, woven roof, giving it the curious feel of a cathedral borne of nature itself. The light of the setting sun filtered through the gaps in the branches, where it joined the glow of polished silver sconces to illuminate the festivities. King Mellawin sat at the center of a long, horseshoe-shaped table. His people and the gentry of the town sat along his right. Myranda and the other Chosen sat along the left. Considerable hushed argument had passed between the locals and the king's spokespeople before Garr and Myn were permitted to enter the hall. Their presence displaced two full tables of locals and created a palpable feeling of tension among the rest of the attendees. This, if nothing else, seemed to be a source of profound entertainment for the king.

"Hah! You see!" King Mellawin said. "Look at them. Listen to their murmurings. All shall remember this day, the day their king brought the mightiest and most mysterious people from across the sea. I, of course, have the greatest of confidence that you shall ferret out the source of our woes to the north, but even if you fail, there shall be no doubt in the minds of my people of the lengths their king is willing to go for their safety."

Servers approached, setting plates before each guest from the inner curve of the oddly shaped table.

"Ah! And how I envy you all. Today, you taste *proper* food for the first time in your lives. And the wine. The *wine*. I ensured that a dozen casks of the finest wine in my reserve was sent here in preparation for our arrival." He stood. "We shall drink a toast! All of us. That is how great deeds begin among your people, is it not?"

Servants filled tall chalices before each of the guests. Ivy sniffed at it, then glanced uncertainly at Myranda. "Are we sure?" she said.

"Do not *suggest* that you would forgo a taste of our wine," Mellawin said.

"Ivy's abilities are such that drinking too much wine could be dangerous for—"

"Fuff! You do yourself a disservice and me a great dishonor if you turn your nose up at our wine. Drink deeply of our hospitality or I shall be *personally* insulted."

Ivy sniffed again and licked her lips. "It does smell interesting. I'm sure *one* glass won't hurt. I'll be careful."

The king reached for his glass, but he paused. His smile widened briefly, then vanished into a rather theatrical scowl. "Where is the steward?"

"Here, Your Majesty," replied an anxious older elf with an inexpert grasp of Varden.

"Was I not clear when I stated that we should *all* enjoy this toast?"

"All of the guests have been served, Your Majesty."

Mellawin pointed to the dragons. They were seated just beyond the edge of the table, each with a pair of troughs. One trough had been filled with water. The other was awaiting the meal.

"Do you intend the grandest of our guests to drink simple *water*? Wine for the dragons."

Myranda turned to Grustim. "I defer to your expertise regarding proper diet for the dragons."

"Wine is, on rare occasion, permissible," he said.

"Then it is settled. Quickly! Serve my guests and let us begin this glorious enterprise in earnest."

Servants hastily hauled away the water troughs, replaced them, and upended casks of wine into the troughs. The king stood and raised his glass.

"To the Chosen, to Sonril and revealing the mystery of the Aluall and making them pay for their crimes!"

All raised their glasses, then drank deeply. Ether, showing remarkable commitment to her goal of experiencing more of what the world has to offer, even joined in the toast. Ivy took the opportunity to drink a bit more deeply than the others, nearly finishing her cup lest she not be permitted another sip. As she licked at the stain on her white muzzle fur that the wine left behind, the king addressed Myranda and Deacon.

"Let me again apologize that we are not able to provide you all with a *proper* tour of the many gems of Sonril's crown, but the length of the journey and the drudgery of diplomacy has squandered quite a bit of time. Until we know precisely who or what is responsible for the attacks to the north, I hesitate to waste any more time than we must before you commence your investigation."

"Of course," Myranda said, nodding in thanks as a plate was set before her. "There will be plenty of time for that afterward, provided we are successful."

"I will not *hear* of the mere *suggestion* of your failure. You are the tools of the gods and fate. If those responsible are D'Karon, then this shall simply be the latest in your clashes with them, battles you were crafted in the forge of the divine to win. And if they are a lesser threat, then there should be no trouble at all in besting them."

"I appreciate your confidence, but I prefer to treat any mission with care and respect."

"Of course, of course. Deacon, as the record keeper, I do hope you shall record the details of your exploits thoroughly."

"I endeavor to be complete in my records," Deacon said.

"Wonderful. If they are suitably heroic, I believe I shall commission a playwright to adapt them to the stage. Already songs are being sung and tales are being told of your triumph in the Perpetual War.

My people deserve to have a thrilling legend of their own to capture their imaginations."

"A play!" Ivy said. She licked a conspicuously fresh dose of wine from her muzzle. "That's wonderful! I do hope you'll let us see a performance. We're only *just* getting things like theaters rebuilt in New Kenvard. Thanks to the war, things like plays and operas have almost vanished. I would *love* to see how you perform here, so that I can help build up our *own* theaters."

The king raised his eyebrows. "Ivy, I do not know what surprises me more. That your people could *survive* without the spiritual nourishment of drama, or that you've waited this long to replenish it. Silla, make a note. When we return to the capital after the Chosen are off to see to the Aluall, we shall stage a special performance of *The Swan and the Thistle*. It will bring you to tears from curtain to curtain, Ivy. A masterpiece."

"Perhaps we could discuss the mission itself for a moment before we plan the victory tour," Myranda said.

"Of course, of course. Silla, if you would?"

"Yes, Your Majesty. As we discussed during the journey, from now until you have either succeeded or failed, the king shall return to our capital, Grandwinn. A sizable contingent of the royal guard has already bolstered the local defenses here and in the sister city of Rendif to the east. We have gathered all troops quartered within three days' travel in all directions and put them on alert on the Sonril side of the isthmus in the event the border must be defended or an assault must be made upon an enemy."

"All merely a precaution, as we all know that your victory is assured," the king said.

Silla continued. "Our formal border is marked by a fortified wall a short distance to the north. No citizen of Sonril has ventured past it since the last of our investigation parties was menaced, and by royal decree no one *shall* until safety is assured. Thus, as we've discussed, you shall be traveling without escort. Ruins of both of the cities that were attacked are clearly marked on the maps we've provided. You shall communicate your findings once per week at the maximum."

"Ah, yes," Deacon said, "communication. I had been meaning to ask you how you intended to maintain communication. I have developed a method that has proved quite effective."

"You've mentioned it. Your notebooks. Inventive though that solution is, our military would prefer to keep to established methods."

"I presume, then, you'll be providing us with ravens or other messenger birds of some sort?"

"Perhaps your own kingdom is limited to such options, but Sonril's natural resources afford us a more sophisticated method than birds." She signaled a servant standing near the doorway. "It is best we provide it to you now, such that you may develop some level of familiarity prior to your departure."

"I am intrigued," Deacon said. "Does it require much training to use?"

"For you? No. It is simplicity itself, but there are some procedures you'll need to be aware of. While we wait for it to be fetched, I need to impress upon you to treat it with great care. Though it is not unique, this messenger pair represents a profound amount of time and expense."

The servant reappeared, carrying a pair of tall, thin cases. Unlike the silver wood that was so prevalent elsewhere, these were stained dark. A lighter wooden inlay labeled each with a unique rune.

"'Messenger' and 'Beacon,'" Deacon read.

"That is correct," Silla said.

She set each case on the table. They were small enough that combined they could still comfortably fit within a decent-size pack with room to spare. She unfastened a small latch on the side of each case and flipped it open.

"Heavens…" Myranda said.

The shallow lids each had a series of thin slips of paper held with a cloth band along with an ink pot and quill. In the cases themselves stood a motionless figure, one per case, both fastened at the waist. One was a male, the other a female, each dressed in simple clothing covered with loops and bands. Delicate, filmy wings upon their backs dispelled any doubt as to what the creatures were. They were fairies, though their unnatural stillness made them seem more like dolls.

"This is a messenger pair," Silla explained. "Compose your message, then unfasten both bands. The pair is linked. The male is trained to read the winds and know his place upon the Crescents. The female is trained for speed and an ability to locate one of a collection of beacon gems, one of which I carry. Once you provide the message and allow the two to converse briefly, the female will leave to deliver the message. At that point you may fasten the male's band to return him to slumber. You can do the same when the female returns. Simple, but we've found it to be far more reliable and useful than magic, which requires training on both ends and can easily be fouled by those seeking to silence it, and falcons or other birds, which are not nearly as clever as fairies when it comes to defending themselves and evading capture."

Silla closed the cases and handed them to Deacon.

"I don't understand," Myranda said, taking one and reopening it. "Did the fairies volunteer for this? Were they recruited? It seems an unsettling life, being carried around like equipment."

Mellawin leaned back in his seat, bemused.

"You do understand that they *are* equipment, don't you?" Silla said.

"That is absurd. Fairies are thinking creatures. Even horses and hounds are treated with care and respect, and fairies are as intelligent as you or I."

"Your compassion is admirable, Myranda, but though they play at such things, they are but shadows of proper creatures." The king said. "More so, they are so utterly abundant in our forests, if we did not find a use for them, they would become too bothersome to tolerate."

"King Mellawin, though I can't speak for her personality, I can say without reservation that my teacher of wind magic, a fairy named Ayna, is among the most knowledgeable and talented wizards I have ever met."

"Exceptions notwithstanding, our ways have been refined and developed over hundreds of generations. Your purpose here is not to question thousands of years of tradition," Silla said, her constant feelings of indignation drifting a bit nearer to the surface.

Myranda shut her eyes. "Of course. My apologies. We shall be certain to provide messages as necessary."

Silla nodded. "Excellent."

Deacon fetched one of his books. "In all our discussion, while you have underscored the fact that your knowledge of North Crescent is limited and your contact with the natives is nonexistent, I notice you've not discussed how you would like us to proceed when we inevitably encounter the natives. Are we to act as representatives of South Crescent?"

"Certainly not," Silla said. "A small but crucial part of the reason we have tasked you with this rather than pursuing it ourselves is precisely that you are *not* representatives of South Crescent."

"Then we are free to pursue diplomatic relations between North Crescent and the Northern Alliance and Tressor?"

The king set down his glass of wine. "If we have not been clear, then I am sure the fault is mine. We have no interest in relations with North Crescent, and nor should you. If we had such interest, we would have pursued them ages ago. Our ignorance is entirely intentional. It is a place of savagery. As we embrace the harmony and majesty of nature, they embrace its hostility and chaos. If and when you find those who attacked my people, bring them to justice. If you encounter anyone else, be prepared to defend yourself. There is nothing north of this isthmus that I would consider even a parody of what we've created. You would be well advised to make your time in the North Crescent as brief as possible."

"There is no corner of the world that is so lost to the darkness that we cannot find something to learn and admire," Deacon said.

"You feel that way only because you have yet to venture into the wilderness to the north. It cannot be controlled, it will not yield, and it cannot be destroyed. Thus, it is best left to its own vile devices," Silla said.

"I tire of such debate," the king said. "You have your means of communication, all that remains is for you to investigate and, if needs be, eliminate those responsible. You may utilize any means you desire, and when you are through, you shall return to be lauded by my people for your heroics. Simplicity itself for warriors such as yourselves. Until then, eat hearty and enjoy the hospitality of our fair land."

#

Myranda and Deacon arose early the next morning, ready to load their equipment onto Myn's back and begin their journey. Grustim was already prepared, having foregone the soft beds and smooth sheets the elves provided in favor of Garr's back. The pomp and ceremony of the night before had satisfied the king's thirst for admiration and spectacle, leaving the morning mercifully free of formality. *That* was the most trying part of the entire night. So many prolonged introductions, so much rigidity and structure. The meal itself had been rather small and reserved by the standards Caya had set during her reign, but it had not been without its toll on some members of the party.

"Ugh…" Ivy moaned, clumsily lumbering down the gnarled root walkway leading from the quarters where she'd spent the night.

She was bleary eyed, her fur still lightly stained from the handful of glasses of wine she'd sneakily consumed during the meal.

"Are you feeling ill?" Myranda asked, realizing the state her friend was in.

"Elven wine… It tastes like honey, but my *head*…" Ivy moaned.

"I *thought* you were acting up a bit last night. Hold still, I should at least be able to ease the pain."

"Was I acting up?" Ivy said, opening one eye to look at Myranda. "Did I do anything wrong?"

"You danced with the king," Deacon said. "Silla didn't seem pleased with the decision, but the rest of the attendees seemed entertained by it, as was the king himself."

Ivy rubbed her eyes. "There are worse things than being entertaining."

Myranda placed a hand on the ailing malthrope's head and allowed some soothing magic to wash over her. It didn't erase the consequences of the night before, but from Ivy's expression it appeared to at least have allowed the worst of the pain to subside.

"I'm anxious to get moving," Ivy said. "The air is so much fresher up there. I'm sure it will make me feel better."

Deacon looked to Myn. They had left all but the bare essentials with the king's escort for safekeeping. They had a bit of food and water, some extra clothes, and some very basic equipment. The plan was to live off the land to lighten the load on the dragons and speed their travel. With a desert and a temperate forest as the two most likely settings for their investigation, they dressed light, with Deacon, Ivy, and Myranda all wearing airy tunics and light cloaks. The dragon seemed impatient, her eyes scanning the handful of locals who had gathered. The onlookers were watching with the sort of interest normally reserved for a menagerie. When Ether rather windily arrived and coalesced before them, it caused a stir and even a condescending round of applause.

"I think we may as well be on our way," Deacon said. "We cannot be of any further use to the king until we've reached the nearest of the two assaulted towns. I believe it was called Dusand. Even with Myn to carry us, it will be several hours."

"Then let's go!" Ivy said, scampering up to Myn's back.

Myranda glanced back toward the town, and to the king's entourage, which was beginning to assemble for his journey back to the capital.

"Ether, may I have a word with you?"

"What," the shapeshifter said flatly.

Myranda stepped closer and lowered her voice, doing her best not to appear as though she were trying to keep others from hearing.

"It is fair to say traveling along with us as we fly atop Myn's back will be a good deal slower than you are capable of moving, correct?"

"I am accustomed to enduring the limitations of mortals."

"And you would no doubt be able to find your way to us quickly if we were to require your aid."

"Is there a point behind this? You seem to be the human *least* inclined to waste my time in such a fashion."

"The apparent ignorance the elves show regarding North Crescent is nothing short of willful, and any questions as to their motivation for such ignorance are met with evasion and dismissal."

"The kingdom, and to a large degree the species, strikes me as dismissive and evasive."

Myranda crossed her arms.

"You've said you came here to experience the parts of the world you have neglected."

"As I was advised."

"I think you should accompany the king back go Grandwinn. If they are hiding something about their history with North Crescent, it could be as important to this mission as anything we will find north of the isthmus."

"You distrust their word?"

"I believe they understandably value their privacy, which may be at odds with the potential success of this mission."

"And you would have me uncover the information they may be hiding?"

"I would ask you to tactfully pursue that information without endangering our relationship with Sonril."

"Though my skills and strengths are beyond measure, I am told that I should not count tact among them."

Myranda smiled. "I have faith in you. And to be perfectly honest, your attitude is near enough a match for theirs, I suspect you will fit in better than any of us."

"I *am* a shapeshifter. Blending among lesser beings is one key among my abilities. Very well. I shall see to this."

"Excellent. Thank you," Myranda said.

She and Deacon climbed onto Myn's back, Deacon behind Ivy and Myranda behind Deacon. He held out his hand, and a book leaped from his bag. Its pages spread to reveal the map of the land stretching north of the isthmus.

"Grustim, we shall lead the way," he called.

The Dragon Rider nodded.

"Let's go, Myn," Myranda said.

Myn took a few long strides to judge the weight of her passengers, then spread her wings and caught the breeze. In the warmth of the sun, she had little difficulty finding an updraft to ease her skyward. The land opened out below them. As the subtle details of the town they'd left behind became less apparent, the elven works blending effortlessly with the countryside, the landscape took on the look of unspoiled wilderness.

"We shall need to take special care to follow the map closely," Deacon said, layering a few more enchantments upon the book drifting beside him. "If these new towns are anything like the old, we could easily miss them."

Myranda nodded, though she'd only half-heard him. Her mind was elsewhere. She rummaged through one of the packs strapped to Myn's back beside her and fetched the first of the two "messenger" cases they'd been given.

"I do not believe it will be necessary to send a message back just yet," Deacon said.

"It is not my intention to send a message. At least not of the sort you are suggesting," Myranda said. She opened the box with care, wrapping a bit of her mind around the looser bits of equipment within the case to keep the wind from catching them. "The elves may feel it is appropriate to pack away these creatures as though they are simple *things*, but I needn't humor them."

The case she opened was the one containing the female fairy. Myranda gently removed the band holding her and felt a small but potent spell lift away. The tiny creature began to stir. Her eyes opened, and her expression drifted through the same flashes of confusion and burgeoning awareness that came whenever one awakes from a deep slumber. After a moment she seemed to snap to attention, like a soldier realizing a superior officer was present. She glanced about, eying the blank pages in the lid of the case, then looked curiously at Myranda.

"There is no message. I simply thought you'd appreciate a bit of freedom," Myranda said.

Confusion continued to dominate the creature's expression, with a bit of concern creeping in at the edges. The fairy seemed to be scrutinizing first Myranda, then Deacon. Oddly, her glances to the open sky around her didn't seem to be a source of much concern. She grabbed the top of the case and climbed atop it.

"I don't think she understands Varden," Deacon said. "Not much of a surprise. There isn't much call for it here, the intended 'usage' for her was to carry written messages."

"Can you speak to her?"

"Human anatomy is not well suited to fairy diction, but I can try," Deacon said, turning a bit to speak over his shoulder.

He produced a few complex, trilling whistles. The fairy's eyes opened wide with wonder and a tinge of terror. From her expression, you'd think she'd just heard a monster attempt a greeting. She squeaked a lilting response.

"She wants to know where the beacon is and why we haven't written a message," Deacon said.

"Try to explain it to her. I'll free the male."

When Myranda started to close the case, the fairy quickly dropped back inside and attempted to affix the band that would put her back to sleep. It took more than a bit of coaxing for Myranda to get the fairy free of the case long enough to close it.

The fairy buzzed between Deacon and Myranda. Myn soared with considerable speed, but a gentle bit of magic kept the worst of it from them and thus left the fairy to flutter without being whisked away.

Myranda stowed the box and fetched its twin. The "beacon" reacted in much the same way as the "messenger," though once both fairies were awake and aware, they seemed more comfortable knowing the other was there. They spoke quietly to one another, then addressed Deacon, both speaking at once.

"I've never quite gotten the hang of the fairy language. What are they saying?" Myranda said.

"They are vigorously assuring me that they are ready and willing to carry any message I require. I am having difficulty making it clear that they need not do so at this time," Deacon said.

"We'll give them some time. I have got to imagine being *stored* rather than being allowed to live their lives has left their minds a bit mixed up. Do we know their names?"

Deacon said a few more words. He shook his head lightly at their response.

"The female says she's Messenger, and the male is Beacon."

"Well that won't work," Ivy said over her shoulder. "We can't have a Beacon and a Deacon."

At the sound of the new voice, the fairies darted up to look past Deacon to the source. They hung in the air over either of Deacon's shoulders, for the first time getting a clear look at Ivy, not to mention Myn's head. Myranda prepared herself for the creatures to panic at the sight of a dragon or a malthrope, but like the extreme height, it seemed the fairies had no fear of the two creatures most others would view as a threat. On the contrary, the fairies flitted forward to investigate Myn's face, then hung before Ivy with a look of wonder and disbelief, practically serenading her before tucking themselves into the hood that hung down behind her head.

"What were they saying?" Ivy asked.

"I… I think they're singing," Deacon said.

The male fairy poked his head out of the hood and addressed Deacon eye to eye.

"One moment. This will become troublesome, constantly translating." He drew his crystal to hand and conjured a pulse of light from its heart. "There, we should all understand each other now."

"We are flying north," repeated the male.

The spell Deacon had cast was a curious one. The fairy was not suddenly speaking Varden, nor had the listeners suddenly learned the creature's language, yet the meaning of the words was clear.

"Wow…" Ivy said.

"If only you'd cast that spell while I was in Entwell," Myranda said.

"But then you wouldn't have learned nearly as much," Deacon said.

"North!" the male said, more insistently. "We are heading north."

"Yes," Deacon replied. "We do so on behalf of King Mellawin."

"No…" the female said in this disbelief. She turned to the male. "How far north? We feel very far north. Too far north. Near the edge of Sonril."

The male nodded. "If we do not stop going north, we will leave the kingdom. The king would not want you to leave the kingdom."

"Again, we have been asked by the king to travel this far on his behalf. And much farther if needs be," Deacon said.

"He wants them to die…" the female said, her voice low.

"What?" Ivy said, her ear flicking as she tried to turn to see them in her hood.

"You are using us wrong," the female said. "He did not train you. He did not teach you. If he sent you north and did not teach you, he wants you to die."

"No, you misunderstand," Myranda said. "We know how he intended you to be used, but I thought it was kinder to release you until you are needed."

"Kinder…" the female said.

"Kindness is not for fairies in Sonril," the male replied.

"Kindness is for everyone in New Kenvard, which is where I am from. Now, what are your names?"

The male pointed to himself. "Beacon."

"No. Not your role. Not your task. Your name. What did your parents call you?"

He looked at her askance. "… You do not need to know this to use me properly."

"I wish to know."

"I am the Warm Dry Breeze that Scatters the Sand."

"Ah, another reason why a translation spell is not ideal. If I recall the means the fairies used in Entwell, that would render to… Freet Scattersand?"

"Freet," he said, nodding.

"And you?" Myranda asked the female.

"The Fragrant Wind that Rustles the Pine Boughs."

"Shah Rustlebough," Deacon said.

"Freet, Shah, my name is Myranda. This is Deacon, that's Ivy, and the dragon is Myn. For the duration of this mission—and if I have anything to say about it, from this point forward—you can consider yourself a part of our party, not a part of our equipment."

Shah's eyes glimmered with hope, but Freet pulled back slightly.

"We wish to be the beacon and messenger," Freet said.

Myranda shook her head. "This is not a trick, I assure you."

He squinted uncertainly. "You are *not* elves. What sort of creature are you?"

"We are humans. You've never seen humans before?" Myranda said.

"No. You are like elves… but different," Freet said.

"Less… elf-y," Shah said.

"We come from across the sea."

Ivy turned again. "You seem to like *me*. Do you know what I am?"

"Malthrope," both fairies said.

"You're from the stories," Shah added.

Freet shot her a stern look, and she ducked a bit farther into the hood.

"Stories?" Deacon said.

"She doesn't know what she is saying. There are no stories," Freet said.

"But…" Shah said, her voice small.

"*There are no stories*," Freet said firmly.

"It's fine," Myranda said. "If you don't want to tell us, you don't have to."

Shah tugged at Freet. "They aren't like the elves. They are going where the elves don't. They're doing things elves don't. Maybe…"

Freet glared at Shah, then turned to Deacon. "If you tell the elves about this, we will tell them you used us wrong, and we will all have trouble."

Myranda smiled. "Understood."

"When we are little, with the other fairies, before the elves make their choices, the older fairies tell us stories," Shah said.

"Stories from their parents, and *their* parents. Stories from before everything," Freet said.

"And there were stories about the fox people, the malthropes," Shah said.

"They did terrible things to elves. Stole from them. Killed them," Freet said.

"They've never heard of humans, but of course they've heard all the same stories about malthropes," Ivy murmured.

"But they don't do terrible things to fairies!" Shah said, leaning back to stroke Ivy's hair.

Freet nodded. "Malthropes are *friends* of fairies."

"That's why I didn't think they were real," Shah added.

Ivy turned, again trying to glance at them. "So in *your* stories, I'm not a monster?"

"You *are* a monster. But you are a monster to the people who command us. And you *don't* command us. So you are a monster who is safe for us," Freet said.

Ivy laughed. "That's still probably the best opinion of a malthrope I've ever heard."

"And dragons?"

"Dragons are the same," said Shah. "The biggest story is about dragons, and how they—"

Freet once again silenced her with a hard look.

"Is something wrong?" Deacon asked.

"The elves do not like the big story. They don't like when we tell *any* of our stories, but the *big* story is the only one they've told us we should never tell. Even if you promise not to tell them, I still don't think we should talk about the big story."

"Yes," Shah said. "But dragons are like malthropes. Bad to elves, but no story ever tells of them being bad to fairies. They are monsters that are *safe* for fairies."

"You don't have any stories about humans?" Myranda asked.

"We don't," Freet said.

"The elves have some. They talk about humans sometimes. You fight each other. You've been fighting each other for a long time. And you have money. You pay the elves to help you fight each other."

"The fighting is over now," Myranda said. "And I'm honored for us to be the first humans you've met. Hopefully, when this adventure is through, the stories you tell will remember us kindly."

"You *did* introduce us to a malthrope and a dragon," Shah said. "And you are taking us north. That's where a lot of the stories take place."

"Really? You know about the north?" Myranda said.

"We have heard things. But I'm a beacon," Freet said. "I only *really* know where I am. Mostly, I get to see little bits of here or there while the messenger asks where we are. The rest of my time I'm just in my home grove."

"I know a lot about the *south*. But *I* only really get to see the things between the beacon and one of the gems and back again," Shah said.

"But the stories, the best stories, are from the north. That's where most of the fairy families started," Freet said.

"Someone attacked the elves in their new cities to the north. The elves think it may be something called the Aluall. Do you have any stories about them?" Myranda asked.

"The Aluall," Freet said, face pinched in thought.

"The elves tell stories sometimes about the Aluall. They sound like spirits," Shah said.

Freet nodded. "Vengeful spirits. I think maybe the elves make everyone mad at them."

Deacon compelled his stylus to jot down some notes. "It *does* seem that the elves have not had much success in earning allies."

"They all…" Shah paused. "You're *sure* you won't tell them anything we say, right?"

"It will be our secret," Myranda said.

"They just seem like they want to be in charge of everything," Shah gushed, as if she'd been fighting to keep the words inside. "Everything has to be *their way*. They always act like just because *they're* elves and everyone else *isn't* an elf, everyone *else* should do what *they* say. Like just being an elf makes them better. Which they really aren't."

"They aren't," Freet agreed.

"They *live* a long time, and they're bigger than us, but most things are bigger than us and live longer."

"Are you slaves?" Myranda asked.

"Every fairy grove that provides a messenger and beacon is protected and cared for," Freet explained.

"And the ones that don't provide a messenger and beacon?"

"I don't know," Shah said. "We all do it. We don't always *like* it, but the elves act as though it is an honor to serve them. If they're so great, why do they need *us* to fly for them? Why do they need to snatch up the best males to make them beacons?"

"And they aren't very good at reading the wind," Freet said. "I'm not sure they can at all."

"Only male fairies are beacons?" Deacon said. "Fascinating."

"Sure," Shah said. "It's because male fairies are so easy to find, because they're so hard to find."

"I'm not sure I understand," Myranda said.

"There are ten females for every one male," Deacon said. "So I can understand why males would be difficult to find, but I must admit to ignorance regarding why they are also easy to find."

"A female fairy can *always* find a male fairy," Shah said simply. "Males protect the home grove. They stir the wind differently than anything else. It's because of male fairies that we can always find our way home."

"Fascinating…" Deacon said.

"If you don't know about the Aluall, can you at least tell us what sort of creatures we can expect to find in the north?"

"All kinds," Freet said. "Except elves."

"It's a wild place. Dangerous," Shah said.

"There is a reason even fairies who *hate* the elves don't go back there," Freet said.

"Sounds like just the sort of place we'd end up," Ivy said.

#

A few hours later, they reached the nearest village that had been menaced by the Aluall, a place they'd called Dusand. Myn and Garr touched down and the others hopped to the ground to investigate. Myranda realized she needn't have worried about missing the city, as unlike the more established elven city they'd left behind, this one was much more like a human settlement. The structures were built rather than grown, though much of the lumber still had a live edge, and the stoutest timbers of some buildings had fresh sprouts.

"It doesn't *look* like it was attacked," Ivy said, cautiously approaching the edge of the town.

It was indeed disturbing just how intact the place was. Myranda had unfortunately become quite familiar with the ruins of whole towns laid low by attacks. This was unlike any she'd seen. The buildings were whole. Not a single door had been broken down, though every door in the village *was* wide open. The only real damage seemed to be the charred remains of the town gate.

"It's been ransacked," Myranda said, peering through the window of the first of the dozen or so houses in town.

Grustim crouched down and peered at the ground. "No footprints," he said.

89

The others scanned the ground.

"None at all," Myranda agreed. "There should at least be footprints from the townspeople. Could the wind have wiped them all away?"

"The wind isn't so thorough," Grustim said. "Or selective. I see animal tracks there, and there. But they vanish when they approach the town."

"Then those who attacked this place took care to cover their footprints," Deacon said, wary but intrigued.

"Or they didn't have feet." Ivy sniffed. "I don't smell anything. No creatures, anyway. I smell a bit of char from the gate, some greenness from the wood, but that's all. There aren't even any fresh trails from woodland creatures. It's as if things are staying away from this place."

Myranda, Ivy, and Deacon stepped inside the nearest house. Cabinets and cupboards had been stripped clean with far more care than a panicked departure of the residents would explain. Not a scrap of food remained, not even a single kernel of wheat or carrot green. And on the back of each door, a carved message.

"'Heed the warnings. There shall be more blood,'" Deacon read, running his fingers over the shallow shapes hacked into the wood. "At least, I believe that's what it says. It is very poorly rendered."

"I guess evil spirits don't care much about penmanship," Ivy said.

"I don't think evil spirits would steal bags of flour," Myranda said, nudging a bit of burlap sack torn free by the edge of a plank.

Deacon copied the complex elven letters etched into the door. He fetched a small knife from his bag and found a discarded plank that had once been a shelf.

"What are you doing?" Ivy asked.

Freet and Shah climbed from her hood and perched on opposite shoulders to watch as well. Deacon carved a word in Elven, then held it up to the carvings on the door.

"I am not certain the person who carved this knew how to write in Elven at all," Deacon said.

"Why not?"

"Here," he said, indicating his carving. "The word 'blood' is very simple in Elven. Three quick marks and anyone who knows the language would be able to read it. But this. Care was taken to try to make the curve here. No one familiar with the language would bother when it would be clear enough as a straight line. The way this is written is like it was an attempt to carve a *picture* of the words, rather than simply carving the words. They didn't know what was important for meaning or understanding and what wasn't."

"And what do you make of this?" Myranda called.

Ivy and Deacon slipped into what must have been the personal workshop of the former homeowner. Myranda held a small painted tile, one of quite a few that were scattered about on the floor.

"What's wrong?" Ivy asked.

"Let us suppose this town was raided. It has been so thoroughly stripped of its goods, it is tempting to believe it was a clan of bandits that was responsible. But why wouldn't they steal these tiles? These could fetch quite a price."

"Maybe there wasn't time?"

"I am willing to believe that there wasn't time to take them, or perhaps they were too heavy, and that's why they were left behind by their creator. But that was weeks ago. Whoever chased them away has had ample time to take anything of value. They've taken the curtains." She peered out the window. "The rope and bucket from the well is gone. They've taken things that aren't worth a fraction of what these are worth, but these have been left behind. Curious…"

"This is a dragon's doing," called Grustim.

They hurried outside and found him beside the devastated gate. Garr had craned his neck, and Grustim was perched atop it, peering at the blackened wood at the top of the single pylon that had remained standing.

"It would stand to reason," Deacon called. "Witnesses of both attacks claim massive gouts of flame appeared from nowhere. Where there is fire, often there are dragons. But are you certain this is the work of dragon fire?"

"The way this burned, the heat was far more intense here, near the top, than elsewhere. This is where the flame was focused. A burning arrow couldn't achieve this, nor could dousing something in oil. This is either magic or fiery breath. And I have seen enough dragon fire in my life to know what it leaves behind."

"Was it an infant dragon perhaps? Or a smaller breed?"

"No," Grustim said, running his fingers across the charred surface. It crumbled beneath his fingers. "This is the work of an elder. Something towering."

"Difficult to miss then," Myranda said.

"It would be massive. Its wings would cast half this town in shadow."

"Then it would have had to be hidden, veiled such that even in the light of day the people of the village could not see it. Powerful magic."

"And powerful magic leaves its mark," Myranda said.

She stepped to Myn's side and carefully slid her staff from where it had been strapped to her back. Deacon summoned his crystal to his hand. They stood side by side and both shut their eyes to focus.

"It wasn't spirits," Deacon said swiftly.

"You know so quickly?" Grustim said.

"Spirits do not come and go as simply as mortals," Myranda said. "This area would still be vibrant with their influence if spirits powerful enough to do what must have been done here were to blame. If anything, the air and land here feel a bit muted, drained."

She tightened her grip on her staff and took a breath. "And I know of at least one magic that could drain the strength of the land like this. This *could* be the work of the D'Karon."

"No…" Ivy said. "But we *got* them all. I'm *sure* of it."

"We were sure we'd gotten all of them in the weeks following the Battle of Verril, and then Turiel arose. Clearly, the D'Karon sowed the seeds of their treachery wherever they could," Myranda said.

Deacon reached out to Myranda. Without opening her eyes, she took his hand. Their focus joined and deepened.

"This is not the work of a D'Karon, but there is the unmistakable stain of D'Karon techniques…" Deacon said.

"Perhaps Turiel did this as well?" Myranda said. "She'd learned to use their portals. And we do not know for certain what became of her after our last clash. She *could* have survived."

"This isn't Turiel's handiwork. Turiel's workings were powerful, but imprecise. This… this feels almost like the opposite. Profoundly weak, but so carefully refined the effects must have been exquisite. These are spells cast by those with poor mystic affinity, creatures who would have had to hammer the spells into their minds to produce any effect at all. I can *feel* the care and precision of endless repetition in the way the spells were cast."

"If that is so, finding them will be difficult," Myranda said. "They aren't powerful enough to be easily tracked. And while having *strong* mystic skill isn't an uncommon trait, having weak mystic skill means virtually any creature of any species could be responsible."

"And the only spells I can feel the residue of all have links to stealth. Hiding their footprints, their scent. Veiling themselves. The only things those responsible for this care about are evasion and stealth."

"In other words, they want to be 'unseen,' the way the lore keeper described," Ivy said.

"Indeed," Deacon affirmed.

"So the Aluall aren't a legend. It seems like *nothing* is just a legend," Ivy said. "But now that we know that, what do we do?"

Myranda released Deacon's hand and leaned heavily on her staff. "There isn't much to be learned from the residual magic. They cover their mystic trail nearly as well as their physical one." She wavered a bit. "I suppose it has been some time since I've focused so intently. I'm wearier than I expected to be."

"We've spent an awful lot of time traveling, and the trail is very cold," Deacon said. "I think we should consider remaining in this town until tomorrow. We can have a meal and continue to investigate. It will also give us time to discuss what this discovery may mean."

Grustim took his place upon Garr's back. "Weeks since the attack. Little since. The trail is very cold. A few more hours won't make much difference. All the same, if I were to attack a place to drive the people out, I would leave someone behind to ensure they didn't return. We should assume we are being watched. And if our foes have a dragon at their disposal, we should be on guard."

"Agreed." Deacon nodded. "We shall need someone to keep watch at all times, even through the night. And we should secure food enough for a few days. The threat could only have come from the north, and thus we shall have to venture onward to get to the bottom of this. Already the forest is thinning and the land is becoming more arid. Even traveling by land, within a day or two, we'll be well into the desert and game will be scarce."

At the suggestion of hunting, Myn trotted eagerly to Garr's side and set her eyes on the woods surrounding the town.

"I think perhaps it would be best if one of the dragons stayed behind, just in case—" Deacon began.

Myranda stopped him. "Go, Myn. Help Grustim and Garr bring back plenty of food, and eat your fill."

Myn practically pranced into the woods beside Garr and his Dragon Rider. As they thumped into the distance, Deacon turned to Myranda.

"Are you certain it wouldn't have been best to have Myn or Garr present to defend us if a dragon were to return?"

"They won't go far, and I honestly wouldn't have been able to bear the look on her face if we asked her to miss an opportunity to hunt beside Garr. She was *so* disappointed she couldn't provide any of the meals aboard the ship," Myranda said. "Ivy, gather some wood, and help the fairies gather enough food for a few days as well. Deacon and I will investigate the rest of the town and find a proper place to spend the night. Stay alert, and be sure to call out or send Freet or Shah for us if something seems amiss. There could still be danger about."

"Will do," Ivy said. "Come on, Freet, Shah. What do you eat, anyway?"

The malthrope bounded off into the woods, her new friends buzzing beside her. Deacon and Myranda paced deeper into the city, casting gems at the ready.

"When do you suppose we should send word back to the king about these developments?" Deacon asked, eying another carving upon the open door of a barn.

"Not yet. We aren't sure of anything yet. Certainly not enough to be of use to them. If our clash with Turiel taught us anything, D'Karon magic does not mean there are D'Karon about. And if they have dragons and the means to move invisibly, that they only scared away the townspeople rather than slaughtering them suggests their aim may not be bloodshed at all. I'd like to understand the nature of the enemy better before we discuss what's to be done about it."

"Wise."

"I hope Ether turns up something as well. I wouldn't mind understanding our 'allies' a bit more either."

"They do seem less… overtly virtuous than I would prefer. But we must remember that they have lived in relative isolation. What we perceive as good and proper may be very different from their own views."

"Everything I'm hearing is painting a picture of the sort of people who believe their only rightful place is in command of those around them. With the exception of their trade with Tressor, it seems they have little interest in learning from or working with anyone."

"But they *did* reach out to Tressor, and now they've sought our help. It is progress. Remember, these aren't mortals. For them, change is a thing of decades, centuries. Lasting alliances take time to form."

"And open minds to form them," Myranda said. "I only hope we have enough of each."

Chapter 5

Far to the south, a carriage rolled elegantly along a packed-earth road. As was the case with all things of elven make, it was more a product of nature than of engineering, looping branches curving elegantly and organically around one another to compose its form. Only those parts that required more strength than wood could provide had been fashioned from metal, and even the wood was used precisely and sparingly. The result was a vehicle that rocked and bobbed with every bump and furrow, always in subtle motion such that the relative unevenness of the road made little difference.

Inside, the king was delighted, managing to artfully keep the wine in his glass with practiced grace. Ether, in her human form, was seated across from him. Silla Lorekeeper was by his side. Ether's arrival and "request" to accompany the king had been poorly received by his entourage, but Mellawin himself had been clearly delighted by the novelty.

"… And thus the sculptor began work on the *third* bust," he droned, completing the third lengthy anecdote that Ether had been forced to endure. "But then, I don't imagine you have requested my company to be regaled by tales of my discerning eye for detail and taste for quality."

"No, I have not," Ether replied.

"Ha! Such directness! Are you *certain* you are a diplomat?" he said.

"I am a Guardian of this world, who, for reasons known only to fate, has been coaxed into acting as a diplomat. It is a trying experience, but I shall rise to it as I have risen to every task, however mundane."

"Yes, yes. It is remarkable how frequently the truly great among us must rise to a task that is beneath us." He sipped his wine. "Ah! Where is my hospitality? Here I am drinking wine from my personal reserve—the finest wine you are ever likely to taste—and not offering you any. Or perhaps some of our dried fruit? Also utterly peerless, I assure you."

"I do not drink, and I do not eat," she said with the tone of someone well past the point of frustration at having had to say so.

"As I've said, it was in deference to hospitality. I would have been remiss otherwise."

"King Mellawin, by mortal standards you are extremely long-lived."

"There are those who would not consider elves mortal at all," Mellawin noted.

"I am not among them. Nevertheless, with age comes wisdom. And you are of an extremely advanced age."

He nodded. "I have seen my people through nearly two centuries of peace and prosperity."

"Your knowledge of your own land is plainly evident."

"It is the purpose of a leader to know his people and his kingdom."

"How is it that you have failed to amass any knowledge of any value regarding your massive neighbor to the north?"

"Well now. This is hardly a mystery, is it?" Mellawin sipped his wine. "You hail from the Northern Alliance—"

"I call no place my home."

He rolled his eyes and stirred the air with his hand. "If we *must* hang upon *semantics*. You currently *represent* the Northern Alliance. And yet the Northern Alliance knew little of *Tressor* during the war. And we have done no small amount of business with Tressor, and they knew little of the Northern Alliance. Is it really so strange that we would have little insight into those places, in our eyes, too savage to venture into?"

"Tressor and the Northern Alliance were at war, King. You are not at war with North Crescent."

"Ah, well, that remains to be seen, doesn't it?"

"The events of the last few months do not explain a centuries-old lapse in attention."

"Permit me to turn the question to you. You call no place your home, as you say. Why then do you lack deep knowledge of North Crescent?"

"My focus was elsewhere. It was evident to me, even when my mind and substance were spread thin, where the Chosen would appear."

"It did not interest you, and thus you did not pursue knowledge of it. So it is for us as well. We all have only so much mind to dedicate to observation and consideration. Best not to squander it on places undeserving of our time."

Ether drummed her fingers on the seat beside her and turned to take in the view. Celia's advice echoed in her mind. The value of seeing what the world had to offer had not been immediately apparent to her at the time. But now that she'd spoken to King Mellawin, the folly of *ignoring* what the world had to offer was perfectly evident.

With regard to her mission, this made her question the sincerity of his replies. The man was full of bluster, but he did not appear to be a fool. Moreover, his words had the feel of the same frustrating dance around the point that so many humans in power used to avoid being backed into telling something others could prove was untrue. Her understanding of the way mortals thought was not as finely tuned as it might be… but she was quite certain that there was more to the story than he was admitting.

As for Celia's advice…

"Perhaps I shall sample the fruit, King Mellawin."

#

Several hours of investigation turned up little new information. Here and there, stronger traces of the D'Karon enchantments could be found, suggesting at least *one* of the practitioners had a degree of skill and power approaching that of a proper mystic. The pillaging and looting of the town had also turned out to be less complete than they'd first thought. There wasn't *much* left behind, but many of the scraps remaining seemed unlikely to have been left behind by someone seeking wealth. Like the tiles, a pair of paintings had been left in one home. Several pairs of boots hadn't been stolen in a cobbler's shop, though every bit of leather and sinew had been taken.

The dragon's hunting had been far more successful. Myn had outdone herself, hauling in two large elk and some manner of *very* large rabbit that Deacon sketched before they'd prepared it, the better to document their journey. When they'd eaten their fill and prepared the rest for travel, Ivy volunteered to take the first watch.

She sipped at a cool cup of water and endured the lingering aftereffects of her overindulgence the night before.

"Never again…" she muttered, rubbing her head as she sat beside a fire they'd built in the town square. "That much wine just isn't worth it."

The sky was clear and the moon was full, so her sensitive eyes gave her a fine view of her surroundings. That was good news, because despite how eagerly she'd volunteered, the stillness of night and the possible dangers it hid worried her more than she was willing to admit. She glanced down and grinned. At least she had company.

Ivy had folded her cloak beside her, Freet and Shah tucked adorably into the hood as if it were an enormous sleeping bag. She rummaged in her small bag of personal items and fetched the pad and stylus Deacon had made for her. Like his books, this one would never run out of space, and the stylus needed no ink to mark the page. Unlike his, the stylus could also render things in any color she wished, making it exquisite for artwork when the inspiration moved her. He'd gone so far as to link it with his own book, such that every image she drew was duplicated in his book as well. She opened it to a clean page and set about sketching her new friends.

She'd nearly finished when something in the air gave her pause. She hadn't heard anything, and a quick sweep of the area around her didn't turn up anyone, but something felt… different. She twitched her ears and took a deep whiff of the air. No humans… No elves… but there was *something…*

Ivy set down her book and stowed her stylus. Her life had been one trial after another. In the time since Myranda had found her, she'd made her share of mistakes, faced her share of dangers. She'd come to trust her intuition, but right then she couldn't make sense of what she was feeling. On one hand, the sudden appearance of a scent she'd not detected before set off warnings in her mind. On the other hand, there was something about the scent itself. She couldn't bring herself to be frightened or concerned. Something buried deep in her mind urged her to follow where it led.

She paced slowly along the single street of the town, eyes wide and ears swiveling toward the slightest sound. Her heart pounded in her chest. Here she heard a grind of dust that could be a footstep. There she heard what might have been a fearful breath of someone hidden from view. Then… whispers.

Ivy didn't recognize the language, and even with her sensitive ears she could only *just* make out the words, but there was definitely a voice. Now her intuition rang loud and clear in her mind. This was not a time for curiosity. Something was happening, and it should not be faced alone. She turned and dashed toward the others again, opening her mouth to call for them. The air between her and the campfire seemed to waft away, like reality itself had been nothing but a wisp of smoke. In its place, a figure appeared. Her heart nearly leaped from her chest at the sudden appearance, but as her eyes drifted to the eyes staring intently into hers, she could only a manage a single hushed word.

"How…?" she murmured, reaching out with her hand.

Her mind slowed to a crawl. She couldn't make sense of what she was seeing. But through the shock and wonder, something else clawed its way to the surface. As haunting and familiar as this creature's form and scent were, there was a more chilling familiarity, a violet glow from a crystal hidden in the folds of a sandy robe.

"*No!*" she cried.

She reached for the blade at her belt, but more forms emerged from around her, more crystals burning with D'Karon power. She felt the pressure of vicious spells spearing at her mind. Flickers of blue and red flared around her as her emotions fought for control, but the mix of confusion and surprise were too much. Darkness claimed her. The last thing she heard before she slipped entirely from consciousness was the tiny voice of Freet groggily waking.

#

Myranda woke with a start. The ground was shaking beneath her, and the door of the house she'd selected to spend the night in was rattling on its hinges. It took her a moment to realize the rumbling was Myn, desperate to rouse her. Myranda threw the door open and rushed outside, staff in hand.

"What is it? What is happening?" she said.

Myn was on her feet, claws dug into the ground and tail thrashing. Her eyes were gleaming with fury and anxiety.

"Ivy…" the dragon uttered.

"Where is she? What's happened?" Deacon asked, taking his place beside Myranda.

"They took her! They *took her*!" squealed Shah.

Both fairies had taken shelter huddling among Myn's horns. Now they looked upon Myranda with raw terror in their eyes.

"Who took her? Where are they?" Myranda said.

"I don't know. By the time we were waking, they were nearly gone," Freet said.

"I saw a glimpse," Shah added. "There were three of them, maybe four. They were dressed in yellow, or maybe tan. Just heaps of rags. And even looking right at them, I couldn't really *see* them."

"Were they humans? Elves?" Myranda said, already pulling to mind the spells that would help her scour the world around them for those responsible.

"I don't know," Freet said. "Like Shah said, even with them right in front of us, they seemed to shift and shimmer."

"How long has it been?" Deacon asked. The gem in his fist was burning brightly. "There is a whisper more D'Karon magic than there was before, but nothing beyond that."

"It wasn't a minute ago," Shah said. "We woke the dragon as soon as we saw!"

Garr dropped from the sky, thumping down beside Myn. Grustim, astride the dragon and armed with his lance, called down.

"No tracks, no scent. Not even the stirring of wings. If this is magic, it is the most effective I've ever seen."

"Why wouldn't she call for us?" Myranda said, shutting her eyes to focus more intently.

The world dropped away, replaced by a shadowy counterpart in her mind's eye. The souls of her friends burned brightly around her. Outward into the trees and plains she could sense the galaxy of lesser spirits, the souls of woodland creatures and the wandering spirits clinging to the land. But as she spread her mind and looked to its very limits, flickering glimmers of the elves to the south asserted themselves without even a glimpse of the fiery, lively spirit of her friend.

"It's no good." Myranda climbed onto Myn's back. "The attacks moved south, so if these things have a camp, it must be to the north. Grustim, Garr, head to the northeast. Myn and I will head to the northwest. Deacon, you stay here and focus on tracking her mystically."

"If they are this skilled at hiding themselves, we must search differently," Grustim said. "We search for places that can hide large groups."

"Agreed," Myranda said.

Myn didn't wait to be told what to do. She took to the air with a few mighty flaps of her wings and caught the breeze, skimming low to the ground, eyes sweeping the thinning woods below for any sign of motion. Myranda split her attentions between attempting to detect D'Karon magic and attempting to wring any new information she could get out of the only witnesses.

"Listen to me, Shah, Freet. I need you to tell me anything you saw. Anything at all. I don't care how useless or unimportant it might seem."

"We already said," Freet said. "There were three or four of them. They were dressed in pale yellow."

"And there was some violet. Some violet light," Shah added.

Myranda's expression intensified. "That color often accompanies D'Karon magic. Did they have weapons? Staffs? Swords?"

"I didn't see any. But it was so *hard* to *see*," Freet said.

"We weren't trained for this, Ms. Myranda," said Shah. "I'm a messenger. I'm supposed to avoid everyone. I belong in my box."

"If it wasn't for the two of you, we might not have known what had happened until morning. You've done well. But anything else, anything at all. Did Ivy try to fight them?"

"She was struggling for a moment, once they grabbed her," Shah said.

"I think she might have just been staring before that," Freet said.

"Just staring?" Myranda said.

"I don't know for sure. I'd only just woken up. But that's how it seemed. Maybe she was entranced. Some say the Aluall are vengeful spirits who lead travelers to their doom."

"She isn't dead, is she?" Shah asked, hugging Myn's horn tightly, eyes twinkling with tears. "I've always wanted to meet a malthrope. I've dreamed they were lovely, and *she* was lovely and I don't want her to be dead."

"She must be dead. Why would they take her? The Aluall wouldn't take her, they would only kill her," Freet said bluntly.

Myranda set her gaze firmly on the ground below. "You do not know Ivy as I do. If you did, you would know that she would not go down without a fight."

"What if she did try to fight?" Shah asked. "What if they were too powerful for her and she succumbed despite her fight?"

A wry smile came to Myranda's face. "If Ivy had truly fought, there would be no doubt in your mind. There's something more to this we don't understand, but I assure you, Ivy is alive. And she…"

Myranda trailed off as Deacon's voice insinuated itself into her mind.

Myranda. Move east. I can't be sure, but I may have felt a flare of magic through the thickest of the woods.

"East, Myn, and lower. Skim the trees. They may be uncanny at hiding themselves, but if they were hiding a dragon, I would feel it. They are on the ground, moving by foot, and carrying Ivy with them. They can't be far."

#

Grustim brought Garr down among the trees. The dragon dropped his head low and sampled the ground with snout and tongue. The Dragon Rider removed his helmet and crouched low. He was no expert in the dark magics the Aluall might have at their disposal, but in his last battle beside Myranda and the others, he had learned that D'Karon magic was not without its cost. If he were a creature making use of such enchantments, he would do his best to use it as little as possible. That meant keeping to those places with the most cover, places where footprints wouldn't show. If they'd seen Myn and Garr, they would also seek shelter where a dragon could not go with ease. That meant the thickest, thorniest sections of forest. He waded through waist-high bushes, trained eyes searching for any sign of something left by their fleeing targets. A part of his mind doubted he would find anything. Creatures on foot, as they were forced to assume their targets were traveling, were no match for the speed of a dragon in flight. But there were worse things than getting ahead of them. If he and the others were lucky, it would force their targets into the open, or the unseen foes would foolishly run right into the dragon and Dragon Rider.

He saw a glimmer of something out of the corner of his eye and rumbled a simple command. Garr raised his head and sent jets of flame coiling from his nostrils. In the brief splash of brilliant yellow light, Grustim saw a cluster of bruised branches, gleaming with fresh sap. If this had been a deer or other wild creature, there would have been more such branches. This was the result of someone moving with care. He touched the sap and tested its tackiness. The plants of this land were not familiar to him, but the damage to the branch was likely several hours old at least. Too old to have been the fleeing creatures, but something about this place spoke to his intuition.

Garr rumbled under his throat and pawed at the ground, and Grustim made his way back to the dragon. The beast's claws had turned up bones. They were picked clean. Even the marrow was gone. They were too fresh and too deep in the ground to have found their way there on their own. He ground the toe of his boot into the soil and unearthed more bones, older but equally stripped of every morsel of nourishment.

"Concealed remains. And I hear water nearby. They made camp here… but no fire. And still no footprints but ours. Such dedication to stealth…"

Leaves rustled. A buzzing approached. Grustim snatched his dagger and turned, but the form darting through the trees was Shah.

"Mr. Dragon Rider!" she squealed, flitting about before him. "Ms. Myranda and the dragon found something. This way, this way!"

Grustim mounted Garr, and the two launched into the sky. Shah led the way, but she needn't have. Myranda and Myn were not difficult to find. They'd set down some distance to the north, where the trees had thinned out entirely to the plains. Garr swept swiftly toward them and alighted on the ground beside Myn. They were in the center of a short stretch of sandy soil between the fringe of the forest and the dry grass of the plains that stretched into the distance. Myn was shifting anxiously from foot to foot as Myranda held her staff over the ground. Its gem illuminated a smooth patch of soil.

"What is it?" Grustim asked, crouching beside her.

Myranda held out her hand. "Ivy's stylus. Perhaps it was shaken loose."

"Or perhaps they were wily enough to know its enchantment might have given us a chance of tracking her," Grustim said.

"Unlikely. If they had sensed that, they would have sensed that the book has a similar enchantment. And more to the point, we only *just* detected it. Whatever is hiding them is powerful enough to shield *this* from us as well." Indicating a spot of earth, she said, "It was in the center of this patch of smooth soil, the same unnaturally smooth soil we found in Dusand."

Grustim turned to the south. "So they *do* move by land, but so quickly. Horses couldn't have navigated the forest as they have."

"They have powerful magic at hand. At least this tells us they aren't using the D'Karon portals. But look. There is little cover between us and the desert, and no sign of them. We shall not find them through simple tracking. Deacon and I shall need to find some mystic weakness in their veil. Did you find anything?"

"Only their camp, or what passes for it. They live lightly, and off the land. No fire, and care taken to hide all else. They are natives of this place, familiar with its bounty and how best to make use of it."

Myranda shut her eyes and lowered her head. "That won't make things any easier. But we have one thing working in our favor. They have Ivy, and there are few creatures less controllable and more visible than Ivy when she is unleashed."

"We should contact Ether," Deacon said.

"No," Myranda said. "They have Ivy. Ether is too reckless. She might be better equipped to find them, but she also might compel them to threaten or kill Ivy. And the same goes for the king's people. They will want swift, sweeping action, and I don't trust them to act with Ivy's interests in mind. Leave Ether to her own investigation for now. This is up to us. And up to Ivy. She's still alive. I can feel it in my bones. And if she's alive, then she is working just as hard as we are to free herself. Now let's go."

Chapter 6

Consciousness came slowly to Ivy. For some time she had been vaguely aware that she was being carried, but some foreign influence was pressing upon her mind, keeping her in the twilight between sleep and wakefulness. That pressure was gone, or at least diminished. Her vision cleared, and she tried to move. Her arms, her legs, and particularly her head felt terribly heavy. Her stomach grumbled and her lips smacked. She felt as though she'd not eaten in days. Though it was impossible for her to know it, it had indeed been three days since she'd been taken.

With some effort, she eased herself upright and took in her surroundings. She was in a warm, dry, dark place. The floor had wooden planks, rough-hewn but walked smooth over years of use. The walls looked to be packed earth. The air was cool, and what little light there was filtered through short windows near the tops of the walls. She'd been lying upon a very simple bed, rough cloth stuffed with hay.

There were no chains, no locks. If she was a prisoner, they were quite certain she would either not awaken or not attempt to escape.

She tried to stand, but her legs wouldn't support her weight and she crumbled to the ground. The sound caused a stir outside the door. Ivy tried to shake the cobwebs from her mind and climb to her feet. She'd made little progress when gentle fingers closed about her arm to help her.

"No. *No…*" Ivy slurred, red weakly flickering around her. "Stay away… Stay…" She raised her head to look her captor in the eyes, and instantly her last foggy memory before being forced to sleep came rushing back. "It's not possible…" she murmured, blinking the sleep from her eyes.

The creature before her was no human. It was no elf or dwarf. Staring at her were soft silvery-yellow eyes. A sleek fiery-orange muzzle offered a reassuring smile, and a bushy tail swished in slow sweeps.

"You're… you're a malthrope…" Ivy uttered, almost afraid to form the words.

She was a female, dressed in the same simple sand-colored clothes as those who had kidnapped her. She murmured something softly, though the language was not familiar.

Ivy tried to stand, reaching out to her. "How can this be? Who are you? What's going on?"

The malthrope raised her voice slightly and eased Ivy back down, then stood, speaking in soft and pleasant tones all the while. She stepped out of the room and called out. A second malthrope heeded the call. This one was somewhat more grandly dressed, a robe topping her rags and a vine circlet resting upon her brow. The two malthropes spoke to each other briefly, then the first was sent away. The newcomer stepped inside. Ivy stared at her, transfixed.

As unprepared as she was to see another malthrope, something about this one seized Ivy's mind almost as rigidly as the night she had been taken. It was something in the way she moved, in the way she smelled. It was in her voice, and more than anything else, it was in her eyes. Ivy simply stared, feeling strangely as though she were seeing a ghost.

"Notta tells me you speak the Varden tongue," said the new malthrope, her voice clear and her diction crisp.

"Y-yes," Ivy said, slow to rise from the depths of her thoughts.

"Ah… It is lovely to hear a new voice speak it. There are few who keep that language alive, but meeting you shows that it was wise to do so. No wisdom should be discarded. My name is Nehri. What is your name?"

"Ivy," she replied.

There was something so calm, so pleasant and kind about Nehri's voice, Ivy found any trace of fear or anger melted away.

"I am sorry for how you were treated, Ivy. Those who fetched you were not expecting to find another malthrope. They tried to help you, but you panicked and they had to put their gems to use, lest your former keepers be alerted. It took far more of the gem's strength to keep you asleep than we had expected, far more than may have been wise. For a time we were not certain you would *ever* awake. You have our profound apologies."

The first malthrope, Notta, knocked at the door. She had a joint of what smelled like raw venison, and a drinking skin bulging with water.

"Ah! Thank you, Notta," Nehri said, accepting the meal and turning to Ivy. "I am sure you must be—"

Ivy snatched the water and guzzled half the skin in a single go, then grabbed the meat and tore into it.

"Yes, you poor thing. Starving." Nehri sat beside Ivy on the bed. "At least your former keepers had been keeping you properly fed. Some of us may not have survived so long without food. They gave you proper clothes as well. You were very lucky indeed… How did you come to be in their clutches?"

"I… I'm not sure what…" Ivy began, her head too awash with questions of her own—not to mention the profound relief of getting a meal—to begin to consider forming any answers.

Nehri smiled warmly and placed a hand on Ivy's shoulder. "Of course. As you are not familiar to us, we must not be familiar to you. And you have had a very trying time. If there is anything I can do to put you more at ease, simply ask."

"Where are we?" Ivy asked.

Nehri's smile widened. "We call this place Den. When you have your strength back, I shall show you. But for now, you need only to know that you are home."

"Home? But I've never been here."

"No. But it is where you were meant to be. Can't you smell it? Can't you see it? We are family."

Ivy shut her eyes and drew in a breath. Nehri's scent *was* quite like her own.

"But I don't have a family. Not in the way you mean…"

"You do, Ivy. We are kin. The scent does not lie. In time we shall learn your story and you shall learn ours, but for now let us simply rejoice in having you where you belong."

"How many of you… how many of *us* are there?" Ivy asked, her voice wavering a bit.

"In all, there are nearly four hundred of us in Den and the surrounding countryside, and eighty of us are of the Sorrel line, and thus kin."

Ivy remained silent. The words slowly sank into her mind. Then, in a flurry of motion, she leaped from the bed.

"Ivy, be careful! Get your strength back first."

The warning fell on deaf ears. Ivy teetered toward the open doorway, carried by the raw will to see for herself what Nehri claimed. She steadied herself on the doorway and gazed outside, blinking in the bright light. When her eyes adjusted, what she saw took her breath away. Malthropes. Males and females. Young and old. Their colors ran the gamut from deep red to tawny brown. Simple homes like the one she'd awoken in were scattered about, each little more than a roof erected over a burrow sunk into the ground. A large communal stew pot simmered not far from her door. In the distance, a river flowed.

Ivy couldn't believe her tear-filled eyes. Dozens of creatures, just like her. Living, breathing malthropes. She turned and grasped Nehri by the shoulders.

"Where is the one who captured me?" she insisted. "Where is the malthrope who came for me that night?"

"I believe there were four. I am not certain which—"

"He was my height, with fur like yours, and I've only ever seen eyes as soulful and fierce as his once before. Please, you must bring me to him."

Nehri nodded. "That will be my brother Reyce."

She called out to a smaller malthrope stirring the stew pot. Ivy couldn't tell if he was a child or simply a diminutive adult, but his fur matched his tan clothes and his ears were almost comically large. He nodded and trotted away. Nehri tugged Ivy back toward the bed.

"He shall be here shortly, but please, do not exert yourself. Sit."

Ivy stumbled back and flopped down.

"Do you think you can answer some questions for me?" Nehri asked.

Ivy nodded numbly, eyes trained on the door.

"I have never seen a malthrope with coloring like yours. Where do you come from?"

"I'm from… I was created in." Ivy shook her head. "Kenvard. I'm from Kenvard, in the Northern Alliance."

"Kenvard…" Nehri tested the sound of the word. "There were three kingdoms. Ulvard, Vulcrest, and Kenvard. Yes, yes, of *course* you are from one of the three kingdoms. That is where Sorrel came from. That is how we are related but have never met. You must have come from Sorrel's line as well, before she arrived."

"I'm sorry, I don't know the name Sorrel."

"Do not worry. I am sure it was before your time. Sorrel came to North Crescent generations ago. Tell me, are there other malthropes like you where you came from?"

"I didn't think there were any other malthropes *anywhere*."

"Ah… So it is as I feared," Nehri said. "You are the first new malthrope we have seen since the joining of the desert and woodland tribes. We had little reason to believe life elsewhere was any easier for us than here, but we at least had hope. Fortunate that we were able to free you from your keepers."

"My keepers. Those people who were with me weren't my keepers, Nehri. They are my friends."

"The friends of the malthropes are few and rare, Ivy. Are you certain they had not fooled you?"

"They *rescued* me. They gave me a family again. They *aren't* my *keepers*."

A figure darkened the doorway. Ivy and Nehri turned.

"Ah," said Nehri. "Thank you for coming so quickly, Reyce. Our new friend has awakened, and she was insistent she be allowed to see you again."

Ivy stared intently at the malthrope called Reyce. He stood at least her height, perhaps a bit taller. Compared to most of the other malthropes she'd seen, he was practically a giant. His clothes were more travel-worn than the others' and hung from his wiry frame as though they were handed down from someone with a far stouter build. He looked upon Ivy as he seemed to look upon all things, with intensity and purpose. Everything, from the color of his fur to the way he stood, cut straight to the core of Ivy's memories.

"Lain…" she whispered.

"My name is Reyce," he said.

"You look just like Lain. You *sound* just like Lain."

"I know no one by that name." Reyce turned to his sister. "Are we certain her mind has recovered? It took more of the sacred magics to quell her than anyone we've faced before."

"She is recovering. She has her appetite back, at least," Nehri said.

Ivy tried to gather her thoughts. "My friend, Lain. I thought he was the only other malthrope left, and he thought the same of me. You look so much like him, it can't be a coincidence." Her eyes darted about. "The mark…"

She tugged at the neck of her tunic to reveal the dark shape of the mark of the Chosen against the white fur above her heart. Nehri studied the mark.

"Reyce… when Sorrel spoke of Teyn, she claimed he had a mark just over his heart as well. And histories claim he had no true name."

"Yes!" Ivy said. "Lain said he didn't have a name! That was just… a title or something. Do you know him?"

"We know *of* Teyn," Reyce said. "Father of Reyna and Wren. Mate of Sorrel. He has an honored place in our history. One of our ancestors."

"He was my friend! He… he had a family?… *You're* his *family?*"

Whorls of yellow aura flicked and flared around Ivy. She struggled to form more words, but when they did not come, she burst from the bed and threw her arms around Reyce in a tight hug. "I'm so happy to get to meet you. I'm so, so happy!"

Reyce returned the embrace, then gently placed a hand on her shoulder and eased her back to the bed.

"We are pleased to have you among us, Ivy, but there is much to be done," he remarked, shaking his hand as if he'd been stung. "Nehri, outside for a moment."

"Don't go," Ivy said. "I have so much to say to you! To *tell* you."

"We shall speak again, Ivy. This evening. And Nehri shall return and remain with you as long as you wish. But the safety of my people is my burden, and one that takes precedent above all else."

He motioned for Nehri, and the pair stepped outside. Ivy tried to ease her racing emotions and focus on what they were saying. Her mind was awash with the whirlwind of revelations, but she'd learned a great deal in her many adventures. These people were *her* people. She felt it in her heart. But they had also taken her. They'd used magic that had the stain of darkness about it. And they were almost certainly the creatures responsible for the stories of the Aluall. She couldn't allow herself to be blind to the threat they may present. She had come to North Crescent with a job to do.

She angled her ears and trained her eyes on Nehri and Reyce, straining to hear them as they spoke beneath their breath. It was no use, though. Whatever language Notta had spoken seemed to be their native tongue. She couldn't understand a word of it… but their tone and

Reyce's body language spoke volumes. They were as uncertain of her as she was of them.

#

"A new cousin, Reyce! A sister, a new daughter. After so long! And she speaks of Teyn," Nehri said.

"Nehri, be calm. It is perhaps a gift from our blessed benefactors and patrons. A time of great turmoil awaits us, and we shall require every able body and sharp mind if we are to succeed. But she came from the south. She was among strangers. Warriors with dragons. Outsiders behaving precisely as Boviss said the elves would when they chose to act. The timing is worrisome." He rubbed his hand and glanced in Ivy's direction. "And she is no simple malthrope. There is more to her, and more to her keepers."

"Reyce, there are so few beings in this world we can rely upon. So few beings that do not mean us harm. We cannot afford to look upon our own kind with distrust."

"I know it, Nehri. And I wish with the core of my heart for it to be true that she is simply a lost sister finally brought home by fate. But we cannot afford to lower our guard now. Our greatest trial is only weeks away. She has power, Nehri. It could mean *everything* for us if she would fight by our side. But she also comes from the outside. We must be vigilant of the wiles of our foes. See to her. I shall return by nightfall."

"Where are you going?"

"I must see Boviss. This is a matter that requires his counsel."

Nehri narrowed her eyes. "If that is your aim, then I shall save you the journey. Boviss knows only blood. And since he's earned your ear, it seems you share his thirst for it."

"Nehri, I do not relish war. But the first lesson he taught us, the first lesson *Sorrel* taught us, was that we cannot always cower in the darkness. Sometimes we must fight if we wish to survive."

She lowered her head. "Yes, I know. But as the priestess, every wound is mine to bind."

He smiled. "You have a soft heart, and strong instincts. I cannot imagine better qualities for our priestess. If one of us must be sullied by dark deeds, let it be me. See to Ivy. Learn all you can. And perhaps more importantly, tell her all she needs to know. She *is* one of us. She deserves to know our history. But until we know she will share our cause, she need not know there is a cause at all."

112

He paused, as if the next words stung him even before he spoke them. "And keep crystals at hand… If she turns against us… you may need to forget your mercy."

#

Ivy finished the food and drink she'd been given while the creatures who were either her hosts or captors completed their spirited discussion. The first malthrope she'd met, Notta, slipped inside to collect the bones and the emptied water skin. Despite the increasing concern and agitation she felt over the circumstances of her arrival here, the wonder of being among creatures like her and the gratitude of their hospitality compelled Ivy to behave herself and show the proper manners.

"Thank you very much," Ivy said. "I haven't had a nice raw meal like that in quite some time. I'd forgotten how lovely it can be."

Notta nodded. "Welcome."

The word was stilted and accented, delivered with the sort of tone reserved for words one had been told to say rather than words truly understood. Notta ducked out the door quickly, perhaps hoping to avoid having to muddle her way through any conversation with a potentially nonexistent knowledge of the language. She nearly bumped into Nehri, who was on her way back in.

"I apologize. You will have to excuse my brother," Nehri said. "We have not been having an easy time of it, here in Den. As the chieftain, his task is to provide for us. Between attacks from the beasts of the wild and the poor hunting we've had in recent seasons, he's been stretched quite thin."

"It sort of reminds me even *more* of Lain… or Teyn, I guess, to hear harshness in his voice. And probably for the same reasons. Lain had a heavy weight on his shoulders," Ivy said. "You don't need to apologize. Not for *that*…"

Nehri lowered her head. "But you *are* owed an apology. You were brought here against your will."

Ivy crossed her arms and narrowed her eyes. "Yes, I was. And I'm *frankly* amazed my friends haven't already come to rescue me."

"Those who were with you will not find you here, Ivy."

"You don't know my friends."

"It does not matter. Den would not exist if it had not remained hidden for the generations since it was formed."

"Then let me go to them."

Nehri folded her hands and sat beside Ivy. "Den *also* would not exist if we allowed people, even *our* people, to leave without being sure they could be trusted."

She narrowed her eyes. "Then I am a prisoner."

"No! Please, Ivy, you must understand. You are perfectly free to explore Den and learn about us. And when we can be sure it will not endanger us, you shall be free to leave if you choose. But four hundred lives depend upon me. I will *not* bend the rules if it means they may come to harm. Are you strong enough to walk?"

"I think so."

Nehri took her hand. "Then come. Let me show you Den and tell you our story. Perhaps then you will understand."

The malthrope priestess helped Ivy to her feet and pulled her arm across her shoulders. They walked out into the village. As had happened in so many other places, all eyes turned to her. But here it was different. In these eyes, she saw excitement. The curiosity was genuine, untempered by fear. All kept their distance, but it was out of courtesy to the newcomer and reverence for their priestess.

Nehri gestured to the community around her. "You spoke earlier of believing there were no other malthropes but you and Teyn. It may well be true in the place you call home, as it was nearly true of North Crescent in the years before Den. First, we learned not to travel south of the isthmus. The elves would strike us down on sight. Then we learned we mustn't travel to the mountains. The dwarfs lurked there, and the dragons. That left only two places we might find sanctuary from those who would see us dead: the desert and the forests.

"There are reasons so few things like elves and dwarfs come to North Crescent. It is a dangerous place. Vicious beasts. Harsh weather. Even with the many gifts of our race, we lacked the strength to thrive. In time, there were but two tribes of us who remained. Those of the desert, like Hana, our best seamstress…"

She gestured to a female of the smaller tan-colored variety of malthropes. Hana offered a bow and a smile before returning to her conversation with one of the taller, red-furred variety.

"… and those of the forest, like myself and Reyce. We live in harmony and fellowship now. But there was a time when each would have counted the other as just as terrible an enemy as the elves or dwarfs. And we owe that enmity to a single terrible foe. A dragon called Boviss. He could have wiped out both tribes with a few breaths, but he saw in us an opportunity. He desired two things above all, the same things that drive all dragons. The first was gold, enough to bury him. The second was meat, enough to fill him to bursting. Our people were clever. We were hard workers, good hunters, and when the circumstances demanded it, skillful thieves. We could go places that even *he* would find troublesome. So he did not kill us. He came to us and demanded his needs be met. At every full moon we would give him gold and meat. Each of us would offer him some, and those who didn't have enough would simply be part of his next meal.

"There was a grim genius to his cruel demands, as those of the forest had meat enough to satisfy him, but little gold. The desert had precious little game, but there were rich veins of precious metals. If we were truly wise, we would have worked together from the beginning, but in our fear for our lives and our desperation, we believed the only way we could survive was by taking what we lacked from the rival tribe. And so it continued for ages. The desert tribe poaching from the forest tribe. The forest tribe stealing gold from the desert tribe. We claimed as many of each other's lives as the land or the dragon did.

"But then came a vixen named Sorrel. She was the mother of twins, Reyna and Wren. Like you, she came from across the sea. She sought only a safe place to raise her young. She feared the land she'd left behind would soon kill off what few of her kind survived, so when she found our tribes, she was overjoyed. The tales of her deeds could fill a hundred nights, but two deeds tower above the others. Through her actions and those of her young, the tribes were united. And through that union, Boviss was defeated. We spared his life, because no creature who had taken so much from us should be allowed to rest until he had repaid it. So we put him to use. We used him to push back the others who would kill us in this land."

As she spoke, the journey had taken them to the center of the village, where the one stone building stood. Unlike the simple homes dug into the earth, this one stood tall and proud. It was a monument, a round building easily thirty feet high. The door was a pair of massive, ancient gray slabs of wood. The left one bore a carving of a vixen, presumably Sorrel. The right had another fox and vixen, her young. All around the village center, malthropes were working, talking, laughing.

"The tribes sent their strongest and best to build a village— Den." She placed her hand on the cool stone of the monument and lowered her head, uttering a few arcane-sounding words with the reverence of prayer. "This is not the *first* Den. Time and the whims of nature have required that we move it from that first site. But always we have moved with it, kept together. Kept united. Until you arrived, we believed every malthrope that remained lived within sight of this tower, protected by its enchantments. And now that you are here… I believe it is true."

Ivy gazed at the bustling village around her. It was almost too beautiful to be true. Families of creatures like her, working and playing out in the open without the hunted expressions or fear of being found out that had plagued her prior to the Battle of Verril. These precious beings, creatures she'd believed were lost… Ivy fully understood the lengths one would go to in order to maintain this safe haven for them. But some actions, however justifiable they may seem, have consequences.

"Nehri, what happened to the towns near the isthmus?" Ivy said.

Pain and doubt passed briefly across Nehri's expression, but resolve chased them away.

"To understand, you'll need to see. There is a hill. This way."

They paced along a narrow footpath heading toward the edge of the village. Some of the shops in this section had the sharp smell of tanning leather, or the herbal aroma of an apothecary. The nearer they came to the row of stones marking the edge of the village, the starker the change of the mood and appearance of the land. With the last of the homes behind them, the ground took on a progressively grayer, dryer appearance. The air felt stale and dead. What tenacious underbrush still grew was gnarled and brittle, snapping as they brushed past to a disused path leading up the slope of a hill. It looked like the result of a creeping drought, or perhaps the aftermath of a seasons-old wildfire. But there was no smell of char, and the lifeless soil felt as moist as in the city. The land didn't seem un*able* to thrive. It seemed un*willing*.

Their path wove up the steepening slope, offering a steadily better view of their surroundings. Ivy glanced at the city opening up below her. As lively and welcoming as it was, even at this distance, the more she saw of what surrounded it, the more it seemed like a single point of color in a lifeless landscape. When they reached the crest of the hill, Ivy's heart dropped.

All around them, reaching halfway to the horizon in each direction, the land suffered the same mysterious blight. A few motes of green marked the struggling fields of farms or pastures of livestock, but they were like stones being eroded by an unrelenting sea of decay.

"The land is failing us. It is the same withering and weakening that chased us from the original Den. We have known since the time of our grandparents that we wouldn't be able to stay here much longer. Every year it becomes more difficult to meet our needs. The good hunting grounds push farther away. The farms are less bountiful. Those beasts nearest to the village have become more vicious and hostile. Once again we need to find a new place to live. But our roots here are deep. This is the only home any of us has ever known, and it took us generations to make it what it is. Even with the proper planning, it will be a terribly dangerous enterprise to move all of these villagers to a new home. We must be certain that the new place will be safe, that it will sustain us for generations more. And so Reyce and others have explored. They've traveled far to the north, the south, and the west searching for land with the mystic and natural bounty we require, while still remaining far from the eyes of our enemies.

"Then, some months ago, he returned with grave news. The elves had crossed the isthmus. They were coming closer. Even single elves braving the dangers of North Crescent were rare, but whole villages? We'd never seen it before. We didn't know what to make of it. Reyce spoke to Boviss."

"Boviss is still alive? Even today?"

"Yes. He is as old as the mountains themselves, and wise. And he has seen this before. The elves came, hundreds of years ago. First there were towns, then cities. Then forts and armies. They tried to take this land. Now they are coming again. And at the worst time. We are at the weakest we have been in years. We couldn't let them get a foothold. We had to push them back."

"So you *did* attack them. You *are* the Aluall."

Nehri looked away. "The Aluall… I suppose that is what we have become. That name has been whispered in the stories of the land since long before Den was founded, but the blessings of our race and of those who watch over us have allowed us to assume that role for the elves. So be it. If it was that fear that kept them at bay until now, then I only wish we *were* the Aluall of legend."

"Nehri… you attacked them. You attacked them unprovoked."

Nehri shut her eyes tightly. "*They* came here, and they would have come farther. Creatures like the elves don't take one step without taking another. We had to stop them," she said sharply. "We had no choice…"

Her final words were flavored with uncertainty, as though she were trying to convince herself of their truth.

"You didn't have to attack them. You could have—"

"What? What could we have done? Should we have sent Reyce and some of the elders to *speak* to them? Do you really believe that would have led to anything but bloodshed? No elf would ever listen to reason if that reason was spoken by a malthrope. If we'd shown our faces, they would have slit our throats. On *that*, Boviss was correct. It could only be force. It could only be fear. We did our best to spill no blood, but… what had to be done, had to be done."

"People died," Ivy said.

"One… One life was taken. It burns at me. But if the circumstances were reversed, would the *elves* have shown such restraint?"

"But it hasn't solved anything, Nehri. Now they have a reason to hunt you. They have a reason to find this place and return the favor. You'd better *hope* my friends find you first. They're smart, and kind."

"But they will not find this place, Ivy. Not your friends, not our enemies. Not unless we allow it."

"We have dragons. We have wizards. We can fly, and see things no one else can see. Even if I didn't know there was a city here, if we were soaring over and I saw a swath of the countryside withering like this, I would investigate."

"You would not have seen it. This place cannot be found by any but those faithful to our patrons, those who speak their words and know their prayers."

Ivy turned back to the village. Her eyes lingered on the monument in the center of Den. Now that her muddied thinking had had time to clear, the pieces were beginning to slide into place. The blight upon the land. The means of her capture.

"Nehri…" she said, hesitating for fear of the answer to the question on her mind. "What are your patrons called?"

Nehri bowed her head, her expression serene and sincere. "Our protectors. Our saviors. May our first breaths and last speak our undying loyalty to them. The D'Karon."

#

The Crescents

Reyce and another malthrope dashed across dusty ground and between withered gray trees. The malthrope chieftain set his eyes firmly upon the cliff side. A freshly slain elk rested heavily upon the shoulders of each. The weight barely slowed them. When there was a job to be done, Reyce refused to let petty things like fatigue control him, and he expected nothing less from his fellow malthropes. The D'Karon magic could speed his motion and increase his stamina. Such things came at a price, but at a time when any delay could be disastrous, that price was a bargain.

He tightened his jaw as he traversed more and more barren land. Wind kicked up loose soil as he passed the first of the craggy alcoves marking the outskirts of his destination. It was a wretched place, a place no normal creature would choose to live. But then, Boviss had *not* chosen to live there. And if the dragon were a normal creature, Reyce would have no use for him. The stone beneath his feet shifted in color as he traveled. There were great swaths stained the brown-red of old blood. Shattered and powdered bones were scattered about, seldom intact enough to offer a hint of what beast they had once belonged to. Finally, there was the cave. It was a yawning maw in the mountain, turned from the sun such that walking even three paces past its mouth would cause an unwary traveler to plunge into inky blackness. The path thus far wound high into the cliffs. Now the air had a terrible chill, and it was so thin that even with the legendary endurance inherent to his species, Reyce had trouble catching his breath.

Reyce heaved the kill from his shoulders and paced to a shallow pond fed by a frost-covered trickle from between the rocks. As he slaked his thirst, a distant jingle rang out from within the cave.

"Another feeding. So soon. You spoil me, Chieftain." The voice that thundered from the darkness was deep and resounding. Each time it spoke, its final words trailed off into a rumble that could grind stone to powder.

Reyce signaled the other malthrope to back away. "This is not generosity, Boviss. It is preparation. You may need to take flight again soon."

The jingling shifted to a metallic grind. Thumping footsteps plodded toward the mouth of the cave. Reyce held his ground as a deep orange glow smoldered inside the cave, hinting at the hulking form within. Finally, the beast emerged, a dragon easily three times the size of Myn. He looked as ancient as the mountain itself. His scales were a stony gray, notched with the scars of a thousand battles and hard as iron. Along his throat and belly, the scales were broad, overlapping armor plates of bone white. Folded wings ran down his back and along the ground behind like the cape of a dark lord. His eyes were small, set deep in his wedge-shaped skull, and pure black. Powerful jaws formed a permanent, menacing grin, but for all of his power, his monstrous form also told tales of disgrace and captivity. Chains thick enough to anchor ships hung about his neck, dragging taut as he reached the light. One massive foreleg had been severed beneath the knee. In its place was a vicious iron replacement, spindly in comparison to its flesh counterpart, but tipped with a cruel, three-clawed parody of a dragon's paw. Half his tail had similarly been sliced away in some ancient battle. A chain, twice as thick as what he wore about his neck, emerged from the remaining nub. It led to a spiked iron ball the size of a small boulder. He dragged the ponderous weapon with ease.

A final touch labeled him as something more, or something less, than an elder dragon. Streaks of red, too bright to be blood, traced out long stripes along his snout and face. The marks were fresh, but the ragged, feathered edges suggested they were merely the most recent iteration of marks applied dozens or hundreds of times in the past. If not for the chains, they might have resembled war paint. Bound as he was, they seemed more like markings meant to label him as a prisoner, should he be seen fleeing.

"Another flight. So the elves have returned. As I predicted."

"No," Reyce said. "But there *are* warriors from the south."

Boviss devoured the whole of the first offering in a single messy crunch.

"Pawns of the elves then." His stout tongue snaked from his mouth and lapped at the juices running down his chin. "The people of the trees are cowards. They would send pawns to fight for them. No matter. One army is as good as another."

"It is no army. But it is not to be dismissed. They came from the south and set up camp in Dusand. Three humans, two dressed and equipped as mystics and a third dressed as some manner of knight. And two dragons as well."

"Dragons."

"A red one and a green one. Smaller than you, but clearly subservient to the others."

"I have never known the elves to command my kind. But I shall deal with them. I have no patience for newcomers treading in my domain."

"In *our* domain, Boviss."

"Of course."

"There was also a malthrope among them. We have brought her to Den."

"Foolish. If she is of the enemy, she is to be killed."

"I will not kill one of my kind. And besides. She may offer valuable information about the pawns of the elves."

"No information *offered* is to be trusted. Only lies are offered. Do not trust wisdom that is given freely. Things of value are protected, secreted away. If you wish to learn from her, you must *drag* the information from her. *Tear* the information from her." The dragon strained at his chain to crunch up the second offering.

"I will do no such thing. She could be a valuable ally. And what's more, she is of the Sorrel line. She claims even to know of Teyn, the mate of Sorrel herself."

Boviss dragged his iron claw across the stone, producing an earsplitting grind and digging deep furrows into the stone. "Sorrel…" he growled, flames rolling from his lips and nostrils. "Bring this new malthrope to me. Let me sample her scent. Let me taste her blood. I will tell you if she is truly of Sorrel's line."

"I shall do nothing of the sort."

"Why do you come to me then?" Boviss snapped. "To make a paltry offering and taunt me with her name?"

"I come to you because all is not in place for the task. We cannot afford to squander warriors upon these agents of the south. Already my force is too small to be certain of victory if things do not go according to plan."

"Every moment you allow them to live, you risk the lives of *all* of your people. Nothing good has ever come to this land from the south. Nothing good will *ever* come from the south. Kill them."

"If it were merely human mystics and knights, or a handful of elves, it would not be a concern. But the dragons trouble me."

Boviss continued as though he'd not heard Reyce. "You should have allowed me to raze the cities. To consume the trespassers in flame. They would never have dared send anyone this way again. Elves have long memories. They remember their defeats, and shrink from those they cannot overcome."

"I have no interest in slaughter, Boviss. I wish only that my people not wither and die while others snatch up the land that should sustain us."

"Pathetic attacks. Harrowing the enemy with pinpricks when you could be crushing them underfoot."

"Offer me advice I can use or be silent."

The dragon growled, sending cascades of stone crackling down from above the mouth of his cave. Reyce did not so much as flinch.

"You are watching them, I trust?"

"One of my best runners. They follow him closely. He has been instructed not to return while they are still a threat."

"And if they find him?"

"He will lead them astray and give his life to protect the rest of us. As any of us would."

"Very well. If you must continue in this weak-willed game, if you refuse to slaughter the lot of them, then my advice is simple. Find these agents. Learn which ride the dragons. And when you are certain, kill the Dragon Riders. No dragon is loyal to an elf or human cause. They shall not continue the hunt. And without them, the others are no threat."

"But to kill the Dragon Riders I must get past the dragons."

Boviss raised the steel paw. "And so you would have me reveal another of my secrets. The way to get past a dragon is to be small enough to slip through its claws."

Reyce shut his eyes and nodded. "The wasps then."

"Yes."

The chieftain considered this. "So be it. Let this be a test. I will spare one wasp. If she can strike down their Dragon Riders, then perhaps they will show the wisdom to turn back. Two deaths are better than five. I thank you for your counsel. And I urge you to prepare. If this does not succeed, I fear the dragons will indeed need to be dealt with."

"Then I pray for failure. It has been too long since I've tasted a proper battle."

Boviss lumbered back into the cave. Reyce paced back to where his helper was waiting.

"Go back to Den. Tell Nehri I shall not return until late evening. I must pay a visit to the forest. And say nothing of what has been discussed here."

His assistant nodded and dashed back from whence they came. Reyce took another long drink of water and made ready to begin a new journey.

"You have magic, do you not?" Boviss crept up to the edge of the darkness. "The crystals you rely so heavily upon."

"I do."

"And the wasps each have one. The better to follow your orders."

"They do."

"Then why do you prepare yourself to run to them?"

"That is not your concern."

"The priestess would see," Boviss rumbled, emerging enough for his grin to catch the light. "She would not approve of the wasps being called into use."

"We spent many months honing the plan. She would see any variation as a rash decision."

"You fear her judgment."

"I have sought and received your counsel. We are through."

Boviss emerged fully into the light, stretching his chain taut. "There are swifter ways to reach the forest."

Chapter 7

Myranda and the others had been moving slowly and carefully in the days since Ivy's capture. Without a definite destination and with no simple trail to follow, flight was out of the question. They had to move along the ground, eyes and snouts scouring the land and air for anything that might hint at a clue. Their journey had taken them across much of an arid plain, and now they were well into the southernmost fringes of a desert that occupied a fair slice of North Crescent. It said much of the elven view of the continent that despite its size the makers of the map the king's people had provided did not see fit to apply a name to the region. It wasn't like the great desert of Tressor, which was like an endless sea of sand. Here the dunes were in motes and clusters spread among vast stretches of burning-hot stone.

The dragons were coping well, suited as they were to extreme heat. The fairies were decidedly less adapted to travel through the desert. At least, travel at the speed and level that tracking the Aluall required. Shah had taken to buzzing about between Myn and Garr, almost without pause. She would linger in the shade of one dragon's great body, flitting between its legs, then dart up and investigate what the riders were up to. The endless buzz of wings and Shah's untrained sense of personal space made it a constant effort to suppress the urge to swat at her as one would an insect. Freet, on the other hand, had taken up a position between Myn's horns, where he sat like a king surveying his kingdom.

Myranda had to keep her mind focused, in part to weave spells that would ward off the worst of the heat and keep the sun from roasting her, and in part to scour the spectral plane for the faint residue of D'Karon magics. The skill of the Aluall in moving without a trace was truly confounding. They'd spent days moving with agonizing slowness, earning only fleeting hints of the nearly nonexistent trail. It was only through constant scouring of both mystic and material evidence, as well as a worrisome amount of speculation and intuition, that they'd followed the trail this far. And every moment the trail grew colder, harder to follow.

Myranda wavered slightly, then felt a hand on her arm to steady her.

"Is something wrong?" Deacon asked.

"Just a bit fatigued. I suppose the desert is taking a greater toll upon me than I realized," she said.

"Do not push yourself. Your mystic endurance is significant, you should have no trouble with this level of conjuring, but one can never be certain of how one's mind and body will react in times of great stress."

"I've traveled through the desert before. And I have dealt with terrible pressure. I've never felt so weary so quickly."

"You haven't been a wizard as long as I have. Your training in controlling your emotions is less complete."

"I can control my emotions," Myranda snapped.

"Of course you can," Deacon said with a deferential tip of his head. "I have every confidence in your abilities with that regard, even the edge to your response suggests the contrary."

Myranda shut her eyes and took a breath. Deacon's tone was free of accusation or condescension. She knew he was not attempting to chide her, merely making a somewhat graceless observation as he so frequently did, but Myranda still felt a flare of annoyance at the implication. The annoyance was compounded by the realization that her inability to push it aside was evidence that he was right.

Deacon pulled a canteen from their supplies and handed it to her. "Drink. And rest. I'll take over on the tracking. You keep your eyes on the sand for physical clues that I may miss in my metaphysical search."

She took the container and sipped at it. "Myn, do you need water?" she asked, leaning forward and placing a hand on the dragon's neck.

Myn didn't answer. Her predatory instinct was focused entirely upon the task at hand. She and Ivy had become quite close in their time together in New Kenvard. The pair were practically siblings. A single glimpse at the heartbreaking worry hidden behind her determined gaze revealed just how knotted up her heart and mind were at Ivy's capture.

"Here," Myranda said, splashing a bit of water into her cupped hand. "Shah, Freet, water."

The fairies buzzed up to the offered refreshment and drank deeply.

"There are very few flowers about," Freet observed. "What shall we do for food?"

"Are you hungry?" Myranda said. "I am certain we can work something out."

"I'm fine. I'm trained for endurance," Shah said proudly.

"I don't need to eat yet either," Freet said defensively. "I am just planning for when I *do* need to eat."

"There must be an oasis nearby," Myranda said. "We'll stop there for the night."

"No," murmured Myn, turning her head to offer Myranda an accusing glance.

"We'll do Ivy no good if we collapse in the desert looking for her," Myranda said. "This path has twisted and turned, coiled back on itself, and looped. I don't care what sort of monsters the Aluall are. The distance they traveled to lead us on this chase would push anyone to the limit. They must have found some way to rest and recuperate. Their trail will lead us to it, and we shall restore ourselves when we reach it." She raised her voice. "Grustim! You've taken to the air most recently. Have you seen evidence of a source of water?"

He called back, "There is a spring to the west. A few hours travel on foot will take us there. A few minutes by air. And just beyond the horizon is the edge of a forest. By air we could reach it by nightfall. And Myranda. Come this way. Approach from behind."

Myn trudged over of her own accord. Any excuse to be a bit closer to Garr was welcome to her. When they reached the green dragon, the riders hopped down and Myn leaned against Garr, a forlorn rumble in her chest. In response, he leaned his head comfortingly against hers. Grustim stepped with slow care to a shallow impression in the sand, and Myranda crouched down.

"It is a footprint," Myranda said. She glanced about. "A single footprint. None leading to it or away from it."

"The third I've seen in as many hours," Grustim said.

"Are they becoming careless perhaps?"

"Perhaps. But what concerns me is that we have found it. The wind is steady, constantly stirring the sand. Our own footprints fade within minutes. This one is not sheltered by stones or dunes."

"So it is fresh…" Myranda narrowed her eyes.

"Our progress has been somewhat slower for the last few hours," Deacon observed. "Trails should be colder, not fresher."

"Then there is no doubt. We are being led astray," Myranda seethed. "And that means they are near us. Something must be done."

She stabbed her staff's tip into the sand and held her hands on either side of the crystal. A powerful glow pulsed within its heart.

"Myranda act with care," Deacon said.

"We haven't felt a glimmer of Ivy's spirit since she disappeared, Deacon," she uttered, eyes shut and mind focused. "Not a glimmer. I could find Ivy on the other side of the *world* if I needed to. The only time her spirit has remained so weak for so long was because the D'Karon were leaching her power. If we had a single thread to act upon, some means to be *certain* we are heading in the correct direction, then I could set aside the concerns and trust that we will find her. But for all we know, we've not taken a single step closer since we entered the desert. We may be playing into their whims, wasting precious time. And I am through with that. We know someone is near. I mean to find them."

Wind began to swirl, spreading out from the base of the staff.

"Everyone, set your eyes upon the desert around us. Call out if you see anything out of the ordinary," Myranda instructed.

The wind churned faster, keeping low to the ground near them but rising up as it traced a circle around them. A wall of wind-blown sand rose. It retreated quickly, forming an ever-widening circle. The wind spared Myranda and the others, but relentlessly scoured an expanding ring of desert around them.

"There!" called Grustim.

Just past the crest of the nearest dune, an odd void in the swirling sand moved with uncanny speed. It wasn't a visible figure, but rather the kind of disturbance in the sand one might leave behind. Myranda lashed out with her mind, focusing intently on the form, but it was slippery, evading attempts at direct spells. Rather than give up the one advantage they had, Myranda redoubled her efforts to stir the sand around the figure, to keep it visible.

Grustim vaulted to Garr's back, and the pair dashed toward the retreating form. Myn snaked her tail around Myranda and her staff, hauling them from the ground and depositing them on her back. Deacon and the fairies joined her. Now that she had her target, Myranda could focus the wind only upon the fleeing form. She turned the wind upon it ever more intensely. Turning her mind to any spells that might stop the retreating spy would mean relenting with the wind, and relenting with the wind would mean potentially losing her target. By now the improvised sandstorm should have coated the foe head to toe in sand, but it seemed whatever splashed against it and clung to its body or clothes eventually faded from visibility.

"Whatever it is, it runs as fast as Myn! And its mystic defenses are every bit as developed as the D'Karon's," Deacon called.

Garr was airborne, gaining on the half-seen form, but it moved in erratic, sudden motions, evading his sweeping claws with astounding nimbleness. Deacon's crystal burned with a white glow. A bolt lanced forward, arcing over the fleeting figure. The ball of energy struck the sand, its glow spreading like quicksilver. Their quarry attempted to dodge and dive, but the widening moat of brilliant light kept pace. Finally, the Aluall bounded over the obstacle. It was a prodigious leap, but Deacon had anticipated it. As the sand-scoured form crested over the churning mass of magic, tendrils of animated sand coiled upward and wrapped about the soaring shape.

No sooner did the tendrils touch the form than they started to erode. Deacon was ready for it, shifting the loose sand to solid stone. What had been a lashing tendril was now a rigid spire, and their invisible spy was locked at the top.

"Grab it! I can feel its magic working against mine. The stone may not hold firm for long!"

Grustim needn't have been told. Garr released a savage roar and wrapped his claws about the still-unseen figure. As the grip tightened, crunching the stone to powder, a howl of pain gave them their first proof they'd not been chasing a phantom. It was a sharp, primal sound, with the barest hint of a male voice behind it.

Garr slammed the thing to the ground. A flicker of violet light hinted at its true form, but only for an instant. Grustim hopped down and drew his blade. Myn skidded to a stop, and the others hopped from her back.

All formed a circle around what looked to be little more than a hollow in the sand beneath Garr's claw. A ragged, pained breath echoed as if it were far away.

"Show yourself, coward," Grustim spat.

The buzzing of fairy wings filled the air as Myranda and Deacon knelt down, staff and gem at the ready.

"Hold him," Myranda said. "D'Karon magic can be just as potent when it ends as when it is in use."

She swept her mind over the enchantments laid out before her. It had been a mercifully long time since she'd had to deal with D'Karon magic cast with this level of precision. She'd forgotten how elusive it could be in the mind's eye and the complex knots it tied.

"Yes," Deacon said. "I can sense traces of vicious spells that will be unleashed if this creature dies."

The weariness and lack of focus that had been creeping up on Myranda during the day was washing over her again, now that the intensity of the moment had all but gone. Every little sound and sensation bored at her mind. The burning of the sand, the sting of her wind-scoured eyes, and the buzzing of the wings. She cast her gaze upon Freet and Shah, huddled among Myn's horns, watching with fascination. But the buzzing was coming from behind.

Not a moment too soon, she raised a hasty shield spell. Something rebounded off it and darted aside with the will and speed of what could only be a fairy, but like their veiled spy, it was barely visible. All she could make out was the buzz of its wings and a faint violet streak of light.

"He wasn't alone. There is a fairy!" Myranda called out.

The streak of light traced random zigs and zags between the assembled heroes. It was uncannily skilled at slipping from their vision, darting in from an unseen angle and pulling back to avoid a swat or spell.

Myranda pulled her cloak from her shoulders. As the fairy buzzed toward Deacon, he raised a shield of his own. The creature struck it hard, causing a ripple, and rebounded back. Myranda heaved her cloak. The creature easily evaded it, but she infused the garment with a splash of magic and guided it after the tiny creature. The makeshift net looped over the frenzied fairy and pinned it to the ground.

Myranda dove upon it and secured the cloak as the bulge of its prisoner shook and jolted about, buzzing like a whole hive of angry bees.

"I have it," she said. "Hand me my staff. This little creature must have some of the D'Karon enchantments as well. I can't put it to sleep. I can't even calm it."

"Wizards!" Grustim barked.

Deacon and Myranda turned. In the madness caused by the fairy, their attention had been pulled from their original target. Now a violent crackle of energy was coiling its way around Garr's claws and up his leg. The stoic dragon squeezed harder, but the searing tendrils of magic did not cease.

"It is the thir stone," Deacon said, approaching as near as he dared and holding out his gem. "It is leeching strength from Garr. Whatever spell he's triggered, it is an order of magnitude greater than what we've seen thus far. Just hold him. I believe I can subdue it."

Myranda's grip upon her staff was weakening. The fairy *certainly* had a thir stone as well, and it was drawing upon the strength that was already beginning to fail her. Something jabbed through the cloak, narrowly missing Myranda's hand, and the fairy once again burst free. It traced an arrow-straight path, heading directly for Deacon before Myranda could shout a warning.

For better or worse, Myn was ready. She lashed her tail. The swift attack struck the fairy hard. As its feather-light body thumped to the ground and rebounded in a twirling trajectory away from the group, her tail continued along its path and knocked Deacon to the ground.

Without his dampening influence, the spell of their captive flashed and activated. Garr threw his head back in a roar of pain. His mighty claw was wrenched open as bands of black and streamers of violet coiled and tore at it. The magic burned with a staggering heat. The others shielded themselves and averted their eyes from a light that soon became blinding.

Myranda raised her staff and threw together a hasty counterspell, pushing back the worst of the attack until its power was spent and it began to fade, but the spell had done its work. A smoldering set of footprints led a few dozen paces to the north, then faded away as the stealth enchantments were restored.

Myn galloped off after the vanished spy, roaring in fury. Myranda helped Deacon to his feet, and they looked to their other allies.

Grustim had been near the spell when it activated, but his reflexes were swift and his armor well-made. Though a patch of the green enamel was seared away to bare metal, he seemed otherwise unhurt. The same could not be said for Garr. His claw had taken the brunt of the attack. Thick blood fell in scattered drops, sizzling the sand where it landed. The flesh was raw and torn.

Myranda put her mind to work healing it. She let her thoughts and the strength of her spirit wrap about the injured limb, and wove her will deeply into his flesh, tugging torn hide together and feeding his own spirit and body with what it would need to repair itself. As she did, she felt a second will work its way in beside her own, moving in concert with her own treatment. It was Deacon, putting his mind to work unraveling the lingering mystic effects.

"The Aluall shall pay," rumbled Grustim as he watched them work. "I will not underestimate them again. Their magic is potent, and they fight without honor."

"No, Grustim. Not potent. Simply very complete," Deacon said. "I can say with absolute certainty that this particular Aluall was barely a novice in the ways of magic. These are not spells conjured from the mind of a fleeing warrior desperate to evade capture. What we witnessed was an assortment of carefully prepared spells stored in thir stones. They weren't a fraction of what might have been wielded by a true D'Karon mystic, but every modicum of magic was used with absolute precision. Whoever readied these spells put every syllable of incantation and every nuance of enchantment precisely where it needed to be. There is a blight attempting to wrap itself about Garr's soul right now. Barely more than a single line were it written in a spellbook, but it was not forgotten or left out. If anyone but Myranda or I had been the one to treat Garr, he might have fallen to it in the days ahead."

Deacon drew his crystal back, and a thread of black energy followed. When it slipped free, it briefly writhed like a worm on a hot skillet before fading away. "But that is the last of it," he said. "Do you need my help with the wound, Myranda?"

"No. No I have it," she breathed, knitting a broken bone and closing the last gash.

Garr tested the motion of his injured paw, then cautiously put his weight on it. When he was satisfied, he turned in Myn's direction. Grustim climbed to the dragon's back, then to his head, and peered off to the north. Myn was utterly rampaging. She was thundering across the dunes, roaring in rage and belching flames. The path of churned-up sand traced out a meandering, aimless search. This wasn't a predator closing in on her prey. This was an animal furious and frustrated.

"She's lost him," Grustim said.

"That he was alone means he wasn't one of the ones carrying Ivy," Myranda said. "And that he was leading us means we certainly weren't heading in the right direction. Do you suppose we can backtrack and attempt to find where this Aluall split off from the others?"

"A trail left to purposely lead us astray was nearly beyond our capacity to follow when it was fresh. I very much doubt a colder trail by more cautious travelers will do us any good," Grustim said.

"No turning back, then. We press forward," Myranda said, brushing the sand from her cloak. "When Myn calms down, we must discuss what we've learned. We'll gather what we know. If they haven't left a trail for us to follow, then we have no choice but to follow what clues we have until we've worked out where they were heading in the first place."

#

Ivy fought to control her churning spirit as she and Nehri approached the base of the monument at the heart of the village. These people, *her* people, did not seem to have a drop of malice in their hearts. Surely fate could *not* be so cruel as to allow them to become entangled with the D'Karon. There had to be some mistake, some other explanation. She had to see the truth for herself. After she'd had time to consider the terrible revelation, she'd asked to learn more of the D'Karon, feigning ignorance. Nehri assured her that with each sunrise and each sunset, there was a ceremony at the monument. It was the only time its doors were permitted to open, but she was welcome to observe it that evening.

"Something troubles you, Ivy," Nehri said as they finally reached the monument. "You have not spoken since you asked to see this place. Have you no more questions? No more curiosity?"

"They can wait until after," Ivy said quietly. "I just… I need to see this for myself."

"As you wish. The ceremony is brief. As the priestess, it is my honor and duty to oversee it. When it is through, I shall answer any questions you may have. I am afraid the ceremony is very precise and rigid. You shall not be permitted to join in it until you have learned the proper prayers, but I shall happily teach you if—"

"No," Ivy said, more sharply than she'd intended. "No, I just want to watch."

"Then I must request you remain outside the circle of stones."

The people of the village formed orderly rings around the tower. None spoke. The jovial atmosphere of the village had shifted to the solemn, reverent tone of a church service. For a few minutes, all waited silently, eyes turned to the west. The trees between the village and the sea had been trimmed, providing a clear view of the sun. It slid slowly toward the horizon. The moment it touched, Nehri rang a bell beside the door. As one, the villagers dropped to their knees and lowered their heads.

Nehri began a recitation. From the first syllable, the words chilled Ivy. They were D'Karon words, twisted and unnatural. She wanted to cover her ears and shut her eyes. Someone who seemed so kind speaking words of such raw evil and darkness was something out of a nightmare. And yet, somehow Nehri's sincerity and grace made them seem almost pleasant. At the end of each line, the villagers repeated her final words back to her. The phrase made the air crackle around the monument, and a purple light smoldered within, visible between the cracks and pulsing brighter as the prayer progressed.

Nehri completed the recitation just as the last of the sun slipped away. Ivy looked about to see that no lamps, fires, or lanterns burned. The only light in the village was the dim glow of the evening sky and the eerie pulse of the monument. Two villagers stepped forward and, at Nehri's direction, unbraced and opened the doors.

Ivy squinted as nearly blinding violet light spilled from within. By the time her eyes adjusted, two of the villagers, each dressed in garb that suggested theirs was a specialized and honored position, had already stepped inside. She couldn't make out what the monument contained, but from the light and the awful, gnawing influence she felt on her very soul when then doors were opened, it was certainly filled with thir crystals. The same thir crystals that fueled all of the D'Karon creations. The specially dressed villagers emerged from within. They supported a slumped form between them. It was a fellow resident of Den.

She put her hand to her mouth, aghast at the sight of it. If the malthrope the others were carrying had truly been inside the monument for half a day, surrounded by those spirit-hungry stones, it was a wonder he was alive at all.

When the weakened villager was seen to, Nehri called out a name and a new villager stood. This time it was a vixen. She stepped forward, spoke a few more words of prayer, and walked freely into the monument.

Ivy almost called out to stop her. Having felt the searing thirst of the gems firsthand, she couldn't bear the thought of someone willingly offering herself to it. But she needed to learn more, to know how deeply rooted in their society the D'Karon were. So she watched in agony as the doors were shut.

With the deed done, the others chanted a final mantra and stood. Just like that, as though some spell had been broken, the life and personality returned to the village. Smiles returned to their faces. Conversations picked up as though they'd never been interrupted. There was no sign that there was anything unusual or upsetting about offering one of their own willingly to feed the workings of beings who had meant to conquer or destroy their world.

Nehri paused to call over a male and one of his children, then led them to Ivy. The priestess crouched to address the child. "Go ahead," she said with a broad smile. "Now's your chance."

The little boy looked to Ivy. "Hell-o, Ivy. Wel-come from… your new… home," he said.

"Hello there," Ivy said, briefly shrugging off the curdling sensation in her stomach to offer a smile in return.

The boy scurried off as though he would die of embarrassment if he had to speak another word. His father laughed, uttered a friendly word to Ivy, and hurried after him.

"The boy is Roma," Nehri said. "He is also of Sorrel's line, and the youngest of our people to begin learning any of her languages. When he learned you spoke only one of those languages, he *had* to test his knowledge."

"He did a good job."

"Did you learn what you wished to from the ceremony?" Nehri asked.

"I learned enough," Ivy said. "That woman who stepped inside… and the man who was pulled out. They… *fuel* those gems."

"Yes!" Nehri said. "So you *do* know something about the D'Karon. We each spend our time in the monument. Our village has grown such that many need only spend a single day or night in the whole of a year. Naturally, the very young and very old are not permitted to offer themselves. Those who begin too young do not grow to be as strong. Those who are too old may not survive until the doors are opened. In exchange for our strength, their magic keeps our village and warriors hidden. We are protected from our enemies. If our hand is forced, their magic gives us the means to vanquish our foes."

"How… how did you learn of the D'Karon? How did they… just *how*? How any of this?"

"Like to Sorrel, it came to us in our time of greatest need. Some among us say that when Sorrel passed away and met with the powers that be, she demanded they provide for her people. In turn, they sent a messenger named Teht."

Ivy flinched at the name.

"You know the sainted educator? The bringer of the D'Karon blessings?"

"Please. Just… continue."

"Teht knew we were hunted and offered us the sacred knowledge. She gave us the first of the gems and the knowledge to make more. She gave us the writings, the wording of the prayers and spells. She gave them to us freely, asking only for our loyalty in return."

"You are loyal to the D'Karon. All of you."

"As I have said, from our first breath to our last. We pledge ourselves to them and offer our undying gratitude for the strength and safety they have granted us."

Ivy covered her face, unable to hide her despair any longer.

"I do not understand your concern. This is the story of our people. It is the way we have thrived in the face of those who would end us."

She forced the feelings away and tried to will a look of curiosity to her face. "It is just that it is so much, so quickly. Tell me… do you have these writings you were given? Somewhere I can see them? I wish to know more."

"Of course you do. It is only right that a newcomer should wish to learn of the patrons of her kind. Come, follow me."

Nehri paced toward a hut a short distance from the shrine. Though it was not built of stone, it was visibly sturdier and better fortified than the villagers' homes. It had no windows, and the roof was of wood rather than thatch. A malthrope of the desert tribe, barely larger than a child but bearing a hefty wooden sword, stood guard outside the door. Nehri exchanged some pleasant words with him. He smiled at both the priestess and Ivy, then fished a small thir stone from his pocket and pressed it to the door. Lines of mystic power pulsed brightly, then faded away. Nehri pushed the door open.

"Second to the shrine, of course, this is our most secure building. We have little need to lock things away here, but if we feel that something must be protected, we place it inside this stronghold."

She stepped inside, Ivy close behind. The lack of windows meant that not even the dim glow of twilight found its way to the dark interior. Nehri reached toward a D'Karon crystal set beside the door, but before she could touch it, it smoldered to life, feasting hungrily on Ivy's strength. Others, spaced regularly about the walls, did the same, soon casting every corner of the large room in light.

"Look," Nehri said happily. "How powerful you must be, to feed the crystals so."

Ivy edged away from the nearest crystal and tried to focus instead on what the light revealed. Anything that anyone might consider valuable seemed to be present in some way or another. Crude chests stuffed with gold lined the far wall. Tables arrayed with everything from carefully rendered works of art to curious artifacts stood in neat rows. A shelf of leather-bound books stood against one wall. Beside it stood a cabinet that even Ivy's weak knowledge of magic told her had been potently warded against theft. Nehri walked to the book shelf.

"Here we have copies of every D'Karon teaching. Part of my training as priestess involves copying them myself from the originals, such that we need never risk using those books penned by D'Karon hands. They are the most precious treasures we have. They must be kept safe, and so they are sealed in the cabinet, to be revealed only when the time comes to appoint a new priestess. But you are free to look upon all else, so long as you do so with care."

Ivy glanced about, her eyes swiftly coming to rest on a small satchel, the one she had been carrying when she was captured. She hurried to it.

"Oh! Yes, my apologies. I had forgotten we had brought your things here for safekeeping. I hope you will understand that we have taken your weapons—you would have no need for them here, and our own people might need them to defend this place. We also cannot allow you to bring any mystic items with you. It is unwise to carry mystical items about when others may be carrying thir gems. Unexpected things can happen if the gems drink too deeply. As such, this book—which has the feel of magic—will need to be kept here. But the rest is, of course, yours to reclaim."

Ivy sifted through the pack. "There was a stylus… I can't find it."

"That is all that we have of your things, I am afraid. If something is missing, it was lost before you arrived."

Ivy pulled her pad from within and opened its cover. Seeing her illustrations brought a rush of relief and calm, as though if these moments frozen in time were still intact, then the world couldn't possibly be spinning out of control.

Nehri smiled broadly at the images covering the page. "An artist? You are an *artist*? That is wonderful! So few of us have the time or skill for the arts." She placed a hand on Ivy's shoulder and squeezed it encouragingly. "You see? You were meant to come here. You are a missing piece to make our village whole. What is this place?"

The image on the page was of the palace of New Kenvard, not in its current state of repair, but as it would be when finished.

"This is part of my hometown."

"A grand place," Nehri said, gazing with interest.

She flipped a page, revealing a sketch crowded with people. "And this is my family…"

The illustration showed Deacon, Myranda and her father, and Myn. They were gathered about a fire, laughing and talking. Ivy remembered the day well. It was the night they'd broken ground on a new hall, the first *new* building to be built in New Kenvard. Myranda insisted they celebrate the moment, as while there was so much more to be done to restore the rest of the broken city, this new hall was proof that the city was not just healing, it was growing.

"Ivy, *we* are your family," Nehri said.

"No… Well, maybe. I don't know. Maybe you *are*. But these people. They earned it. They chose it." Her eyes lingered on the page before she shut the book. "May I have some time to look into these D'Karon books?" she asked.

"Of course," Nehri said. "I am afraid I cannot allow you to remove them from this place, but you are welcome to remain here and learn their teachings. I do not suppose you understand the D'Karon language. I have some matters to attend to now that the ceremony is done, but if you would like, I can begin to teach you personally beginning tomorrow."

"Maybe. But I'd really like to start looking over them now. Even just to see how much is there."

"Then by all means. I shall leave you to it."

Nehri paced out the door. Ivy looked around her. Every precious item they had, and they allowed her to remain inside without supervision. Even with a guard at the door, such implicit trust from her own kind was astonishing. It was not lost on her ailing conscience that to serve her friends and her mission, she would have to betray that trust. Ivy wasn't entirely certain what she hoped to achieve in coming to where they kept the D'Karon writings. A part of her was hoping that she would discover some sort of misunderstanding, that the D'Karon they worshiped were not the same ones she and the other Chosen had fought. That hope was dashed upon looking over the very first page. Ivy felt the hot sting of unwanted knowledge, something she had mercifully been spared since shortly after her rescue. She could read the D'Karon writing. When she had been in their clutches, they had prepared her to be a warrior for their own purposes, and to that end they had forced knowledge into her unwilling mind. How to fight. How to act. How to follow their orders. Much of their "teachings" had fallen away, failing to take root. Much more had not. And now, the knowledge they had lodged in her mind made sense of the dark, twisted words on the page. They were genuine D'Karon writings. This was all-too real. She felt a flicker of anger, causing a rush of red around her and a pulse of intensity from the crystals. The thought crossed her mind that she should destroy these books. Destroy the originals. Do her best to cleanse this place of their tainted influence. But it would do no good. The people of this village were behind the assault on Dusand and Treadforge. They had plans. Somehow, Ivy needed to determine what those plans were, and she couldn't do that if she roused their anger or suspicion.

Everything of any value was locked in this place. If she were launching a dangerous campaign against an enemy, this is precisely the sort of place she would lock the things that might damage the mission if they were known. But what could those things be? And where would she find them? Ivy quietly wished Myranda or Deacon were here. They were so much better at this sort of thing. She wasn't nearly as clever as they were… but she *did* have stronger senses. She shut her eyes and took a deep whiff of the air. The mustiness of the books dominated the room, but beneath it was the subtle scent of fresh ink. She followed the smell and found, to her disappointment, a small inkpot filled with gummy black ink.

The Crescents

Too much to hope I would have found a list of freshly written marching orders, she thought to herself.

Again she sampled the air, asking herself questions about what her senses told her, hoping they would lead her somewhere. What were the freshest scents? A few sacks of things likely brought from the raids on the elven cities. What sort of scents would she expect to find but hadn't? This was perhaps the only place in the whole of the village that didn't have the lively, wholesome smell of people living their lives. Aside from her own scent and that of Nehri, there was precious little evidence of any other malthropes in this place. Even the guard's scent came only from the doorway. But as she sifted through the complex, layered aromas surrounding her, she detected the faintest remnant of someone else. It was mixed with the dry scent of the desert and even a lingering hint of the strange trees where the elves made their home.

She followed the scent to a small leather bundle hung on a hook near the back of the strongroom. It was certainly one of the more recent acquisitions to this place. She carefully removed it and unrolled the bundle on a nearby table, checking the doorway every few moments to be sure she wasn't being watched. Inside were some crude pages of paper. A careful but uncertain hand had covered both sides of the first sheet with writing, a mixture of the looping, complex writing of the elves and another language she didn't recognize. The way the elven letters were formed, much like the ones in Dusand, she suspected they were copied by someone who didn't know what they meant. Ivy wasn't certain what they meant either, but she knew they were fresh, so they were the closest she was likely to come to finding a clue.

Other pages in the bundle had similar writing, but in a different hand. This was beginning to look like the result of maybe a dozen different villagers being sent off to the elven lands…

Ivy hastily snatched the ink she'd found and scrounged up a stylus from near where it had been kept. She flipped open her own book. With an artist's speed and care, she transcribed the contents of the mysterious sheets. She desperately wanted to jot down what had happened to her, what she'd discovered here, but she couldn't risk it. There was no telling how much she would be able to write before she was discovered. Worse, not knowing what the writing said meant that any bit of it could be something important, and if she left it unrecorded because she'd wasted time on other messages, it could mean disaster or failure. So she copied as swiftly as her fingers would allow, hoping that the magic of the book was strong enough to reach her friends.

#

Myranda and Deacon sat around a small fire, warming food and mulling over their next steps. Myn, perhaps exhausted by her fruitless rampage and brief battle, had been showing considerable fatigue. They'd made it as far as the oasis they'd spotted that morning, where freshwater and a scattering of flowers provided refreshment for human, dragon, and fairy alike. Though there was enough dry wood for the campfire, it came in the form of stubby bramble and other such plants that offered little in the way of shade. Luckily, the dragons thrived in the baking sun. Myn was more than willing to bask in it while the others sought relief in her shadow until the sun slipped from the sky. Unlike the Tresson desert, which could become terribly cold as soon as the sun set, here on North Crescent the heat seemed to linger into the night, just as the cold lasted longer into the morning.

Deacon gazed at the night sky. Garr was circling overhead, riding the rising air currents to search the area with Grustim on his back.

"Should we await his return before we discuss what is to be done?" Deacon asked.

"I cannot imagine he'll return having learned anything we don't already know," Myranda replied, sipping at a simple tea she'd prepared over the fire.

The heat of the day was such that Shah and Freet had abandoned their cozy little roost among Myn's horns once they'd arrived at the oasis. For a while they'd been swimming in cool, clear water. When Shah had had enough, she climbed to the shore, flicked most of the water from her wings, and buzzed over to join Myranda and Deacon. She drifted above the steaming cup and peered in curiously, accidentally spritzing Myranda with drops of water as she flitted about.

"You are drinking hot water?" Shah said.

"Hot tea," Myranda said.

"But it is so hot here. Wouldn't cool water be better?"

"The elves gave this to me to settle my stomach when we were at sea. It helped a bit."

"You still aren't feeling well?" Deacon said.

"I feel well enough. We have greater concerns right now than my constitution." She turned to Shah. "Have you detected any hint of that fairy that attacked us?"

"No. She had magic to hide her, the same as the larger creature."

"Such was my concern," Deacon said. "A fairy is a bright bit of magic in the mind's eye, but the D'Karon magic could easily snuff it out."

Freet darted from the water and joined them.

"I am certain she is not about. Even *with* that magic, she would still have to stir the air, and we would feel it."

"Yes," Shah agreed. "I suppose that's true."

"Is there anything else you can tell us about the fairy?" Myranda asked.

"She was young. Very young. Not a child, but close," Shah said.

"A forest fairy," Freet said. "Certainly a forest fairy."

Shah nodded. "Yes. Not from the desert."

"How can you tell?" Myranda said, shading her eyes as Myn shifted positions and her shadow moved.

Shah shrugged. "You just can! We… bring our wind with us. That wasn't a desert wind. That was a wind through the—"

"Shah!" Freet snapped.

She shrank away from him. "Right… I'm sorry."

"What's wrong?" Deacon asked.

Shah looked sheepishly between Deacon and Freet.

"You do not reveal another fairy's home to a dangerous creature," Freet explained. "You have treated us well, but they do not want to be found, and that isn't our choice to make."

"Shah, Freet—our friend has been taken. She may be with these other fairies."

"The malthropes are friends of the fairies, Freet," Shah said quietly. "The *stories*. We should help find her in any way we can."

Freet was unmoved. "No. There are more bad people than good. I would not want these fairies to lead bad people to our grove. I will not lead others to their grove. But… if you find the grove on your *own*… I cannot stop you. And I would be sure to visit with the fairies there. That is only proper, when passing through their groves."

"When Grustim and Garr return, they shall tell us which forest is nearest," Deacon commented. "A group of fairies, even a large one, is not likely to be easy to find if they are in some way associated with the Aluall."

Myranda squinted skyward. "We mustn't wait. Every moment is a moment wasted, and we've yet to feel a glimmer of Ivy's strength. Myn, quickly."

She turned to her friend. Something was wrong. Myn's eyes were half-lidded and unfocused. Her head sagged; her wings drooped.

"Myn," Myranda said, taking the dragon's chin in her hands and trying to raise her head to look her in the eye.

The dragon's eyes darted vaguely, but she did not focus on Myranda.

"Deacon!" Myranda said.

He already had his crystal raised and his eyes shut. "She is *not* well," he said, his mind scouring her body and soul. "From the looks of her, she's been fighting this for some time and not letting it show."

"No! Not the dragon too!" Shah squealed, covering her mouth. "Can we do something? Can we help her?" The tiny creature darted about fretting aloud.

Myranda fetched her staff and focused her mind, sweeping it over her friend. "Her spirit is strong. It isn't magic. Certainly not D'Karon magic," she said.

Deacon nodded. "Indeed. This feels like poison."

"Yes. Like cutleaf, but faster…"

Myranda had been working her way slowly along Myn's powerful slumped body, waving her brightly glowing gem. She did her best to be dispassionate, detached as she tried to help her friend. It would do Myn no good if Myranda allowed her emotions to distract her, or to rob her of the nuance necessary to catch a potentially crucial detail. But it was difficult. Far more difficult than it had been when she'd last been tasked with healing someone in dire straits.

"Here!" she cried.

Her thorough search had gone from snout to tail, but it wasn't until her mind had pored over her friend's entire body that she finally found something out of place. She dropped to her knees and leaned low. There, between two scales near the end of the tail, was a tiny shard of something. It was little more than a splinter, snapped off almost flush with her hide. Myranda wrapped her will around it and eased it out. Myn stirred weakly. When the foreign object finally slipped free, it was as long as Myranda's finger and came to a cruel point.

She did not risk touching it directly, allowing it to hang in midair before her under the influence of her magic. Deacon stood and set his own well-trained mind upon it.

"Certainly poison. But not poison from the thorn itself. At least, not in its original state. This was prepared, distilled. Potent. That thorn was a weapon."

"We can discuss what it means later. I'll extract the poison, you treat her."

Myranda's hands were shaking as she drew upon the unpleasant but well-learned skill of withdrawing toxins. This was the first time she'd had to perform it on a creature so massive with a dose so small. It didn't matter. Without knowing how badly the poison might affect Myn if it lingered, the cost of failure was too high to even consider it.

Working magic alongside another, particularly someone as skilled as Deacon, was a profound experience. Were the circumstances not so dire, she might even have enjoyed it. They each extended their will, complementing each other perfectly, weaving through the body and spirit of the ailing dragon. Deacon's steady, sure mind was comforting and inspiring. Having it present was like having a shoulder to lean on, a hand to hold.

The poison gathered. It drifted toward the wound through which it had entered. All around it, she could sense Deacon's spells undoing its damage and soothing Myn into a deep, healing sleep. It was impossible to know how much time had passed since she'd started the procedure, but again, it didn't matter. She had no intention of stopping until she was through. Her bleary eyes focused on the pinprick on Myn's hide. It still trickled blood, evidence of the terrible potency of the poison. With a final nudge of her mind, she drew out a fleck of the terrible stuff. It was barely the size of a grain of sand.

"Here. We mustn't risk poisoning the oasis," Deacon said.

He extended a slip of parchment. Myranda dropped the speck of poison upon it, and he carefully folded and stowed it.

"Will she survive?" asked Grustim.

Myranda turned with a start. She had no memory of him returning from scouting, but now she discovered both he and Garr were back, and from the looks of it, they had returned some time ago. Despite Myranda and Deacon's distraction, the fire had been tended to. Garr was also lying beside Myn, one wing draped over her and his head resting cheek to cheek with hers. Even behind his armored mask, the dragon's anguish was heartbreakingly evident. Both fairies had also returned to their perches among her horns. Freet was dozing fitfully. Shah sat, hugging her knees, beside herself with worry.

"She will recover," Deacon said. "The poison is gone. The damage is being healed."

"She should rest until morning. And it may be several days before she has her full strength back," Myranda said.

Deacon held out his crystal and willed the poison thorn from the ground. "This was wielded by the fairy. A single jab of so tiny a weapon nearly brought down a dragon. I hesitate to think what would have become of one of us if we'd been struck."

"The Aluall are a potent threat. The elves were right to summon aid," Grustim said.

"Why don't you just turn back?" murmured Shah. She flitted from Myn's horns and darted back and forth between the humans, addressing them each in kind. "This isn't your battle, right? This is the elves' battle. We are sworn to serve them for the good of our grove, but not you! Not the dragons! Just go back! Put us in our boxes and bring us back. Tell them what you found. Let *them* do the fighting. You are *good* people. You shouldn't have to die fighting for other people."

"Shah, this *is* our fight," Myranda said. "We knew it was dangerous. But these creatures, whoever or whatever they are, are a threat on a far larger scale than even the elves imagined. They are using D'Karon magic. We were only narrowly able to push the D'Karon back when they attacked before. If there are any D'Karon here, or if these people share their goals, then it could mean war and bloodshed the world over. In the face of that, there is no other option."

Shah looked uncertainly back to Freet, who was beginning to stir as well.

"Then you need to go to the east. The northeast. The fairy that did this comes from—"

"Shah, don't!" Freet scolded. He buzzed up. "It isn't our place to tell an outsider where other fairies hide!"

"Fairies *did* this, Freet!" Shah proclaimed. "It was a fairy holding that thorn. Myn was stung when she defended herself against the fairy. She attacked a *dragon. Dragons are friends to fairies.* The stories taught us that, and Myn and Garr prove it. Did any members of our grove ever use a weapon like that? No! Would any of us attack *anyone*, let alone a dragon? No! And Myranda and Deacon and Grustim, they are good. They didn't keep us in our boxes. They introduced us to real dragons. It seems to me that maybe humans are friends to fairies as well. At least *these* humans are. So the fairy who did this, she doesn't deserve our protection. The wind she brought with her was the wind from the east over the brook and through the brambles." She stared at Freet, as if challenging him to object.

After a short contemplative silence, he spoke. "These fairies do *not* deserve our protection. But there are *many* fairies here. Fairies in every corner of every forest. What if we lead them to the wrong ones?"

Shah darted to the thorn Deacon was still investigating. "The *brambles*," she said, pointing at the weapon and glaring at Freet. "The wind, from the east, over the brook, and through the *brambles*. We will know when we've found the right fairies. And Myranda and Deacon and Grustim, they won't do anything to fairies that we don't say are the right ones. Right?"

"We wouldn't dream of it," Deacon said.

Freet nodded once. "Very well. If you *all* promise not to go a *step closer* to any fairies that are not *these* fairies, then we shall lead you."

"Agreed," Myranda said.

"I've never heard of fairies working with other creatures outside of Entwell. It may be that the Aluall are not a single group but an alliance of sorts. We need to be prepared for anything," Deacon said.

"I think it is time to summon Ether," Myranda added. "Her powers are such that a weapon like this would be of no concern. Having her would give us a chance, even if faced with this poison again."

She tightened her grip about her staff again and tried to draw her mind together. Deacon placed a hand on her shoulder.

"You did the most trying portion of the healing. Let me seek out Ether," he said.

"Yes," Myranda said, blinking her weary eyes. "I think that would be best."

He readied his mind, coaxing a faint amber light within his gem. For the moment, Myranda found herself with nothing expected of her. It would have been wise to rest and consider what she'd learned, but the ragged weariness and overall lack of focus and energy that had plagued her since shortly before they'd left New Kenvard were beginning to affect her ability to fulfill the mission. Healing Myn would have been difficult in any situation, but she'd *barely* been able to achieve it. If there was some sort of affliction weakening her, next time she could falter at a critical moment. Better to spend this time seeking what, if anything, seemed to be wrong with herself.

She turned her mind inward, first sweeping her soul for the dark stain of D'Karon workings. There seemed to be nothing out of the ordinary. Next she searched her body. The days had been long and taxing. Even a healthy person would have been weary. But the weariness went so much deeper. And it was more than that. To a tiny but undeniable degree, the whole of her body seemed, for lack of a better word, *distracted*. It was almost like when someone was suffering through a potent disease, how every system in the body would labor to defeat it. But there *was* no disease.

Slowly, something did reveal itself. When Myranda realized the truth, that *this* was what was ailing her, a flood of emotions shook her mind from its state of focus. If she were anywhere else, if it was any other time, she would have felt very differently. But now was the worst possible time. Concern for what it would mean for her, how she could risk going forward now that she knew, wracked her mind.

"Myranda?" Deacon said.

She looked to him and saw concern in his eyes. Now new thoughts and concerns rushed in to join the others, worries about how Deacon would feel, what he would say. How it would all effect the mission. She grappled with herself in the moments before answering.

"It's nothing. I'm fine," she said.

Worse than speaking the lie was what she had to do next. Deacon was a wizard, more able than most to know the truth of a statement, as he had insight into the souls of those around him. And with Myranda, he had a link. Until this moment they had been entirely open with one another. But now she had to quietly tuck away the truth, guard it in her mind and mask it from her soul. But it was the only way. Anything less could endanger the lives of all who were depending upon them.

"I have contacted Ether. She informed me she made some limited discoveries regarding Sonril's history with North Crescent," he said. "It strikes me I should record our location and what we've learned. I have been terribly distracted."

He coaxed his book from his bag and flipped it open. Pages riffled and came to a rest. He held his stylus over the blank page but paused. "There... there is something here..." he said, looking closely.

Freet darted over the page. "I don't see anything," he said.

"There isn't anything to be seen, but there is certainly something here. Or something *intended* to be here."

Freet looked at him curiously. "Do all humans speak in riddles like you?"

"Deacon does so more than most," Myranda explained. "What seems to have happened?"

"I believe there was an attempt to copy pages from one of the other books, but something interfered with the spell. I believe I can repair it."

He held his stylus over the page, shut his eyes, and released it. The enchanted writing instrument hung in the air, then wandered vaguely about the page, drifting this way and that as if drawn to certain parts of it. Deacon deepened his focus, and the shuddering, darting motions became sharper and more frequent. The tip of the stylus touched the page, conjuring a line, then jumped to another part of the page to produce a curve. Momentum built and the stylus was soon dancing across the page, tracing out words a letter or two at a time, though often on opposite edges of a page. The contents of the page populated in this piecemeal fashion, such that it wasn't until the page was nearly full that any individual line was complete.

"That is Ivy's writing. I'm sure of it. Or, at least it is the work of her hand!" Myranda triumphantly threw her arms around Deacon. "I knew she was alive! Can we track the origin of this message? I can't seem to feel that aspect of the spell."

"No. This wasn't written with the stylus I made for her, so it was already a weaker version of the spell, and something has confounded the magic terribly. We are fortunate I was able to retrieve the message at all."

The stylus traced out the last few lines on the opposite page, then came to rest.

"There… I am not certain this is the whole of the message, but I cannot seem to retrieve any more of it. Curious. It seems to be more than one language…"

"What does it say?" Freet asked. "That looks like the writing the fairies make."

Deacon nodded. "Yes. They appear to be names. Locations. This here says Mellawin of Grandwinn. The king of Sonril in its capital. And I distinctly remember this name below it coming up in our briefings during the voyage from Tressor."

Myranda looked aside and gingerly fetched the thorn she'd removed from Myn.

"They have potent poison, nearly impenetrable stealth, and a list of Sonril's nobles. This does not bode well… Contact Ether again and tell her to warn the nobles. Shah, it may be time for you to deliver a message. The elves were rather insistent that we use you and Freet for messages." Myranda tugged Shah's box from Myn's back as she slept. "I don't want to risk that they are bullheaded enough to disregard a warning simply because it did not come through their preferred means."

Shah darted up to her and floated rigidly at attention. "I'm ready to do my job!"

#

For a second time in very short order, the voice of Deacon faded out of Ether's thoughts. She was still simmering with anger that Ivy had been taken and they had neglected to share it with her until now. Another of the Chosen taken by an unknown enemy, and she was not immediately informed. *More* frustrating was their insistence that she deliver a message to the nobles. A message that apparently would be repeated by one of their *own* messengers. It was possible, though she would never admit it to herself, that a large part of her frustration was owed to how little progress she had made in her investigations in Grandwinn.

She paced through a hallway, a part of the sprawling palace the king called home, that rose and fell to follow the shape of the land. If the bulk of their structures were formed from trees, the palace was formed from a forest. Rooms seamlessly transitioned to outdoor groves. It was as near to a perfect union of society and nature as she'd ever observed. Unique among nobility, at least in her observation, was the nearly total lack of anything resembling true security. If home to someone of any level of importance, most cities of Tressor and the Northern Alliance had fortified themselves against the risk of attack. There was little evidence that the people of Grandwinn considered attack the remotest of possibilities. Nowhere was this more apparent than in the fact that Ether was allowed to walk the halls without accompaniment. She was an outsider. All other kingdoms treated outsiders with some level of justifiable caution. But she saw very few guards and felt very few enchantments.

Ether paused… Something in her mind clicked into place. Of the few guards she saw, she did see *some*. And of the few enchantments she felt, she did *feel* some. They were far from the central grounds of the palace, and thus far from those she had been interviewing and investigating. Until this moment she had simply assumed they were guarding some manner of valuables, which Ether had little interest in. But the king had expressed no small amount of joy in endlessly presenting and prattling about the most precious treasures of the land.

If she was going to leave this place, she wasn't going to do it without seeing just what they felt warranted protection. She shifted to wind and relaxed her form, reducing herself to a gentle breeze rather than the raging gale she typically assumed in that form. Some time ago she had been lectured by Lain that she wasted her capacity for stealth. Like so many attempts at advice, she'd failed to take it to heart until recently. As it was made clear that tact was called for, and her repeated attempts to pry information from the people of Grandwinn had established that direct methods had a way of raising their suspicions, this was a moment for avoiding detection.

Her subtle form drifted past a trio of elven sentries, each of whom didn't offer so much as a glance toward the leaves she rustled in passing. A thin veneer of magic, however, was becoming stronger. Deacon had a knack for unraveling the intent of unknown spells. From the texture of this enchantment, she noted it seemed too weak to hold her at bay, but nonetheless offered a degree of resistance. That put her in mind of a spell of detection. She tested the edge of the enchantment and found that it encircled a large section of the palace grove, one thick with trees but undeniably an "outdoor" portion of the grounds.

Ether's impulse was to simply overpower the spell, to sever it with raw force of will, but as she could not restore it when she was through, all it would do would be establish that someone had entered the protected land. They would be fools to suspect anyone but her. Instead, she drifted near the ground and surveyed what clues nature had to offer. Almost immediately, she discovered the paths of woodland creatures that had passed through the perimeter of the enchantment. Obviously, such coming and going had not brought sentries running, so it was likely such creatures were exempt from the spell's influence. A short investigation turned up a bit of fur caught on some bramble, and a brief flex of her mind allowed her to resolve into the little creature's form. When she was, to all outward appearances, little more than a rabbit, the pressure of the enchantment dropped away.

She hopped among the trees, sharp eyes and sharper ears sifting her surroundings for some indication of what they were protecting. It wasn't until she was well into the guarded woods that shapes very subtly differentiated themselves from the growth of the forest. They were trees, mighty oaks, each centuries old at least. At a glance they might not have seemed much different from the other trees of the woods, but strange looping patterns, each with an oddly metallic sheen, suggested that something had become embedded in the tree. She hopped up and looked over one of the strange patches and discovered it to be the pitted and badly tarnished tip of a silver blade. Elsewhere, trees held shields and bits of armor. Most mysterious, names in elven script seemed to have been formed out of the natural whorls of wood and bark.

It took a bit of thought before Ether reasoned out what she was looking at. To a mortal, the answer would have been apparent much sooner, but she was timeless, and seldom had cause to think about death. These were monuments, grave markers. Trees planted to mark the resting places of warriors. Their weapons were placed among the growing tree, and the growth was enchanted to immortalize their names. And if the age of the grove was any indication, they all had fallen within a few years of one another, hundreds of years ago. It painted the tale of a battle. A battle that neither King Mellawin nor his people had seen fit to mention even in passing during their many discussions.

Ether twitched the ears of her current form and ventured deeper. She had learned much about the people of Sonril in the last few days. And chief among those revelations was their predilection toward self-aggrandizement. In the current circumstance, that meant two things. That they had not mentioned a battle, or perhaps a war, that apparently had taken hundreds of lives suggested it was a point of shame. Had it been a victory, they would have proclaimed it at every opportunity. Second, it would very likely not be enough for them to simply mark the graves of their fallen. There would be more.

She ventured through the thickening overgrowth. This land had been left to its own devices for quite some time. It was not tended to, and thus lacked the sculptural aesthetic of elven horticulture. She had to struggle through some very dense bushes to reach the center of the memorial, but it was worth the effort. After startling the very rabbit whose shape she had borrowed, she found herself at the foot of a statue that reached nearly as tall as the trees that surrounded it. The grove had all but reclaimed it, cocooning it in vines that bloomed with sweet-scented flowers. But still visible was a trio of elves, each standing heroically with weapons raised. Their heads were craned, looking upon the final figure that dominated the image. It was a dwarf, rendered more crudely and monstrously than the elves. It was many times their size, and set back from them such that she suspected it was intended to be larger still.

Ether did not know precisely what it meant. On the surface it was symbolic of a ruinous clash against dwarfs. But she wondered how much was artistic interpretation…

She set the matter aside and hopped back toward the palace. No doubt she would be missed if she was absent for much longer; and there was, after all, a message to deliver.

Chapter 8

Hours later, Nehri sat in her own hut. Despite her honored place among her people, her home was no larger or more ornate than those of the other villagers. The only indication of her status was the abundance of artifacts associated with her role in the village. Her robes hung with care on one wall. She had stacks of texts, painstakingly copied from her predecessor as part of her training. And of course, she had several of the precious thir gems, the better to focus her mind upon their worship and practice their teachings. As the priestess, she also had the duty to become as skilled as possible in the D'Karon teachings. She knew each of their spells by heart, and could recite every word of their many invocations and mantras backward and forward. It was the entirety of her purpose, the focus of her life.

Right now, though, she'd shifted her attention to a small mark, the curve and point that Ivy had revealed when they'd learned she had known Teyn. She'd scrawled it with care on a bit of parchment, duplicating it from memory. It really was a simple insignia, but something about it had lodged in Nehri's mind. Ivy was visibly reluctant to embrace the D'Karon teachings. And she claimed that those approaching from the south, warriors clearly in service of Sonril, were her friends. Any of these things separately would have been cause for varying degrees of concern, but Nehri could have set them aside. The combination of them set the wheels of her mind in motion, and she did not like the direction they were heading. She set the parchment aside and consulted one of the sacred texts. On a well-worn page, she found a short passage discussing the enemies of the D'Karon, a group the D'Karon called the Adversaries. It was said they would all bear a mark.

Nehri reread the words on the page, the warnings that the mark could "defend itself" against the D'Karon and those who served them. The defense was described as a soul-deep burning, something that would come at a single touch and injure any who were loyal to the

D'Karon way. Nehri steeled herself. She lightly touched her palm to the page.

The pain was immediate, and piercing. She pulled her hand away and gasped, the mystic burning lingering briefly. She felt as though she'd touched a branding iron, yet this was a simple mark, ink on a page and drawn by her own hand. Worse than the pain, though, was the realization. Ivy was an Adversary, and her friends more of the same. One of her own kind, welcomed into the heart of their precious safe haven, was a tool of the powers opposed to their own patrons. And if she spoke the truth… Teyn bore the same mark. The mate of Sorrel, progenitor of her own bloodline, an Adversary…

"No…" Nehri breathed. "There must be some other explanation."

A sound came as a welcome distraction from her worrisome thoughts. It was the massive flap of leathery wings and the jingle of heavy chains. She felt her jaw tighten.

"I've asked him not to do this…" she fumed.

Nehri grasped a thir stone. It drew weakly at her spirit, but it was fresh from the shrine and thus its appetite was nearly sated, so there was no need to make an offering of herself to it. She stepped outside into the dead of night and turned her eyes and ears to the sky. The dim form of Boviss swept over the sleeping town. He came down with an earth-shaking impact at the fringe of the village. Nehri rushed up just as Reyce hopped from the dragon's back.

"Reyce, I have asked that you not bring him here. Boviss frightens the children," she said.

"That is good," Boviss rumbled. "It is a fine lesson for them to fear dragons."

"Better the children be frightened than our village fall," Reyce said.

She glanced angrily back and forth between them. "What are you talking about? And where have you *been*?"

"Doing my best to deal with the agents from the south. Haven't you been watching the gems?"

"I have been doing my best to see to Ivy."

He held out a depleted thir gem. "Rishrim contacted me. He was nearly killed by the party we rescued Ivy from. His wasp struck one of the dragons. I've sent Norrim to watch them, but it seems the dragon may yet recover."

"Nothing has ever survived that poison." She narrowed her eyes. "Why was a wasp even present?"

"Our foes are more formidable than we'd imagined. They are powerful, they are resourceful, and they are dedicated. I needed to act quickly, to strike hard. That is why I needed Boviss. I refuse to risk underestimating them. Though we have always been able to avoid detection before, they may find something there that could lead them here. I need to know more. Where is Ivy? I have questions, and if she cares for her race, she shall answer them."

"Ivy is in her hut…" She clasped her hands together, wringing her fingers. "Reyce, there is something you need to know. About her, and about the others. It may explain why our foes seem so much more powerful than we'd imagined."

"What is it?"

Nehri fetched the parchment with the mark. "Touch it."

He did so and recoiled in pain. She watched as his expression changed, his mind working out what this meant.

"The Adversaries…" Reyce's fists tightened. "How could I be so *foolish*?"

"We couldn't have known, Reyce. She is one of our own kind. It was *right* to bring her here. And perhaps it is not too late for her… Perhaps you can convince her of the truth."

"We shall try." He shut his eyes and lowered his head. "I pray to our patrons that fate has not condemned one of our own to die in service of their foes…"

"As do I. As do we all…"

He marched away, leaving Nehri beside Boviss. The hulking beast swiveled his head and fixed his piercing gaze upon her.

"Nehri," he said, his permanent, unnerving grin shifting ever so subtly to a sneer. He drew in her scent. "I recall your mother. A female chieftain. Rare. So seldom do I deal with females."

"That is because the role of priestess falls more commonly to us, and you refuse to swear your loyalty to the D'Karon. Or had you forgotten why you are kept so far from their blessings?"

"I have no need for their blessings. Such magic is for the weak."

"The weak. I would suggest you have forgotten just how you came to be among our subjects, but you have no shortage of reminders. Half of your scars came from the day you were bested. And both of your missing limbs."

Boviss scratched at the ground with his prosthetic claw. "I remember. I remember all."

"Then remember that my people nearly struck you down once. You live because of our charity and mercy, and you would do well to remind us of your gratitude." She tightened her grip about her gem, bringing a renewed glow to its heart.

There were few beings Nehri had a deep, personal distaste for, but Boviss was chief among them. In all the years he had served the people of Den—far longer than she or even her grandparents had been alive—he had never acted against them. But his demeanor was vile, and his words were poison. Every time Reyce traveled to his lair to seek counsel, the chieftain returned with his mind more firmly twisted in the direction of conquest and battle. The dragon was a terrible influence, but an invaluable tool in their continued safety, as when all else failed, it was by his tooth, claw, and flame that Den was protected. In a way, there was a balance to his unwillingness to embrace the D'Karon, as he was only truly needed when their bountiful gifts fell short.

Nehri thought for a moment. "Boviss. I require your aid," she said.

"To be of service to a priestess. An honor."

"Don't waste your hollow words on me, dragon, and remain here." She once again revealed the page containing the mark and beckoned. "Offer me your paw and tell me if you feel any pain."

"Does the priestess wish to practice her magics upon her lowly servant?"

"Do as I say," she said firmly.

Boviss turned his flesh-and-blood forepaw over and angled it toward her. Each of his claws was nearly as long as the whole of her body, and within the cracks and crevices, rusty-brown stains told the tales of a thousand creatures who had fallen before him. She steeled herself, unwilling to show fear, and pressed the page against the thinnest patch of hide she was aware of, the flesh between the claws.

"Do you feel anything? A burning? Some working of magic?"

"I feel only your touch. And barely that."

"Then it is true," Nehri said. "The mark burns only those loyal to the D'Karon."

"A potent weapon against your kind. A creature with such a weapon comes to you, and you let it live. Curious…"

"We do not share the same lust for blood as you, Boviss."

"And so few of you remain. Perhaps if you did, there would be more of you left. No matter. In your brother, there is hope."

#

"Vesk, Manca," Reyce said, noticing two of his better warriors readying themselves for a late-night patrol. "Follow me. Eyes sharp and ears sharp. I shall have a word with Ivy. She may not like what she hears. Be ready for anything."

The other malthropes nodded and fell into a march behind him. They each clutched ornately carved wooden clubs. Reyce reached the hut and stepped inside. His sudden appearance stirred Ivy from her sleep.

"Reyce…" she murmured, slow to rouse from rest. "Is something wrong?"

Reyce turned aside. "Vesk. A light, quickly."

The malthrope dashed to a flickering lantern hung beside the communal stew pot and fetched it. Reyce took the lantern and lit the lamp in Ivy's hut. What the light revealed was fascinating. Ivy had taken one of the twigs used to light the lamp the previous night and had scrawled complex designs upon the tabletop with its charred tip.

"I have spoken with Nehri. Ivy… I truly thought better of you than to deceive us in this way."

"What have I done?"

"The mark on your chest. You are an *Adversary*. A foe of the D'Karon. An enemy of our patrons."

Ivy shut her eyes and slumped a bit. "That's just what Turiel called us…"

"Then it is true."

"The D'Karon books call us Adversaries. The rest of the world calls us the Chosen."

"And you hid this from us. Ivy, we brought you here. We rescued you, introduced you to your proper home!"

"You kidnapped me, Reyce. Those from whom you took me are my friends. My allies. If you'd just take a moment to *talk* to them, you would understand they aren't here to hurt you."

"Weren't here to hurt us? I sent one of my best and most skilled stalkers to watch them, to keep me apprised of their actions. Not half a day ago they nearly killed him."

"You've taken me and they don't know why! And then you send someone to *stalk* them? You can't say you wouldn't do the same in their place. You took me for the very reason they are coming for me. Because they care about me. They are good people. They only want the best for everyone."

"The Adversaries are enemies of the D'Karon!"

"And the D'Karon are enemies of our *world*, Reyce. You don't know the truth about them. They orchestrated a *war* in my home. It lasted for over a century. The lives lost… they all but usurped the throne of the Northern Alliance and conjured an endless horde of monstrous warriors to attack the south. They were hoping to weaken both sides until they could open the door for more of their kind to sweep through and conquer the world! They are agents of other gods. Reyce, the D'Karon were *evil*."

Reyce gave her a hard look. "Do not speak such blasphemy in the village that owes its existence to their gifts, Ivy." He crossed his arms. "I have questions for you. Questions about your 'friends.' Will you answer freely? Will you answer honestly?"

"Of course." She matched his pose. "I have nothing to hide. And they have nothing to fear from you."

"Nothing to fear from us? Do you really think so little of your race?"

"I think so highly of my friends. Together we defeated the D'Karon. We ended a war."

He hammered the wall. "I will not hear it! The D'Karon are not to be defeated, and *could* not be defeated. But I haven't got the time or inclination to debate you on such matters. Nehri is our priestess. In time she shall set you straight. If there is even a fragment of hope for you, we will see you brought back into the fold, onto the path of truth. You are a malthrope. You deserve nothing less. But right now, I want to know about the rest of your party. What can I expect from them?"

"Myranda is a wizard, and so is Deacon. If one of them isn't the finest wizard to have ever lived, then the other certainly is. Myn is a dragon, strong and true. She would do anything for us, practically a daughter to Myranda and practically a sister to me. You'll never find another creature as mighty and as loyal and as sweet and kind as Myn. The other dragon is Garr, and his Dragon Rider is Grustim. No one knows more about dragons than Grustim, and Garr has finer training than any dragon in the world. We have faced undead hordes. We have faced armies. We have faced fierce creatures, and D'Karon creations. If you'd seen the monsters the D'Karon made, the monsters me and my friends destroyed, you wouldn't dream of calling the D'Karon *good*."

"Ivy," Reyce fumed, voice shaking with barely controlled anger. "If you will not speak of the D'Karon with reverence, do not speak of them at all."

"Gladly."

"What will it take to turn your friends away?"

"They won't turn back. Not while you have me. If you want them to stop, you have to let me go. Let me talk to them."

"I cannot risk releasing you. Though you do not know enough to lead them here, after all that we've done to shield Den from discovery, I cannot abide you leaving this place having seen it."

"It wouldn't matter if you did. No one is smarter than they are, and if they learn about whose magic you're using, they'll stop you. What you need to do is be open to them. Talk to them. They'll listen."

"You would have me negotiate with agents of the elves, with the foes of our patrons? No. I have come too far to submit now."

"There is nothing else to be done. They don't want to hurt you. You have to trust that there is a peaceful solution."

"Peaceful? A peaceful solution between the malthropes and the other races? You, who come from a place where none has survived but you?"

"But I *have* found peace with them. I am a diplomat at home, an ambassador. It isn't perfect, there is a long way to go, but I walk among them without fear. The elves sought *my help*. Reyce, I know all too well what sort of a past you and the others must have had, but I've also seen Dusand. Your hands aren't clean."

He lowered his head, regret of his dark deeds hanging over him like a shadow. "No… No my hands are not clean. But that is all the more reason for them to refuse anything resembling peace. After what we have done, they would be fools to offer it. Why should they accept a hand extended in friendship? And why should we be the ones to extend it?"

"Because it has to start somewhere. In order for things to change, *people* need to be willing to change. Blood always leads to more blood. The only thing that can lead to peace is friendship. If you battle my friends, and you don't give them a chance to help you, you *will* fall to them, and I desperately want to keep that from happening."

He clenched his fist and tightened his jaw briefly. "We captured you. We've kept you here. We are more powerful than you think."

"You captured me because I was taken by surprise. I never expected to see another malthrope, and I didn't know what to make of it when I had. And you've kept me here because staying here is the only way I could learn the nature of this place and its history. Now I'll stay because it's my only chance to talk some sense into you. But I assure you, if I think my friends need me, I will go to them. You won't be able to stop me." She leaned forward, her voice bordering on threatening. "You don't know what I'm capable of, what I really am. And I hope you never find out."

"You haven't learned what *we* are capable of either. But you *will* find out. Everyone will. Come." He turned to the doorway. "Follow."

He walked out into the village, Ivy in tow. His guards followed close behind.

"You say you have dragons. The mightiest of dragons. I have seen them. And if you believe yours are the mightiest, then you don't know what true power is." He pointed to the edge of the village. "Do not look away. *Boviss! Flame!*"

A low rumble rippled through the town, then a rush of flame roiled over the village. The heat, even as far into the village as they were, was scalding. Brilliant orange light flooded the village and offered a glimpse of Boviss in all of his terrible glory.

Reyce turned to Ivy. A weak stir of blue swirled around her, and her eyes widened in surprise.

"There, Ivy. That is power. And there is more where that came from. I can protect my people. I *will* protect my people."

Ivy looked around, then looked Reyce in the eyes. "You're right, Reyce. I hadn't seen the power you have. But I *have* seen what it looks like when a village feels safe. Have you?"

Reyce scanned the village. The commotion had stirred several residents from their beds. They had their eyes locked upon the edge of town, where the dragon was lurking. There were terrified.

Ivy turned her back on him and marched back to her hut without being dismissed. Reyce burned with anger. He stomped back to Boviss. Nehri was still at the dragon's feet, but there was fury in her eyes.

"What is wrong with you!" she snapped.

"I had to demonstrate our ability to defend our home." His voice had the tremble of fading anger, and the flicker of regret.

"And to do so, you risk burning it to the ground and send up a flare in the night for any to see?"

"The enchantments will keep us hidden."

"They likely will, but that is no reason to push their limits. We are already leaching away far more power than we ever have to ready for your assault. Every extra crystal we drain in hiding this village is one that will need to be filled from the souls of our people and the life of our land."

Reyce took a breath. "Yes. It was unwise. I apologize."

"Don't apologize, Reyce," she said, her anger beginning to ebb. "Just *think*. Please. You are better than this. This isn't you. You have been away from your people for too long. First watching the elven city, then seeking and fetching Boviss again and again. You are tired, and your people miss you."

He looked away. "My task is not through. Boviss must feed. He must be returned to his lair. Further plans must be made for those who seek Ivy. Now is a moment of reckoning for our people. I can rest when our plans are through. A sated gem, please."

Nehri handed him the gem she was holding. Reyce climbed to Boviss's back. The chain affixed to the massive beast's neck had a small hollow, sized for the gem. He slipped it in place, touched the surface, and unleashed a D'Karon spell. A violet and black mist rushed from the gem and coiled about both Reyce and Boviss. He shuddered at the cold, eerie sensation of the enchantment taking effect. When the mist had entirely enshrouded them, they faded from view. Reyce blinked away the stinging in his eyes. He was briefly without his vision, but it returned in a shifting, ghostly form. The enchantment ran its course and nothing remained to suggest there had ever been a malthrope or a dragon.

Boviss unfurled his unseen wings and took to the sky, a breath of wind offering the only evidence of his movement. Even the deep footprints and claw marks he'd left behind shifted and slid until there was naught but level ground.

Reyce watched the village under his protection slip away beneath him. When they had risen to twice the height of the shrine, the flickering lanterns and cozy huts vanished as well. To even the most carefully trained gaze, the sprawling grounds of Den looked to be nothing more than a lush stretch of wilderness.

Boviss pitched aside and drifted south.

"We shall do our hunting to the north," Reyce said.

"The better prey lies south," Boviss rumbled.

"Yes. And that prey must feed my people. You shall feed to the north."

"Of course," There was the tremor of irritation in the dragon's voice. "Your newcomer. She is powerful."

"You haven't met our newcomer."

"My kind sees more than what our eyes may show. I sensed when you had only just signaled for me to land."

"Impossible. That is beyond the veil that conceals our village."

"Yes. And others seek her. The other dragons. The humans."

"The rest of her party. As I have said. Two of the humans are wizards."

"They shall find her. Den shall fall."

"They shall not. We shall stop them."

"No. If they are wise, and wizards are wise, then they shall find her. Den shall fall."

"We will kill them before that. The dragons are no match for you."

"A single dragon. A single wizard. Perhaps. I can crush any who face me. But a pair. I cannot crush both. Not if they do not face me as one. And they shall not. They shall attack from two sides. Their flames will claim your homes. Their claws will trample your people. Their magic will unravel your protections. Den will fall."

"Enough! Den will *not* fall."

"You lack the fortitude to protect your people."

"I will do *anything* to protect my people!"

"Then you finish what you have started. Now. Before they reach Den. You must begin the attack. The dragons and wizards are agents of the elves. When the attack begins, they will turn back. And in the face of the attack, they will succumb. But it must begin now. If they draw too near, it will be too late."

"We do not even know if the attack will be necessary. Perhaps if we defeat these agents, as you and your kind defeated them in the ancient past, then they will honor the isthmus once more and we shall be safe."

"Then you forfeit the lives of your people."

"The attack is not ready! We have many more crystals to fill."

Boviss was silent for a time. When he spoke again, it was with a far more sinister edge. "The newcomer is very powerful."

Reyce considered his words. He gripped the chain about the dragon's neck and tightened his jaw. Finally, the chieftain shut his eyes tightly and hung his head low. "May the D'Karon forgive me for the things fate demands… To the southern hunting grounds. Eat your fill. Restore your strength. Then take me to Ironcore Mountain. Preparations must be made…"

#

Myn thumped along, her plodding pace slow and her breathing heavy. She was recovering well, but it was clear she had not yet been fully restored to her strength. Nevertheless, what she lacked in speed she made up for in determination. As the sun rose, they had covered the narrow strip of desert separating them from the near edge of the northeastern forest. Myranda swatted at the buzzing of insects as they traveled deeper into the muggy heart of the woods.

The dragon's paw caught a loose bit of soil, and she nearly toppled over, but Garr leaned aside to support her with a well-placed leg and a curve of his neck. The male dragon had not allowed himself to be more than a half step away from Myn since she'd awoken, except for brief trips to catch food enough for himself, the others, and especially Myn. While they walked, Garr spent as much time watching her as the path ahead, mindful of any sign of weakness or discomfort. If the circumstances had not been so dire, it would have been almost adorable to see the concern and affection simmering just below his hard, military exterior.

"That's enough, Myn," Myranda said, hopping down from the dragon's back once she had steadied herself. "Come here."

The dragon lowered her head to be level with that of the human.

Myranda looked her in the eye and spoke with all the authority of a mother to her child. "You need rest, and you certainly shouldn't be carrying Deacon and I upon your back. You've made your point, you're the strongest and most dutiful dragon anyone could hope to know. But now that we've reached the forest, we must move slowly anyway."

"I very much agree," Deacon said, stepping down onto the lush undergrowth of the woods. "Fairies have a way of hiding themselves in the most cunning of ways. Better to be slow, and to take this time to tend to your condition. Even with Shah and Freet to guide us, it will be no small task to find them."

The two fairies were nestled among Myn's horns. Shah, exhausted from her astonishingly fast trip to and from the capital, was sound asleep.

Myn huffed a breath at Myranda, then looped her tail around Deacon to return him to her back. With him in place, she leaned low, offering her back to Myranda as well.

"Fine. But at least take it easy," Myranda said, climbing back into position.

Garr rumbled something. Grustim uttered a gruff reply.

"Is something wrong?"

"He wants to hunt. He's caught the scent of new prey."

Myranda grinned. "He's hunted three times. Myn's never eaten so well."

Grustim nodded. "Fresh meat, new prey, and Myn's strength and favor are difficult for him to ignore." He indicated a bush with familiar thorns. "But the fairies may be near."

"They are," Freet said. "I can feel the same wind as I felt from the bad fairy's wings."

Myranda took her staff in hand. Deacon fetched his crystal.

"And the poison?" she asked.

Garr raised his snout and sampled the air.

"Nothing," Grustim said. "Yet…"

"At least there is that mercy," Deacon said. "It would have been helpful if Ether had come directly to us instead of pursuing her own search, as her unique talents would be extremely useful in this situation. There are many small points of magic about. Weak. Difficult to pinpoint. And moving quite quickly."

They cast their eyes upward, toward the canopy. The leaves of the trees here were broad and waxy, the air heavy and humid. Insects larger than any Myranda had seen in the Northern Alliance or Tressor crawled and fluttered about. But from out of the corner of her eye, Myranda was certain some of the things that appeared to be dragonflies had the hint of a human form.

"They are all around us," Myranda said.

Garr tensed and dug his claws into the soil.

"Perhaps we can open a dialogue," Deacon suggested.

"Will the spell you cast for us to speak to Shah and Freet work for these fairies?" Myranda asked.

"Only if they speak the same dialect. To my knowledge, fairies all speak similar languages, but the dialects can vary widely. As the fairies of Entwell likely came via the Northern Alliance, and thus via Tressor, and in turn via trade from South Crescent, it stands to reason that all of their languages would be similar…"

"Deacon, I think we may not need to speculate much longer," Myranda interrupted.

The wind around them was rising, moving with a clear will. It was different from the wind Myranda had conjured to reveal the spy in the desert. That wind had been focused, direct. This was much more turbulent and chaotic. It wasn't the result of a single mind. This was the work of many working together, but not in perfect harmony. That made it weaker than it might have been, but also rendered it nearly impossible to counter with her own magic, like trying to catch a handful of sand instead of a single stone.

"No fire, Myn," Myranda called. "I don't want to hurt them, and even if you are careful, this wind will make it difficult to control."

Freet roused Shah and they both flitted up, trilling in a language different enough to escape the effects of Deacon's enchantment. A few of the darting forms of the fairies came close, then one of them snatched Shah and pulled her into the intensifying wind. Freet cried out and pursued. Myranda could just make out Shah's struggling form pulled into a thorn bush at the edge of the clearing. Freet charged in after them.

"We should spread out," Grustim called, his eyes scanning his surroundings with swift efficiency. "Better to split their focus."

"Indeed," Deacon replied. He had to raise his voice to be heard over the growing wail. "And if they work together, they may be able to blow down one of these trees. We don't want to present a single target."

Garr rumbled.

"Garr still does not smell any of the poison."

"That is a relief," Myranda said.

The current of both wind and magic was growing ever stronger, each fairy now faintly visible as a dim streamer of light.

"They do not glow very brightly at all," Deacon said. "It implies they are mystically weak. Among the weakest I've ever felt from a fairy."

Dust, soil, and leaves were beginning to fill the air, along with more than a few small branches and stones. Garr unfurled his wings and lowered them to deflect the debris from Grustim. Myn imitated for Myranda and Deacon.

"They seem powerful enough to me," Grustim said.

"I believe it means there are a *lot* of them," Myranda said.

The wind and ribbons of light wove in more interesting shapes, fairies lining up into strings of a dozen or more. They darted toward Deacon, then curved upward at the last moment. A stuttering patter joined the wailing of wind, and a sequence of dusty bursts worked their way along the ground in front of him. He conjured a shield just in time to see a line of thorns clash against the mystic barrier. Lines traced across the ground toward Myranda and Grustim.

"Impressive coordination," Deacon said.

Grustim raised an arm to shield his face. The thorns peppered his armor, but did little more than scratch it.

"Deal with these creatures before they find a way to become more than a nuisance!" Grustim demanded.

Something long and brown whizzed toward Grustim. He swung his sword, but the shape darted down and swept at his ankles. He cried out in pain as it was revealed to be a thorn vine stretched between a pair of fairies. They whirled around his legs. There were few gaps in his armor, but thorns found their way into every one.

Deacon's and Myranda's shields were sparkling with constant impacts from thrown thorns. The dragons, notably, were spared the attacks. Garr took full advantage, stepping over Grustim and surrounding him to protect him. Myn stood behind Myranda and Deacon, shielding them from behind so they could focus on a single direction.

"Wind magic will be of little use to us," Deacon called. "I believe levitation will be our best chance at sparing them injury."

"I care not if you spare them injury. Just end this!" Grustim growled, unaccustomed to being in a position of weakness, particularly in the face of so diminutive a threat.

Deacon held up a hand. One of the blurred forms came to a sudden and complete halt. It was a female, and she was different from any fairy they had ever seen. A bundle of thorns hung at her waist. She was wrapped head to toe in thorn vine, the barbs strategically angled outward. Myranda raised her staff and wrapped her will about a fairy as well, then another, and another.

One by one, they split their focus to hold more of the little creatures. They soon numbered in the dozens, struggling in place and terribly taxing the capacity of the wizards. When a unique fairy was locked in place, however, the gale ceased in an instant. The darting forms hung in the air, eyes turned to Myranda and Deacon, their faces looking shocked and concerned. Finally, Myranda realized that the final fairy she'd captured was a male. His tiny form was bristling with thorns even more than the rest of the fairies, and chips of amber and other glittering stones suggested he had a position of importance.

After the initial disbelief wore off, the air filled with angry trilling.

"I am afraid I don't understand their words," Deacon said. "Formulating a translation enchantment requires a good deal more time and concentration than I can spare at present."

"Don't! Wait!" called Shah.

She and Freet burst from the bushes, none the worse for wear but quite frazzled.

Freet's voice warbled between half-understood syllables and completely unfamiliar fairy-talk. Slowly, the fairies surrounding him turned and paid attention. His speech slid entirely to the same trilling as the other fairies. When he was through, they fluttered to high perches among the trees, watched, and waited.

"You've got to release their war chief," Shah said quickly. "They've agreed to stop their attack, but only if you release their war chief."

There was no question which of the fairies she meant. She and Deacon released the fairies held in place by their will, leaving the war chief for last. When he was released, he drifted up and took a place on a nearby branch. A phalanx of other fairies joined him, thorns at the ready. He uttered a few rolling whistles. The rest of the fairies reluctantly assumed less hostile postures.

Grustim unleashed a quiet torrent of Tresson profanities as he climbed to his feet. Garr fixed a small cluster of fairies in his gaze. The dragon's burning anger was enough to make even the fearless fairies squirm a bit.

"Everyone be calm. Freet's able to make himself understood."

There was a short exchange between Freet and those fairies nearest to him. Shah acted as a go-between so that Freet could keep his attention on the temporarily pacified fairies, lest their calm demeanor come to a sudden end.

"They want you to leave immediately," Shah said.

"Tell them we just need to ask them some questions," Myranda said.

"They say they are forbidden from dealing with any but the Children of... some word he doesn't know."

"Who are these Children?"

Shah listened intently as Freet and the others spoke, with the thorn fairies becoming progressively more agitated.

"They don't know how we don't know who the Children of Whatever are. They say they are simply the Children of Whatever. And they want you to leave, because the longer you stay, the more angry the Children of Whatever may be with them."

"Tell them we just need to know anything they may know about the Aluall."

"They don't know that word. They say they don't know anyone like that."

"Ask them if they know of creatures who are able to make themselves invisible."

"... They say the Children of Whatever can do that."

"I can't imagine there are an abundance of creatures with that ability here," Deacon said.

"So it would seem," Myranda said. "Shah, Freet, please ask where we can find the Children."

The fairies trilled for a bit. The answer came almost as a chorus, all of the fairies angrily buzzing and shouting.

"They can't say. They say their alliance is very old, and they dare not threaten it."

Grustim tugged a stubborn thorn from a joint of his armor. "Tell them their alliance has caused them to assault us, and we demand retribution. We know that a fairy, similarly armed but far more deadly, was in service of the Aluall and that we hold them personally responsible."

"No!" Myranda said quickly. "I don't want to use threats or force if I don't have to. We should at least learn what we can first. Ask them what the nature of their alliance is."

"They say the Children help them to learn new magic. They help make them stronger, and protect them. In exchange, the fairies keep their eyes and ears open, scanning the forest and the surrounding places for those who would hurt the Children. And the Children say *all* but the fairies, some… he thinks she said 'dwarfs,' and one dragon would hurt the Children."

"The Aluall fear humans, elves, most dwarfs, and most dragons. Either they are not principally composed of those races, or perhaps they are outcasts…" Deacon mused.

Shah continued, as the other fairies were quite passionately listing off the details of their partnership with the Children, and Freet was hard-pressed to keep up. "He says the fairies who learn the new magic best are allowed to join the Children. They call them… some kind of bug. They want to know why you travel with dragons. They didn't expect those who would threaten the Children of Whatever to travel with dragons. And certainly not with fairies…. They used a bad word for fairies. I don't think they think very highly of us for traveling with you."

"Because like them, we are allied. Tell them that we need to find our friend Ivy, and to stop further attacks and needless bloodshed," Myranda said.

Freet launched into a lengthy exchange with the fairies, but he was having clear difficulty having his message heard as they all spoke at once around him. Many had grown bolder, darting about among Myranda and the others again, more with curiosity than hostility. Grustim kept his hand tight about a knife and his back to Garr's chest.

"If these creatures attempt to attack us again, by my word, I shall slice each one in half," he seethed.

"It won't come to that," Myranda said.

"Curious, from their behavior, I would have thought their war chief was some sort of leader, but he's done none of the speaking. I wonder if their society has anything resembling diplomacy, or even a true hierarchy of leadership," Deacon said.

"There must be some level of leadership and discipline. That level of combat coordination requires training, and training requires leaders," Grustim said.

One of the fairies, who had been investigating Myn and Garr with the same wonder and awe that Freet and Shah had upon being introduced, suddenly pointed and cried something out. The fairies erupted into a frenzy, filling the air with the buzzing of wings and the trilling of tiny voices.

"What is happening, Shah?" Myranda asked.

"They saw the boxes and they're yelling something about being kidnapped. I guess they tell stories about what the elves do down south. They're all shouting," Shah fretted, more than a bit frazzled.

"I can get them to listen," Freet called. "Give me time!"

Myranda wavered between the feelings of helplessness and frustration at the thought that, for the moment, these rather chaotic creatures were their best chance at finding Ivy and determining the degree to which the D'Karon had infiltrated the North Crescent. The fate of so many hinged upon this information, and they were at the mercy of a language barrier and a tribe of creatures who were the definition of flighty.

Though the fairies were getting noisier by the moment, none were brandishing their thorns or otherwise acting in a threatening manner. Myranda flashed briefly to her time in Entwell, and Ayna's proclivities when arguing with the other master wizards.

"Once a fairy, always a fairy," she muttered.

Freet was making *some* progress, so Myranda held her tongue and hoped for some measure of order to be restored, but it would take some time. The whole tribe was flitting and darting about now, with the exception of those flanking the war chief and a few scattered among the lower branches.

Myranda gazed at the stationary fairies. The solders seemed as hearty and healthy as one could expect for their race, but the others seemed different. They had sallow expressions, withered physiques and wilted wings. They were the only of the fairies who didn't wear the thorny armor. Strands of gray wove through their hair, though they seemed too youthful to have earned them. The specific nature of their diminished state was hauntingly familiar.

"Freet, ask what is wrong with these fairies here," Myranda said. Her voice was unheard amid the shouting. "Freet, this could be important," she repeated, raising her voice.

Still she was unheard. Myn drew in a breath.

"*Stop,*" the dragon bellowed.

Though the fairies did not understand the word, nothing spoken with that level of power and authority could be ignored. Silence descended upon them in the wake of the echoing command.

"Freet, these fairies here. What happened to them?" Myranda said quickly.

He asked. "They tried and failed to become the… bugs," he reported moments later.

"The ones that help the Children? How does it happen?"

The answer was longer this time.

"They aren't strong enough to carry one of the gems. They failed the test against the gem in the dry place," he finally explained.

"A thir crystal…" Deacon murmured. "It would stand to reason. It would take a very special fairy to withstand more than a few moments in contact with a D'Karon gem. They are intrinsically mystical but don't necessarily have the strength of will to resist being sapped dry of their strength."

"Ask if they can take me to the gem."

"They won't. They say it is for allies only. A secret of the Children of Whatever."

"If we can cure these fairies, the weakened ones, will that prove us to be allies?" Deacon offered.

"They say it cannot be done," Freet said. "They are the weak ones. Each will be dead in weeks. Their fate is sealed."

"But if we can do it, will they take us to the dry place to see the gem? Will we be allies?" Myranda repeated.

"… They say we will all be allies if we do that impossible thing."

Myranda nodded. She thrust her staff into the soft earth of the forest floor and stepped to one of the branches where the weakened fairies were resting. Her outstretched hand frightened several of them, causing them to scurry or flutter away from her. One was either too brave or too weary to flee. The ailing creature stepped from the branch to Myranda's hand. She was practically weightless, underweight even for someone her size. Myranda carried her carefully to the staff and set her atop it.

The fairy sat and looked almost defiantly at Myranda as the wizard raised her hands to either side of the crystal. There was an air of resignation to the creature, the sense that she'd come to terms with her plight and there was nothing more for her to fear. Myranda shut her eyes and looked upon the tiny thing instead with her mind's eye. It was barely a glimmer amid far brighter embers, a soul drained of strength. To a trained mind, healthy spirits felt like flames of various sizes. Some were roaring blazes, like Myn or Deacon. Others were like a cozy fire in a hearth. Even the weakest was like a candle, casting some light and some warmth upon those nearby. This poor creature felt like a point of cold and darkness.

Myranda let some of her own strength flow into the gem, focusing and clarifying it. She could not simply force the magic into the creature's soul. She could merely provide the nourishment her soul so badly needed and allow it to restore itself. When she'd done what she could do, she opened her eyes, watched, and waited.

At first there was little evidence of recovery, but the mere chance of it was enough to keep even the most scatterbrained of the fairies watching intently. When the change came, it came first in her wings. They straightened and strengthened, their wilted sag replaced with a much healthier sturdiness. The fairy stood and held out her hands, watching their drawn, shriveled skin recover. Her sunken features became plump and healthy again. A sparkle and liveliness came to her once-dim eyes.

It was really a wonder to behold. Fairies quite literally lived and died on the strength of their magic. A fairy with little mystic affinity might only live a few years. One with a strong soul and proper training could live longer than a human.

Myranda shut her eyes again and focused on the fairy's spirit. It was burning bright now. Not as strong as the others, but vastly improved. The point of light darted upward. Myranda opened her eyes to find the little creature face-to-face with her, buzzing in the air with the unsteady but enthusiastic expression of someone taking their first steps after being bedridden for too long.

It was clear, even now, that a toll had been taken, but the only thing that truly set her apart from the others was the lingering streak of gray in her hair. She flitted toward the branches, where some of the healthier fairies buzzed around her, trilling with glee. Then she flitted back and grabbed Myranda by the fingers, tugging her desperately toward a branch where several of the other ailing fairies sat.

Deacon stepped forward as well. He set his focusing gem in the crook of a tree branch and a pair of weakened fairies climbed atop it. Freet and Shah flitted over to Myranda, whose staff had become the eager roost of three more of the ailing fairies. The healthier residents of the tribe were flying rings around her, trilling and shouting at the tops of their lungs.

"They say you are all friends of the tribe. They shall be your eyes and ears from now on, and will help in any way that will not injure their other allies. But only if you can cure *all* of the weak ones," Freet said.

Myranda shook her head a bit. She could already feel the weight of a single restoration, and there were many more to be done. It didn't matter. If this was what was necessary to take the next step toward finding her friend, then so be it. She would not fail.

#

Two hours later, Myranda and the others approached their destination. The Bramblebreeze fairies, as Freet had taken to calling them, were all on the mend, and the rescue of so many of their kind had completely eliminated any hint of the fear and hostility they'd shown toward the group. Now Myn had acquired a veritable crown of fairies among her horns. No less than a dozen of them had joined Freet and Shah there. Sheer persistence and stubbornness had even worn down Garr's willingness to chase them away from his own brow. But the goodwill they'd earned was not without its cost.

Deacon, at Myranda's request, sat in front of her while the rode. At first he'd been confused, but the reason soon became clear. She was terribly fatigued from the restorations of their new friends. Far more so than he or she had expected. If not for her tight grip around his waist, she might easily have been tipped from Myn's back. The dragon, always mindful of Myranda's needs, walked smoothly and slowly as they traveled, the better to keep her in place.

"Myranda, there are any number of things that could be causing this weariness, but it is crucial that you treat it with all proper respect. It could be as simple as an unfavorable affinity with local spirits. This *is* the first time either of us has traveled this far from the place of our birth and training. The nature of the land and its mystic makeup can often produce strange effects. But it could be more sinister. A D'Karon curse, a withering disease. It could be dire."

"Deacon, I don't care *how* dire it is. Until we have Ivy back, I will push myself as hard as circumstances require."

Deacon was silent for a few moments. Then Myranda felt the calm, steady influence of his will upon her, sweeping her for injury in the same way they had searched Myn for ailments after she was poisoned.

"No," Myranda said. "Save your strength for other things."

"What harm is there in trying to learn more?"

"We need at least one of us to be alert and refreshed. If I need your help, I will ask for it. Your time would be better spent focusing on the task at hand. Search for Ivy; contact Ether and see what she's found. Craft some means of speaking directly to the fairies. I am the least of our concerns."

"… As you wish," Deacon said.

"Here, here! The dry place. This is where they say the gem is," Shah said.

She needn't have troubled herself with pointing it out. The D'Karon influence upon the place was subtle but unmistakable. A single gnarled tree stood at the center of a dense cluster of thorn bushes. It had died long ago, and the bushes around it were all either dead or a twisted shadow of their natural state. The tree had a small knothole some distance up from the ground, and it was smoldering with violet light.

The recently restored fairies shrank from the sight of it, but the rest beamed with pride, as though it was some manner of monument they'd worked hard to erect.

"They say you may look, but you may not touch. That is reserved only for the Children of Whatever," Freet said.

"Very well. Myn, if you would? Pardon me, please," Deacon said.

He climbed to Myn's neck. When she approached the tree and craned her neck, Deacon caused a flurry of departing fairies by climbing to her head.

"What does it look like?" Myranda called to him.

"Quite well done… but not of D'Karon make, I don't think."

"Not of D'Karon make? I wasn't aware anyone but the D'Karon could create those vile things."

"The secrets of the techniques are buried deep within their writings. Very selfishly protected. I only just discovered them recently, and we've got access to the general's personal collections." He raised his crystal and watched as the glow intensified. "Interesting…"

"What is it?"

"Evidence of their flawed make. They aren't as greedy as their genuine counterparts." He took his crystal away, and the glow faded. "And they do not hold to their stolen power as tightly either."

"What does that mean for us?"

"It means they likely can't be overfilled and made to burst in that way. They simply can't consume energies to that degree. But it also means they never truly stop drinking in the power. Even when filled they still wick energy away from what surrounds them. It explains how a single gem could have damaged this tree without anyone draining it so that it can feed again. They are like a rain barrel with a leak, always making room enough for the next shower. In the short term, in small quantities, it wouldn't make much of a difference. But on the scale of years, and in any reasonable quantity, this would have a *pronounced* effect on the landscape at least, and likely the people if they did not exercise extreme care."

Myranda turned to Freet. "Ask if they know of any other places that are dry like this."

Freet trilled to them. The answers came amid a flurry of anxious trills and uncertain looks.

"Slow down. Not so fast," Freet said. "They're arguing…"

The twittering and whistling became heated, then a single voice spoke up with authority. Freet translated.

"They say there's something they call the New Place. It is one of the stories. None of the fairies here remember a time before it was here, but it is said they… it is said *it* appeared one day. A distant patch of forest that became dry in a single day. They have been told by the Children of Whatever they must watch it closely, and to tell them if any enemies find the place."

"Will they lead us there?"

"She says… she says you are allies to the fairies, but they do not know if you are allies to the Children of Whatever. They can show you, but they will have to tell the Children of Whatever that you went to that place."

"How will they tell the Children?"

"… The war chief can use the gem to send a message."

"So be it. The Aluall know we are coming regardless. If they send more people for us, we will be ready for them. Every run-in we have with them is another chance to capture and question one of them. Tell them we agree."

"What do you hope to find in the other place blighted by the D'Karon gems?" Grustim asked.

"Something. Anything. If they've arranged for it to be watched, there must be something to find. And even if not, if going there allows us to lure them into another attack, we know their tricks now. Time is running out, Grustim. I know it. Something is happening…"

Chapter 9

Reyce peered down at the icy mountains drawing steadily closer. The mere sight of them turned his stomach, and not due to the dizzying height. These were the mountains where, until their assault upon Treadforge, he had taken the greatest chance and made the most regrettable concession to the safety of his people. It was here that he had enlisted the aid of the dwarfs.

Dwarfs felt no differently about malthropes than any of the other races. If he had come to them seeking aid, or even simple peace, it likely would have meant bloodshed. But the gifts of the D'Karon gave him a means to approach without revealing his race. The might of Boviss gave him power enough not to be ignored. That meant he could take advantage of the one thing that would blind a dwarf to all else. Gold.

A familiar stretch of mountain came into view. Once one had seen it, there was no mistaking it. Seven stone statues had been carved into the landscape. They were truly massive, rivaling the height of the tallest castles and built with the stout, powerful stature of a dwarf. The center dwarf was the largest of all, and was seated atop a throne the size of a cathedral.

As the ground neared, Reyce lessened the strength of the stealth enchantments upon him. He allowed Boviss to become visible. Having the dragon looming over a negotiation helped to keep it short and favorable. He allowed an indistinct shade of his form to become visible as well. Not enough for his malthrope nature to be known, but enough for a conversation to take place.

Boviss dropped down at the feet of the statue, hard enough to shake frost from its beard. Reyce stepped from his back and set his eyes on a door half-buried in snow in the base of the throne. There was no need to call. If a dragon touching down on one's doorstep was not enough to summon someone to the door, nothing was.

Reyce hunched his shoulders against the biting cold. Den seldom had weather cold enough to warrant the kind of clothing suitable for the mountains, and he certainly didn't intend to spend enough time away from his people to have heavier clothing made. His fur would do.

"Who is that knocking at my door unannounced?" muttered a gruff voice from within.

The door shuddered and pulled open. A dwarf, short and fat even for his people, emerged. He was heaped with bearskins and topped with a fur cap. Coupled with his beard and bushy eyebrows, a bulbous nose and the gleam of hidden eyes were the only bits of him not hidden by hair.

"Ah. This one. The boy with the lizard and no face. What brings you to the court of the Seven Brothers?"

"The time has come," Reyce said.

One of the massive eyebrows raised. "By my count, you're a good few moons short."

"Plans have changed. We need to move now."

"Then we need to talk about the gold."

"You have been paid."

"You coming here today, months before we agreed? That's not part of the plan. And when you change the plan, you reopen negotiations."

"This change costs you nothing."

"You're right about that, but we are talking about what it'll cost *you*. Call it… my weight, twice again, in gold. And a nice ruby I think, for the missus."

"Why should it cost me an ounce more? You need only drop the tablet now instead of later."

"Because you pulled me out of bed. Because I'm freezing my nose off here talking to you, searing my eyes in the sun. Because I *decided*. And because you don't have a choice."

Boviss lowered his head, his permanent grin smoldering with the beginnings of a fiery breath.

"I do not like the dwarfs," Boviss rumbled. "They riddle my mountains with their tunnels. They claim my gold for their own. You have given them my hoard. Perhaps I shall eat this one as compensation…"

"You can try it, lizard. You'll get a mouthful of dwarfish iron, and your keeper here won't get what he paid for. And if there were anyone but me that could give it, we wouldn't be talking. So you've got your price. Agree to it and I'll drop the tablet. If not, whatever it is you're looking to get done can wait."

"You vile, greedy—"

"Sling all the insults you want, dragon keeper. But I am the one who wrote out the tablet. I am the one who knows what you're up to. So you'd best thank whatever dark god you worship that I'm as greedy as I am, because if your plan doesn't work, it'll mean war for me just as surely as you." He rolled his head, cracking his neck. "Then, I'm protected by the brothers. So that's no concern. But there is the principle of it."

"… You shall have your gold."

"And to think I doubted you had a proper head on your shoulders. Now, normally I would demand payment before delivery of services, but this payment is *for* expediency, isn't it? And by now I think we both understand just how much of a fool idea it would be to promise the keeper of the Seven Brothers a payment and not deliver." He scratched his head. "Now, I wouldn't be doing my diligence if I didn't ask you to think this over good and hard. Once I drop the tablet, there's no going back until the deed is done. No room for second thoughts."

Reyce had almost hoped he would be given this chance to back away. Until now, there had been little life lost. He and his people had spilled blood, and planned to spill more. But nothing could compare to what would begin when the dwarf fulfilled his end of the bargain. A large part of him, one he had pushed down and attempted to silence, screamed for him to abandon this, to toe the line of peace and decency, to find another way. As though he could hear that voice, Boviss offered the opposing view.

"Your people live or die by this moment," he rumbled. "Do not shrink from your responsibilities. Destroy your foes or be destroyed by them."

Reyce tightened his fists. "The decision has been made."

The dwarf eyed Boviss before addressing Reyce's hidden form. "Seems to me you might not be the keeper here… Bah. That's not for me to bother myself about. Off with you. Our boy needs room to stretch his legs."

"How long will it take?"

"Not less than a week to get where he's going. Not more than three to get back. At least, if my grandfather is to be believed. Best to give me my payment before he takes his seat again, or he's liable to find a new place to visit."

"Understood."

The dwarf disappeared into the doorway. Reyce turned to Boviss. The dragon looked coldly upon him, fire spilling from between his teeth as his grin took on a more self-satisfied tone.

"You have done well."

"I have set in motion something that will end more lives than any battle in my lifetime…" Reyce said, the gravity of his decision not lost on him.

"In your lifetime, perhaps. But not in mine. We are hunters. We cannot fear blood. Blood is how we feed."

Reyce climbed to his back, and the beast launched into the air. He rose into the sky, nearly to the clouds, then spread his wings to catch the mountain winds. He hung in the air and watched as a tiny figure emerged from a passage in the mountain near the seated statue's head.

"Let us go. We have work to do."

A wisp of smoke wafted from his nostrils. "No."

"Boviss, remember who you serve."

"It is because I serve you that I shall not permit you to turn away from this sight. You, who have made a weapon of me, should give this moment its due respect. For you now wield the only weapon greater than I."

Reyce, with little recourse, squinted into the rushing wind and watched the mountains below. The figure approached the head of statue. Reyce knew that in the dwarf's hand was a bronze tablet. It was etched with simple instructions written in ancient Dwarfish. He held his breath. The figure hurried away, having dropped the tablet into a slot in the statue's head. The mountain began to tremble. Layers of ice and snow, accumulated over decades if not centuries, fractured and tumbled away. A deep, fiery glow smoldered in the statue's eyes. Joints ground and crackled. Boulders sloughed away from the mountainside and tumbled down the slope. The statue climbed to its feet. It was a thing of grim awe. Nothing so large should ever move of its own accord, and yet there it stood, sturdier and taller than the mightiest fort. It turned to the south and took a step, shaking the slope and sending a rolling thunder through the countryside.

Reyce tried not to think about the havoc it would cause. A part of him had hoped the stories had been false, that the Seven Brothers were nothing but statues and that this fearsome working of dwarfish magic would never stand. But now it stood. Now it had its orders. There was no going back. It would take the whole of the elven army and the full attention of its many wizards and mystics to keep the statue at bay. The elves were powerful. And their agents, the outsiders combing North Crescent for Den and those it protected, were powerful too. Together, perhaps they could turn the golem away. But not before the rest of the plan could play out. With this act, a kingdom would fall.

Finally, the dragon had watched its fill of the awesome sight and shifted to the south and west. Reyce must return to Den. There was little time to move the rest of the pieces into position. To fail now would mean… No. He would not fail now…

#

The war chief himself served as their guide as Myranda and the others made their way toward the so-called New Place. Myranda never would have injured their pride by suggesting it, but she suspected that sending the war chief along was a way for the fairies to give them more time before the Aluall would appear. The war chief was the one who could use the gem to alert them, and thus he could not tell of their arrival until he returned. The other fairies were initially reluctant to leave their place among the horns of the dragons, but with each step away from their home grove, they became more uneasy. Eventually, only the war chief, Shah, and Freet remained with them.

It was a relatively short journey to find the New Place, but the trip was through forest so dense and lush it would have taken them weeks to find it without guidance. The surrounding woods had done their very best to reclaim the place. Even viewed from above, the creeping canopy of nearby healthy trees would have all but swallowed up the damaged section. But at ground level, the scars of the ravenous D'Karon magic were horribly apparent.

Deacon and Myranda hopped down to investigate. Myranda's mind and body had largely recovered along the way, and she was eager to contribute.

"No telling just how long this place has been free of the magic, but it must be years. Ten at least. Perhaps as many as fifty," Deacon said.

Myranda crouched and leaned heavily upon her staff to run her fingers through the soil.

"All that time and the shoots and weeds are only just beginning to grow again," she said. "The D'Karon gems must have been drinking in the strength of the land for ages to do this damage."

"Something lived here," Grustim said. "A great many things."

"Yes," Myranda agreed. "These furrows and pits. The way they are spaced so regularly, and dug to the same depth. And I see timbers here… I've never seen a home like this, though."

Garr lowered his head and sniffed at the ground. Myn plodded over to his side and imitated. She pawed at a bit of ground, then dug deeply with her claws to bring up some ancient, powdery bone that had been buried a fair distance beneath the surface. She and Garr dug a bit more to turn up a seemingly endless amount. Grustim selected one of the longer bones and turned it over in his hands.

"Prey animals," Grustim said. "But not butchered.… No. This *has* been butchered. I can see the clean cut here, but this has certainly been gnawed. They've all been gnawed. Perhaps they kept hounds…"

Myranda looked about and tried to put the pieces together, but something at the edge of her mind nagged at her. It wasn't intuition, or any sense she could identify, but something nearby almost called to her. She shut her eyes and let her mind ease outward. Mostly, she felt the stale deadness of D'Karon-ravaged land. But there was something else. Not a spirit. Indeed, spirits seemed to have abandoned this place. It was something of that ilk, though. Something beyond the physical. She shifted her focus outward and held out her hand. In her palm, her mark smoldered in her mind's eye. It was always a point of focus, a brighter part of her own soul, but it was pulsing a bit, glowing more powerfully to an almost imperceptible degree. She stepped forward, navigating the remains of what had certainly been a village at one time. As the others investigated in their own way, she followed this strange feeling. It led her past the edge of the more obvious features of the former village. She paced a short distance. Behind her, she could feel that Myn and the fairies were following, but keeping their distance as if they might somehow foul the scent if they came too near.

She stumbled, catching herself with her staff and allowing herself to slip from her trance. The edge of her boot had caught in a slight mound of earth ahead of her. Myn came closer and sniffed at it while Myranda scanned the forest floor around it. Not far from the mound was a large, flat stone. It seemed out of place, too rounded to have come from anywhere but a river. As Myranda flipped it over to investigate, Myn began to paw at the mound.

Myranda's eyes widened. "Myn, don't!"

The dragon quickly raised her paw and looked to the stone. The underside was etched with care, tracing out simple letters. A name.

"These are graves…" she said.

Deacon stepped up to the edge of the graveyard.

"Interesting. I've never seen a graveyard so near to trees and yet so near to the surface," he said.

Whatever power was leading Myranda, it was somewhere within the graveyard. She stepped lightly, avoiding the mounds and flat stones. Ahead, there was a mighty tree that still grew strong and healthy despite the withered nature of those around it. She approached it and knelt down. There were three graves, clearly in a place of honor. One seemed considerably older than the others, but all three were traced out with stones, unlike the others, and the facedown grave markers were cut and polished. Myranda gently flipped over the stone of the oldest grave.

"Sorrel…" she said.

When she reached for the grave marker of one of the other graves, her hand tingled and the subdued sense that she'd followed this far became stronger, more acute. These were the graves she was meant to find.

"Reyna. Wren," Myranda said, turning over the stones one by one. "I think… I don't know how to put it to words… I can feel the same sort of power lingering here that I searched for when I was trying to join the Chosen. It isn't the same… But I think these two graves… I think Reyna and Wren may have been of a Chosen bloodline."

"Chosen? Fascinating…" Deacon said. "Their connection to the divine must have been extremely strong for such an aura to linger so long after death. From the way the roots have grown, they must have been buried when the tree was much younger."

"Look here," Grustim called.

He and Garr had approached the same tree from behind. Graves spread out around it like the petals of a flower, and one of them had been churned a bit more by the tree's growth than the others. It had pushed some of the bones to the surface. Most seemed broadly human. But the skull was certainly not.

"It looks canine. Or… vulpine," Deacon said, realization in his voice.

"This is a malthrope," Myranda said. "*These* are malthropes. Malthropes of a Chosen bloodline," Myranda said. "These are relatives of Lain. They *must* be."

"D'Karon influence, decades old. The presence of those worthy of being Chosen far from the site of the war. The questions this raises—" Deacon said.

"Can wait," Myranda added. "We aren't looking for questions, we are looking for answers, and this has provided some. If the Aluall are malthropes, it explains much. They have much the same reputation, and even without magic they would be peerless at remaining unseen."

"A valuable discovery perhaps, but one that is of little help in our search," Grustim said.

"Perhaps not…" Deacon said. "Forgive me. I prefer not to present a theory that relies so heavily upon speculation and supposition but—"

"Speak," Myranda urged. "A guess of yours is nearly as good as a certainty from someone else."

"If we suppose that these *are* descendants of Lain, then they are touched with the divine, perhaps more strongly than even you or Myn. And if the Aluall of today are indeed descended from those who once lived here, then that divinity has been bred among them. Look around us. We know that the D'Karon magic is central to their culture. I cannot imagine that any, even those touched with the divine, could have avoided it."

"And unless they were born with the mark, then utilizing D'Karon magics, even serving a D'Karon cause, would not have killed them," Myranda reasoned, following his logic.

"You and I have become intimately familiar with what happens when D'Karon magic and the divinely Chosen are mixed. It is like tinder and flame."

"Of course!" Myranda realized. "Until now we've been searching for D'Karon magic, which is devastatingly difficult to detect if properly cast, or trying to detect Ivy, who could similarly be hidden by that magic. But if we were to search for the conflict between the divine and the D'Karon, not just as it might apply to Ivy but as it might apply to other lesser examples of a Chosen bloodline…"

"We could easily have missed it before. We've focused so intently upon what we *should* have been seeing. We could easily have disregarded clues as subtle as this, things we didn't know to watch for."

The Crescents

"Enough talk. We have a new thread. Let us pull it and see what unravels."

#

Ether drifted across the landscape, spread as thinly as she dared, in hopes of catching even a glimpse of something out of place, or a hint of Ivy's power. Her consciousness spread for miles, but that was still but a pinhole's view of the sprawling continent, and a thorough search required her to move slowly and deliberately. The other Chosen were conducting their search to the east, so she focused on the western shore. What opened below her was a veritable feast of sights and sounds. There was flora and fauna here that was utterly unlike the creatures of the Northern Alliance. This was a place wholly untouched by civilization of any sort, unspoiled from the dawn of the world. Experiencing nature in the absence of society stirred distant memories of her earliest times, the time not so long after the gods had crafted her. It was a time when *everything* was fresh and wild. A time when chaos reigned, sculpting things according to its own whims. As her mind dwelled upon the distant past, she finally felt something, a twist of magic that certainly was not inherent to the land. She coalesced into her more focused windy form and approached.

Even the sharpest eyes and keenest mind could have looked upon the small cluster of trees not far from the beach and seen nothing of note. Prior to her rather frustrating stay in Grandwinn, Ether might not have noticed it herself. But the trees here, a silver-barked variety present on both North and South Crescent, were not entirely as nature decreed. The residual magic was impossibly faint, its effects almost entirely wiped out from centuries without maintenance. Nonetheless, to Ether's eye, these trees bore the unmistakable touch of elven architecture. The branches curled toward each other. Had they received a few more years of gentle guidance, they might have interwoven to form the roof of a grand hall. Tiny indents in the surface of a stout-trunked tree were the abandoned beginnings of a doorway.

Ether shifted from wind to stone and knelt beside one of the trees. She pressed her fingertips into the hard earth as easily as the surface of a lake. A curl of will caused the ground around her to shudder and tremble. As the soil shifted, fragments of rough-hewn wood and bits of stone that had seen the touch of a mason's chisel emerged from below. This had been an elven town, one well established enough to have been in the progress of moving beyond its brick and timber infancy into the more harmonious form present in the more established parts of Sonril. That implied it had been *years* old when it had suddenly been left behind by its residents.

She continued to sweep her mind over the place, but hundreds of years of nature had swallowed up and eased away nearly any evidence of what the place had once been. There was little of it left, certainly not enough to provide any meaningful information… But there was something *else* out of place. Her stony fingers crackled against a thin layer of glossy black stone, hidden a fair distance beneath the surface. She scooped up a fragment of it. It was glassy and smooth, entirely unlike any of the other stone. This sort of rock didn't belong here. It took the heat of a forge to produce stone like this. A cooking fire, even a forest fire, couldn't leave a fragment this size behind, let alone what appeared to be an inch-thick layer. That sort of quantity was the work of fiery mountains. Something had come to this place and baked the earth to a molten state. Even *she* would have to expend a great deal of her strength to manage such a feat.

Something truly terrible had happened here…

Chapter 10

Nehri paced about in her hut, eyes flicking back and forth between the sky and the crystal she'd taken from the shrine that morning. Reyce was late. Days late. Again. She was not concerned about his safety. No one in the village was better able to take care of himself in the dangerous world beyond Den's borders. But every moment he spent with Boviss was trouble. The dragon had been indispensable throughout their history, it was true. He had yet to betray his loyalty—or at least his servitude—to the malthropes, but the hatred boiling beneath the surface was unmistakable. His words dripped with manipulation. Nehri worried Reyce might bend to his whims. She worried he already had.

A curious sound outside briefly tugged her from her concerns. It was a lilting melody played upon a flute. The pleasant tune floated softly through the village. There was nothing strange about that. Many of the children liked to fashion and play flutes from the reeds by the river. But she'd never heard this melody before, and it was being played so beautifully. She stepped from her hut and looked toward the source. A small collection of children had gathered around the door to the hut where Ivy was being kept. Some danced and capered about to the complex melody. Others simply sat and watched as Ivy crouched in the doorway of her hut, merrily playing the flute.

As Nehri approached, Ivy's eyes drifted to her and she quickly took the flute from her mouth and pushed it into the hands of the nearest child, gently whispering and pointing. The children turned and, upon seeing Nehri, scattered. Nehri took two long strides and caught the flute-bearing child by the arm, then held out her hand. The child sheepishly offered up the flute before scampering off.

"Please don't be angry with them," Ivy said as Nehri approached the hut. "They were curious. And when I saw one of them had a flute, I *may* have coaxed him into letting me try it. It was my fault."

"There are worse things than sharing an instrument or a song," Nehri said.

She glanced behind her as the children slowly edged closer to the hut. Technically, Ivy was a prisoner. It was made clear to the others in the village that she was not to move about freely until further notice, and those normally charged with patrolling the edge of Den instead kept an eye on her hut. But Ivy had yet to attempt to leave, or in any way disobey or misbehave. This, coupled with the fact that they'd never truly had need for a prison or to hold prisoners, left the villagers somewhat uncertain of how to deal with Ivy's current status.

"I'm not accustomed to my own people running when they see me," Nehri said, looking to the child she'd taken the flute from.

"I'm a bad influence, I guess," Ivy said. "I couldn't help it. It's getting awfully lonely in here, and it's been so long since I've properly played a flute. The ones back home just don't work for malthropes. They're made for a different sort of mouth. I'd given up on them. But these work perfectly."

"Of course they do," Nehri said, admiring the crude but adequate flute the child had fashioned. "We've made this place for ourselves. This is the one place were things work as they should for us. Which is why it is so important your friends and those they work for not be allowed to disrupt it. If Den falls, then there will be nowhere left for us."

"Den can survive without making enemies of my friends, Nehri."

Nehri considered the flute for a moment. "Perhaps it is time we discussed it. I have ruminated upon the mark you bear. It does seem that only those faithful to the D'Karon teachings are injured by it. I have tested it both against Boviss and, with great care, against a child who had not yet pledged her faith. There is no doubt in my mind that its power is directed wholly against those enemies of the D'Karon. But I refuse to believe that this is evidence that the D'Karon are evil. Their teachings and protection have done too much for us for me to believe that. Neither do I believe that this mark labels you as our enemy. Though it is possible your behavior may be a ruse, my heart and mind tell me that your intentions are good, however misguided and ill-informed they may be. But that does not change the fact that your friends have not been turned away. I have received a message that they have reached Old Den. And since then, they have been moving slowly but steadily in our direction. They, therefore, represent a terrible threat to Den and its future. They must be stopped… And I believe I am willing to face them personally if that is what it takes."

"Yes! Please do! Just promise me you will approach them in peace. I assure you they will do the same…. Except maybe Ether. Be careful of Ether. But for Myranda and the others, you just have to *meet* them. Show them who you are! Let them *talk* to you. I'm sure you'll see that they don't mean you any harm."

"My hopes are low. But if there is one chance in a thousand that my words and actions may keep them from coming here, then it is worth the risk. I will leave immediately. There may not be much time left."

"Wait! Do you have paper? Anything to write or paint on? And something to write or paint *with*?"

"I'm sure someone can find something for you, but—"

"I need to send it *with* you," Ivy said. "If they know I'm alive, that I *vouch* for you, then they'll be sure to listen."

Nehri called through the doorway. Notta approached. After a short exchange, the other vixen hurried off. She returned in short order with some rough sheets of parchment and a dense bit of charcoal.

Ivy snatched them eagerly and went to work.

"Quickly," Nehri said.

"I'll be quick as a flash," Ivy said, glancing in Nehri's direction and tracing out a few basic shapes. "And when I'm through, there will be no doubt in their mind that I'm alive and well…"

#

Nehri squeezed her gem tightly and let its strength flow into her. She scolded herself for using one of the precious charged gems for this purpose. How many times had she given Reyce an earful for using a gem he didn't need to? But the outsiders, the friends of Ivy, had come so far in such little time. If she trusted her own endurance, they might be too near Den for her to hope to turn them away. It was for the best. The D'Karon magic pushed away the fatigue. It sped her movements and wiped away any trace of her travel. Under its influence, she was swifter than any horse and didn't so much as cast a shadow or raise a cloud of dust in her wake.

Sprinting in such a way gave her little chance to put her sharp eyes or sensitive nose to work to attempt to locate the outsiders, but it seemed they had no interest in avoiding detection. As she'd suspected, they were moving in a perfectly straight line from where they'd last been spotted. The whole party had mounted their dragons and flew slowly and low to the ground. The green dragon was fearsome and armored, smaller by far than Boviss, but with his thick scales augmented with iron. The red dragon was a similar size, and though unequipped, she carried two wizards, each with gems burning bright. The color of their magic was different, an eerie white-blue rather than the deep violet of the D'Karon workings. She felt a flutter of revulsion that they would flaunt something other than D'Karon magic in North Crescent, but she forced those thoughts away. If she were to have a chance at getting them to listen to reason, she mustn't approach them with anger or hate in her heart. She was a priestess. It was her purpose to right those who had gone wrong, to lead them in the proper direction. You cannot take someone by the hand if you first clench your fists.

She slid to a stop and took a breath. If they were the trackers she knew them to be, she wouldn't need to do much to get their attention. Sure enough, she'd only just begun to ease the enchantment concealing her when the heads of both dragons shifted in her direction. They angled their wings and dove toward her with a nimbleness and agility she had never seen Boviss demonstrate.

Nehri steeled herself and allowed her many protections to drop away. As soon as the gem's commands were gone, it hungrily drew upon her soul, but she warded herself from its hunger and set the gem at her feet. It might be the last mistake she would make, but she was determined to face these people with empty hands and an open mind.

The dragons landed on either side of her, eyes intense and teeth bared. Their riders hopped down, weapons held defensively. Two wizards, a male and a female, and a male warrior. All human, or at least as she'd imagined humans must be. This was the first she had personally seen of their kind.

To have them look upon her, to have them *see* her, made Nehri feel like an insect suddenly cast into the light. She wanted to snatch the gem again, to hide away as she always had. But the time for that was past. She held her head high and waited.

The warrior had the wary look of a man ready to strike her down in a heartbeat. The green dragon seemed stoic and measured. But the others… they behaved in a way that she hadn't anticipated. They were cautious, yes. Their defenses were high, but the female in particular seemed to have a look of wonder tempering her expression.

"You *are* a malthrope…" Myranda said. "I almost didn't believe it could be so."

Deacon looked to the gem at her feet. "And she indeed makes use of D'Karon magic."

"At this moment, I do not. And I am assured by your friend Ivy that you are reasonable, that if I do not act, neither shall you."

"Where is Ivy?" Myranda said, her expression and tone sharp.

"She is safe. If you will permit me, she provided me with a message for you," Nehri said.

"Slowly," Grustim warned.

Nehri slipped her fingers into her robes and produced the parchment. Myranda stepped forward to accept it. The "message" Ivy had composed was a simple but exquisite sketch of Nehri herself. There were only two words beneath it. *Trust her*. She hadn't left anything resembling a signature or other mark to identify herself, but Myranda and Deacon both nodded after a single glance.

"No mistaking her style," Myranda said.

Myn stepped forward and glared at Nehri. She held her ground. The dragon took a deep whiff, then plopped down on her haunches and locked her eyes on the priestess. It didn't feel like an act of intimidation or threat, but it was a loud and clear statement of her distrust and disapproval. If the dragon's opinion was any indication, this was going to be an uphill struggle. A pair of fairies between the dragon's horns buzzed down and orbited Nehri, joyful to have found another malthrope.

"So many friends of fairies in North Crescent!" Shah trilled.

"I imagine we both have a great many questions." Myranda stepped back and loosened a strap holding a bundle of firewood that Myn had been carrying. "I am Myranda. This is Deacon. That's Myn, and those are Grustim and Garr."

The fairies took it upon themselves to do their own introductions.

"I am Shah!"

"And I am Freet!"

"I imagine we will very shortly be joined by Ether," Myranda said, concluding the introductions.

Nehri took a half step backward. "I was warned about Ether."

Myranda smiled. "Probably wise on Ivy's part. We will be sure she behaves. And your name?"

"… Nehri. High Priestess of Den."

"Are you hungry? In my observation, meetings like this are better held around a warm fire and a hot meal."

"I would prefer to keep it brief," Nehri said. "You are outsiders, and you are not welcome in North Crescent. I respectfully ask that you leave this place, and leave Ivy with us where she belongs. To do otherwise can only end in sorrow for you."

"I am afraid it won't be as simple as that," Myranda said. "If you want our cooperation, you'll need to give us more than orders. We shall need answers, and assurances. Are your people the Aluall?"

"That is the name the elves have chosen to apply. As it kept them at bay, and wary of us, we saw no need to correct it."

"And did your people attack the villages near the isthmus?"

Nehri stared at Myranda evenly, but did not answer.

"I already know it was your people who were spying on us. And who nearly killed Myn."

"You are unwelcome in this land. Your presence here invites war," Nehri said. "You pursued our 'spy.' It was not my decision to send a wasp to aid him, but clearly that choice was a wise one. They were within their rights to defend themselves."

"I know a thing or two about war, Nehri. I've had my fill of it. And the greatest friend of war is silence. Your people attacked those villages. A watchman was killed. Not a word of warning was offered until *after* the attack. And nothing else until this moment."

"Look at me, Myranda. What elf would have listened to any words uttered by a creature such as I?"

Myranda lowered her eyes and shook her head woefully.

"There is truth to that, perhaps." She looked up. "But it does not change what has been done."

"Yes. Our people retook the land from the elves. And we spilled blood, but far less than they would have spilled of ours, and only what was absolutely necessary. If the elves could be trusted to remain south of the isthmus, no more lives would need to be lost."

Myranda arranged the wood into an orderly pile on the ground before them. Myn twisted her head just enough to huff a breath of flame upon the wood without taking her eyes off Nehri.

"You have the ears of someone who will listen now, Nehri," Myranda said, fetching some provisions and taking a seat on the ground. "Are you certain you don't want something to eat?"

Deacon took a seat beside Myranda. Myn shuffled aside to provide shade. The fairies buzzed in slow circles around Nehri, observing her with the same wonder and excitement they'd offered Ivy, though with a degree more caution. That caution visibly grew as they simultaneously glanced aside. The source of their concern became apparent as grass and brush around them fluttered in an ever-increasing unnatural breeze. A whistling form of raw, chaotic wind dropped from the sky and shifted to flesh and blood before Nehri's eyes. A fourth human, this one with the distrustful, vicious gaze she would have expected, now joined the others.

"A malthrope? So it is true." Ether's eyes drifted to the gem at Nehri's feet, and a new fury flashed through them. "And a user of D'Karon magic!"

"Calm down, Ether," Myranda said. "She was about to explain herself."

"If she must speak, let her speak of the elven settlement to the southwest," Ether said.

"The what?" Myranda said.

"I found evidence of elven magic twisting the trees near the coast, but seemingly abandoned some time ago. It, along with an apparent clash with dwarfs that the elves memorialized but seemed unwilling to acknowledge, represents the entirety of the fruits of my investigations."

"We know of the trees you speak of," Nehri said. "But if there were ever elves there, it was before our time here."

"Then tell us what you can. What you *do* know," Myranda said.

Nehri crossed her arms. "What needed to be said has been said. This is not your fight, and it is not elven land. Leave this place."

"I won't go anywhere until I hear Ivy speak with her own lips a desire to stay. And if I am to find some way to keep the elves from demanding vengeance for your attacks, I am going to need to know beyond a shadow of a doubt that your people can be trusted not to squander my efforts with *another* attack. Perhaps most pressing of all— I'll need to know about the D'Karon."

Nehri stood in silence, enduring the continued gaze of the dragon and the shapeshifter.

"Nehri," Myranda continued, "the last thing I want is to see harm come to your people. Ivy is one of my dearest friends and closest allies. I personally, and the world in general, owe a debt to another malthrope, Lain, that may never be repaid. It makes my heart *sing* to know that they aren't the last of their kind, and it makes it all the more important that we learn how to avert further war, and how to protect you from being destroyed by the D'Karon."

"The D'Karon are our saviors, not our destroyers!" Nehri asserted.

"Then tell me how. Explain to me how you came to be, and why you believe they would defend you."

Nehri recoiled at having to defend her faith, to prove to these interlopers that the patrons of her people did not mean them harm. She drew in a breath to voice her outrage, but as she did, she detected something in the air. A scent she hadn't noticed before. She looked upon Myranda with a measuring stare, then slowly took a seat. If nothing else, the moments spent here delayed further battle or danger to her people. And if a woman in Myranda's condition could find it in herself to come to this dangerous land and speak with someone who by all rights and evidence was her enemy, then perhaps she *was* owed an explanation.

Myranda offered a bit of meat. Nehri sniffed it and detected no poison, nor did she sense any dark enchantment about it.

"It began as a battle between two tribes…" she began, for the second time in as many weeks beginning the tale of her people.

#

"… And so it continues to this day," Nehri finished.

She'd told the story with care, making certain not to hint at just how near Den truly was, or the specific nature of the enchantments that protected it. Myranda listened intently, and Deacon feverishly recorded her words in his book.

Ether stepped forward. Nehri eyed her warily. The shapeshifter reached out and barely brushed the fur of her hand. She then shut her eyes as if savoring the aroma of a heavily spiced meal.

"It is true. It is woven and folded with generations of lesser beings, but Nehri has the blood of Lain in her past."

"Amazing…" Myranda said. "I never dreamed Lain might have had children. And that they could have survived and thrived. It breaks my heart to realize he never knew… And that… Forgive me if my words are unkind to those you credit with protecting you, but it is further heartbreaking to know what your loyalty to the D'Karon cost the bloodline, and nearly cost the world. Lain was Chosen. His children, their children, and so on down the bloodline could have been Chosen as well. But loyalty to the D'Karon robbed them of their right to be. It was darkly brilliant of the D'Karon, and it nearly left the world without enough Chosen to defend it from them."

"Ivy spoke of this. And she showed me the mark. You'll understand if I do not abandon my faith on the word of a few outsiders."

"Of course we understand. But I've seen where you and the others must have lived before. And I've seen how the land is barely recovering from the damage the D'Karon did."

"There is no other way. We would have been wiped out if we did not hide ourselves."

Myranda held out her hand. "Then perhaps the time has come to stop hiding yourselves."

Nehri glanced at the offered hand uncertainly. "The elves sent you here, not knowing what we are. Now if they knew, you cannot believe they would do anything less than exterminate us."

She lowered her hand. "The elves reached out to us, *including* Ivy. Things are changing. That you've killed some of their people will not go unanswered, but there is no shortage of your blood on their hands. D'Karon magic is not the answer anymore. Relying upon it is killing your people just as surely as the elves would. If you need an advocate among the elves, I will speak for you."

"First you offer your aid to our enemy. Now you offer your aid to us. How can anyone trust you?"

"My goal in life is to heal the damage of the last war and prevent the damage of the next. What I do for you and what I do for them are only to further that cause. It is the right thing to do. It is what must be done."

Nehri looked at the position of the sun. They had been speaking for some time. "Soon I shall need to return to my home," she said. "I drained the gem in my attempts to reach you before you reached my people. Do I have permission to charge it sufficiently to make the return trip?"

"As you wish," Myranda said.

Nehri took the gem in hand and felt the familiar hunger tug at her soul. With practiced focus, she choked off the flow of energy, lest it drink too deeply, but for once she allowed herself to fixate on the physical and spiritual sensation. What Myranda suggested, even if it was an impossible dream, was a world where she would never need to feel the withering touch of a D'Karon gem again. A world where the shrine would need no offerings, where lives were not shortened and the land was not weakened by the endless hunger of the gems. It was a tremendous risk, certainly. But was it really more dangerous for her people than the plan looming over them?

"Your words have the ring of sincerity, Myranda. I dearly want to believe what you say can be so. And it speaks to your dedication that you would risk searching us out despite your condition."

Myranda's expression became more serious. "My condition?"

Deacon spoke. "Myranda hasn't been feeling well. Do you have some insight into this?"

"I may not be familiar with humans, but I am a malthrope, and a priestess besides. I would be a poor example of either if I did not know the scent of a female with child."

Myranda placed her hand upon her midriff, eyes distant and expression complex. Beside her, Deacon practically threw his book aside and fumbled for his crystal.

"It's been… it must be nearly three weeks since… And the way you've been feeling…" he said.

She shut her eyes. Deacon's crystal flared. After a brief moment of analysis, Myranda opened her eyes again and looked Deacon in the eye. There was the shortest moment of tension, as though something very important had been left unsaid, but the moment passed and Deacon threw his arms around her.

"This is wonderful. This is *wonderful*!" he said.

Tears came to Myranda's eyes, and she returned his embrace. The two sobbed joyfully.

Nehri smiled, bemused that two who seemed so wise and powerful could miss something so precious. It was heartwarming to see the layers of diplomacy and negotiation dissolve into the simple joy of pair of parents learning of the blessing they had received. She had seen the same look upon the faces of her own people a hundred times over. These were humans, creatures who in her mind stood beside elves, dwarfs, and nearly all other species in their monstrous and ravenous desire to see malthropes killed. But in this way, they were the same. Perhaps in other ways as well.

"You have given me a great deal to consider, Myranda. All of you have. But even with all you have said, this is not a decision I can make alone. Too many lives hinge upon the wisdom of the choice to be made. I must return to Den. I must speak with the others of my village.

I ask that you remain here. Give me two days. Cease your searching and do not try to follow me. I shall return with my answer."

"Of course. Of course, you shall have your two days," Myranda said, her voice still thick with emotion.

The priestess clutched her gem tightly. It had not drunk its fill—doing so would have weakened her greatly—but it had borrowed enough of her strength to cast the spells she would need to return to Den before the setting of the sun. She let the spells fall into place. They did their work, fading her from visibility. The world around her shifted to the ghostly form she perceived when hidden. For a moment she lingered, waiting to see if these strange outsiders would gather their mystic paraphernalia and attempt to follow, but they merely continued to rejoice. The only exception was Grustim, who after a few seconds, voiced his concern.

"Two days gives them ample time to plan for us," he warned.

"If they choose to act, we shall act, but trust must begin somewhere," Myranda said.

Nehri turned and dashed toward home.

Trust must begin somewhere…

#

Reyce watched the sun sink in the sky as he stood outside the door of Ivy's hut. Boviss loomed at the edge of town, licking the blood of a recent kill from his chin.

"What is keeping her…?" Reyce rumbled. "If your allies have hurt her…"

"They *haven't* hurt her, because they wouldn't hurt *anyone* who didn't deserve it," Ivy said.

"It is nearly time for the ceremony. Our people are already beginning to gather."

Ivy crossed her arms. "Maybe she'll have come to her senses and there won't *be* a ceremony."

Reyce looked in the direction of the shrine. "There *shall* be a ceremony."

Voices rose and heads turned. Nehri sprinted toward the edge of the village. She'd abandoned the veil of invisibility when she'd crossed into their territory, but the violet glow of D'Karon magic accompanied her preternatural speed. The glow and the speed slipped away as Nehri approached Ivy's hut. She was dusty and winded, but her expression was unmarked by the shadow of anxiety and conflict that had hung over her for months.

"Reyce!" she called, stepping up to him. "I am relieved to find you here and see you're unhurt. You were gone far longer than you had indicated."

"There were matters that needed tending to," he snapped. "Is it true that you abandoned your village to seek out these *Chosen,* these former keepers of Ivy?"

"If I hadn't, they would have reached Den by now. Reyce, we need to discuss the assault. I realize it is an act of profound optimism to suggest it, but I believe it may not be necessary."

"The assault is not for discussion," Reyce said. "Ready yourself for the ceremony."

"Reyce, I have spoken to them. Dragons, wizards, a warrior. They even had fairies with them. They listened to me. Their ways are different than ours. They are steadfastly against the D'Karon and their teachings—but they say they are willing to stand for us. There is already no going back, after what we did to the villages to the south. But at least this way we may avoid further violence. Or perhaps we can at least delay it."

"There shall be an assault, and it shall not be delayed."

"If there is the chance that our people do not have to go into battle, then isn't it our duty as their leaders to pursue it?"

"The D'Karon will protect us. Our victory is assured."

"If we throw ourselves off a cliff, the D'Karon shall not protect us. They give us strength. They do not reward the foolhardy. Meet these people for yourself. Hear their—"

"The golem is already on the move, Nehri," he shouted.

Nehri stepped back as if struck. "Already… But we aren't nearly prepared."

"We have the weapons. We have the training."

"But we haven't got the magic yet. The plan for the assault required us to use the D'Karon portals to reach the isthmus en masse. In our current state, we won't be able to deliver *half* of our people there."

"We have the means to charge the crystals we need and hundreds more," Reyce said. "We could even prepare a gem to bring the golem to his target in hours rather than days."

"How?"

He looked to Ivy.

Nehri's expression hardened. "No… Reyce, that is not our way. Our people freely offer their strength to the shrine. Ivy has not embraced the D'Karon teachings."

"We do not have the luxury of holding fast to our beliefs anymore, Nehri. The golem is walking. It will reach South Crescent, and it shall leave a trail of devastation behind. The elves will respond. There will be war. What we do now shall decide if we survive the war or not."

"But to draw that much power from a single person. It will *kill* her. She is one of us."

"Lives were always going to be lost. We knew that when we formulated the plan. But if sacrificing an outsider means saving the rest of us, then it is a noble act and one that any malthrope should gladly perform for her people."

"At least let me talk to her. If she will do so willingly—"

"Whether she will do so willingly or not, she shall be given to the shrine."

"Reyce, please. We are better than this—"

"Not today, Nehri. Don't think it doesn't tear my heart from my chest, but today we must be the monsters of nightmares, or tomorrow we shall be nothing at all. You are the priestess, I am the chieftain. It is your place to protect our souls, it is my place to protect our bodies. I need you to be strong. If we live to see tomorrow, it will be the work of a lifetime to cleanse our souls of the stain we earn today."

Reyce turned to the doorway and set his gaze on Ivy. She had been watching with increasing concern, unable to understand their words but horrified at the story their body language told.

"Take her to the shrine," Reyce ordered.

The two guards at the door turned and took Ivy by the arms.

"What is going on? What are you doing?" Ivy insisted. "Just tell me what you are doing! Nehri, talk to them! You met my friends, didn't you? You know they'll help."

"… I'm sorry, Ivy," Nehri said, tears streaming down her cheeks. "We are beyond help now…"

The priestess hurried forward and shouted orders to the keepers of the shrine. Reyce kept pace with the guards and endured Ivy's pleas. As they wove through the city, the bell rang for the evening ceremony. The people of the village began to gather, but rather than the reverence and serenity they typically showed at this solemn time, there was confusion stirring among them. When Ivy saw the doors of the shrine opening, she realized what was happening.

"I won't let you do this," Ivy said.

Her voice was serious and steady with the hint of threat. She dug her heels into the soil and effortlessly brought both guards to a stop.

"It must be done. If you wish to protect your people, then you must offer your power."

"Not like this. Not with D'Karon magic."

Reyce barked an order. Several more villagers peeled off from their places around the shrine to help. They lifted Ivy from the ground. Red light flickered around her in thin, fast-moving streamers. When they crossed the stone threshold encircling the shrine's grounds, she visibly shook in pain. The shrine door was wide open, the day's offering already being helped away. From inside, violet light from half-filled crystals swelled into a brilliant glow, feeding hungrily on the energy pouring from Ivy.

"*No!*" she cried. "You will *not* offer me!"

A rush of red aura accompanied the outburst, pushing back those who carried her and dropping her to the ground. The villagers backed away as she stalked viciously toward Reyce. He drew a blade from his belt and brandished it, but she darted forward and swatted it aside with a swift backhand. He retreated cautiously as she stepped forward.

"*You…*" she fumed, eyes radiant with the building anger. "Ever since I was rescued, and all through my youth, I heard about what *monsters* malthropes were. I heard about their dishonesty, their viciousness. I heard that they were thieves and killers. But I never *dreamed* I would meet a malthrope like you. The damage you've done to your land has been out of ignorance and necessity. But this… to push away the hand of friendship and embrace the forces that are sapping the strength of your own people. Seeing what you are capable of makes me ashamed to be what I am. And I am through with you."

She moved suddenly. Reyce prepared for an attack, but she rushed past him and quickened her pace toward the edge of town.

"Stop her!" Reyce ordered. "By any means necessary! She must be offered to the shrine! Today is the day of battle. Without her, we shall not be prepared!"

The bravest of the villagers fetched ropes and nets. Some gathered gems to cast spells. Every attempt to capture her or slow her brought a fresh rush of red aura, a surge of energy, and a snarl of mounting anger. She quickened to a sprint, easily outpacing the villagers rushing from the shrine. Reyce snatched a bow from one of the guards nearby and readied an arrow. He doubted it would have been possible to strike someone with an arrow and not risk killing them, but the raw power and strength of this outsider made it clear anything less than a direct strike to her heart would be unlikely to do her much harm at all.

Reyce let the arrow fly. His aim was true, but Ivy's speed took her farther out of position than he could have predicted. The arrow tore a gash across her side. She cried out and turned. Her eyes were piercing points of red light now, her face a mask of rage, but she shut her eyes tightly and forced some measure of control over herself. She continued her escape at a still-quicker pace. Ahead of her brilliant form was nothing but the open fields surrounding Den. Then, in an earthshaking crash, Boviss dropped down before her.

The massive dragon was enough to stop her in her tracks, but the aura around her didn't lessen. She glared furiously at the beast. He grinned back at her and addressed her in her own language.

"There is the strength I felt," he rumbled. "Such a sorry beast to hide such power away."

Ivy growled and dashed aside to get around him. He leaped with a speed that seemed impossible for so enormous a creature and swatted her to the ground. She cried out, more in anger than in pain, and the aura intensified. Boviss brought his iron claw down atop her, pinning her to the ground. She cried out again, her voice almost lost behind an unholy roar of anger.

"Do you really have more?" Boviss taunted. "Can you really be so pathetic that you have so much power inside of you, but you refuse to *use* it?" He snarled, pushing more weight atop her.

"Let me go!" she screamed.

Reyce finally reached the edge of the village, but he could come no closer to the spectacle awaiting him there. The energy pouring from Ivy's body was unbearable. The ground was sizzling, and her aura was so bright he had to shield his eyes. Behind him, the shrine was glowing brighter than he'd seen it in years, and each moment fed it more of the rush of energy.

"Boviss, we need her alive," Reyce called.

The dragon's eye shifted to Reyce, his unnerving grin widening a bit.

"You want her power. I want to *see* her power. I will release her when she shows it to me." He looked to her and lowered his snout until it nearly touched hers. "I want to see what the best of you can do against me. I can *learn* from that. I can use it to destroy her friends."

Ivy screeched again. This time there was no voice, no mind at all. It was a sound of distilled, unbridled fury. She lashed at the claw holding her to the ground, and Boviss's whole massive frame lurched into the air. He toppled aside with enough force to buckle the roofs of the nearest huts.

She rose from the ground and drifted a few inches above it, baking the soil beneath her black. Any thought of escape had been washed away by the need to destroy this beast who assaulted her. He rolled to his feet and swatted at her, but she darted nimbly aside and raked her claws along his flank.

Reyce watched in awe as the clash played out. He had never seen Boviss move with such speed and power, nor had he ever seen such raw fury in his eyes. Each blow the supernaturally empowered warrior delivered did the work of a siege weapon. Armored scales that had turned away a thousand arrows and endured the claws of dragons a match for his size split and splintered. Thick, dark blood began to flow, fueling the dragon's rage all the more.

Ivy's power became more savage, more potent, but it came at the cost of speed. Boviss landed a few devastating blows of his own. Ivy struck the ground, then launched skyward again, leaving a smoldering crater behind.

The battle thundered nearer and nearer to the edge of the village. Boviss, in a bid to gain some time to recover and plot his next blow, flew from one side of the village and set down on the other. Combat had sapped enough of Ivy's strength that she could no longer will herself from the ground, so she thundered toward him.

Reyce didn't think; he acted. If Ivy didn't change her path, she would carve a fiery swath of destruction through the whole village. He threw himself in front of her and made ready to take the first blow himself. It likely would do no good, but if giving himself would spare one of his people, then so be it.

He braced himself and shut his eyes, body angled for impact. The blazing heat felt like it would roast him alive, but moments before Ivy would have struck him, the pounding footfalls came, then gave way to a grinding slide.

The Crescents

Reyce opened his eyes to find Ivy standing before him. The fiery aura had diminished greatly, and for the first time since the battle began her face had an expression other than blind rage. She was fighting the emotion. As she looked about and saw the fear in the eyes of the other malthropes, she visibly struggled to control herself, to push away the anger.

He turned away from her as he heard the flap of ponderous wings. Boviss had taken to the air again. Ivy's distraction and willful subversion of the emotion that fueled her had visibly weakened her, and the ancient dragon was far too savvy to let an opportunity like this pass. Reyce called for him to stop, but Boviss swiped once more with his iron claw, narrowly missing the chieftain and striking Ivy full force. The blow threw her into the wall of the nearest hut, punching her through and collapsing the roof on top of her. After a few moments more, the smoldering red glow beneath the ruined roof faded away.

Reyce snapped into action, rushing to the damaged hut and issuing orders.

"You, get Notta and Nehri. You three, help me clear the debris! The rest of you, to arms. And gather the wasps. I want everyone ready for the final assault within the hour."

Boviss touched down just outside the village and waded among the huts, his heavy iron tail dragging a furrow through the walkways and scraping at the walls of the huts. Fire was billowing between his teeth, and though the battle was over, from the look in his eye he had unfinished business with Ivy.

"Back, Boviss. You've done too much already," Reyce called over his shoulder, heaving at a beam and throwing it aside.

"Not enough. Not enough by *far*. That thing made me *bleed*," Boviss fumed. "You have your power. Let me finish this one…"

Reyce spared a glance toward the shrine. It was gleaming like a violet sun, every crystal filled to capacity. For a moment he wondered, if not for its mystic thirst drinking away Ivy's power even at a distance, if the raging malthrope might have actually *won* the clash with Boviss.

"She is still a malthrope, Boviss. You will *not* kill one of my people. Remember what happened all those years ago when you threatened us."

Boviss glanced about, raising his intact paw as if surrounded by rats when he realized how many of the malthropes had come to help Ivy.

"Yes. *They* made me bleed as well."

"Then go. I'll send Nehri to heal you when we've seen to Ivy. The battle begins in hours. We shall need your claws and flame."

"Keep your healing," Boviss said, spreading his wings. "I shall be ready when the time comes to do what has been coming for far too long."

He flapped hard, almost scattering those below him, and flew off. Reyce and his people finally uncovered Ivy. Whatever mystical power had protected her in the battle had absorbed the brunt of the final attack and impact, but she was still much worse for wear. Blood trickled from her nose and lip, staining her white fur. The edges of her clothes still smoldered, and the slash from the misaimed arrow was wide and horrid. But despite her bout with Boviss, she was barely conscious and still breathing.

Nehri arrived as they made ready to move Ivy from the broken remains of the home. Notta was with her, bandages in hand. The priestess worked feverishly to treat Ivy. As she did, she spoke to Reyce, not sparing the moment to look him in the eye as she did.

"The shrine is burning bright. Brighter than I've ever seen. What would have taken our own people weeks to provide, she provided in minutes, and from afar." She gritted her teeth. "She could have been such an *asset* to Den…"

"She will survive."

"Oh, I'll see to that. But I do not think you will be happy that I did." She tightened a second layer of bandage over the wound from Reyce's own arrow. "After what happened here, what would *you* do when you awoke? Would *you* help the people who would use you to fuel a war against her own friends? You have made an enemy of the creature who could have been our savior."

"She has fueled the gems. She already *is* our savior. I did what had to be done."

"You did what Boviss *convinced* you had to be done! I came to you today with what may have been a solution. But you decided that war was preferable to peace, that blood now was better than blood later." She shook with anger but forced herself to calm lest unsteady hands foul her work. "I don't know when it happened, but somehow I lost you to this war before it even began…"

Both were silent as Nehri struggled through the incantations that might close Ivy's wounds. The D'Karon offered many gifts, but their healing magic was limited.

"I shall consult the texts and ready the portals. You stay here and tend to her."

"You will need me during the battle. No one knows the D'Karon magic better than I."

"I am going to war, Nehri. Even if things go precisely as planned, I am more likely to die in battle than to return to Den. The village will need a leader if I do not return. When Ivy awakens, if there is any who can quell her wrath, it is you.... And when the Chosen arrive, tell them where we've gone. Tell them the assault has begun."

"They'll come for you."

"Better they come for me then destroy Den."

"If that is your wish. I only hope their sense of duty to those they serve is greater than their thirst for revenge for what we've done to their ally," she said. "Notta, we've done what we can do. Take her to my hut. I shall need to watch her closely."

As Notta gathered some others to carry Ivy away, Nehri stood. She took Reyce's hands in hers and pressed her forehead to his.

"May the blessings of the D'Karon protect you. And may the generations we preserve with this terrible act redeem us all for its darkness."

"Farewell, sister," Reyce said.

#

For the hours between Nehri's departure from their camp to her arrival in Den, Myranda and Deacon had been free to embrace the joy of the discovery for their future child. Deacon oscillated between remaining guarded and cautious—pregnancies did not always end in happiness—and being utterly elated at the thought of raising their child together. Myranda joined in his joy, even though she knew that when the emotion of the moment began to subside, he would have questions for her that it would pain her terribly to answer.

Their dreams of growing their family and continuing to make a safe, happier world for their child to inhabit were thrust aside when they felt an unmistakable upwelling of power. Ivy, and she was angry. Knowing they couldn't afford to ignore it, they'd taken to the air and followed the bright, burning point in their minds' eyes. Ether surged ahead of them, determined to find her ailing ally. Even when it faded, they traced a straight line to where Ivy's presence was felt. Grustim and Garr struggled to keep pace as Myn sliced through the air. The dragon fully understood what was at stake. If Ivy's anger had destroyed its target, people may have been terribly hurt in the process. If it did not, she was helpless with a foe still alive.

"Are you certain we are heading in the right direction?" Garr called, his voice barely audible over the rushing wind. "We should have seen something by now."

In the failing light, it seemed that there was little but rolling hills and green fields between them and the horizon.

"We are dealing with D'Karon magic. You cannot trust your senses. I've never seen it used so effectively at this scale, but I have learned never to underestimate it," Deacon called back.

"Lower, Myn," Myranda said. "We are close. I can feel it…"

#

Reyce stood inside the shrine and finished his preparations. It was a veritable gallery of brilliant indigo and violet gems. Ancient runes marked those created months before, the gems set aside for the day when the offensive could begin. They'd been filling one by one, but now they were fully charged and ready for any with the knowledge and will necessary to unleash their might. Rows of his soldiers were assembling outside. He stepped out to address them.

They were the best Den had to offer. The fastest. The smartest. The wisest. He had asked for volunteers, those willing to risk their lives to protect Den now and forever. Nearly every malthrope in the village had obliged. Most had been trained in the D'Karon blessings and in the ways of battle as a matter of course. If you were a species that was the target for all other thinking species, failure to learn to defend yourself was a death sentence. All but the oldest and weakest had crafted weapons and trained for this day. Now they stood before him. The weapons were simple, but deadly. Wooden swords, honed to cruelly sharp edges thinner than paper. Heavy spiked clubs. Thin, needle-sharp spears and javelins. They were, perhaps, not a match for what the dwarfs might have fashioned, but they needed their gold to bribe the keeper of the Seven Brothers to offer up a golem to their cause. They did not wear armor. With the D'Karon magic, they would be unseen, unheard. They would leave no scent. An army of spirits with no need for layers of leather or metal. They would be better served by speed.

The air filled with the buzzing of wings. One by one, fairies landed on the right shoulders of the soldiers in the front row. The wasps, summoned from the small grove near Den where they were trained and equipped. Each held a thorn tipped with deadly poison, distilled according to D'Karon teachings. Reyce directed one of the soldiers to begin handing out the gems.

"The day has come. Sooner than we would have liked, but that cannot be helped. Another malthrope than I might mark this moment with speeches of glory and honor. You shall not hear such from me. There is no glory in what I ask you to do today. This is about survival. The survival of Den. The survival of the malthropes. We must act quickly. We must act decisively. We must cut deeply and take as many as our blades will allow. We must be relentless and leave behind a legacy that will last in the minds of our enemies until the end of time. When the sun sets tomorrow, I want the very thought of ever setting foot upon North Crescent to be unthinkable. If we do this properly, our children need never know the fear of war. If we do it poorly, Den will fall, and take the last of us with it. Do not fail us. Give all you have. And may the D'Karon protect us."

They finished equipping themselves from the shrine and marched past the edge of the village, far into the surrounding fields. Boviss set down before them, his wounds scorched black by his own fiery breath. Reyce selected a large, intensely glowing gem and held it aloft. After a steadying breath, he willed it to release its enchantment. The air shimmered and sparked before them, then swirled in a mixture of darkness and violet light. The ring of churning magic spread into a portal. Others began to appear beside it as it grew large enough for Boviss to pass through. The view through the center of each churning magic ring was a different stretch of the border between the desert and the fertile fields of the isthmus.

Reyce gave a final look to the people of his village, ready to wage war on the unsuspecting and unprepared elves to the south. He wondered how many would live to see their homes again. In the distance, strange winds seemed to be blowing, and low to the horizon, two dragons approached... The Chosen... The Adversaries... He needed to be gone when they arrived, a distant target to draw them away from his home. He prayed it all would be worth it. Soon, he would know.

"Forward, to your destiny," he ordered.

The malthropes marched through the portals. He selected the one nearest to where the golem would be, the better to reach it quickly, and ordered Boviss through.

#

Myn angled her wings and dove, sweeping forward again only when the grass brushed her claws. The air had an unnatural, eerie tingle. If there was an enchantment upon this place, they were nearing its fringe. The mark upon Myranda's palm itched, reacting to the D'Karon influence around her. Then, in the distance, a sequence of powerful bursts of magic. Myn didn't need to be told to follow them. They were potent enough it hardly took a wizard to notice them. Ether's blustery form joined them. The new path clearly took them deeper into the enchanted patch of land, intensifying the unsettling feeling it brought.

When the change came, it came slowly. Thriving, flourishing trees seemed to wither before their eyes, leaves vanishing and bark fading. Hearty bushes turned gnarly and dry. The landscape shriveled and decayed, as if years of terrible drought had come upon the land all at once. There were other changes as well. Where moments before there had been nothing but wilderness, now paths became visible. Isolated fields still clinging to life showed where carefully tended farms grew. And ahead, wrapped about a tall stone shrine, a village revealed itself.

"We are through the enchantment," Myranda said. "I'd never imagined it would be so substantial."

"Something terrible happened here," Deacon said. "Look at the edge of the village, those scars in the ground. And those others, off in the distance. Those are the craters left by D'Karon portals closing. The residue of power is like a stain on the land."

"I shall look to the site of the portals," Ether said, streaking off to the south.

"I can feel Ivy. She's weak, but she is alive, in the heart of that village," Myranda called.

The words put new life into Myn. She quickened her pace and left Garr behind. They swept over the village. Half-seen figures dashed for cover in paths between huts. Here and there, fresh damage told the tale of Ivy's outburst. Myn touched down, effortlessly shifting from flight to a sprint. She navigated the huts nimbly until Myranda and Deacon both called out when they reached the hut that held their friend. Garr touched down a moment later, and the humans dismounted to approach the doorway. Inside, a violet light sparked to life. Nehri stepped from the doorway, clutching a gem. Her expression was hard, held rigidly in place but failing to hide the torment inside her.

"Leave this place, Chosen," she warned. "This is a place for malthropes. You do not belong here."

Myranda looked past Nehri, where Ivy was just visible resting fitfully and heavily bandaged.

"You have our friend, and she is hurt."

"She is of our kind and thus she is ours to care for. Go. I do not wish to fight you."

Myn lowered her head and glared at Nehri. "Move…" the dragon warned.

"We won't leave our friend until I know what has happened," Myranda said.

"There is dragon blood here… fresh," Grustim said. "And potent. This is from an elder dragon."

"That is the blood of Boviss. He serves our people. If you continue to threaten my people with your presence, you shall have to deal with him," Nehri said.

Grustim stalked forward. "If you believe you can exert any authority over an elder, you are fools. Elders are old as the mountains. They have survived since the land was young, battled their own, fought off generations of challengers. They are wiser and stronger than you can imagine. If you have seen one and lived, it is because you were beneath their concern, or because they have use for you."

"Do not come to my home and question our ways. Leave us. Please. This village has already seen more battle than I ever wanted it to," Nehri said.

Myn's patience was waning. Her claws split the ground, and her muscles tensed.

"*Move*," she rumbled. Her tone suggested it would be her last request.

Myranda looked about. "Your village is nearly deserted. Where have your people gone?"

"To assure our future. To begin their assault, the very assault you were called upon to stop. And if it means my death, I shall ensure there is a place for them to return to." Her voice wavered. "Please… if you have any mercy… leave this place. Things are in motion that cannot be stopped."

"It isn't too late to find another way, Nehri," Myranda said.

"*It is!*" Nehri tightened her grip on the gem, and it crackled with dark energy. "I am sorry, Myranda, but it is. It was already out of my hands when we spoke. The troops are moving. The plan is unfolding. You should never have left your home. Go back while you can. You have a mate, and soon, fate willing, a child. Don't make me take that future from you."

The threat was more than Myn was willing to bear. In a terrifyingly swift motion, she snatched at Nehri with a forepaw, but the malthrope deftly dodged into the doorway. She held out her gem and summoned an all-too-familiar blast of curling darkness. Myranda struck the ground with her staff and raised a shield, dispersing it. Deacon raised his own gem and wrapped his mind about Nehri's crystal, willing it from her hands. She rushed forward, chanting an incantation that made the stolen gem shudder and flash with a forthcoming attack, but a few words and a moment of focus from Myranda snuffed it out. Myn struck. With a swift, carefully measured blow, she pinned Nehri to the ground. The priestess wheezed as the air was forced from her.

A scattering of malthropes who had been watching from the shadows emerged brandishing weapons. With the strongest of the village already gone, those left to defend their homes were the oldest, the youngest, and the weakest. Some were withered by years of offering themselves to the D'Karon shrine. Gray fur threaded among the red or tan. Others were little more than toddlers, pudgy vulpine paws barely able to clutch their weapons. They held their ground, but from their body language, it was taking all of their resolve to do so.

"Easy, Myn." Myranda crouched down to Nehri and spoke softly. "Nehri, you worship the D'Karon. We *fought* them. And we won. I admire your dedication to your people, your desire to defend them. I would *do* and have *done* the same. But the way to protect them now is to tell me everything about this plan so that I can stop it before it escalates to a full-scale war. And let us see to our friend."

Myranda nodded to Myn, and the dragon reluctantly lifted her claw away. The Chosen stepped back. Nehri's people rushed in to help her to her feet and raised their weapons against the Chosen. Nehri hissed some orders angrily at them. They slowly backed away.

"Very well. You, and only you, come inside. The rest of you, lower your weapons. Stand down. My people will do the same."

Deacon pocketed his gem. Grustim slowly and deliberately sheathed his blade. Myn was the last to stand down, glaring at Nehri long and hard before thumping down onto her haunches and huffing in irritation. With the tension of the moment somewhat lessened, the fairies drifted from Myn's horns and hung in the air, eyes wide and hands clasped in delight.

"So many malthropes…" Freet said.

"So many friends of the fairies…" Shah murmured.

#

Nehri led Myranda inside the hut. Notta sat beside the bed. She looked uncertainly to Myranda, but Nehri whispered something to ease her concerns. Myranda swept her eyes and mind over Ivy's form. The worst of her injuries had been tended to, perhaps not as thoroughly as she or Deacon might have done, but well enough to keep her from deaths' door. Her spirit was terribly weak. She had certainly transformed, as they'd felt. There was no helping that, save giving her time to recover.

"Tell me what happened," Myranda said.

"Reyce… the chieftain… he moved faster than we'd agreed upon. He… began something we couldn't stop, did something we could not undo. It forced our hand. We needed power to make our plan work, and the only way to get it fast enough was Ivy. She refused. She became angry. I've never seen something so destructive, so filled with fury. If not for the power of Boviss and the thirst of the shrine, I don't know how she would have been stopped. But her strength gave us what we needed. And now the battle has begun."

"You opened D'Karon portals. Where did they lead?"

"Where do you think? To the isthmus. For weeks we have been carefully placing gems to serve as beacons, destinations. They were coming to our homes, threatening us. What could we do but the same in return?"

Myranda took a breath, disbelief and disappointment in her eyes. "Your plan is to attack? To send all of your people to do battle? Even with the D'Karon spells, this village isn't large enough to contain the force it would take to defeat the elves. Tell us the rest of the plan."

"You know what you need to know already. Enough to know Sonril is in danger."

"You attacked us, nearly killed Myn using fairies and a poisoned thorn. And you have a list of Sonril's nobles and where they linger."

Nehri's eyes flashed with anxiety. "How…"

"You shouldn't underestimate Ivy. She got a message to us. There is only one conclusion I can come to. Those are the ingredients for assassinations. We warned the nobles."

"It won't do any good." Nehri hung her head. "I do not know what to fear more, that you might be able to stop what we've started, or that you won't. Whether we succeed or fail, something of our people dies today…"

"Nehri, if you feel something you have done, something that you are doing, needs to be redeemed, now may be your only chance. Tell me the rest of the plan."

She shut her eyes tightly and turned away. "D'Karon forgive me… We promised all of our wealth to a dwarf in the northeast. He is the keeper of the Seven Brothers—huge, terrible war machines that have slumbered since some war before our time. We awakened one of the machines and sent it to the south. It is as nearly unstoppable as anything wrought by mortals or gods. It will reach their capital, turn it to rubble, and then return to its keeper."

"What manner of war machine…?"

"A golem. A great stone dwarf that knows only the orders it has been given. It will smash the cities. And then the wasps… even if you warned the nobles, when the golem arrives, any and all mystics and warriors will be summoned to face the golem and to try to stop our people and Boviss. Our stealthiest people spent nearly every moment from the formulation of the plan to this day infiltrating the cities of Sonril, finding the most important nobles, learning their defenses, and reporting them back to us. We know all we need to know. There will be nothing to stop the wasps from striking. Generals. Nobles. Anyone of importance. They will all fall…"

"A swarm of fairies as assassins…" Myranda said. "And a major assault to split their resources…"

"You'll never be able to stop it all. Now do you understand? Once the war machine rose, it was victory or death. Do not interfere. I beg of you. It will mean death for us all."

"I won't let that happen. I won't let any of it happen. You'll get your people back, there will be no war."

She lowered her head and shut her eyes. "But that's impossible."
"We are the Chosen. We've done the impossible before." Myranda stepped outside just as Ether returned. "What did you find?" she asked the shapeshifter.

"The sting of D'Karon magic is strong, and the spells were cast curiously. The path between where the portals opened and their destination still hangs in the spectral realm like a line on a map. There are a dozen points, each just north of the border."

"Deacon, we need to find a way to get to where those portals opened, and swiftly. Time is running out."

"I may be able to reopen one of them with the help of Nehri's remaining thir gem."

"Do what you can. And what do you know about golems?"

"Cresh used to talk at length about them. The pinnacle of dwarfish magic. But they were considered too dangerous to be used. His final task before braving the Cave of the Beast was to dismantle the last one in the Rachis Mountains."

"Did he teach you how it was done?"

"Not specifically. He mostly bragged about the difficulty. It took him years."

"We have hours."

"There is a functioning golem!"

"And it is heading toward the elven capital with orders to destroy it."

Realization dawned on Ether's face. "This has happened before…"

"What do you mean?" Myranda asked.

"The elven memorial I found had a stone rendering of a dwarf. As it was a statue, there was no indication that the dwarf was *intended* to be stone rather than flesh and blood. But if a massive stone working of dwarfish magic is on the move, it seems clear that such a mechanism attacked and defeated the elves so savagely that they collectively chose to conceal it from us."

"Were the circumstances less dire," Deacon mused, "this would be a tremendous learning opportunity. Magic so ancient and powerful. I ruminated on the operation of such a creation. The amount of magic necessary would require focus of the sort—"

"Deacon."

"Right, yes. Time is wasting. Is there anything else?" Deacon said.

Myranda turned to Grustim. "The elder dragon is with them. We may need to fight it."

"Then we may need to prepare ourselves for death," Grustim said.

"Would such a creature have any weaknesses?"

"They have the same strengths as normal dragons, but amplified to an unimaginable degree. Immense strength. Near-impenetrable hide."

"And magic may be of little use," Deacon said. "The strength of the mind and spirit grows more with time than anything else."

"Then we have too many problems to solve and not nearly enough time to solve them. We've been here before." Myranda turned. "Nehri, two of the dearest friends and strongest allies I've ever had were malthropes. One lost his life ending a war that would have claimed my people. The other sleeps on the bed behind you. I am ready and willing to make the same sacrifice to keep you from succumbing to another pointless war. If troops reach the village, know that it is only because I have fallen in the attempt to stop them. I see that you truly care for Ivy, and I cannot afford the time to help her or the risk of bringing her with us in this state. I leave her in your care."

She stepped to Myn's side and unfastened some straps, freeing a pair of cases.

"When you came to me, Ivy provided a message to convince me you could be trusted." She presented the cases. "When Ivy awakens, give these to her. She will know what to do."

She turned to the others. "Deacon, work on the portals. We'll need one large enough for the dragons. Then you and I see what can be done about the golem. Grustim, Garr, it will be up to you to warn the others what may be coming and hold off the elder dragon if it attacks. Somehow, along the way, we'll need to find a way to defeat the spells that hide the malthropes. Perhaps if they are no longer hidden, they will forgo their part of the attack. But even if that is not the case, we need to do it so that the fairies can be stopped. They will be difficult enough to find without magic veiling them."

"I can find them!" Shah crowed. "I can find them, I *know* I can. After being among the Bramblebreeze fairies, I *know* I could follow their wind if I need to. It isn't *so* different from having to find my way back to Freet!"

"Then you shall be with Ether. The two of you can move the most quickly, and Ether is the only one of us who will be safe from the poison the fairies carry," Myranda said. "Deacon can give you the locations Ivy discovered. Knowing where they are heading may just allow you to get ahead of them."

"Shall I kill the fairy assassins?" Ether asked.

"No!" Shah trilled. "Please don't kill them! They're just helping the wrong people!"

"Deacon, the ribbons in the cases, the ones that put Shah and Freet to sleep when bound…"

"I, yes, I see what you have in mind. It is a simple matter to duplicate them," Deacon said.

He drew a length of twine from his bag and, under his influence, sections of thread began to reel out, separate, and faintly glow as he enchanted them. As he did so, he spoke.

"I would be remiss if I did not make it clear that each of the insurmountable problems we face today could serve as fuel for a months-long debate among the Entwell masters, at the end of which there would be little hope for a solution that could be relied upon, and even if we *do* find solutions, it is doubtful that any could be executed without endangering you, and with you, our unborn child."

Myranda took a breath and shut her eyes. "The lives of whole nations, of the whole world, have hung upon our shoulders too many times already. A single precious life has been added, and somehow it has doubled the burden. But it doesn't change anything. We must solve these problems, we must face these foes. It is why we are here. And our lives are no more important than those that will be lost if we relent. If the gods are with us, then someday we shall tell our child of this adventure. If they are not… then we won't live to regret this. Now let us delay no longer. There is work to be done."

#

Reyce soared through the sky, following the coast toward the mountains, far from the isthmus where the first blood of this filthy campaign had been drawn. His people had already spread far and wide, using the power of their gems to run tirelessly to their assigned places along the border. If this plan was to work, it must appear as though the attack was coming from everywhere at once. Fear and uncertainty were weapons every bit as crucial as poison and blade. Only he and Boviss were heading in the opposite direction. If things had gone as planned, this would not have been necessary. But their hand had been forced. Both the deployment of the golem and the deployment of his people had come too close together, and thus he had to waste time and expend a tremendous amount of power to speed the golem's journey. The D'Karon must have been watching over them, though, as they had provided their most favored children with more power than they could have hoped for. With what they had collected from Ivy, they would not miss the power necessary for this next step.

The time away from the battlefield, however, did not suit Boviss's tastes.

"The others are in a place where the wind is heavy with the scent of elves. Their claws and teeth are tasting the blood of our foes," Boviss rumbled.

"The attack will not begin until the golem arrives," Reyce said.

In truth, Reyce was eager to be back beside his brethren as well. He and Boviss could move most swiftly and hit with the greatest strength. They were the ones who would serve as the grim finale to any attack that might tip in the wrong direction. The longer they were away, the greater the chance they would be needed but unable to reach the others in time. He poured magic from the cache of gems he carried, increasing Boviss's already prodigious speed to something truly astounding. A journey that would have taken weeks by foot and days by normal flight was, with barely an hour gone, nearly complete. Already he could see the massive, lumbering form of his target.

Reyce selected the largest gem that he'd yet to put to use and judged the golem's path. He shut his eyes and coaxed the beginnings of a spell from its heart. Finally, he dropped it. As it plummeted, intense streamers of light lanced outward, then a swirling darkness grew. It expanded, an inky void swelling among the mountains and trees, directly ahead of the golem. A point of light spread from the center of the void, revealing the sandy fringe of the fields north of the isthmus. It was the nearest destination available to him, as the portals could only lead to where they had been targeted, and their targets were few and precious, as each one was another chance to be discovered. At the speed the golem lumbered, mere hours separated it from Rendif, the first of many targets to which it would lay waste.

Boviss hung in the air, watching the war machine as it flattened trees and pulverized stone. It stepped through the portal and paused, perhaps to get its bearings and to seek its target through whatever mystic means it used. After a moment, it marched stoically onward. Boviss swooped through the portal behind it.

"Now, take me to Rendif. When the golem arrives, you shall have your blood…" Reyce said darkly.

"We should begin the battle now. Let me raze their twisted trees and slaughter their soldiers. Let them test themselves against *me* before that thing of stone and magic finishes the job."

"We shall follow the plan, Boviss."

"Each time you ignore my counsel, you find yourself regretting it."

Reyce selected another fresh gem. In his haste, he had neglected to restore his invisibility. Though soon enough the dragon, at least, would be revealed, for now they should both remain hidden. He conjured the proper spell. The dragon shifted uncomfortably, his image the ghostly shadow visible to one hidden by D'Karon magic. Reyce looked to the dragon's fresh wounds, still clearly paining the massive beast.

"And each time you clash with malthropes, you earn new scars," Reyce said.

"That thing resting in your village is no more a malthrope than that statue marching toward Sonril is a dwarf. She is a creation. A weapon. And when the elves are crushed, you would be wise to crush her as well. She will be the end of you."

"I do not care about her past. My duty is to ensure the future of my people, and she is among them."

"If you continue to rule with a weak hand, then your people shall have no future."

"And if you do not hold your tongue, this shall be the last time I permit you to leave your lair."

Boviss rumbled in suppressed fury but kept silent. For several minutes he moved with speed only D'Karon magic could manage. Already the golem was far enough behind to be barely visible, and the city of Rendif was just over the horizon.

The dragon did not speak again until, seemingly unprovoked, he snapped his head aside. "Do you feel that?"

"I feel nothing."

Boviss fixed his eyes on a point to the distant west. "A new portal stirs."

Reyce matched his gaze, and sure enough, the first sparks of a D'Karon portal were swirling to life. It was barely visible, even to Reyce's sharp eyes, centered on one of the more distant portal beacons. Reyce put his fingers to his gem, ensuring the enchantment that hid them was secure. The portal's opening was slow, and a measure less chaotic than he was accustomed to. This allowed Boviss to cover a considerable amount of the distance toward it. When it was fully open, two dragons and their riders came spilling out.

"No... *No*..." Reyce growled. "They are using the blessed magic!"

"They have pillaged Den. They have stolen your secrets."

"They have not..."

"They are agents of the elves. They will have ruined your homes. You should have struck more quickly."

"It cannot be so!"

Reyce clutched his gem and attempted to contact Nehri. The spell would not activate. It could mean any of a dozen things. It could mean Nehri's gem was drained, or that she was unable to reach it to complete her half of the spell. But it could also mean something far worse, that she was dead, or that her gem was in the hands of someone else...

Boviss's rumbling voice put words to his fears. "Your village is gone. Your people are dead. The agents of the elves have destroyed the priestess of Den and smashed her gems."

"It is not so until I have seen it with my own eyes," Reyce affirmed.

Myranda and Deacon guided Myn to the northeast, no doubt heading for the golem which was now *just* out of sight. Grustim and Garr soared due south, toward Rendif.

Reyce held Boviss tightly. "Let the others destroy themselves in a clash against the golem. But follow the green dragon and his rider. When he nears the first of the elven settlements, we end him."

"I can easily end him now."

"No. Let it happen before their eyes. Let them see that their hired blades are nothing against us. And do not end him quickly. I want them to see that even the best of them is helpless against us. And when the golem appears, grind him into paste. I shall signal the others to deploy their wasps and join us here. This Dragon Rider and the others deserve nothing less than our full, focused fury for daring to violate the sanctity of our village and turn the D'Karon teachings to their blasphemous will..."

Chapter 11

Myn soared through the sky, eyes locked on the looming form on the horizon. Myranda, Deacon, and Freet all rode on her back, observing the same terrible sight with varying degrees of awe and wonder. Myranda had worried it would be difficult to spot the golem. That, it turns out, should have been the least of her concerns.

"My heavens…" she said. "It is enormous."

"Like a monument come to life," Deacon said. "I can feel the mystic energies animating it even at this distance. Astounding. It is will, but in the absence of *consciousness*. The wizards who crafted it managed to forge raw obedience and servitude without any of the other trappings of thought."

"Does it give you any insight into how to defeat it?"

"Only that something so large shouldn't be able to move. The power required to simply keep it in motion without falling to pieces means that it won't be as simple to destroy as a like-sized statue."

Myranda squinted at the form as it seemed to grow ever larger with their approach. "It would be far more useful if your observations revealed weaknesses rather than strengths," she said.

"I very much agree."

"I don't like it," Freet said. "I don't think dwarfs are friends of fairies. Not *big* dwarfs, at least…"

Myn caught a cross-breeze and gave the golem a wide berth, circling and surveying. Even by doing little more than walking, the thing had left a trail of devastation. A path of footprints, each large enough to be the foundation of a house, flattened patches of earth and turned trees to kindling. As it paced along the foot of the mountains, several rockslides knocked loose by the earth-shaking steps littered the landscape.

"Closer, Myn," Myranda said. "But carefully."

She obliged, sweeping inward until she was perhaps the monstrosity's arm's length away. It ignored her or, more accurately, seemed utterly unaware she was there.

Myranda shut her eyes and focused her mind, dredging up her knowledge of earth magic in hopes of immobilizing it, or perhaps banishing the enchantment that gave it this semblance of life. No sooner had she begun than she felt a sharp metaphysical pain slice through her mind and soul. She winced and relented.

"I've never felt anything like it. It isn't like trying to move and sift stone back in Entwell. It feels like it is actively pushing back," she said.

"Without knowing the nature of the spell that animated it, I would advise against using earth magic directly upon it, then. The dwarfs are ancient masters of the art. We can't hope to best them at their own game without more time," Deacon said.

"Very well, there are other elements," Myranda said. "Fire, Myn. Aim for the face."

Myn's chest puffed out, and she belched a column of flame that splashed against the impassive stone face. Myranda funneled her own power into it, and Deacon did the same. In moments they stoked the flame to an unimaginable intensity, its brilliance too painful to look at, and its heat enough to force Myn herself back, lest her riders be scorched.

The golem did not lose a step. When the flames faded, the stone face was glowing cherry red, but showed not the slightest sign of damage or melting.

"We may as well be trying to melt a kiln," Myranda said.

"Focus on wind. I shall focus on water," Deacon said.

They swept still closer. Myranda felt Deacon's mind tug and draw at the air, sky, and soil, gathering first a mist, then a swirling ribbon of water. Above them, the mix of wind and water magic churned and darkened the clouds. As she had in her final test in water magic, Myranda worked with Deacon to bring forth a storm. Fat drops fell all around them, hissing and spitting as they struck the golem's cooling face. Myranda spurred the already wailing wind to a terrifying velocity, splitting it around Myn and blasting the lumbering giant. It leaned into the wind and plodded onward, its broad form catching the brunt of the gale but barely slowing. Deacon blasted the grinding joints of its knees and hips with the conjured water, saturating them.

As one, Myranda and Deacon sapped the heat from the air around the joints. The water froze, encasing most of the legs in a thick crust of ice. The sound was bone rattling: wailing wind, crackling ice, rumbling stone. But it was working. The layer of ice wasn't enough to immobilize it, but it was enough to turn its steady stride into a shuffle.

Myranda relented first, her endurance once again failing her. Deacon stopped a moment later, shaking his head a bit. The air continued for a few moments more, Freet having silently pitched in with his best effort at sustaining the gale. All three watched intently as the wind and water tapered off. For a few more steps, the golem remained hobbled by their attack. Then the crust fractured and sloughed away, and it returned to its former speed.

"We can slow it, at least," Myranda said.

"Not the most efficient means of doing so, and it would at best delay the inevitable," Deacon said.

Myranda took a breath. "So long as we've got the storm, this has saved our lives once before…"

She hefted her staff and heaved it like a spear, guiding its flight and bringing it to a stop just above the golem's head. The crystal took on a piercing white glow, and Myn wisely put some more distance between herself and the stone monster. A forking bolt of lightning split the sky. Searing light swallowed the world around them, and the air shook with a prolonged peal of thunder.

Myranda sustained the bolt for as long as she could manage, and when she began to flag, she felt Deacon take the reins of the spell and stretch it out for a few seconds more, until the clouds themselves had no more to give. Dragon and wizards alike blinked away the afterimages of the dancing bolt. When their vision returned… the golem still walked.

"Thank the gods the D'Karon never learned of this power…" Myranda said, wiping the rain from her eyes. She held out her hand, and her staff drifted to her side. The rain was still squealing against its searing-hot surface.

"Land, Myn. I have an idea. Again, it may not defeat it, but it should give us options," Deacon said.

Myn looped about and swooped several dozen strides ahead of the golem. Myranda and Deacon stepped off.

"Focus on the shaking of its footsteps," Deacon said. "If we can split the earth ahead of it…"

"Of course," Myranda said.

She drove her staff into the earth; he crouched and dug his fingers into the muddy soil. Earth magic was largely about the heartbeat of the earth, of taking the trembling present in the land and combining it with one's own strength to amplify and direct it. The punishing blow of each footfall provided them with a substantial head start in that regard.

Myranda felt the shaking earth strum up through her soul and back down through her staff, joining peak to peak and feeding back upon itself. The trees around them shook and shifted. The ground ahead of the golem rolled and roiled like an angry sea. Its steps became unsteady, but it did not slow. Deacon released his crystal, leaving it to float in the air beside him, and clutched Myranda's hand. Their minds worked as one, directing the trembling earth to do their bidding.

The golem continued toward them, stumbling but refusing to fall. Myn thrust herself into the air, catching the stormy breeze and climbing high above the stone behemoth. She rose to many times the golem's height, then swept her wings and dove toward it. Myranda knew what she was planning and carefully adjusted the timing of her own attack. Myn pulled up, flexed her legs, and delivered a punishing blow with her hind legs. Myranda and Deacon heaved the earth beneath the golem at the same moment. The combined attack finally pitched the colossus far enough forward that it could not recover. It came crashing down, the impact sending a wave of muddy slurry toward Myranda and Deacon, nearly burying them.

They let the trembling subside, then wove their spirits and minds with the plants in the soil. Stout tree roots burst from the ground and entangled the stone figure until it was barely visible beneath the writhing mass of woody tendrils.

"Quickly," Deacon said, letting his focus fade and rushing toward the figure.

Myranda tried to shake the haze from her brain as he helped her keep pace. The golem was anything but defeated. Already the roots binding it were crackling and splitting, its arms nearly free.

"The golem acts on orders." Deacon said. "I don't recall the specifics, or even if I was ever *told* the specifics. But I am quite certain the orders are written, and then slipped inside the golem somehow. Perhaps if we can remove them, it will go still once more."

Their attack had left the ground difficult to traverse, but Myn touched down to sweep them up. Myranda and Deacon focused their eyes and minds on the carved stone head that shifted and rumbled before them.

"I cannot see past its surface. They have warded it against the mind's eye," Myranda said.

"Such should have been expected…" Deacon said.

"There! It's blackened by the lightning blast, but there is an opening," Myranda said. "I… can't squeeze a spell past it. The defenses are astoundingly secure."

"Nor can I." He pocketed his crystal and physically climbed to the stone head.

"Be careful!" Myranda called.

Clenching his teeth in pain, he tried to squeeze his hand into the opening. "The head hasn't quite cooled, I'm afraid. And the opening isn't large enough. Perhaps Freet—"

The male fairy didn't wait to be asked. He had already darted from his place atop Myn's head and, in a flash, squeezed himself through the slot.

In a loud sequence of snaps, one of the golem's arms broke its bonds.

"Quickly, what do you see?" Deacon said.

"There is a bronze tablet," Freet called from within. The little fairy grunted, then a flash of light and squeal of pain burst through the opening.

"Are you all right?" Myranda called.

"When I tried to touch it, it sparked and burned me."

"More warding magic," Deacon said. "One must admire their comprehensive defenses."

The other arm broke free, and the golem heaved itself from the ground. Deacon, still holding on tightly, was drawn up with it.

"Myn quickly, we need to get them down," Myranda said.

The dragon leaped into the air, circling around the golem as it unsteadily righted itself.

"No!" Deacon called back to them, clinging to the slot for grip. "Leave us here. Go help the others."

"Are you mad?" Myranda called back.

"For all we've done, it has paid us no mind," he said, crouching to hold a bit tighter as a sudden motion nearly threw him free. "If we stay with it, I can continue to work out a way to deal with it. There is much to be done elsewhere. Go help the others."

Myranda wanted to argue further, but if their adventures together had taught her anything, it was that Deacon could be depended upon, and they simply didn't have the time to waste.

"Very well. But please, be safe," she said.

"I shall take no unnecessary risks," Deacon said. "Beyond those implicit in riding atop an ancient war machine. Now go, quickly, and be careful!"

"I will take good care of him!" Freet called. "Just wait until I tell this story to the others in the grove!"

Myn gave Deacon a lingering look of concern, then rolled aside to return from whence they came.

#

Ivy shifted uncomfortably. The leaden weight of unconsciousness was slowly lifting, but her head felt heavy, her eyes were almost unwilling to open, and her hearing was throbbing with a soft voice that whispered words she couldn't understand. As she had too many times before, she searched her memories for what could have left her in this state. There was fire and heat. Anger and combat. She could only recall flashes, moments, but they were fierce and terrible. She'd lost control… That she was still alive suggested she'd won her battle. That this appeared to be a hut in Den suggested otherwise, since she was quite sure she was trying to escape when she'd transformed.

She heaved herself into a sitting position and winced at a cluster of sharp pains. The voice she'd heard was coming from the doorway of the hut, where Nehri sat cross-legged, head lowered in prayer. A small gathering of the village's youngest and oldest had formed a semicircle around her. The crowd stirred when they noticed Ivy had awoken. The priestess turned, then stood and approached her.

"What happened?" Ivy asked, wiping the sleep from her eyes.

"You fought Boviss—with a power I've never seen before," Nehri said. "You were badly hurt, but the upwelling of your spirit fed the shrine enough for the assault to begin."

"Then it's happening," Ivy said, trying to stand.

Nehri eased her back to the bed. "Rest. Recover. It is out of our hands now. Your friends came. They know what is happening. They say they will try to stop it."

A moment of relief fluttered across Ivy's face. "They came. Then they *will* stop it… But they'll need my help." Again she tried to stand, this time making it unsteadily to her feet despite Nehri's protests.

"Ivy, right now terrible things are happening. Things terrible by design. Your friends are strong. It seems impossible, but perhaps they *can* stop the battle. Perhaps they can even quench the flames we have ignited in the hearts of our enemies. But I am not so foolish as to trust that it shall be so. If you have ever cared for your people, then rest. Stay with us. We will need every healthy malthrope we can get once the blood has been spilled."

"My friends are out there."

"But your *people* are here."

"Nehri, Myranda and Deacon are the wisest people I know. If they have chosen to fight, then it *must* be the only option, the *best* way to help everyone. Did they say anything to you? Did they tell you what I should do?"

"They only offered a pair of cases. They said you would know what they were for."

Ivy's eyes brightened. "My cases! Please! Bring them here!"

"One contains a weapon. You are dangerous enough empty-handed. I will not allow you to have it among my people."

Ivy waved dismissively. "I don't care about that one right now. Bring me the other one."

"What good will it do?"

"Bring it to me and you'll see."

Nehri signaled to one of those assembled in the doorway. A moment later one of the children arrived, carrying the sturdy wooden case as if it were a rare and precious treasure. The priestess took it and ran her hands over the surface, eyes shut.

"I feel no magic, no enchantment about it. Not like the case with the weapon." She clicked the case open to reveal a somewhat worn fiddle. "What value does such a thing have at a time like this?"

"Oh, it's got magic in the right hands, Nehri," Ivy said, plucking the instrument from the case. "Just you wait and see."

Ivy shut her eyes and, moving stiffly at first, put the bow to the strings. Almost in sympathy for her battered body, the instrument seemed unsteady and out of tune. Plucks, twists, and strums gradually coaxed it into correct musical pitch, and then came the long, clear note of a simple ditty. Nehri watched and listened in confusion, but around the doorway the curious onlookers pressed closer. The song wove back upon itself, repeating its simple beginning amid layers of new melody. It escalated and evolved, and Ivy's spirits rose with it. A deep golden light was conjured around her. The raw exaltation of the music flowed through her, and with it the revitalizing power of her own joy. The aches eased, not just for her, but for those around her. Fatigue and exhaustion burned away like morning mist in the rising sun.

Perhaps the most powerful, most astounding effect of them all was the influence on the huddled, uncertain people of Den. These poor creatures, withered by their dependence upon the D'Karon, had life in their eyes again. After watching wives and husbands, brothers and sisters, sons and daughters, and mothers and fathers march forth to commit terrible deeds from which they might never return, they were able to briefly lose themselves in the spirited melody and the contagious joy.

Finally, the song reached its rousing climax. Ivy took a deep, cleansing breath after the final notes. She stood tall, her sharp pains all but gone. A quick tug of her claws removed the bandages to reveal the stain of blood around a wound that had almost entirely healed. Nehri looked upon the results with awe. She touched where the wound had been.

"If only you had been with us from the beginning… It might never have come to this."

"We can still fix it. I need two things." Ivy clutched her stomach. "I need something to eat, and I need to know where the others went."

Nehri sent one of the others to fetch some food. "By now, the warriors of Den have already spread out and taken positions across the isthmus. The golem could already be attacking the first of the cities on the way to the capital. And you have no dragon to ride, nor do we have enough power to open even a single portal. What good will it do you to know?"

"Do you have any crystals at all? Even exhausted ones?"

"The only gems left are those keeping Den hidden."

"Can you use one to open a portal to my friends?"

"That would leave us exposed until I could restore the crystal sufficiently!"

"Nehri, your people can't hide anymore. What you have done *will* bring people to this place. I am asking you to trust me now. Help me to help my friends. If you do, maybe you can finally live without this magic that is killing your land. You can keep hiding your village, but the handful of people here may be the only ones left."

Ivy watched Nehri consider the words. She did not envy the priestess's decision. She was being asked to abandon everything she'd come to believe was necessary for the safety of her people in exchange for the narrow thread of hope offered by someone she'd just met. Nehri's face was twisted with worry and uncertainty. The rich red fur of her face was dusty and stained with tears. She turned and cast a look to her people. When she looked back, she had an expression of resolve.

"… Follow me…"

#

At the northern edge of Rendif, Garr stood ready, Grustim astride his back. Ever since the attack that had compelled the king to seek the help of the Chosen, the town had been home to triple its normal complement of guards and soldiers. They stood at the ready, eyes turned to the north. Grustim had done his best to prepare them for what was to come, but working as he was through an interpreter, he suspected the urgency and scope of his warnings were not conveyed with the gravity they deserved. No matter. Words alone could never prepare them for the battle ahead. An elder dragon, a thing he'd only read of in his training as a Dragon Rider. And a golem, a thing he'd never even *heard* of. If he and Garr survived the day, it would be a testament to their conditioning, and more than that, to their good fortune.

Garr rumbled and lowered his head. Around him, the elves were beginning to stir. From his perch atop the dragon, it took Grustim a moment longer to realize. The ground was quaking. It was subtle and rhythmic, like the beating of a heart. More accurately, it was like massive, plodding footsteps. The golem was not yet in view, but if they could feel it already, it must have been enormous.

"*There*," Grustim called, pointing.

All eyes turned to follow his gesture. A form in the sky was approaching. Both dragon and Dragon Rider knew at first glance it was Myn. It did not bode well that she was returning while the golem still moved.

"Remain here, and remain alert," Grustim called. "That, at least, is an ally. I shall meet her and see what news she carries."

"No…" rumbled a voice.

The voice was powerful and deep, loud enough to be right in front of them, but seeming to come from thin air. A moment later, the air shimmered and a mystic veil wafted away. Standing before them, near enough for them to feel the heat of his smoldering breath, was

Boviss. For the first time since he'd earned a Dragon Rider, Garr had to look up to meet the gaze of his foe. Boviss wore the same permanent sinister grin, but his teeth were separated slightly, making the horrid expression seem wider and more demented. His eyes gleamed with anticipation. He was a creature who wanted nothing less than blood, and his thirst for it was unquenchable.

"Do not go. I want you here. A *trained* dragon. So curious to me. Will it be more of a challenge? Or have the humans ruined you?" Boviss rumbled.

Though they did their best to keep their composure, a ripple of palpable fear spread through the elven soldiers. Boviss was so much larger, so much more powerful than even Grustim had prepared himself for. That they'd not turned tail and run proved the elves had a greater fortitude than the Dragon Rider had given them credit for.

For a moment, Boviss remained where he was, sweeping his eyes across the row of soldiers, selecting where his meal would begin. Grustim took that time to train his eyes on Boviss's back, searching for the rider. He knew better than anyone that killing a dragon's rider would do little good. Garr and his fellow mounts would fight on long after their Dragon Riders had fallen if the mission or their own whims demanded it. This was an elder dragon. That he allowed himself a rider at all was unimaginable. He would not be here if he did not wish to be. In that way, the rider was meaningless. But the magic that had concealed him? That was the work of the rider. Even Grustim's untrained mind could sense that. If such magic was at his disposal, knowing where the rider was and what he or she was doing could be the difference between life and death. Alas, the rider must have been mindful of this as well. While Boviss was revealed in all of his terrible glory, the rider remained a flickering, half-visible form, still obscured by magic.

For seconds, all remained still but for the sweeping predatory gaze of the massive dragon. When the stalemate was broken, it was by a single archer of the elven force. He released an arrow that hissed toward the elder dragon's eye. The beast twitched aside, causing the arrow to slice a shallow divot out of his armored cheek, then locked his eyes on the archer responsible. With that, the battle that had hung threateningly in the air descended all at once. Garr launched himself into the air. Arrows flew, thick and rapid. Boviss charged forward and belched flame across the field. Soldiers scattered and raised their shields. Had they been any slower, the whole row of them would have been a pile of ash. The heart of the flame baked the earth to a glassy black char. Those nearest to its curling fringe had to dive to the ground for fellow soldiers to smother the flames.

Garr looped downward and delivered a blast of flame of his own along Boviss's back. The flickering image of the rider rolled aside. With an elder dragon as a mount, he had room to leap and dodge without ever leaving the creature's back. The magic that hid him made it confounding to track and target him. Shimmering afterimages lingered for fractions of a second after he moved. Garr's flames, potent though they were, barely darkened the scales of the larger dragon's back. Fire alone would do no damage to the creature at all. Dozens of archers firing hundreds of arrows made the air around Boviss too dangerous for Garr to venture near enough for an attack with tooth or claw. Though many of the exquisitely made arrows met their marks, most shattered and fell away. The peerless elf-made arrows barely bit deeply enough into the dragon's scales to stick. It was no use. With the weapons available, they may as well have been throwing pebbles. Their only hope was to target his weakest points and try to last long enough to wear him down.

Boviss slashed his claws and breathed flame in sweeping swaths until the archers were too scattered to give him anything meaningful to target. He may as well have been a cat losing interest in the mouse he'd been batting about. Instead, he looked to Garr as he circled above and harried him with flame. Grustim held tightly to Garr's back as he saw their target's eyes lock on to them. A dragon with many targets could be evaded. A dragon with a single target was another matter entirely. Now that he and Garr had Boviss's dedicated attention, the end could come with a single slash of his tail or snap of his jaws. Together, they were too inviting a target. Grustim leaned low.

"Lead him from the town. Whatever it takes, keep him from moving south," the Dragon Rider instructed.

Garr rumbled in reply and hooked sharply around a column of flame hurled in his direction. Grustim took the moment and leaped from Garr's back, sword in hand. He came down hard upon Boviss's neck. The elder dragon growled in anger and reached up with his iron claw to rake at the unwanted rider, but Grustim nimbly evaded, sliding down the jagged scales of the beast's neck. He charged at the flickering form of Boviss's rider. Above him, Garr took full advantage of the distraction and slashed at Boviss's face.

Grustim trusted his mount to do his job. He had his own target to worry about. The scaly hide beneath his feet quaked and shifted as Boviss spread his wings in pursuit of Garr. Though he had been trained since childhood to navigate the sky by dragonback, he had never had to cope with a beast of this size, and one so rigidly dedicated to Grustim's death. The ground dropped away. He gripped a craggy split in one of Boviss's scales tightly with his gauntleted hand. If he fell, Garr would not be able to catch him. Before him, moving with a confounding sureness of step, the flickering rider approached.

"I know what you are," Grustim said. "I have seen your home and your people."

"And for that, you must die," Reyce replied, his voice ghostly and at the edge of hearing. "For my people to be safe, others must know only fear for what lurks to the north."

The obscured form rushed at him, but Grustim rolled aside, keeping his grip with one hand and raising his sword in a preemptive block. A half-seen weapon thumped against his. A follow-up attack might have met its target, but Boviss pitched to the side to lash at Garr, and in doing so, nearly dumped Reyce from his back. Grustim used the moment Reyce took to recover to gain more solid footing. If victory was possible, this would be how it would be achieved. The malthrope was swifter, more agile, and had magic at his command, but Grustim had more experience doing battle while clinging to the back of a dragon. It wasn't sure to even the odds, but it was the best he could hope for.

#

Far away near the center of the isthmus, Ether stood at the ready. She was in her human form, as she'd become familiar with and comfortable enough in that form to expend very little effort to remain in such a state. This freed a greater proportion of her focus to scan the surrounding countryside for their prey. She knew their targets would help them soon, but for now they had to linger midway between Rendif and Twilus, both of which had targets and either of which could be the first to need defending. She was aware of the battle going on to the east. She could feel the power of the foes her friends battled. But this was not her first battle. It had taken longer than it should have, but she understood that even when circumstances seemed dire, the other Chosen often knew how best to divide their assets. That did not, however, make it simple to stand idle while she knew others were fighting.

In one hand, she held a small bundle of twine cut into short lengths, the threads prepared by Deacon. The other was clenched into a fist as she did her best to set aside the urge to hurl herself into the distant fray. Shah hung in the air before her, darting to and fro, scrutinizing Ether from all angles.

"You look so human, but you are not human," Shah said.

"That is correct," Ether said.

"You can take any form. Even the form of wind."

"That is correct..." Ether said, her patience already nearing its end.

"That must be *wonderful*..." Shah said, twirling about. "We fairies already feel as one with the wind, but to *be* the wind..."

"I have a task, fairy. It will be trying enough without your distraction."

"Yes. Yes, you are right."

Shah flitted up and stood upon Ether's shoulder, face serious and eyes scanning. Now and again her wings stirred the air. To a casual observer, it may have seemed like an idle motion, but Ether could feel a weak swirl of magic each time she did. It was more akin to a scent hound stirring up the dust to catch a better scent.

"You are dedicated to this task."

"Yes I am, Ms. Ether."

"Why?"

"Because it's what we must do."

"But it is not *your* task. If I understand correctly, to the elves you are merely a tool. And a tool not intended for this task."

"I'm not doing it for them," Shah said.

"Surely you do not owe your allegiance to Myranda."

"She's a lot nicer than them. I'd rather listen to her than them. She's a friend of the fairies."

Ether shook her head. "Myranda seems to have no trouble gathering new allies..."

"She's nice. And she does good things for the right reason," Shah said. "I haven't really had the choice to do anything since I volunteered to be a messenger. It's nice to be able to *decide* to do something nice."

"Even if it means risking your life? And fighting against your own?"

"Myn and Garr will fight other dragons for what's good. And *they* are friends of the fairies. I think, if you know what you are doing is right, and you know what someone else is doing is wrong, then sometimes you have to go against them. Even if they are like you."

"So you help us in this simply because you are permitted to choose, and you wish to make the moral choice?"

"I suppose."

"You do not fight for glory? For wealth?"

Shah shook her head. "After this, I just want to go home to my grove."

"I imagine you find fulfillment in your family, as so many—"

"Ms. Ether, now you are the one who is being distracting."

Ether's expression hardened. She tightened her grip around the twine.

"And please be careful with those strings," Shah said. "Mr. Deacon worked very hard on them, and we will need them if we want to do our job."

"I will not be lectured by a fairy. I have existed—"

She stopped suddenly, and both she and Shah turned to the east. There was nothing to see, but fairy and shapeshifter alike knew that there was something there.

"I felt it. The way the air moved. There is a fairy there. Only a fairy moves the air like that," Shah said.

"Yes. It is time."

Ether shifted to wind. Once immersed in the element that formed her, she could feel every motion that stirred it, like the whiskers of a cat brushing against a doorway. The fairy, reading the breeze with her wings, followed the same clues. A single but very definite curl of wind told the tale of a fairy darting to the south. Ether launched forward, dragging along the bundle of twine. Behind her, Shah rode the currents Ether stirred up. Ahead, a tight point of focused wind swirled about a tiny, unseen form skimming low to the ground. The first of the fairy assassins.

She was heading east, to the city of Rendif. The D'Karon magic must have not only hidden her but also given her speed, as she was streaking at an astounding speed. Ether had to work to keep pace, and if not for her ability to hitch a ride, Shah would have fallen behind. Ether gathered her will and tore across the sky. By the time she closed the gap, they were approaching Rendif. Ether could feel the distant burn of the assassin's gem and realized getting much closer would not only cause her further pain but would fuel the enemy fairy's magic as well, potentially giving her the capacity for far greater acts of enchantment.

"Shah, you need to separate that fairy from her gem," Ether said.

"Me!?" Shah objected. "Those fairies are trained to fight. I'm just trained to fly fast!"

"I shall help you, but I mustn't get any closer, or she shall only become stronger," Ether said. The shapeshifter separated a single thread from the tangle caught up in her windy torrent and offered it to the little creature. "Now go."

Shah nodded shakily, taking the thread and working her wings for all she was worth. Though she did not share the same speed enchantment that fueled the assassin, her own gifts of training and breeding more than made up for the difference with Ether pushing her along from behind. Now that their quarry was aware she was being followed, she took evasive action. The nimble creature wove between tree branches, dipped under carriages, rushed through tall grass and among leaves. Shah, to her credit, stayed on the assassin's tail. Ether found herself having to scatter and loop around as they squeezed through progressively tighter gaps.

The people of the village recoiled and jumped as what appeared to be a single messenger fairy rushed by amid an impossibly strong gust of wind. The battle at the edge of the city and the sight of the approaching golem had already caused its share of chaos, but an invisible chase served to elevate the hysteria considerably.

The fairies zigged and zagged their way through the city until they reached the outside of the elven equivalent of a large and stately manor, no doubt the home of this assassin's target. Spurred forward by the realization it would soon be too late, Shah finally overtook the other fairy, snatching at her feet. They physical contact caused the stealth spell to falter slightly, offering the slightest hint at their foe's form. The warrior fairy pivoted and drew one of her poisoned thorns, slashing at Shah. The messenger was swift enough to dodge the first attack, but only just, and she was entirely unprepared for the second. Ether threaded her will into the air between the two creatures, churning it with a potent gust that forced the two apart. Even that short burst of magic within range of the assassin's crystal gave her a surge of speed.

For the better part of a minute, Ether did her best to help Shah without empowering her opponent. It was a bit like combat by proxy, her contribution limited to shoving and tugging the opponent out of position. After too many close calls, Shah finally found herself in position to strike. She looped the thread around her opponent's waist and hastily pulled it tight. Once the thread was cinched into place, the same enchantment that kept Shah and Freet immobile and asleep within their cases fell upon the assassin. She plummeted to the ground like a puppet with her strings cut.

"Quickly. Destroy the gem," Ether instructed.

Shah tore the little crystal from the harness affixed beneath the fairy's wings and darted high into the air… but once it was in her grasp, the same enchantment that had affected the fairy fell over her. She vanished from view. As the spell lingered on the fallen fairy, Ether could see neither of them any longer.

"Ms. Ether!" came Shah's voice from thin air. "I can see her now! She's faded and dull—and so is everything else—but I can see her."

"The spell must allow those to see others it affects," Ether said.

"Sh-should I break the crystal still?"

Ether considered the question. Having the working of D'Karon magic so near to her was like having a hot coal pressing against her… but there was value in its effects.

"No… Keep the gem. If it will allow you to see the others, and perhaps help you to match their other feats, then for now we can use it."

"It… it won't wither me like it did to the Bramblebreeze fairies, will it?"

"The gem won't drink your strength. Mine is far more abundant."

Ether looked down. Her target was finally sharpening into visibility, sound asleep on the ground. She shifted to her human form again and picked up the sleeping fairy. A few deft tugs tightened the enchanted cord to ensure she would not accidentally be awakened. As the poisoned thorn could not very well be trusted to be left about, she plucked it from the ground and, with a thought, incinerated it.

She looked about. The sudden appearance of the sleeping Bramblebreeze fairy, the disappearance of a messenger fairy, and a blustery patch of wind turning into a human had attracted a crowd of bewildered onlookers.

"Come. We need to move quickly," Ether said, once again shifting to wind. "There was only one target within this town, but many elsewhere. The other fairies will have to pass nearby. We may be able to catch the next one quickly."

"You aren't just going to leave her here, are you?" Shah asked, eying the sleeping assassin.

"She is our enemy. If I had my way, I would have incinerated the creature along with her weapon."

"She's still a fairy, and she is *just* doing her *job*. Helping people *she* thinks are right, just like *we* are. Please take her with us!"

"There will be dozens of them before we are through."

"They're light!"

If Ether's present form had had teeth, she would have been grinding them. "Very well…"

A curling loop of wind snatched up the fairy. Without further comment, Shah darted skyward. Ether followed the stir of wind and the burning of the gem from her partner. Similar sensations blazed through the landscape around her, both near and far. If she was to succeed, she would have to catch them all. They gave chase to the nearest one.

#

Myranda held firmly to Myn's back as she watched the midair clash playing out in the distance. It didn't seem possible that any creature could be as large as the dragon doing battle with Garr. Grustim's mount looked like a hatchling compared to the beast. Nonetheless, the monstrosity swooped and swept with the focus and precision of a seasoned predator. Ponderous motions and apocalyptic gouts of flame barely missed the nimble target.

She leaned low to speak to Myn, to motivate the creature for the battle ahead, but there was no need. Myn saw the predicament Garr was in just as plainly as Myranda did. The young dragon scarcely needed to be told what to do. Get to Garr. Help him. Protect him.

The distance between them closed swiftly. Myranda focused her mind, doing her best to force away the concern for Deacon. He had been left behind with an insurmountable task, but he was equal to the challenge. She set aside the fear for her own life. This was worth risking it for. Most trying of all, she set aside her concern for the safety of the precious life growing inside her. She would need every ounce of focus, every scrap of strength if she were to triumph.

She held tightly to Myn and gripped her staff, shutting her eyes and reaching out with her spirit. In her mind's eye, the elder dragon was, if anything, even *more* fearsome. His spirit burned like the sun before her. Its light dwarfed the smolder of Garr, Grustim, and Reyce. He was a rival even for Myn's soul. That meant his spirit may as well have been as heavily armored as his body. At her best she would have had trouble penetrating such a potent defense with her magic, and she was far from her best right now.

There were other things for her to consider. She felt the corrupt burn of D'Karon magic wrapped about Reyce. It wasn't masked anymore. At least, not very well. As Myn tucked her wings and dove into the fray, Myranda knew her role in this battle would be to deal with that sorcery. Her one asset in this clash was that Reyce depended upon the crystals for his magic. They were little more than a tool for him, limited in their function. If she tugged at the threads of his magic, he would not know how to keep the enchantments from unraveling. The spell was in use before her, and in a weakened and labored state. If she could take a lesson from Deacon and intuit its workings, she might be able to snuff it out, and other spells like it.

Searing heat flashed across her skin as she delved deeper with her will. Myn was fully entrenched in the battle now, and Myranda had to trust the dragon could do her part. The familiar twists and knots of mystic power pulsed at the edge of her mind. Under her scrutiny, the pieces of the spell resolved in greater detail. Like bricks in an arch, they traced out the structure… and at the peak… the keystone.

She interwove her will with the central focus of the spell and wrenched at it. The ribbons of D'Karon magic rippled and recoiled, struggling like a stricken serpent and sending jolts of painful energy through her mind. She did not relent. Another mighty flex of her will finally severed the link, and she felt the spell fall away. She had not merely broken the enchantment. That would have done little good, as the malthrope could have commanded the crystal to restore it. She had torn the very spell from the crystal itself, stolen that weapon from his arsenal. Perhaps Nehri or another more skilled practitioner could restore it, but not an untrained warrior.

Myranda opened her eyes. The battle had not relented in the least while her focus had been elsewhere. Myn had curled herself about the base of one of Boviss's wings, teeth clamped tightly and hind claws slashing. Boviss was trying to curl his neck to snap at her, but each time he tried, Garr dove and swiped his own claws at the massive beast's eyes. The wizard tried to get her bearings and find a new task to set her mind to. The last flickering violet light of the veil formerly obscuring

Reyce fell entirely away. A heartbeat later Grustim seized the opportunity of a clear and open target, jabbing his weapon at the malthrope.

Reyce leaped aside, but even on a beast as large as Boviss there was precious little space where one could be sure of foot. The edge of Grustim's blade caught his side and he faltered. He slid painfully along the jagged scales of Boviss's back until his flailing hand grasped the iron links of the chain dangling from his abbreviated tail.

"Lose them!" Reyce barked. "The D'Karon magic has failed me."

The elder dragon acted swiftly, ignoring the attacks of both dragons and their riders. Instead, he pivoted into a dive. The clash had climbed higher and higher into the air, such that they were near the clouds now, and thus the dive would be a long and swift one. As he dove, he worked his wings, flapping to speed his descent and rolling to put himself into a spin. The wind felt thick as syrup as it blasted against them, and his twirling spin forced them to hold ever more tightly or be thrown aside.

Garr pursued, but he steadily fell behind. Myn was still holding firm and doing her best to tear a hole in Boviss's hide, but soon it was all she, Myranda, or Grustim could do to keep their grips.

The Dragon Rider worked his way toward Myn, moving hand over hand as though he were climbing a mountain. "I have seen dragons do this to Dragon Riders. It is a death plunge. We need to be free of him before it is too late to recover," he called.

He climbed to Myn's back. After a final, vicious bite and a blast of flame for good measure, she spread her wings to catch the air. Boviss continued downward faster than either Myn or Garr could pursue, though now free from attackers he ended his twirl. Reyce clamored along the tail and up his back, making his way to the base of the elder dragon's neck. His massive wings spread and he leveled out a bit, striking the ground with a force that must have knocked the air from his rider.

The battle had done its job, at least. Garr's and Myn's harrying attacks had drawn Boviss some distance from the city, and even after his dive, they were far enough that it was barely visible to the south. The two smaller dragons landed at a safe distance, edging near enough for Grustim to transfer to Garr's back but never taking their eyes from the looming behemoth. The battle had left both Myn and Garr terribly winded and badly battered. Even their mighty hides couldn't completely shrug off the intensity of Boviss's fiery breath. Myranda held her staff low and healed the worst of the blackened and burnt scales. When the open wounds had sealed, she raised her head to match their gazes.

Boviss was staring at them. It would take no more than three powerful strides for the monster to close the gap and begin the battle anew, but instead he watched, horrid grin agape and teeth curling with flame. Myn's and Garr's best attacks had done little damage at all. Fresh, bright scrapes marred the rusted iron of his replacement limbs. Nicks and gashes along his scales didn't even show a tinge of blood. It would take so much more than what they'd done so far if they hoped to hold this monster at bay, and they didn't have much more to give.

His rider was another story. Reyce climbed painfully up Boviss's neck and perched atop his head. Once there, he clutched his crystal tightly in his hand and held his injured side with the other.

"What have you done?" he cried angrily. "Why will the gem not obey me?"

Myranda did not answer. Not immediately. This was the first time she'd seen Reyce clearly, without the madness of battle or the confounding veil of D'Karon magic to hide him. His face, his bearing, even the curl and glow of his soul… If she'd not known otherwise, she would have believed it was Lain, that he'd clawed his way from the clutches of death to return to them. Beside her, Myn took a single tentative step forward, her eyes fixed upon Reyce, and her nostrils breathing deeply of his scent. Both wizard and dragon were at the brink of tears. It was as near a reunion with their fallen friend as they were ever likely to get.

"Keep your distance and answer my question! What have you done!" he cried.

The tone of voice was the first thing to shatter the illusion. Lain could be cold, even cruel. But he was always in control. Reyce was at the end of his rope, struggling to maintain a grip on the situation.

"I've undone the spell. Taken it from you," Myranda called back. "You can't hide behind the D'Karon veil any longer. Now that I've done it once, I can do it again. I can teach the elves to do it. Your soldiers will be revealed. And once they are, the elves will know who they are facing. You must end this now. Call them back, or you will force my hand."

"Tiny wizard," Boviss murmured. "I can feel your power. *You* are the one who might have stopped us. You are the one who might still. But that power fails you. You are like a lame bit of prey. You lack the strength to do what must be done. Let me end your misery…"

He took a single plodding step forward.

"Hold," Reyce said.

Boviss took a second step.

"*Hold*," Reyce demanded.

The elder dragon rumbled in anger, but held his ground.

"You would condemn my people to oblivion," Reyce said.

"I do not wish to see anyone killed. Some of my most cherished friends and allies have been malthropes. My heart ached at the thought that the race had been snuffed out, and it sings at the revelation that you and your kin have survived. But you use the tools of my enemy, the enemy of our *world*. You seek to kill, to destroy, even when a hand is extended in peace. If I must choose, I can only choose to help those who wish to defend themselves."

Reyce bared his teeth. "*We* are defending ourselves!"

"You are seeking to slaughter thousands out of fear. That is not defense." Myranda tightened her fist about her staff. "I won't let it happen."

Reyce squeezed the gem tightly, then turned to the east. The lumbering form of the golem was drawing near. Soon it would reach the city. He lowered his head. "Then you must die," the chieftain decreed.

"A wise decision," Boviss said.

Myn did not wait for an order. She burst into the air, summoning all of the remaining strength and speed she had left to keep Myranda from harm.

"To the east," Myranda ordered. "I do not know if we still have a chance, but if we can lead him to the golem, if we can reunite with Deacon, we will have more options. And if the beast stays on us, the city will be safe. So long as Ether is doing her part…"

Chapter 12

Mellawin, from his throne in Grandwinn, looked upon the other nobles. In the time that the Chosen had been north of the isthmus, he had returned to see to the affairs of state. As he had hoped, his decision to recruit the heroes of prophecy had stirred a great deal of discussion. Many heaped upon him the praise that such an inspired decision deserved. Of course, as with all challenging decisions, there were naysayers.

"I, of course, defer to the greater knowledge of the court mystics when they say that these so-called *Chosen* do indeed seem to have been touched by the divine, but I am simply not certain so drastic a measure was necessary," remarked Lady Morrilyn, a representative from the southerly reaches of the kingdom.

"I ask you, milady, what are we to do if our people are assaulted by unknown aggressors? Simply lay down and allow them to trample us?" Mellawin said.

"We have an army of our own, and though I would *never* trivialize the death of any of your subjects, there was but one life taken. And it belonged to someone who unwisely chose to break with tradition and cross the isthmus. I am uncertain anything more than a return to the wisdom of remaining within the safety of our own land is called for."

"I wonder, milady, if perhaps you would feel differently if the attack had come from the *southern* reaches of our fair land. If the people whose lives were lost were under *your* protection. And let us not forget that all of the people of Sonril are under *my* protection. While I am king, I will not shrink from the task of keeping us all safe. If doing so means crossing an angry sea and securing the aid of the representatives of the gods, and through them the gods themselves, then I shall do so. It is long past time those above us turned their eyes to our people. Perhaps in bringing their warriors to our shores we can remind them of the greatness of our land."

She raised her hands. "Again, my king, I would not *think* to second guess your wisdom. But what evidence have we that what awaited them north of the isthmus was *worthy* of their attention? Attacks by ruffians and barbarians? We knew they made their homes in that terrible land."

"They turned up a plot of potential assassination."

"They *claim* such. We cannot be certain they are correct. Suppose there is nothing to be found but the same wilderness and lawlessness that our people left behind when we turned our backs on the place. I very much doubt the gods would look kindly upon those who waste the time of their representatives."

He clucked his tongue once, as if in disappointment at her lack of understanding. "Milady, North Crescent is a vast place, and *of course* the Chosen would be thorough. It is as wise to send word of the *threat* of assassination as it is to provide evidence only when it is certain. I, of course, *hope* to see proof of their claims as soon as something worthwhile is found, but if they do not contact me for a *month*, I would not be surprised."

Morrilyn leaned back and sipped her wine, formulating her next carefully phrased jab at her king's plans. This all was to be expected. Elven diplomacy was complex and nuanced, but a large proportion of it was aimed at taking a subtly contrary stance such that points could be scored if and when even the slightest negative resulted from them. It was a game of waiting and remembering, perfect for those with centuries of rule to maneuver themselves.

While waiting for her further comments, Mellawin had turned to a lesser lord who had been particularly articulate in his praise, with the express desire to receive another helping of it. Alas, he seemed distracted, as were several others at the banquet table. The king didn't need to ask why. A horrid, wailing wind could be heard outside the palace. It might not have seemed so out of place if there had been a storm raging, or even one brewing, but the sky was clear and the air had been still until that moment. The pair of guards near the entrance stepped outside to investigate. They shut and secured the door behind them.

"Curious," the king said.

"No matter, Your Majesty," Morrilyn said. "I am certain it is nothing of concern. I *did* wonder, however, how you would—"

The door burst open, bringing her passive-aggressive comment to a sudden and startling end. Wind filled the hall, hurling plates and glasses about. Guards shouted warnings, ordering everyone from the room, but the intensity of the gusts was such that every door rattled and slammed dangerously on its hinges. The palace mystics struggled to formulate some sort of defense, or even to comprehend what was happening, but it was all too powerful, too swift. Forms flickered at the edge of vision, the beat of tiny wings buzzing in their ears and the shouts of still-smaller voices echoing as if from miles away.

In one monumental gust, the wind shifted from swirling all around them to blasting in a single direction. Nobles struggled to keep from being dragged to the far wall. A sharp thump rattled one of the curving branches that had woven to form the structure. A flickering, glowing violet form struggled there, then in a flash, became visible. It was a fairy, dressed in thorn armor. The long, sturdy thorns of her equipment had bitten into the wall and pinned her there. Before anyone could investigate it, a second and third thump signaled the impact of two more fairies. Flashes of shattering thir crystal revealed them, then a mystically concealed blur fastened a cord about their waists to render them still. The wind became more focused, and it seemed to be following the king as he retreated farther into the corner.

Two crystals dropped to the ground at his feet, both glowing so brightly he couldn't look directly at them. Simultaneously, a pair of fairies appeared inches from his face. One was dressed in the same thorny equipment as the other unexplained ones affixed to the wall. The other was dressed as one of the elves' messengers. The fairies were shouting at each other in a twittering, trilling cacophony. Behind them, a swirl of wind so intense it was visible to the naked eye resolved into a disheveled female form, who snatched the thorny fairy out of the air. Easily a dozen other thorny fairies, motionless save for the breeze that kept them aloft, drifted behind her. The messenger fairy grabbed one of a handful of threads being tossed about in the lingering wind and tied it about the waist of the struggling fairy, rendering her still.

Ether stalked silently to the wall, plucking off the pinned fairies one by one.

"I don't feel any more of them, do you?" Shah trilled breathlessly.

The little fairy was red-faced and ragged. Here and there, tears in her clothing and dabs of blood marked where struggles with the fairies had taken their toll.

"I believe these were the last," Ether said.

"What is the meaning of this?" Mellawin demanded when he finally found his voice.

The fairy turned and gasped, realizing for the first time just who was standing before her.

"The king!" she squealed. "Er, I mean *my* king. Uh, My Majesty. No, no, *Your Majesty*. I, hah… This is Ether, it is an honor and—"

"We don't have time for this, Shah. Speak quickly. We must return to the others," Ether said. "And destroy that crystal."

"Yes, right!"

Shah darted down, grabbed the crystal that had been strapped to the final assassin, and hurled it out the door to shatter on the ground outside.

"Your Majesty, er, I have a message for you," Shah said. "There is a terrible battle at the isthmus. The Chosen are doing battle as we speak. It is all to do with—"

"Speak more quickly!" Ether said.

The shapeshifter pulled the cloth from a nearby table and gathered its ends into a sack. She rather unceremoniously dumped the immobilized fairies inside, then looked impatiently to Shah.

"I have to go back to them. I'll tell you later. Er. Your Majesty," she blurted.

Shah grabbed her own crystal and strapped it back into place, using the loops normally used to carry messages. She, Ether, and the improvised sack vanished from view once more, her empowered crystal now powerful enough to encompass the entire group in its stealthy magic. A final savage gust of wind whipped from the room.

The chaos, though brief, had left the room in an utter shambles. The food from the banquet was as much on the walls and ceiling as on the table. Nobles had been splattered with wine, their carefully selected outfits twisted and torn, their hair in disarray. Outside the door, guards still barked orders at one another, uncertain what had occurred and unconvinced the danger was over.

Mellawin took a moment to collect himself, then turned to Morrilyn. "I do believe you were passing judgment on my precautions regarding the danger from the north. By all means, continue."

#

Deacon held tightly to the side of the golem's head with both hands. His stylus and one of his books drifted beside him, awaiting the next moment it would need to be used. He'd been able to slow the golem a bit, thanks to the continuing rain keeping it soaked, and thus giving him something to freeze to foul its joints. That was the only thing he'd managed. His additional exposure to the golem and its enchantments had offered little in the way of additional insight into weaknesses or flaws. The obvious next step was to find out precisely what the tablet containing the instructions said, but that was more easily said than done. He could not see it himself—it was shielded against any potential mystical viewing—and while Freet could see it, he could not read. They had attempted to have Freet bring the stylus and a page inside to copy the symbols so Deacon could read them, but as soon as the paper contained any writing whatsoever, the same enchantment that rendered the tablet incapable of being removed did the same for the page. The only evident solution was turning out to be a time-consuming one.

"The next symbol please!" Deacon called.

"I'm looking. It is complicated!" Freet called from within.

A moment later the fairy darted out and carefully traced a few more lines.

"There, that is everything," he said.

Deacon analyzed what Freet had transcribed. He'd been watching the message as it was assembled, but it was the first time Freet had ever written or drawn anything—and it showed. Even with all of the runes copied to the best of his ability, it was not immediately clear what the message was supposed to say.

"It is… well, it is definitely Ancient Dwarven. That last symbol is the symbol for 'home,'" Deacon said. "I haven't written anything in Ancient Dwarven in quite a while, but I think I can recall enough for some simple instructions."

He shut his eyes, and the stylus plucked itself from Freet's hands. The book turned to a fresh page, and the stylus traced out a far more precise sequence of runes.

"There. Stand still. Simple enough," Deacon said. He pulled himself up to the slot, tore the page free, and slipped it inside.

"Did it work?" Freet said insistently.

The golem continued to thunder along.

"It appears it did not," Deacon said.

He scrutinized the poorly transcribed order, trying to work out what it said. As he did, he thought aloud. "There are a thousand things that could prevent the golem from following a fresh order. Likely, it follows its instructions in some defined order, and it probably wouldn't follow the next until it was through with the first…"

Freet glanced ahead. "We are close to the city, Deacon."

"… If I were to design a mechanism of this sort, it would be simpler and safer to limit it to only a handful of known commands. I would also see to it that the golem would take some safe action if something goes wrong. Though, for a war machine, perhaps that would not have been preferable…"

"We don't have much time, Deacon!" Freet urged.

"Little good can come from rushed thinking, Freet."

"But no good at all can come from slow thinking that doesn't get anything done."

Deacon ignored the statement and continued to blink through the pouring rain at the page drifting before him.

"This… this looks like a number… or a rank. Freet, this line here. Did it look like this?"

The stylus darted up and scrawled a more precise shape beneath the one Freet had scratched down.

"Yes! Yes, it looks like that."

"Edict One, Edict Two…" Deacon said. "I see. It has four commands. The last looks to be 'Return Home,' and the first is likely the instruction to walk to its target."

"We already know what it was ordered to do!"

"I know. But now we know *how* it was ordered… I have an idea."

With visible dismay, he willed over a dozen pages to tear free. His enchanted stylus moved in a blur, filling each page with writing within a few moments. Once both sides of a page were covered, he stuffed it through the slot in the golem's head and began the next one. Freet looked anxiously from Deacon to the golem and back again.

"It isn't stopping, Deacon. It isn't working!"

"We won't know if it will work until it seeks out its next command. Not until we reach the city."

"But if it *doesn't* work, then there won't be any more time to try other things!"

"Then we shall simply need to devise a worthwhile contingency plan in the meantime."

#

Myranda's mind was stretched to the limit. If she'd not been trained in the ways of magic, she would have been dead moments after she and the others had attempted to evade Boviss. Knowing where he was wasn't enough to know where he was going. Though he was but one creature, he was so large and moved with such deceiving speed that in the blink of an eye he could seem to be everywhere. Flame rained down from above. Wings curled around on either side. Claws slashed from the sides. Even the morning star of a tail swung up from below. Hasty shielding spells shattered, barely deflecting a blast of flame or a rake of claws. Garr did his best to distract and draw the attention of the beast, but now that Myranda was his sole target, he would not be swayed.

In the fleeting moments that she and Myn were not in imminent danger, she looked to the east, to the approaching golem. It would reach the edge of the city soon. Perhaps not long after they reached it. It had already trampled a section of the border wall and ignored the soldiers stationed there, leaving them far behind with its ponderous strides. At this distance, Deacon's continuing efforts to destroy or delay the thing were more than apparent. It was layered with frost. Stout vines conjured from the earth cocooned its limbs. Flame had blackened and charred sections of it, and even radiant bands of pure energy flickered in and out of being in hopes of binding it. Still it labored on, barely slowed by all these efforts. That they continued unabated at least meant that Deacon still lived.

The icy drops of the rainstorm they had conjured stung Myranda as she and Myn swept along, rolling to avoid scything claws. She shut her eyes and reached out with her mind, seeking Deacon's clear, sharp thoughts. They reached out in return, and his frazzled, fatigued voice echoed in her mind.

Are you hurt!? he asked.

Not yet... She narrowly diverted a blast of flame. *But I cannot be certain I can keep ahead of this beast's attacks. What of the golem?*

Freet and I have devised a plan, and an admittedly rather drastic supplement should it fail, but I would be lying if I said my confidence in the success of either plan was very high. It is fascinating how varied and potent the threats can be from one continent to—

Deacon, please.

Yes, of course. Thoughts for another time. How can I help?

The elder dragon is trying to kill me, under orders of the rider. The longer we can keep him focused on me, the better chance we'll have of protecting the city. But Myn is tiring, and I can barely maintain focus.

I understand. A thought occurs, though I hesitate to suggest it. The risk is too—

I am intentionally *keeping the attention of a predator the size of a fortress, Deacon.*

Yes... Yes, I suppose the time for risk management is behind us as well.

Rather than putting the plan into words, Deacon's thoughts wove with her own in the form of images and notions. It *was* a long shot, and an unwise one, but if it could be made to work, then it would be worth everything. She called out to Myn, swiftly and efficiently explaining the plan. The dragon huffed in acknowledgment.

Myn dropped low to the ground. Weaving between trees and swooping near enough to the hills to ruffle the blades of grass. She kicked her legs against the ground and dragged her claws to dodge attacks that now, at least, could not come from below. Without any altitude, they had precious little insight into what lay ahead, but the one thing they needed to be most mindful of could not be missed. The golem towered above all else in the area. In minutes it would reach the wall of the city. The thunder of its footsteps steadily boomed louder with their approach. By the time their plan was ready to be hatched, each calamitous stomp drowned out even the whistle of wind in their ears.

From here, timing was everything. Myn tucked her wings and switched from skimming flight to a frenzied sprint. Boviss overshot, but dug long furrows into the soil with his claws as he skidded to a stop and doubled back. The ground quaked with each pounding stomp. Their mad rush sent them across the packed-soil road leading to the town. Out of the corner of her eye, Myranda saw the town guard and its military supplement approaching. If this did not work, more innocent blood would be spilled. Myn darted left and right, for the first time in her life having to use the same tactics of those creatures she preyed upon during a hunt. Myranda judged the length of the golem's stride and guided Myn, then put her mind to work fully on the task of working the spell, trusting Myn to keep her safe and do her part. Deacon, high atop the lumbering golem, united his will with hers. This spell would have to be swift and strong. Even with both of them working at it, she couldn't be sure it would hold long enough.

The ground thumped one last time, the golem's foot pulverizing the earth not a stone's throw away. Myn turned, rushing directly across its path. Boviss followed. Myranda and Deacon struck. More stout vines split the ground beneath Myn, weaving upward as she rushed past. Boviss's iron claw came down among the conjured thicket and was instantly ensnared. More vines shot up along his other leg, coiling tightly around his stout torso and thrashing neck. Deep roots pulled free as the dragon was brought to a sudden stop, but Myranda and Deacon conjured more. Boviss belched flame, roasting the vines, embrittling them. Another heavy step of the golem shook more of them free. The wizards redoubled their efforts, replacing each of the snapping, tearing bonds with a fresh one.

Realization dawned upon Boviss, but it was too late. As the golem took another step, the enormous, pendulous swing of its trailing leg struck the dragon's head with a devastating kick. Huge and powerful though the dragon was, to the veritable mountain that was trudging across the landscape, he was nothing at all. The blow tore him free of the vines and threw him aside. Reyce tumbled from his back and rolled across the broken ground. The golem lumbered on, not a stumble or a pause to show for the impact. Boviss was barely moving at all, eyes unfocused, jaw slack.

Having seen the beast's power, Myranda knew better than to believe the blow had killed him. It would have been best to take advantage of this moment, to make one final effort to permanently incapacitate him, but circumstances forbade it. The golem had reached the town. It had to be stopped. Nothing else mattered.

#

Ether and Shah, after making certain all of the fairy assassins had been gathered into the makeshift sack drifting along with them, had shifted all of their strength and effort to returning to the isthmus. Through Ether's power, Shah's training, and copious amounts of D'Karon magic, they had managed to dart and dash across nearly half the continent. During the return, Shah worked out how to end the stealth enchantment in the gem, allowing for still greater speed from the little D'Karon crystal. Few other beings could have achieved the task in weeks, let alone the relative blink of an eye that they had. Despite this, the greatest task, the task their friends still struggled with, lay ahead of them.

"We're almost there!" Shah said breathlessly. "Wh-what do we do now, Ms. Ether?"

"I shall find the others and render aid. You should seek shelter. You have reached the end of your stamina."

"N-no! I can still help!" she wheezed.

Ether squinted into the distance and felt the loathsome sting of more D'Karon magic. "Another portal has opened since we left…" she fumed. "I can feel it…"

"Where? From where? To where?" Shah asked.

Ether focused on the lingering sensation. "It opened where the golem first appeared…" She paused as she realized another sensation. "This needs to be dealt with."

Even now, the golem was shambling through the outskirts of the city, and the elder dragon seemed to be motionless in a field to the north. Both would benefit from her attention, but this, perhaps, was more important. She blazed past the battlefield and onward along the path of destruction the golem had left behind. Not far from both the dragon's dazed form and the edge of the city, sprinting as best she could over the broken earth, was Ivy.

Ether dropped down beside her. "Ivy, you should not be here," the shapeshifter said.

"There's a battle, isn't there? We're the Chosen aren't we?" Ivy huffed, taking advantage of Ether's arrival to take what was clearly a much-needed break.

Shah landed on Ivy's shoulder and hugged her neck. "You are better!" the fairy trilled. "I am so glad!"

Ivy held out her hand, and Shah stepped onto it. The malthrope looked the fairy over in dismay. "What happened to you?"

"I helped Ms. Ether stop the assassins!" she said, glowing with pride.

Ether held out the sack. "They are here. Look after them, and Shah as well. There is no room in this battle for the weakened and infirm."

"I've fought in worse condition than this, Ether," Ivy said, a pathetic wisp of red aura flickering.

"And you were lucky to survive." She looked to the south. "I don't have time to argue. See to the fairies."

Ether shifted to wind again and streaked into the sky.

#

Ivy blearily watched as Ether whisked away, then looked to the remnants of the city's wall. The golem had crunched through as if the structure were made of twigs. Myranda, Deacon, Grustim, and the dragons had all turned their attention to the hulking stone behemoth, to little avail. If she were to attempt to aid them, she would only be a liability; that much Ether was right about. But she hadn't come this far to stand idle while the others risked their lives. She set her eyes upon where the dazed dragon and the injured chieftain lay. Not far to the south of them, a small contingent of soldiers was approaching.

She shook her head and tried to gather her wits. There had to be something she could do. Her brain wasn't ready to cooperate, so she chose instead to focus upon her heart. Ivy hurried to Reyce's side and helped him to stand.

"You…" he murmured, face contorted in pain. "How…?"

"You of all people should know there are no limits to what you can and will do when the people you care about are in danger." The sound of shattering stone and splintering wood split the air. "Reyce, this has gone far enough. You've got to call it all off."

He coughed. "No. I can't. And I mustn't. The golem will perform its task regardless of my desire or anyone else's. The only way is forward. The mission is everything."

"Open your eyes! Too many people know the truth. This won't be some attack from enemies they don't know. This will be an attack from the malthropes! You are *killing our people*. Marking us once and for all as the monsters they believed us to be!"

"The wasps will kill their leaders. The unseen soldiers will do the rest. They will know that to attack the malthropes is to invite death into their homes."

"The wasps are *here*!" Ivy held out the sack. "And I don't care how skilled they are or how much D'Karon magic they can use, the people you've sent out there won't be coming home if you ask them to fight a whole kingdom alone."

He raised his head to watch as the golem came to a stop at the first massive sculpted tree of the town.

"What is done is done. Now, it is in the hands of fate."

"That is something you need to understand about us, Reyce." She turned to watch her friends as they circled and assaulted the golem. "We are the Chosen. We *are* the hands of fate."

#

Arrows sparked and clanked uselessly off the massive stone form as it leveled its smoldering eyes upon the towering tree the elves had crafted into their town hall. Ether arrived and immediately assaulted it with ice and wind. Its joints ground slowly, like the wheels of a mill. Its arms rose.

"We've got to do something!" Myranda called out from her place atop Myn. "It isn't going to stop!"

"It may. I've done what I can," Deacon called, still atop the golem's head, a mystic shield raised to block errant arrows from hitting him and Freet. "Only time will tell if it will do any good. In the meantime, if my backup plan is going to work, I'll need a pair of D'Karon crystals. I have the one we took from Nehri, but the plan won't work without a pair."

"Shah has one," Ether called. "A small one taken from one of the assassins."

"That will do!"

"I will fetch her!" Freet announced.

He whisked away, his wings a blur as he moved. The crude fists of the golem reached the top of their arc. Myn and Garr, as a final effort to stop the attack, each landed atop a fist, dug in their claws, and worked their wings. The fists began to descend, but slowly. They stopped a moment later with an unnatural jerk, then rose again. The head twitched and turned slightly. One foot shuffled backward. The whole of the golem seemed to be making tiny, innocuous adjustments, never quite finishing a motion before beginning another.

"What is happening? What did you do?" Grustim said, calling down to Deacon.

"The mechanism seemed to be operating on numbered edicts. I couldn't undo them or remove them, but I knew the whole of the journey was only the first of the edicts. So I added several minor edicts of my own, and numbered them all as the second."

"How many did you add?" Grustim asked.

"Four hundred and fifty."

"The golem is attempting to do over four hundred things at once?"

"Yes." A labored joint fractured, and one of its arms sagged. "We should be mindful of how it progresses. It is possible this will be rather destructive."

"Hopefully, that damage will be limited to the golem."

"In the event it is not, we had best have the contingency plan ready to deploy."

Myn dropped down and snatched Deacon from the golem's shuddering head. With him safely gathered, both Garr and Myn flew to a safe distance. Freet streaked back with Shah in tow. She carried her stolen thir crystal.

"Here it is!" she trilled.

The gem was glowing brightly with absorbed magic. Between Myranda's and Deacon's spells, Ether's presence, and quite possibly even the spells animating the golem, the area was positively *bathed* in energy.

"Good, good," Deacon said. "Myranda, do you think—"

"I can make the smaller one the target, but I've never quite understood the portal magic."

Deacon flexed his left hand and adjusted his ring. "I believe I've worked out that aspect of their magic sufficiently. At least, I hope I have."

They shut their eyes and set to work. It turned Myranda's stomach to know that the spells she wove had been born of a D'Karon mind. Even utilizing their magic for good was distasteful to her. The mark on her palm tingled and smoldered, as if to remind her of the thin ice she was walking upon, but she pressed on. She forged her will into the proper shape and imposed it upon the crystal. It pulsed and flickered, but finally the prepared spell took hold. It pressed like a coiled spring into the crystalline prison. With just a hint of will, it would consume the stolen energy and become a beacon for a D'Karon portal to open upon.

Deacon's work was more complex. All others watched in concern, fearful that the golem's twitching and rattling might become more violent. Fragments of its otherwise impervious body cracked and dropped away. A dim but undeniable light was shining from some of the deeper fractures.

"Listen carefully," Myranda said to Shah. "When Deacon is through, we need someone to be ready to carry the entry point of the portal somewhere far away, very quickly, should it be deemed necessary."

"Me and Ether are the fastest! At least, when we're together," Shah said. "I'll do it!"

"Are you certain? You've risked your life so many times for us already."

"It's right! It's right to do it!" Shah said. "And I want to do what's right."

"There," Deacon said, holding out the crystal. "It is done."

The crystal's glow was different now. It had less of the piercing violet appearance and more of a warmer golden glow. It was as if the presence of Deacon's spell had imbued the crystal with a purity that had not been there before.

Shah took if from his hands. It was a struggle. The palm-sized gem probably weighed more than she did, but she buzzed her wings and remained aloft. "What do I do when I get far enough away?"

"Focus your mind and think of the word 'open.' And don't forget to drop it and fly clear once you activate it. The spell will do the rest. But do it *only* if we say so. Far too much D'Karon magic has been used today already."

"All right!" Shah said, hefting the gem and awaiting further orders.

"What can I do?" Freet asked. "I want to do right too!"

"This isn't a game, fairy," Ether snapped. "Not everyone gets a turn."

Myranda held up her gem. "We need to keep this near the golem's feet. It needs to be beneath the golem when it opens, and it cannot be crushed before then."

"And we can't be sure of when it will open, as that will be triggered by Shah," Deacon added.

Freet looked to the golem, which continued its odd, rattling attempts at fulfilling all of its orders. "I'll do it!" he said.

He snatched the thir crystal and launched toward the golem. Myranda wasn't entirely comfortable placing so dangerous and important a job in the hands of the fairies, but they had shown themselves to be capable and dedicated—and right now, they needed all the help they could get. Now that the soldiers had determined their attacks weren't doing any good against the golem, and at the moment it seemed to no longer be advancing, a healthy proportion of them had split away from the city and were marching toward where Ivy, Reyce, and Boviss were waiting and watching.

"Come on," Myranda said, "Our job isn't through yet…"

#

Reyce watched the troops as they approached. They were readying their bows. He looked to Boviss. The dragon was barely stirring. By the time he was able to do battle once more, it would be too late. Reyce fought a breath into his lungs with a telltale hesitation.

"I know that sound," Ivy said, pulling his arm over her shoulder to take a bit more of the weight off him. "That's a broken rib. You need treatment."

He pulled his arm from her grip and pushed her away. "No… This is the moment I have planned for. I knew I would be giving my life today. I am ready."

Ivy clenched her fists. "People like you are always so ready to *die* for something. Don't you understand dying is the *easy* part? If you die here, your troubles are over, but the people you leave behind have to live on, knowing they've lost you and that they'll lose everything else *because* of you. If you want to do your people some good, *live*."

"Even with the blessing of the D'Karon, it cannot be."

"What are you going to do? Fight them alone?"

He lowered his head and took another breath. "I am not alone."

Reyce raised his hand and spread his fingers, then dropped it with a slicing gesture. One by one, forms unseen until now flickered into vague visibility around him. The others of his force, arriving after heeding his call. Just as when he'd done battle with Grustim, they maintained the greatest part of their mystic veil. They made their numbers known, but not their nature. Almost two hundred of them stood with weapons ready. A match for the force approaching them. The sudden appearance of the greater force caused the elves to pause, but only briefly. Now with their targets in sight, they began to form ranks and draw bowstrings.

"On my word," Reyce said. "Not before…"

"No!" Myranda called from above.

Myn touched down. Myranda and Deacon jumped from her back. Garr landed beside them, though he and Grustim were more concerned with the dragon.

"Leave us or be struck down as well," Reyce said.

"*No one* will be struck down!" Myranda hissed angrily.

She gripped her staff as she spoke, a twist of magic raising her voice and carrying it for all to hear. Deacon added his own twist to the spell, allowing the words to be understood by elf and malthrope alike.

"Listen to me! I know, with what you have seen, it may be difficult for you to believe it, but we have yet to pass the point of no return. War is not, nor should it ever be, inevitable. Terrible things were planned. Regrettable crimes were committed. But they were committed from a place of fear and anger. If you put your weapons to work now, any of you, a worse crime by far will be committed. Soldiers of Sonril, if you fire your arrows first, I shall defend this force. And you, the people of Den. If you move against the soldiers, I shall defend *them*. I am a representative of the Northern Alliance. I am the duchess of Kenvard. I am an ambassador of my people. And I am a warrior. If you wish for peace, I will broker it. But if you make war, you will find me a powerful foe."

Reyce watched the elves as Myranda spoke her stirring words. He watched as she spoke them fearlessly, knowing full well that she risked not just her own life, but the future of peace for her entire nation. And yet she stood with her back to him. She stood with an army of his kind behind her. It was true, what Ivy had said. For him, for his kind, there was no longer anything to be gained by the war he'd hoped to begin and end today, and everything to be lost. He still had Boviss, if he recovered. The dragon could rain devastation upon them, but not enough to end them. Not enough to keep them from the task of hunting down his people, of extinguishing the last of the malthropes.

In the middle distance, the golem's rattling and malfunctioning began to slow, fresh fractures fouling its joints. The most potent of his weapons was gone from his grasp. His assassins had been stopped. His golem had been stopped. This woman and her friends had done the impossible against him. Perhaps… perhaps she could do the impossible *for* him. Again, he took a painful breath.

"Lower your weapons," he ordered.

The half-seen forms of his people obeyed without hesitation.

Myranda called across the field to the elves. "They have as much as extended their hands in peace. Will you do the same?"

With good reason, the elves were more reluctant. Boviss, though still laid low by the golem attack, was clearly alive. But the words of a noble in service of their king carried weight. Their arrows did not leave the strings of their bows, but they relaxed the tension and lowered their aim.

Myranda's posture eased slightly. "Good. If there is room on the battlefield for wisdom, then there is a chance for us all."

Reyce swept his eyes across the battlefield, unwilling to believe what he saw. The history of his people, and his own two eyes, had shown time and again that dealings with other creatures ended in disaster for his kind. What few allies they had came at a terrible price, or required constant vigilance lest they turn viciously against them. But here—in a place he had personally and willfully turned into a battlefield—humans, malthropes, fairies, elves, and dragons all stood face-to-face. The windy form of the shapeshifter coalesced, her eyes set resolutely upon him with the same emotional intensity that had shaken the others when they had first seen him, mortals, immortals, even creatures supposedly touched by the divine. And they were all ready to meet each other as equals. For so many years, his entire life, something like this had seemed like a childish dream. And for months he had crafted this terrible scheme, trying all the while to remind himself that those he targeted did not consider his kind to be anything more than animals, and would be better off slaughtered like them. And during all that, a single voice whispered in his ear, coaxing him, goading him.

The ground trembled as though the mere thought of the elder dragon roused him from his daze. Boviss got his feet under him and stood. The motion brought the elven soldiers to attention again, their weapons quickly raised, targeting the dragon. He widened his stance and dug his claws deep into the earth, teeth bared and fire hissing from his nostrils. The raw anger in his expression turned his natural grin into something wholly other.

"Reyce," Myranda said, her staff gripped tightly, its gem glowing.

"Boviss, be still," he ordered.

"Be still?" he rumbled. "The enemy is at hand."

"Perhaps there need not be an enemy here today."

The dragon's eyes narrowed. His gaze slid toward Reyce. "After all of this time. After all of this planning. After keeping me on a short chain for generations. After seeking my wisdom and relying upon my strength. You would turn coward at the final moment?"

"How I choose to lead my people is none of your concern. Stand down."

Boviss growled. For a smaller predator, such a sound was frightening enough. For the elder dragon, the sound was almost beyond hearing. Pebbles at their feet shook and rattled. Trees in the distance lost leaves. It was as though the land itself was trembling in fear. Myranda, Deacon, and the others set their eyes firmly upon the dragon. Gems burned with mystic light. Reyce stood tall and met Boviss's gaze.

"*Stand. Down.*" Reyce stated.

Boviss's answer was a single word, spoken through a gout of fiery breath.

"… Die."

\#

Myranda and Deacon each raised a shield. Though they'd done their best to prepare for his attack, they never could have anticipated its raw intensity. The flames rippled against the conjured barriers. Sheets of brilliant fire splashed back upon Boviss. The air seared and sizzled against all present and filled the whole of the field with a blinding, brilliant light.

Boviss rocked the ground with a powerful leap, taking to the sky before those on the ground could recover. Myranda blinked the afterimage of the flames away. The defense she and Deacon had raised against the breath of flame had not been enough. The worst of the attack had been deflected or absorbed, but the shields had broken. She looked to where Reyce had been, fully expecting to see him roasted to ash… Yet, he still lived. Between him and where Boviss had been stood Ether, her form smoldering as she drank away the last of the flame. The shapeshifter looked Reyce in the eye and reached for his face.

"So much like him… You could *be* him… I cannot allow you to fall as he did…"

The raw intensity and torment evident within Ether at the sight of someone so like the creature she'd cared so deeply for was nearly a match for the flames she'd absorbed. But there was no time to indulge them. Boviss was already looping around, maw agape and flames ready for a second blast. All warriors on the battlefield, elves and malthropes included, acted as one. A hail of arrows peppered the dragon's open mouth. Reyce's soldiers looked to him for orders.

"Spread out! Ready your weapons!" he bellowed.

Myranda and Deacon hopped onto Myn's back to join Garr, who had already launched after Boviss. Even Ether burst into a whirl of wind and roared skyward. Only Ivy and Shah lingered beside the chieftain. Though he had been spared the dragon's flame, the battle thus far had left him in no shape for battle against the beast. Shah landed on Ivy's shoulder as she stood beside him.

"Reyce, please, take shelter. If Boviss realizes you are still alive…" she urged.

"My people fight, and so I must fight," Reyce said. "The beast has shown his true colors. We've come this far on his counsel. If his aim was to wipe us away, he has come shamefully close under my watch. He shall come no further. Your friends fight well, but they do not know Boviss as I do. They do not know his strength, his tenacity. They may survive, but they will not keep him from blood if that is what he seeks. If you care for them, help them. I intend to do the same.”

Sparks and flares of brilliant white stirred around Ivy. The blue of fear, the red of anger, and the yellow of joy were quite common, but white was rare. White was duty. Focus. She reached to her belt and slid her hands into the grips of special blades, punch daggers made specifically for her. She was exhausted, drained by the D’Karon crystals, and battered in her last clash with Boviss. There wasn’t much left for her to give, but as the certainty crystallized, she knew she had to strike down this beast before it took those she treasured most.

“Stay safe,” she insisted. “*Please*, just stay safe…”

Ivy dashed along with the other malthrope soldiers, eyes raised to the sky. Shah darted along after her, determined to be ready if they decided she and her portal gem were needed.

At last, only Reyce remained. He gripped his injured side and clutched one of the D’Karon gems. He *would* be of little use in battle. His every plan had depended upon the weapons he’d been able to amass. The D’Karon magic, the golem, the wasps.

His eyes drifted to the sack Ivy had left behind. Perhaps he could yet save his people…

#

Boviss roared forward, enduring the endless bolts of magic and blasts of flame without any sign of weakening. If he’d chosen to do so, the elder dragon could easily have burned Rendif and a dozen cities like it to cinders before they could stop him, but for the moment, general devastation was abandoned in favor of a single focused target for his rage. If not for Myranda, his machinations would have succeeded. For spoiling his plans, he was clearly determined to make her pay with her life. His jaws snapped, barely missing Myn’s tail as she dove away from him. As Ether buffeted him with wind and Ivy slashed at him whenever he ventured near enough to the ground, he kept his eyes on Myranda.

“This is *your* doing, wizard,” he roared. “The work of decades, ruined by the words and actions of a pathetic spell caster and her allies.”

“Myranda, we need to get you to safety,” Deacon called.

“No. I won’t abandon the battle.”

“But the child!”

"I won't abandon the battle."

Boviss hissed. "Humans had no place here. You should not have come! This would have rid me of the malthropes. It would have rid me of the elves. It would have made them all pay for *daring* to call my land theirs! To wound me. To imprison me. And it was ruined by *you*."

This voice thundered around them, but more potent was the raw intensity of his anger. It was like a broiling heat in Myranda's mind, rivaling even his burning breath.

"I don't understand it. If he had such hatred for the malthropes and the elves, and he has such power, why not attack them ages ago?" Deacon said. "He could have easily wiped out Den in a single day."

Myn swept upward and planted her claws on Boviss's head, springing off him to get some distance. This brought them terrifyingly close, and gave them a clear view of the forged replacements for his limbs.

"I think… I think somehow, ages ago, it was the elves and the malthropes who injured him. Grustim said that a dragon can be consumed by fear. It happens when something proves to be a threat even when they believe themselves invincible. I think he is afraid of them."

The spiked flail attached to Boviss's tail whistled through the air, missing Myn's belly by a hairbreadth.

"If we do not do something soon," Deacon warned, "we may not survive to learn if you are correct."

"I have an idea. But it will take all of us. Help me contact the others. We may not get a second attempt at it."

#

Boviss's frustration grew as the blasted wizard remained tantalizingly beyond his grasp. The young dragon she rode was no match for him. A single blow would shatter her, but she was nimble. More irritating were this bizarre, swirling knot of magic and wind that harried him from one side and the more skilled dragon and Dragon Rider who attacked from the other. It was like flying through a cloud of insects. No one of them was enough to be anything more than a bother, but combined they were pushing him close to madness.

Myn drifted nearly to the ground, skimming along with both feet and wing to better dodge, but he'd seen her do it before. It would not work so well this time. Whipping his wings and surging forward, he closed in on her. She was near enough for him to practically taste her when Garr swept in and directed a blast of flame into his eyes. The attack did little more than obscure his vision, barely singeing his scales and stinging his eyes. He swatted away the beast and turned back to his prey. Myn had set down and dug in her claws, ready to make her stand. Myranda had dismounted and was focusing her strength. It would do no good. He lashed out with his iron claw, bringing it down upon her. The air above her wavered and rippled, a conjured mystic barrier barely preventing the blow from hammering her to a paste. Other warriors swept in, pounding at his hide to little effect. His grin widened as he watched the wizard's form struggle to keep the spell protecting her in place.

"Perhaps I shall allow your friends to survive. If only to tell the tale of what happens to those who tread upon my land."

He took a deep breath and let the flames well up within him. The others redoubled their efforts, to no avail. He belched a blast of flame. The shield shattered, and his claw came down upon her, pinning her unseen form to the ground to writhe beneath the iron as he roasted her. She was powerful, more powerful than even *he* may have realized, so he would not be so foolish as to relent until she was nothing more than a pile of ash. He sustained the flame for as long as he could manage. His iron claw was glowing cherry red by the time he finally relented… but when he ceased the rush of flame, it lingered. Not in the smoldering glow of baked earth, but as a white-hot roiling ball of fire.

"What is this?" he rumbled, taking a step back.

Boviss stole a glimpse of the surrounding field. Myn was gone. He'd not seen her leave. It was as if she'd simply vanished…. or that she had never been there. Illusion? Deception? Perhaps. But the fire was genuine. He could feel its heat. Shapes within the flame began to coalesce. It looked almost human…

A moment later, something burst from the ball of flame and wrapped around his throat. It was so hot it seared even *him*. Fingers closed around his neck. A face and body resolved before him. It was the same ball of magic that had pestered him with wind, her face smug and defiant as she squeezed his throat.

"A lesson even immortals can be slow to learn," she said, wrapping a second hand about his throat. "It is unwise to squander your power when you are not certain of the outcome."

She stood. Her brilliant flaming form had been strengthened by his breath. She was now a match for his own size. The heat about his neck was becoming painful. It was difficult to breathe. He spread his wings and worked them hard. Though she was large, her body was composed of flame and had little weight. He dragged her into the air, but this small victory was short lived. The brilliance of her form darkened. Wind rushed in around her. She shifted from flame to stone, and suddenly was far more than he could ever hope to lift. Her feet struck the field. With a fluid shift of her arms, she slammed him to the ground, pinning his chin to the earth.

"I give you a chance to yield," Ether said.

Boviss rumbled with fury but didn't allow it to burst free in a fresh breath of flame. If this creature could draw strength from it, the last thing he would do is feed her. "I will never yield!" he roared, struggling against her grip.

"Then you will die."

"If you could kill me, I would already be dead."

He attempted to raise his head. She forced it back down, but with far greater effort.

"The power you use against me. It is stolen *from* me." He struggled again and heard the stone of her hand begin to fracture. "You arm yourself with the powers of others. Just like the malthropes with their precious gems. But if you rely upon the strength of others. You can never become more powerful than they. You will *always* fall to them."

Ether leaned low, her massive mouth beside Boviss's head. "There was a time I would have believed that, dragon," she said. "But I am wiser now. Because you forget. I do not fight alone."

As he focused his eyes on the field before him, the flickering half-seen forms of malthropes rushed toward him. They let their enchantments drop away, revealing dozens of creatures, weapons in hand. Memories from over a century ago dragged themselves from his mind. The searing pain of when he'd lost his claw. The agony of losing his tail. And it had been at the hands of these creatures. They were swarming, vengeance in their eyes. Emerging from among them, Reyce. He moved with pained determination and barked orders causing his soldiers to fall into line and separate into waves. And Boviss was held, helpless, as they approached.

The thinking part of his mind abandoned him, instinct insisting he not allow the horrid creatures to have their victory again. He tried to pull away, but Ether held him firmly. The other dragons dropped down, tearing at him. The malthropes leaped to his neck, hacking with their weapons. Punishing blows from Ivy's blades raked him. He felt the distant prickle of elven arrows peppering his sides, the crackle and burn of magic as the blasted wizards cast their spells.

Boviss thrashed and struggled, making slow progress against both the stony grip around his throat and the unfamiliar feelings of panic and anxiety. They were focusing their blows on old wounds, hacking and blasting away at scars. Reyce scrambled atop his head and over his horns, dropping into the place that he had for too long ridden like a king atop his royal steed. A chain jingled. Reyce lifted the same plate he used to mount the gem that had concealed him and the dragon alike. Then, the blow. Reyce drove home his blade in a place between two scales on his neck, a place weakened by generations of exposure to those wretched gems. The pure, sharp pain of it finally pierced the cloud of panic. He gathered himself, dug his hind claws into the earth, and thrust himself back.

Ether's stony grip literally crumbled. Malthropes rained down from him like ticks exposed to flame. A field littered with elves, malthropes, dragons, and wizards stood ready to finally face his might once more. But Reyce remained, driving the blade deeper and twisting it savagely.

"I will not be defeated again. Not by your magic. Not by your weapons," Boviss roared. "None of you have the power to defeat me. You will all fall!"

He launched himself skyward, streaking up more quickly than the other dragons could follow. Ether was still shedding the excess mass of her hulking form and fell far behind. But Reyce had been trained almost from birth to endure the rigors of traveling atop the elder dragon. He worked his blade still deeper.

"You would betray my people!" the chieftain hissed. "You would lead us all to ruin! I will remind you why you were locked away. Why you were right to fear us!"

Boviss lashed at his neck with his flesh-and-blood claw, wrenching Reyce away and clutching him tightly. He held the struggling, broken form of the malthrope before his eyes.

"You are nothing! You are *less* than nothing! A mewling, pathetic *insect*."

The claws squeezed down. Reyce's body was broken beyond hope of recovery. He was breathing his last. And yet he kept his eyes fixed on Boviss, unafraid.

"Perhaps we are nothing…" he breathed. "But we have beaten you…"

Tiny forms, almost too small to see, buzzed on either side of Boviss's head. The wasps, released from the sack that Reyce had carried, which even now was pinned to the behemoth's neck. He snorted, ready to heave a final column of flame that would roast his hated former master to nothing. The breath carried with it a tiny, familiar scent. Poison.

Reyce had opened a deep, raw wound. And even now, he could feel where the fairies had driven their thorns into it. A single thorn had been enough to lay Myn low. Many dozens of times that dosage now coursed through his veins. He could feel the withering weakness. His wings were already beginning to fail him. Perhaps it would be minutes. Perhaps it would be hours. But the poison *would* be enough to claim him. He was already dead.

He looked to Reyce.

"You have killed me…" the dragon rumbled. "But know this. With my final breaths. I shall take the lives of *all* that I can. And you are the first."

#

Myn and Garr streaked skyward, Ether surging up from below. High above, Boviss had faltered. His wings rustled and slackened, like a ship suddenly without the wind to fill its sails. The elder dragon curled his head and belched flame into his claws. Boviss seemed more focused on heaving ever more flame into his claws than gaining control of his wings and ending his uncontrolled descent.

"The dragon has killed him…" Ether uttered. "The dragon has *killed him…*"

She launched past the dragons as Boviss discarded the blackened remains of his former master like so much refuse. Ether snatched up the form and spirited it earthward.

"The dragon is weakening," Deacon said, clutching tightly to Myn's back. "Can you feel it?"

Myranda clenched her fist about her staff. "If he's given his life to give us this chance, let us not waste it."

Boviss struggled to catch the air again, angling his wings to glide toward Rendif once more.

"He's heading for the city," Deacon said.

Myranda narrowed her eyes. "He won't make it."

She pulled the edges of her ragged mind together and reached for teachings she was loath to use. Black pulses and tendrils of energy formed about the head of her staff. Black magic—the simplest, purest form of mystic attack. It was not evil, no more so than a sword or a hammer was evil, but it represented the failure of all else in Myranda's mind. Sometimes there were simply no better options.

The bolt of black lanced forward and curved under the guiding influence of her mind. It struck Boviss at the base of his wings. She'd seen this attack pierce some of the stoutest defenses she'd ever encountered, and with the force she'd cast it, most creatures would have been struck down. Not so for Boviss, but even the mighty elder dragon was not immune. His jaws spread in a growl of pain, and what little control he had over his wings vanished in a wave of shudders and spasms. He flailed and writhed in the air as the ground swept closer, and finally, he struck.

Dirt spewed around him, launched like water by his heavy form as it struck with punishing force. Malthropes and soldiers alike, wisely having kept their distance, dove for cover as stones the size of melons were heaved in all directions.

It would be too much to hope that the landing would have killed the beast. Though his iron claw was bent by the impact, he dragged himself to his feet and lumbered forward, eyes fixed on Rendif and fire curling between his teeth with every breath.

Myn and Garr tucked their wings and dove toward him. Below them, two red streaks flared across the landscape. One was the fiery glow of Ether, vengeance in her radiant eyes. The other, the crimson aura of Ivy, anger having seized her once more.

The two Chosen struck the dragon one after the other, each splitting the air like thunder. Ether was a blur, burning off the power she'd absorbed in the form of a thousand shifts and changes—now wind to evade an attack, and now stone to pelt Boviss with heavy blows. Ivy had already squandered strength on her previous clash, but what she had left, she poured directly into an assault, heedless of counterattacks.

She drove her daggers deeply into his hide and swatted him with blows that staggered him, but Boviss shrugged off the attacks. Enough of them would end him, just as surely as Reyce's final act and the rain of arrows from the forces protecting Rendif might. Any sane creature would have been turned back by the savagery of the attacks, but survival was clearly no longer Boviss's aim. His hide was leaking blood from a half-dozen savage wounds. A tooth was shattered. His horns were splintered and damaged. Still he thundered forward. They simply lacked the strength to deliver enough damage to the dragon to stop him before he reached the city and did in the space of moments what it would take an opposing army hours to do.

"Shah…" Myranda said. "Where is Shah!"

She shut her eyes and found the clean, pure pinprick of light, the fairy's soul in her mind's eye. It was paired with the corrosive influence of the D'Karon gem she held.

"This way Myn. We can end this now!"

#

Ether could feel her power waning. Not since her earliest battles had she consumed such power in pursuit of a single target. She didn't care. Lain had been taken from her, and the one responsible had been killed before she could make him pay. For a brief, precious moment, seeing Reyce had been like getting a glimpse of Lain again. Fate had seen fit to take him away as well, but at least it left the creature responsible. She'd existed long enough to know that second chances of any sort were too rare to let pass.

Ivy leaped and bashed Boviss's jaw, shattering another tooth. Her gleaming red aura was flickering. Soon even *her* mighty soul would reach its limit.

"Ether!" Myranda called. "Just slow him."

The shapeshifter looked to the sky. A smile came to her face. Yes… that would do. Below, Ivy was streaking toward the dragon's tail. It wasn't clear if she'd heard Myranda's instructions or if her anger-drenched mind simply latched on to a new target, but she threw down her daggers and grasped the spiked ball at the end of Boviss's tail. Her feet sank deep into the ground as he dragged her like a plow through the tough earth, but sheer strength and raw will slowed him slightly. It was Ether's job to finish the task.

She dropped to the ground and shifted to earth. The soil and stone parted beneath her as she sank down, and a twist of will sent a spire of stone up from below. It passed through one of the thick chain links of the dragon's augmented tail. When the chain drew tight, he continued walking, fracturing the stone, but with a second curl of will, she shifted herself and the spire to iron. Boviss came to a sudden and complete stop. He turned his head and roared, pulling with all of his considerable might and beginning to bend and tear the very links of his tail. She summoned additional spires to spear the rest of the links.

For the first time since he'd struck the ground, Boviss took genuine notice of the attacks. He curled back and swatted at Ether, knocking her metal body aside.

"I will have this city. My dying breath will be a gout of flame to blot it from this wretched world."

"You are wrong," Ether said calmly. "Because *this* is your final breath."

A flash and surge of violet light poured down from above. Boviss looked up to find a portal had opened quite far above him. A form dropped through the portal and picked up speed. It was the golem. Deacon's sabotage had done its job, as it had become entirely motionless. Even the smolder of its eyes had dimmed. But that did not change the fact that it was a titanic mechanism, gaining speed as it plummeted toward him.

He gathered his strength and dove aside, attempting to pivot around his pinned tail. Ivy, with the last glimmer of her strength, surged forward end delivered a blow to his chin, staggering him. Ether delivered a second, knocking him back, then collected Ivy and retreated.

#

The golem struck. The sound was like something from the end of the world, a deafening rush of shattered stone and battered flesh. The whole of the field vanished in a cloud of dust and debris. The impact shook the ground and caused the nearest section of the wall to collapse. The echoes lasted for minutes, and the dust cloud lingered for minutes more.

All around, the warriors watched and waited. Bowstrings remained taut. Weapons remained at the ready. Myranda and Deacon held their crystals high, spells coiled to strike. Ivy's strength gave out, and she was resting peacefully. Finally, Ether summoned a wind.

Clouds of dust cleared away. The golem was little more than a pile of rubble, the dragon buried beneath it. All watched and prayed. There was no stir of motion. No rise and fall of breathing. Myranda shut her eyes and reached out with her mind. The mighty furnace of the dragon's mind and soul had gone cold.

"It is done," she said.

A cheer rose in a single voice. The Chosen, the elves, the malthropes, the fairies, all of them joined in. In a field churned and scorched by battle, beings who minutes before would have been after each other's blood rejoiced in mutual victory.

It would have been nice to believe that, in that moment, any bad blood or ancient hatred could have been forgotten, but fate is seldom so obliging. Old distrust stains the heart and mind. It takes more than the rise and fall of a common enemy to wipe it away. This was a truth the malthropes knew well, a wisdom to which they owed their continued survival. One by one, while the others still reveled in victory, the malthropes and their fairies vanished.

Myranda leaned heavily on her staff. Her soul and body were drained from the experience, and now that the danger was gone, the raw force of will she'd conjured up to endure the trials until now seemed to vanish, its job done. Deacon wasn't much better off, but he loaned her his arm for her to steady herself. A heavily panting Myn wedged her head between them.

"*Safe...*" she rumbled.

Myranda scratched the dragon's brow. "For now."

She turned to the elves. As the exhilaration of victory faded, they reformed their ranks, seeking orders from the most senior among them. A few nervous gazes sought out the conspicuously absent malthropes.

"There is a lot more to be done," Myranda said. "But for today, the battle is over. Tomorrow, we begin the healing."

Epilogue

The glorious silvery flagship stood proudly in the harbor outside Twilus. A lengthy and rather tedious ceremony had been completed amid much fanfare, and the crew was simply waiting for the tide to be right for their departure. Myranda stood on the edge of the pier, watching the workers load the last few crates packed with the precious leaves that could speed the recovery of the land back home. Myn was beside her, sitting on her haunches and watching the sea distrustfully, as though if she were not vigilant, it would try something nasty. Ivy stood to the other side, gazing at the complex shapes of the clouds over the sea.

Deacon stepped up to Myranda and placed a hand on her shoulder. "How are you feeling?" he asked.

"Almost a week since the final battle and I still don't feel like myself." She placed a hand on her stomach. "Though I suppose that has more to do with the little one than the battle."

"Yes..."

Deacon became silent for a moment. When Myranda looked at him, he seemed to be deep in thought, and whatever those thoughts might have been, they must have been quite trying.

"Is something wrong?" she asked.

"... When did you know...?" he said.

"About the baby," she surmised.

"You must have known. And worse, you must have hidden it. You stopped me from treating you, but that would not have been enough. You kept the truth from me, shielded yourself from me..."

"Deacon, there was worked to be done. If you'd known..."

"I understand the importance of the things we must do, Myranda. I have known that since Entwell. If you had chosen to fight, I would have fought beside you. I trust your wisdom. I trust your competence. I trust *you*."

He took a breath. "I am your husband. The duke to your duchess. It has been my honor and privilege to stand beside you, and I have been blessed to have a place in your fabled life. Since the moment we met, I have done my level best to aid and advise you. What we did here had to be done. Of that, there is no question. It is the duty of a Chosen one to serve her world when called upon. But the duty of the Chosen extends far beyond the present day. You have an obligation to the future as well. You aren't just an exceptional wizard, stateswoman, and warrior. You are the first in a bloodline. And should a threat worthy of the Chosen arise in the unknowable future, the line we have started together, represented by our child to be, will be called upon to defend the world once more. It may be a difficult choice to make, but until we are certain our child can go on without us, we may need to leave battles such as these to others. For the sake of our world, and for the sake of our child."

"Deacon, I spent most of my life without a mother or a father. I assure you, I would move heaven and earth to make sure our child is cherished and protected. I should have told you. I should have trusted you. I was wrong. But from this day forward, this child, this *family* shall be first among my thoughts. I won't forget that we are joined in this as in all else."

One of the lines hauling a crate caught on the edge of the pier, pulling taut and creaking before popping free. The loud slap of settling cargo caused Myn to snap to attention. She plodded over to the offending crewmen and glared at them while carefully positioning herself between the crew and Myranda.

"Something tells me Myn is going to be taking the protection very seriously as well." Myranda looked about. "Where are the others?"

"I believe Ether took her leave early. Before the ceremony. Grustim and Garr were granted access to a royal hunting ground not far away…"

Myn reluctantly paused in her intimidation of the noisy crew to glance in his direction at the mention of both the words "Garr" and "hunting."

Myranda turned to the city. It was still bustling, filled to capacity with both soldiers and diplomats. Ivy stepped up beside her.

"It seems like this place is still awfully busy," she said. "I would have thought all of these extra people would have started to clear out, now that we're leaving."

Deacon consulted his book. "As I understand it, without our departure the diplomatic delegation that has been focused upon us will be shifting to the matter of Den."

"Den…" Myranda murmured. "Such a revelation… At home, when the battles are through, we are there to heal the wounds and clean up the mess we leave behind. But Den… If a village of malthropes was to be discovered in Tressor *or* the Northern Alliance, it would take constant vigilance to keep frightened and superstitious people from doing something horrible. Our actions here revealed them, even if it was their own machinations that forced us to do so. What will happen to them now?"

"We have to believe that wisdom will prevail," Deacon said.

"Unfortunately, it tends to need a little help. Do we know anything of how they intend to proceed?"

"It is a Sonril matter. They did not share their intentions."

"Do the malthropes even have a representative?"

"I very much doubt it. Not an official one. One wonders how the elves intend to open contact with the malthropes."

"This could go very poorly for them. They are weaker than the elves. They are the aggressors, with things to answer for. They will need guidance if they are to survive this. If we could stay a bit longer…"

"Myranda, if we stay much longer, you would be in no condition to make the journey home."

"Um…" Ivy said.

"What is it?" Myranda asked.

"What if… what if I stay? I *am* a diplomat. I've done two whole missions as an ambassador. We ended up fighting during them, which I guess isn't the best way for them to go, but they turned out well in the end. And I'm a malthrope. I've spent time among the people of Den… I think I might be the only one for the job."

"It could take a very long time. It could be very difficult," Myranda said. "I am sure there will be more to it than simply speaking on behalf of the malthropes. The presence of the golem will bring the dwarfs into it. This all may be the final laugh of Boviss, dragging the many peoples of the Crescents to the brink of war through his horrid insidious counsel."

Ivy crossed her arms and nodded firmly. "I don't care." She paused. "Just so long as I get to come home and visit when the baby is born."

"They may not look kindly upon you imposing yourself upon their policies," Deacon said.

"If they can call on us to fight their battles, they'd better be ready for us to talk their talks too. Ether saved the king's life! That should count for *something*." She perked up and clasped her hands. "Oh! And staying means I'll be able to play with the fairies some more! Can you believe what happened?"

"I do believe they are the first fairies to be asked to become personal bodyguards to a king," Deacon said.

"And the first to turn him down," Myranda added.

"You can't blame them for just wanting to go home. Saving a king's life *once* is enough. Oh, but there's so much to do. I've got to talk to the king's people!" She gave Deacon and Myranda a hug and kiss each. "Have a good trip! I'll miss you."

Myn lowered her head for a scratch. "*Bye, Ivy*," the dragon said.

Ivy giggled gleefully. "You'll be talking so *well* when I finally get home again. I'm going to teach you a song! Can you just imagine that voice *singing*? *I can't wait!*"

She waved farewell and practically pranced off to the task she'd assigned herself. Aboard the ship, the crew signaled readiness, and a gangplank was lowered for them to board. Myn spotted Garr approaching and leaped to the deck of the ship to await him, plopping down where the conspicuously absent cages had once been set.

Myranda and Deacon stepped aboard. As they readied to set sail, Myranda found her heart lighter than it had been in ages. In the time since she'd discovered her destiny, it seemed she'd not had a moment to reflect upon all the good she'd done. Her eyes had always been set upon the future, the many things yet to do. But for once, the future held real promise. The days to come were offering more than they were threatening to take away. She and her friends had traveled far to make their world safer, stronger.

Now, it was time to go home.

#

Two months later…

Just as she did at the end of every day, Celia climbed the steps to her cozy little home. The day's tasks had been pleasantly light, so she wasn't nearly as weary as she normally was. The next day the inn would not need her, so this was a rare opportunity to rest her bones and take a moment for herself. She was already making a list of things that needed doing as she shoved her door open and stepped inside.

"Hello, Celia."

She gasped and stepped back, nearly tumbling down the steps behind her. Ether was seated at the edge of her bed.

"Ether!" she breathed, catching her breath. "Good heavens, you mustn't startle me like that!"

"I apologize. It was not my intention. You had suggested that I experience more of the world, and return to you with stories of what I have seen and done. I have done so."

"So I've heard." She removed her shawl and stepped to the little heating stove. "Have you been sitting here in the cold, waiting for me? You must take *care* of yourself."

"You say you have heard?" Ether said.

"Yes. Gracious, did *that* ever set me off on a tizzy. The duchess herself came, asking after you. And with *child*. Such a lovely girl. The way she was glowing with pride when she spoke of the child. She will be a *fine* mother…"

"Myranda came to you, asking about me?"

"She did. She was concerned. You vanished, she said, after the deed was done overseas. You ceased to answer her calls. Huddled yourself away."

"That is not her concern. I shall instruct her not to trouble you with questions of my well-being."

"You do nothing of the sort! What other washerwoman can say that the duchess of Kenvard has come to her and sought counsel! You should set her mind at ease when you are through here. It isn't right to make your friends worry. But you didn't come here to be scolded by a silly old woman. I understand you succeeded in your quest?"

"We did. A terrible scheme, hatched by an elder dragon. Without us, there would have been assassinations, destruction. But we prevailed. And as I believe is customary when returning from travels, I bring gifts."

Ether tugged open a sack she'd brought, and one by one, in a rather mechanical manner, detailed their origins. Wine from the royal vineyard of Grandwinn. Fine cutlery from the finest silversmiths of Sonril. They were grand gifts, far too grand to have been intended for anyone but Ether herself. Celia tried to refuse the gifts, they were far too much for her, but Ether insisted she had no use for them herself. With each new gift, she told a piece of the adventure. This battle, that discovery, and how they had all come to fruition.

It should have been overwhelming, and the tales of exotic places and wondrous experiences should have been enthralling, but there was something missing. Celia had known Ether long enough to know that she was by no means warm and enthusiastic. As a storyteller, she left much to be desired. But even with that in mind, her words and demeanor was strangely hollow. Subdued. She was restraining herself, holding something back. For the moment, perhaps the best Celia could do was keep the shapeshifter talking.

"This is all *very* lovely. But it seems you've left the story half-told."

"I have not. From inception to victory, I have told it all."

"Things don't *end* with victory, dear. What of this Den place? They're without a chieftain, and the elves must be rather cross with them."

"Ivy is still among them. She has argued quite vigorously on their behalf. To my knowledge, no further battles have resulted, and the people of Den have been wise enough to keep the D'Karon enchantments dormant."

"So they aren't hiding any longer?"

"More importantly, they aren't stripping themselves or their people of strength."

"And what of the elves and the dwarfs? Surely there have been words about that."

"According to Ivy, a trio of dwarfs approached Rendif unannounced and dropped one of their own, bound and gagged, at the foot of their town hall with a note."

"… Well?"

"Well what?"

"Well what did the note say?"

"I believe it identified the bound dwarf as the one who had done business with Den, against the wishes of the others, and surrendered him to whatever justice they saw fit. It also gently reminded any who might consider an act of military retribution that there are six other golems waiting to defend them."

"Shrewd. And what else?"

"That is all."

She looked at Ether knowingly. "No. I still haven't heard what I have been waiting to hear."

"I do not know what you are speaking of."

"What of you? Why do you come here speaking like you've been hollowed out? Like you've thrown a wall up between us?"

"You are imagining things."

"Ether, a mother knows her child's voice. We hear the words that aren't being said. It is nice to think you come here to share a tale and give some gifts, but not once have you come to me without something weighing upon you. Speak. What else am I here for?"

Ether sat in silence for a moment, but for a being who could perfectly imitate any form she chose, she was doing a terrible job hiding the torment going on beneath the surface.

"… There was a malthrope. His name was Reyce. I encountered him only briefly on the battlefield before he lost his life. It should have meant *nothing*. He was just another creature. Worse, one sullied by the magic of the D'Karon. But from the moment I saw him, I knew him to be of Lain's bloodline."

"Lain. The Chosen who died."

Ether looked down. "It was uncanny, Celia. He was like Lain himself, back from beyond. Walking this world again." Tears began to trickle from her eyes. "And before the day was done… he was struck down. It was a cruel trick of fate. A fresh blow to open an old."

Ether paused for a moment, then raised her eyes. The tears flowed freely now.

"I loved Lain. I truly did. First, I convinced myself I was above such things. Then, I believed I was offering him something that *he* needed. A target for his own affections. But now I know that it was something I needed. Something I'd never known I needed, and something I didn't know how to give or receive. Before I could come to terms with it, he was gone. And now seeing someone so much like him, in body and soul… I'm not strong enough to keep it inside, to force it away. It *scours* my *soul*…"

Celia stood and threw her arms around Ether. "The strength isn't in keeping it inside, Ether. The strength is in letting it out."

And so, for the first time since her creation, Ether allowed the sorrow to claim her. She wept openly, and when the moment passed, she spoke again, long into the night, sharing the thoughts that had been too long denied.

The Crescents

\#

In New Kenvard, Deacon paced the halls of the cozy cottage that served as the official quarters of the duke and duchess. The palace was nearly ready for them to move in, but for now they remained in the same home that had been readied for them in the earliest stages of the rebuild.

He found his way to the study. Myranda was well into the pregnancy now, beginning to show. Despite it, she'd maintained doing all she could to continue the recovery of the capital. She'd drifted to sleep in an overstuffed chair, surrounded by parchment scratched with updates on this or that aspect of the city's reconstruction. He held out a hand, and the pages gathered into an orderly pile upon the table beside her. He then rested his hand lightly on her belly before pulling a blanket over her.

When she was more comfortable, he continued to pace. The house seemed empty at the moment. Her father was away, overseeing one of the many farms that had been treated with the nara leaf. Ivy was still with the people of Den, providing updates daily on her progress. He shut his eyes and listened. The calm, regular breaths of Myn tucked away in her stable were reassuringly present.

He stepped out into the coolness of night, his mind heavy with what lay ahead. He would be a father. In a way, it was precisely what he'd always prepared for in Entwell. What was a parent but a teacher, someone to train and prepare you for everything the world might require of you? Until recently he couldn't have imagined anything more important than to pass on his wisdom as best he could. But it was his own child… It was a whole new level of responsibility.

Deacon held out has hands and looked upon them. He flexed the fingers of his left hand and gently eased the focus that he'd not allowed to flag for the last few months. The flesh of the hand flickered and shuddered, eager to shift chaotically despite the enchantment upon his ring. The D'Karon magic, jumping through portals, or nothing more than time… for whatever the reason, his affliction was getting worse. Harder to control. The progress was slow. He was in no danger of losing control in the near future. But he would be a father soon. And that was a task that lasted a lifetime.

Something would need to be done.

Joseph R. Lallo

From The Author

Thank you for reading! If you liked this story, or perhaps if you found it lacking, I'd love to hear from you. Below are links to some of the places you can find me online. For **free stories** and important updates, join my newsletter at http://www.bookofdeacon.com/contact/

Discover other titles by Joseph R. Lallo:

The Book of Deacon Series:
Book 1: *The Book of Deacon*
Book 2: *The Great Convergence*
Book 3: *The Battle of Verril*
Book 4: *The D'Karon Apprentice*

Other stories in the same setting:
Jade
The Rise of the Red Shadow
The Redemption of Desmeres

The Big Sigma Series:
Book 1: *Bypass Gemini*
Book 2: *Unstable Prototypes*
Book 3: *Artificial Evolution*
Book 4: *Temporal Contingency*

The Free-Wrench Series:
Book 1: *Free-Wrench*
Book 2: *Skykeep*
Book 3: *Ichor Well*
Book 4: *The Calderan Problem*

Collections:
The Book of Deacon Anthology
The Big Sigma Collection: Volume 1

NaNoWriMo Projects:
The Other Eight

The Crescents
Other Stories:

Between
Fallen Empire: Rogue Derelict
Structophis

9 780999 708132